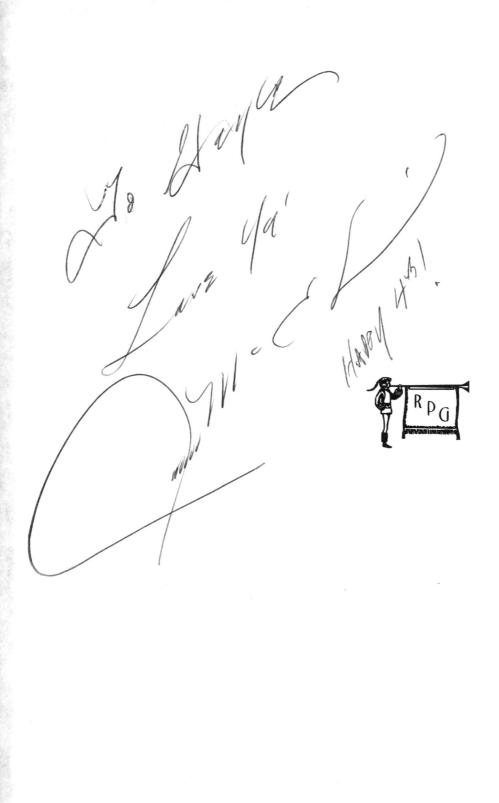

SAY GOODNIGHT

to the

BOYS in BLUE

James McEachin

The Rharl Publishing Group
16161 Ventura Boulevard, #550 Encino, CA 91436-2523
rharlpub@aol.com

Rharl and Colophon
are registered trademarks of
the Rharl Publishing Group

Printed and bound in the United States of America
Library of Congress Catalog Card Number: 98-68156

1 3 5 7 9 10 8 6 4 2

ISBN 0-9656661-5-8
CIP data available

Printed on acid-free paper

The Boys in Blue, circa 1898

Here come the darkness men done cuss'd;
Methinks the whole thing is gonna get wuss'd.

— Soldier Boy

Tuesday, December 19, 1950.
11:31 p.m.

1

I t was a good night to be nice and comfy. It was post-World War II, and the lights were on again all over the world. The boys were back home, Rosie the Riveter had returned to the kitchen, and a feel-good mentality swept through the nation's capital. It was the beginning of a new decade, broken threads had been mended, innocence renewed, baby-booming tots were teething, and apple pie and roses complimented the national menu. Bread could be purchased at 13 cents a loaf, eggs at 62 cents per dozen, and, for a country on the move, the price of gasoline was holding at a respectable 24 cents a gallon. The economic outlook was high; the entrepreneurial spirit was fresh and vibrant. It was the American dream come to life. In the suburbs, crime was down, misdeeds were few, and ill-will and incivility was laid to rest by images of chummy neighbors pruning flowers and hedges behind picket fences that fronted rows and rows of happy little prefabricated homes. And most sanguine had been the change of seasons. Abetted by a benevolent summer, fall had passed the baton on to an engaging winter, nursed it through to mid December, then released it so that the final month of the year could claim the glory of Christmas all its own.

All was right in an untroubled world. Or so it seemed.

That said, in a remote little slice of northern New Jersey a melodious clock sat atop a library that was strong on nostalgia and sent its Roman numerals spewing off in four different directions. It was performing its last chore of the night. Signaling midnight, it was bonging out 12 strokes. Nicely done, but the bold old clock with the weatherbeaten hands was wrong. There were still 29 minutes to go before the witching hour and, save for the boys in blue and a few up-all-nighters, the good citizenry of Elton Head had long since gone to sleep.

Weather-wise it was an utterly splendid night. Unlike the series of bad nights that had preceded it, nights that had been ushered in by a series of weird and seemingly satirical winds that had pranced into town, sucked up what little bit of atmospheric cheer there was, left an impolite deposit in the air and danced away like the clown prince of a black comedy, the night was sumptuous.

Like a greeting card promising something to the '50's that the '40's hadn't delivered, a light snow was brightened by a translucent, silvery-blue moon that looked as if it lit heaven's way and appeared so close to Earth that it seemed almost touchable. It hung there like it was God's pendant. It was magnificent. Even the Elton Head trees, normally flat, denuded, and zonked in winter, benefited from the setting. They stood with their limbs stretched and swooped as though in holy worship.

Not exactly fitting, yet not necessarily out of place, slowly, as if adding a gentle nudge to the card, cutting lazily through the light falling snow were a pair of headlights that belonged to a dated Chevy pickup truck. It was taking its time threading through lonely and silent streets.

Danny Carlsson was behind the wheel. He was on his way to work. Almost handsome, Danny was a pleasantly shy, sandy-haired, 22-year-old Scandinavian whose thin and undernourished look belied his occupation. Less than three months on the job, he was one of eight men on the midnight shift. Because he had been on the department for less than 90 days he was not yet a full-fledged policeman. He was a rookie, not yet, as the saying goes, a *regular*; not yet embraced by Elton Head's boys in blue.

It was a status that didn't displease him.

The wheels of the pickup crunched around a few corners, hit Essex Street, and eased past a series of low-angled storefronts that, even if they didn't appreciate the splendor of the night, should have at least gained glory from the season. Since it was that time of year, they should have been bedecked with the merriment of twinkling lights and shiny Christmas ornaments. Except for a store or two, they did not. They should have had promise, cheerfulness — seasonal zip and zap. Except for a front or two, they had nothing.

But sleepy little Elton Head was like that. It had a look — nothing to write home about, but it had a certain something that said, sleepy or not, little or not, it was an independent sort and was not about to be pressured into change. Even during the war, when the rest of the world was tilted on its axis and had gone haywire with civic pride and nationalism, it hadn't changed much. It assumed somewhat of a warlike posture by having a few star-banners in the windows of the widely spaced few who had a relative in service, and it did suffer through a few blackouts and some rationing, and, to its credit, it had been responsible for selling a few war bonds and having an "A, B, or C" gas-tax stamp plastered on the windshields of the few cars that traversed the streets, but still Elton Head hadn't done much. It never raised the ol' patriotic hue and cry; didn't lift its head in righteous indignation over having the country's peace assaulted, and, as had been denoted by the scarcity of red, white and blue window banners, it hadn't sent many of its men off to fight the nation's battle. And so it was not surprising that, nine years later, the stores and storefronts merely stood there — indifferent; choosing to remain cold in the night, giving mute testament that they were nothing more than an uneven line of downers amid a host of failures in a sleeping city.

As if on tour, as though he had all night to get to where he was going, Carlsson nursed the vehicle to Main Street, Elton Head's central artery. The central artery was dead. Even at the height of summer the old yawner didn't bristle with activity, but it did have a little something on those hot, musty nights — nights that at least warranted the occasional, bug-dodging, mosquito-swatting stroll. But not so in winter. Particularly this winter.

The vehicle moved on. It slowly crossed Railroad Avenue, rounded a few more streets, then touched State and Mercer. Later it eased onto Balanta Place. It finally came to a stop in a yard where a post-high lamp vaguely illuminated the area that was adjacent to the town's only police station.

Small and weathered, the station stood alone.

Slanted a slot or two away from where the pickup had parked were the cars belonging to the men who would soon be getting off from the evening shift and to the men who had already reported in for the midnight watch.

Although the snow flurries had covered the cars that belonged to the 12 men on the evening shift, one could see that the cars were of similar vintage. It appeared that they all suffered from an assortment of dents, bangs, chipped paint, and overall neglect. On the opposite side of the yard, closest to the building, were six Hudson patrol cars. None was new.

Since the cars had been used on patrol only minutes before, they hadn't yet fully benefited from the purifying flakes, and it was easy to see that they were more banged-up than the civilian cars. White-topped with midnight-blue bodies and a single-beam, rounded red light on each top, they were in the yard because of the change of shifts. Being Hudsons, they were clunky and slowest of the slow, but because they were bullet-shaped, they found favor with the chief. He particularly liked car 107. It was the newest of the group, stolen, as the chief and the city fathers liked to say, in an *"as in,"* too-good-to-be-true, post-WW II, once-in-a-lifetime deal. The city fathers couldn't resist making the purchase.

The post-WWII, too-good-to-be-true, once-in-a-lifetime *"as in"* deal was through the courtesy of the Paterson, N.J., P.D. — itself no monument to law enforcement.

On its third odometer, fifth transmission, and fourth clutch, and at four years old and with so many miles on its third odometer that the mileage count no longer registered, the car, again the best of the bunch, leaked oil, the shocks were bad, the radiator was in trouble, and the clutch needed work. According to records, recently started, it had been the victim of two almost-drownings, eight collisions, and any number of "fender-benders." But the chief was happy, Ernest Mulkey, the city manager, was happy, and two years later, the six-member city council were still congratulating themselves over the "steal."

Despite its troubles, and like the rest of the Hudsons, the "steal" never lost its original bullet shape, and no one wanted to jeopardize it by allowing it on patrol at night with the other five cars. According to Mulkey, the chief, and the city council, it was that streamline look that foretold the police department's straight-ahead future.

The Elton Head officials were not known for accuracy in prophecy.

Although he was not privileged to drive because he was a rookie, Danny Carlsson didn't like the Hudsons. Nothing new there — Danny Carlsson didn't like the Elton Head Police Department. Danny didn't like being a *part* of the Elton Head Police Department. As he had done every night for the almost 90 days he had been on the department — on time, creased and polished — he remained in the pickup, looking out at the pitiful surroundings, thinking about his job while idly listening to the car radio. It had been a Walter Winchell re-broadcast from New York. Winchell, a clattering, all-mouth, eyes-'n'-ears newscaster, had just mentioned something about an increase in troop activity in Korea's Port of Embarkation, in the city of Pusan. With the volume low and his mind drifting, Carlsson hadn't fully caught what had been said. It was an oversight. He chided himself for not paying more attention. Although the action over there had been termed a United Nations *police action,* lives had been lost and the United States was certain to upgrade its involvement since it involved fighting the dreaded Communists. Having replaced the newly defeated Germans and Japanese, and reportedly responsible for every ill from the bubonic plague to flying saucers — owned and operated by ray-gun toting, bug-eyed little green people with legs too short to reach the brakes — the Communists were the nation's newest enemy.

But as the recently discharged Navy veteran firmly believed, the whole Korean conflict would be considered a waste. It had never captured the public's concern; never did, never would; and, in the end, knowing the quick-to-forget Americans, the entire episode would be relegated to the back pages of history. And the nation's leader, President Harry S. Truman, all he would be remembered for was authorizing the dropping of atomic bombs on Nagasaki and Hiroshima in Japan. Maybe even that would be forgotten.

And so Elton Head's incredibly gorgeous night appeared to be of no help to a young man of foreign extraction whose thoughts slowed his every move; no help to a quiet young man who was in the wrong place, had the wrong job, and was missing something in life.

In a way, though, Danny Carlsson had to consider himself lucky. After a four-year stint in the Navy that covered a number of European ports and one or two quick trips to Asia, he had been discharged at the end of June. One week later, because of the growing hostilities in Korea, the military froze all discharges, and he found himself back in his adopted country, back in his adopted state; and back in the city of Elton Head. But, considering what the young sandy-haired Dane had gotten himself into — becoming a policeman on the Elton Head P.D., maybe he hadn't been so lucky after all. And besides, there was nothing wrong in a young man having a war under his belt. In fact, if the country was in trouble a young man *should* have a war under his belt. It didn't have to be as big or as breast-beating as WWII. Any conflict would do.

The young man spent the remaining minutes in the pickup with growing thoughts about re-enlisting. He wouldn't "re-up" in the Navy, though. This time he would try the Air Force. And, as he had done while in the Navy, he wouldn't be too keen on talking about his home town.

In that regard, though, Carlsson was like a lot of others. In service, a lot of young men were somewhat reluctant to discuss their home towns when they were away. It was never fully understood why, but little towns were out; "bigness" seemed all-important. A favorite in the military was to look on a map, find the ol' home town, stick a pin in it, and brag about its greatness. With cities like Elton Head, it couldn't be done. It could hardly be done with the State of New Jersey, even on a big map. The best one could do in trying to find Elton Head and all such little northern New Jersey hum-drummers on a good-sized map, was to find "the city so nice they named it twice" and backtrack across the Hudson River. It was a bother. And it was not that anyone from Jersey wanted to renounce citizenship and move to, or even be a part of, the nation's largest city. Far from it. Despite being slighted by the map, New Jersey was the Garden State — pretty in a lot of aspects, and, except for a weed here and there — such as Elton Head sometimes appeared to be — it could hold its own against the best of them. New York, with its overabundance of traffic, hostile air, rude people and other things the city was noted for, left a lot to be desired, and most of the Jerseyites would have been quite content if they had neither seen nor heard of the place.

A scant 13 miles west of New York, and mistakenly named after a roguish, fast-talking Dutch explorer who literally lost his head to a tribe of

Indians whom he had fleeced in a wampum/Bible/land exchange — a deal wherein the rogue got the land and the Indians got two water-stained Bibles and a handful of Jersey-made wampum — some said Elton Head suffered in the shadows of the big burg. It was a view that came mainly from the insecure city fathers. They didn't want the big-city woes, but they did feel that being so close to New York, it miniaturized them and left them without an identity, as if they were left to view the world from under a damp blanket. The cliché went that when New York sneezed, Elton Head caught the cold. It was sentiment that didn't seem to bother anyone but the city fathers, and it was sentiment that seemed to have plagued every administration. In fact, some of Elton Head's earlier city fathers, in an attempt at assertive affirmation, had been so influenced by the shadow of the big burg that, from inception, both the police and fire department uniforms had that same Gotham look.

But not so with the police department's building itself. The Elton Head city fathers wanted a different facade — i.e., a New York front — but the aged building couldn't stand it, and, even if it could, the budget couldn't cut the mustard. And so, through the years, the weary building had remained unchanged.

The Elton Head P.D. building had a look all its own. With a set of weedy railroad tracks cutting precariously close to its rear, it was an architecturally destitute small-timer, with its most prized feature being the Elton Head P.D. brass plaque in front. Highlighted by a lone blue-green bulb, and with Roman-style lettering patinated by age, the plaque was supposed to give the building at least the *feel* of a New York precinct. It didn't get the job done. What was interesting, though, and perhaps could have been used as a testament to the old-time city fathers' imagination, was that 35 years earlier the brownish brick building had been the site of horse auctions. Even though that had been a long 13 years before he was born — and a long way from where he had been born — Danny Carlsson felt sorry for the horses.

Whether it was the imagination, or whether tinged by the forces of the great unknown — influenced, perhaps, by the series of weird, frolicsome winds that had pranced into town several nights before, on this particular night the former home of horse auctions looked a tad different. It maintained its customary lethargy, but, as if queued by the retarded hands of the library

clock, or, better still, aroused by the moon's low-hanging, silvery-blue lumi-
nescence, the building seemed to radiate an inkling that there would be a
change taking place. It wasn't much, but there was a hint — a pinch — a
smidge of something that said — and it said it ever so vaguely — that in the
offering of another dull, plodding, nothing-ever-happens, slow-moving night,
there would be change riding with the hours, and that by morning there would
be room for a changing of the guard. A *complete* changing of the guard, it
said. It was a change that was to be in Elton Head's favor.

It was like an omen.

The snow was receding. The minutes ticked away; the rookie had to
go inside. He disconsolately withdrew further thoughts about Korea and re-
enlisting in the Navy, put his midnight-blue police cap on and slowly got out
of the pickup. He adjusted his uniform, got his nightstick and walked slowly
from the yard to the front of the station. He wouldn't allow his face to show
it, but, as he had said to himself every night, excluding the desk sergeant,
whom he didn't really have a handle on, and patrolman Tetrollini, whom he
did, he was all set for another night with a bunch of bozoid cops whose col-
lective IQ's couldn't reach room temperature in the dead of winter.

Carlsson didn't like it, either, that the men laid claim to the notion of
being home town heroes, but none of them had been in the service.

Every man in the Elton Head Police Department had managed to avoid
the draft.

When the rookie arrived in front of the building, he routinely stopped
under the dim blue-green bulb for a last-minute check of his uniform. Before
finishing, he sent an incidental eye out and caught an old, muffler-hanging
Henry J that happened to be putt-putting by. It was abused by a hand-painted,
powder-pink paint job. A dumpy, compact car, it looked as if it were still
dripping with paint.

Carlsson started to go inside, but, thinking it odd to see the car, he
hesitated for a minute and watched as it eased to a stop and backed up a bit. A
blonde and wholesomely cute teen-age girl with baby-blue eyes was behind
the wheel. Not particularly noticing the junior policeman, she flicked an eye
out on the parking lot, scanned both the patrol and civilian cars, and drove on.

The girl's name was Carol. Carol was all-American. After having ditched school and taken in a movie, all-American Carol had spent the rest of the afternoon painting the car. She had not done a good job. With a touch of pink paint still on her cherubic cheeks, she was now on her way to the park. She would go there and wait. It was almost 20 minutes to midnight. Time, however, was not a factor. The all-American teenager in the hand-painted car with the hanging muffler had all night.

⌛

The interior of the Elton Head station held the hope of a metropolitan police department but succeeded only in being tiny, dull and dreadfully un-imaginative. It reeked of the gaslight era. Up front, stale, teal-green paint blistered the walls and clashed pitifully with a New Yorkishly high, brass-railed desk that sat forward of dated mug shots and a series of faded *Wanted* posters. They were carelessly tacked above an old, infrequently clattering teletype unit. Next to the unit were a series of alarms and tiny red lights, all miraculously wired to an aged radio system that accommodated more wires, jacks, and a rounded, chrome-plated RCA microphone. The mike was centered on the desk. Made in 1937, and the newest item in the station, it was the heart and soul of the Elton Head Police Department. Over the door, next to a big clock, hung the lone speaker. It was a big one, and both clock and speaker were hanging on by a thin wire and an even thinner prayer.

A built-in switchboard sat left-front on the solid oak desk, and sitting behind the desk and switchboard was Sergeant McShayne. A dispirited veteran, he was in charge of the midnight shift.

Dempsey O. McShayne was a puffy-faced, heavy-eyed Irishman with hair that was as white and refined as spun silk. If he had chanced dressing in a red suit and hadn't been so worn and dour-looking, even without a beard he could have passed for Santa Claus. He would have fit right in with the four-foot, light-less Christmas tree, that stood weakly in a bare corner just inside the door. It was underneath a sad, stationhouse picture of old-time cops.

The Elton Head P.D.'s Christmas tree was intentionally unadorned and sparse-looking. The placement had been designed for easy access. It was there for the merchants. By tradition and by strong and frequent hints from the uniformed men on patrol, the merchants were expected to drift in and out of the station during the Christmas season with their best wishes sealed in small, dollar-sized envelopes. The envelopes would be pinned on the spindly little tree. A well pinned tree would be taken down two days before Christmas so that the contents of the envelopes could be divided and put into larger manila envelopes for equal distribution to the men throughout the station. If the tree still had that skimpy and under-fed look two days before Christmas, it wouldn't come down. The boys in blue would get a little testy. Letting an envelope-starved tree stand meant that in the days and weeks that followed there would be an unsettling police presence flooding all over town, particularly on Main Street. The merchants would get the message. If they didn't hear about the tree's anemic condition directly, it would be reflected by an increase in parking citations — or tickets, as they were more commonly known. Disgruntled shoppers on Main Street were not a merchant's delight. And, too, it had to be remembered, Elton Head was surrounded by other little cities. Buses went to the other little cities. Even if not, since the end of the war, quite a few Elton Headers had acquired cars. The postwar boom had seen to that.

Over the years, sometimes the parking tickets and the Christmas tree connection worked; sometimes it didn't. One year the bones of the tree didn't come down until the Fourth of July.

Nobody was happy.

2.

A lot of it had been eroded, no doubt having succumbed to departmental apathy and ineptitude over the years, but Sergeant McShayne still showed traces of having once been a decent and determined man. Despite a gruff, hard-edged exterior, deep down he was just an old-timer, shaped by solid, old-fashioned values, and who, despite a salty tongue, still had a soft spot in his heart for those golden-oldie, profane-less *gee whiz, aw shucks* days.

Because the sergeant still had a job to go to at his age he was reasonably content with life, but he would never know the unqualified heights of contentment ever again because he was still inwardly grieving over his departed wife, Eleanor. She had been a deeply religious, loving woman who had died a few years ago after gamely enduring a long and painful illness. It was one of the few times the sergeant had wished he had had a different occupation. He wished he could have been a doctor. He would have saved her.

On the department for over 40 years, the glum but grandfatherly-looking veteran had long since been eligible for retirement but, as he asked himself time and time again, with the wonderful woman gone, what else was he to do? He didn't want to face it, but it was no secret that his heart was weak, and he was worn down by the midnight hours and by a department that, at times, seemed to be falling apart at the seams. But lately he had been thinking of a time when he would call it a day. He was procrastinating about a date, and more than once he wondered which would give out first — his heart or the department.

Something told him they would expire at the same time.

He should have been a prophet.

Like clockwork, the sergeant of the desk would arrive at the station at 11:20 p.m., or to use the correct term, 2320. Bucky Simmons, his selected assistant, should have shown up at the same time, but McShayne had become accustomed to his lateness, and so he would start the unhurried night alone, going over the day shift's events and double-checking those that had been logged in the thick blotter by the desk sergeant he would be relieving. In most cases the evening shift's desk sergeant would be the smug and cryptic Sgt. Elmore Zemora. Neither sergeant was overly communicative, principally because they didn't like each other, and so the procedure would take only a few minutes. Zemora would put on his coat, and say a sullen goodnight. Once outside, he'd light a cigarette and get lost in the dark, looking like the cat that ate the canary.

Zemora, a big man, always looked as if he knew something McShayne didn't.

For the past month or so Sergeant McShayne had developed a rather curious routine. He would wait and make sure that Sergeant Zemora had gone, and, as he would do all through the night, he would spin his chair to the telephone that was next to the switchboard, stare at it for a moment or two, then place a call. The call would go unanswered. Stifling irritation, he would re-cradle the phone, swivel the chair back around, and lose himself in the morning edition of the New York Daily News. By the time he would get to the comic section, comic-looking Bucky Simmons would come in carrying a Thermos bottle full of soup, correctly assuming that he would be selected to spend the night assisting on the desk. He would go through the ritual of giving the sergeant a quick "Evenin', Sarge," and duck inside the parking-ticket-violations office, or, as it was sometimes called, the citations office, that was adjacent to the desk. Bucky would go in there to put the Thermos away, sneak a nip of rum, and stash two pint bottles in the bottom drawer of the violations desk. While he was still in the citation room — or, as it was referred to, the parking-ticket-violations room — the switchboard at the desk would start buzzing. After about the eighth buzz an annoyed McShayne would swing around in the chair and holler for Bucky to come out and answer it. He would. The voice on the other end was always old; always musical. *"Hell-luuuu,"* it would say. *"Is that you-u-u-u, Buck-e-e-e?"*

It was the unofficial start of the midnight shift.

Reed-thin Bucky Simmons was an out-and-out alcoholic who was on the verge of being swallowed by delirium tremens — or the DTs, as they were known. He had the additional misfortune of being plagued with ill-fitting dentures. For convenience, he carried them in his hip pocket.

Younger than McShayne but older than the other patrolmen, Bucky was unshaven and had somewhere around 12 strands of hair that bounced independently from a face that looked as though a tractor-trailer had run over it, backed up and tried it again — sideways, this time achieving more success. But it was his denture problems that would have McShayne smoldering. As he did every night, Bucky pressed the telephone close to his chest and bent his alcoholic breath into the desk sergeant's ear. McShayne, already stiffened by the penetrating odor, said nothing. Bucky leaned down farther and sent his breath closer. "Mrs. Ina's on the line, Sarge."

His rummy breath swept around the sergeant's ear, curved around his face and settled up his bibulous nose with more discomfiture than a body with the odor of scurvy. But the sergeant held on.

Bucky said it a third time. McShayne finally laid the paper aside, lowered his head and began drumming his fingers on the desk. He was tapping out *Zippo lighter. Zippo lighter. Zippo lighter.* He was wondering whether breath could burn.

"Sarge…?"

"I heard you, Bucky."

"What should I tell her?"

"First of all, Bucky, back up. Just get back."

"What, Sarge?"

"Give me breathing room! When my wife was living, she didn't get into my face as close as you do. And she smelled a hell of a lot better. Now, back off."

Bucky moved the curled and extended switchboard cord away.

The sergeant hesitated, and said, "Now, tell me something, Bucky. Are you stupid or something?"

"Me? No, I'm feelin' fine."

"No. Are you really that stupid?"

"I'm feelin' fine, Sarge."

"I didn't ask you how you're feeling. I asked you...Oh, never mind," McShayne said. He couldn't afford to get too riled up so early in the night. He directed his attention back to the caller. "Tell the woman what you've been telling her every night; tell her the same thing you will be telling her for the next umpteen calls she'll be making before the night is over."

"What's that, Sarge?"

"How are you gonna ask me that?! You don't remember what you've been telling this nut who's been calling this station every single night?"

The bean-pole policeman shook his head in the negative.

"You don't remember that for years — every night — for nine solid years — we're talking even before Pearl Harbor..."

"Pearl Harbor?" Bucky said, thinking that the sergeant was speaking of the one, lone woman of the night who had left town twenty-odd years ago because of a lack of business. "Is she back in town?"

"Pearl Harbor, Bucky! It ain't a goddamn *she!* It's an it! *Pearl* Harbor. Can't you remember *Pearl Harbor?!*"

"Oh, now I know."

"I'm glad you do," McShayne said. "Now, do you remember what happened at Pearl Harbor?"

"They dropped a bomb on it," Bucky said, proud that he could remember.

"They dropped *several* bombs on Pearl Harbor. In fact, Bucky, they dropped a *ton* of bombs on Pearl Harbor! They were trying to erase Pearl Harbor from the face of the Earth!"

"Really?"

"Oh, yes, Bucky. But, now, do you remember who the *they* was?"

Bucky gave it some thought. He was stuck for an answer.

"The Japanese," McShayne helped. "The Japanese bombed Pearl Harbor. And do you remember what year it was when the Japanese bombed Pearl Harbor?"

"Thirty-eight?"

"No, Bucky."

"Thirty-seven?"

"The Japanese dropped bombs on Pearl Harbor on December 7th, 1941. Nine years ago!"

"What was it, some kinda accident or somethin'?"

"Nobody in their right mind is gonna think Pearl Harbor was an accident!"

"That's too bad."

"I'll say it is. Now, do you remember what happened *after* the Japanese bombed Pearl Harbor?"

"Er...let's see now..."

While Bucky was thinking, the old lady's voice filtered through the phone and bounced off his chest again. *"You-u-u-hooo...?"*

"Hang on, Mrs. Ina," Bucky answered, without moving the phone from his chest. "She's still waitin', Sarge."

"I don't care if she is. My question to you is, *what* did the country *do* after the Japanese bombed Pearl Harbor?!"

"I got an idea it was somethin' I shoulda remembered," Bucky said. "When'd you say it happened?"

"Nine years, one week, and five days ago."

"An' you remember it?"

"A lot of people do."

"Musta been somethin' big."

"We went to war!" McShayne roared. *"The country went to war!"*

"Oh," said Bucky without equal concern. "But didn't somethin' bigger than that happen in '38?"

McShayne started tapping his fingers again. *Zippo lighter. Zippo lighter. Zippo lighter.* This time he was tapping in deeper befuddlement. He was wondering whether the whole body could burn. "Something bigger than the country going to war."

"Yeah," said Bucky. "Seems to me it had the whole town rockin'." Suddenly he blinked. "Oh, I know what it was. I got it, Sarge. I got it! You made sergeant!"

"And in your mind that was bigger than the country going to war?"

"Absolutely."

"If you had a brain, you'd hurt yourself! You'd kill somebody!" McShayne sighed heavily. He stopped tapping on the desk and leaned forward in the swivel chair. "Bucky," he said, getting back to the point. "Put the telephone speaker to your lips — and remember you have two of them — and tell the woman what you've been telling her since before Pearl Harbor. Tell her that we'll be sending a car to the house. And after you've told her we'll be sending a car to the house, pull the jack out of the switchboard, hang the phone on the receiver and log the call in the blotter, like we do with every activity and call. Then get in back, and get ready for lineup."

Bucky Simmons knew he would be working the desk, and that lineup was just a formality. Still, he disliked lineup, and, after delivering the message to the old lady, he hung up. But instead of going in back and waiting in the patrol room, joining the others, he went in back and headed directly upstairs to the bathroom. After a quick stop in there, he'd sneak to the end of the hall where the chief's office was located. He'd spend the rest of the stolen minutes sipping on the chief's bourbon.

Carlsson, the last and clearly the neatest and youngest of the seven patrolmen who would be working the midnight watch, had already come in, uttering an unacknowledged but respectfully routine "Good evening, Sergeant," nodding and saluting McShayne. He continued through to the narrow corridor that ended at the patrol room that was squared in back.

The Elton Head Police Department's patrol room was miniaturized by sixteen dark green wall lockers and a long, linoleum-inlaid table, capable of seating 12. Next to the water cooler and a bulletin board that had been hammered onto the wall there was an unopened door leading to two 16-by-48-foot jail cells and the Identification Bureau. On the same side, almost splitting the dark corridor, were the dark creaky stairs that led to the detectives' room and, down from there, a combination interview and waiting room. At the opposite end of the hall, except for Bucky's excursions, was the sparingly used chief's office. Above it, nestled under the pitched roof, was a hayloft. It was a tiny, garretlike addition that had been made into three tiny jail cells for females. Since female arrests were relatively rare in Elton Head, the cells were used for storage.

On this night, however, a haggard, crocked and crooning 81-year-old woman occupied one of the cells. She had been arrested by the day shift well before noon, and the alcohol that wafted from her frail frame was still almost strong enough to bubble paint.

Back downstairs, Curley Spagg, an empty-headed, thin-haired, beefy, veteran patrolman was at the patrol-room bulletin board. He was wearing sunglasses and was wrongly dressed in motorcycle gear. The butt of a cigar in his mouth, cap cocked on the side, he was running a finger across an item of dubious interest when Carlsson came in and went to his locker for his ticket book and few other unimportant items needed for duty. When he unlocked and opened the locker, the rookie policeman saw that someone had stuffed it with rags, a bucket, and a police-capped mop. It was designed to look like a man. The rookie got the meaning, but didn't say anything. He quietly removed the items and took his regular seat at the table, joining the five other patrolmen. They were all older than he, and, except for Tetrollini, who was only about eight or nine years older, he couldn't truly identify with them.

From left to right, there was the gum-whacking Frank Pippilo, graying, ruddy and short. He had a sad, puppy-dog face. There was Georgiovone "Georgie" Tetrollini, a handsome, quiet younger man with black, curly hair and a heavy problem nibbling hard from within. Sitting next to him was Mickey Corbbo. Sloppy and talkative, Mickey was a childish 30, and devilishly pranksterish. He looked like the model for the Pillsbury doughboy — and laughed just as much. He was seated directly across from Johnny "the Dutchman" Van Dreelan. A pugnacious giant, Van Dreelan was a blondish, middle-aged man with a soprano voice, sturdy spaced teeth and a quirky face. All uniformed patrolmen, yawning, scratching, picking noses, and making ready for the midnight watch, except for Curley Spagg at the bulletin board, they were seated and alternately taking notes from the "flyer sheet."

When the junior policeman came into the room, his "hellos" were not as crisp and sharp as they could have been. It made no difference. As always, the responses were slow and grunt-like. Only the full-of-mischief Mickey Corbbo was lively. Carlsson knew he had been the mop culprit, and he knew Mickey could be counted on to lift his head from the flyer sheet and say something crude or come up with another prank, all in the attempt to tease and arouse. Carlsson's grandfather was the station janitor and Mickey was always on him about it, but the rookie promised himself he would never let anything Mickey said or did get to him.

Seating himself at the far end of the table, the rookie quietly said to no one in particular, "Anything new on the sheet?"

Van Dreelan mumbled, "Naw, same ol' stuff. Never no change."

"Never, never no change," a sad-looking Pippilo echoed. "Boring, boring, boring."

"An' even if it was somethin' new on the li'l flyer, it wouldn't concern you, li'l baby blue. It's for *real* policemen," Corbbo sniggered, and went back to scribbling in his notebook.

It was silent when Bucky prematurely came down from the chief's office. He was reeking of alcohol and fiddling with his dentures, but he was not quite as shaky as he had been before going upstairs. "Anybody got any sandpaper?"

"What do you gotta have sandpaper for?" Van Dreelan asked.

"I got somethin' stuck on my dentures," Bucky said, seating himself and clomp-clomping the off-colored whites in Van Dreelan's face. "See?"

"Get outta here with them things," Van Dreelan said.

Spagg moved away from the bulletin board and reclaimed his seat. He looked over at Pippilo. "Nice night out t'night. Frank, you ever see weather like that, Frank?"

"Ummhuh."

"Great-lookin' moon," Spagg said. "Frank, y'ever see a moon like that, Frank?"

"Yesterday afternoon," Pippilo said, dryly.

There was more silence for awhile, then Spagg said to Van Dreelan, "Dutch, you go bowlin' last night, Dutch?"

"Naw," said Van Dreelan. "Been savin' up to take the wife an' kids over to the drive-in in Teaneck this weekend. Hope the weather holds up."

"Wha's playin'?" Pippilo asked, not really concerned.

Van Dreelan mentally shrugged, "I dunno."

"Now *that,*" emphasized Spagg, "is a *real* good movie. Lotta action. No kissin'. An' noooo sissies."

"You ain't got no car," said Van Dreelan. "When'd you see it?"

"Last week. Took the wife."

"What'd you do, Spaggy?" Corbbo giggled. "Take your bicycle and let her ride on the handlebars?"

"Up yours," answered Spagg. He swung his look over to Pippilo, "Hey, Pip, you go bowlin' last night, Pip?"

"Umhuh."

"Where'd you go? 'Mercun Legion?"

"Umhuh."

"Slow?"

"Dead."

"Same at the Elks," concluded Spagg. "Dead-o."

It was silent again. Bucky was still fiddling with dentures. He leaned over to Carlsson. "You gotta paper clip?"

"No," said Carlsson. "Not on me."

Bucky clomped the teeth in the air for inspection, brought them down and pumped Tetrollini. "Hey, Georgie-Porgie, you gotta paper clip?"

"No, I don't," Tetrollini said quietly.

"Bucky, why don't you put them things back in your mouth where they belong," Pippilo said.

"Hey, I got problems," Bucky retorted.

"Damn right, you got problems," Pippilo answered.

"Hold it a sec, Buck," Van Dreelan said, moving his chair closer to the string-bean policeman with the few strands of hair. "Open y'mouth."

"Wha'cha gonna do, John-John?"

"Staple 'em in."

"Will it hurt?"

"I'll put some ink on 'em," Van Dreelan said. "Kill the pain."

"Good thinkin'," said Bucky.

"Bucky, you idiot, you," Pippilo squawked.

"Wha…wha…what?" said Bucky.

"If you wanna be that stupid, then go ahead."

With Van Dreelan laughing, Bucky finally got the point and put the dentures back into his hip pocket. Corbbo leaned back in his chair and tossed another teasing look to Carlsson. "I wish my Grandpoppy-poo had some pull. Tee, hee, hee. If my Grandpoppy-poo had some pull, I'd pick somebody's behind to kiss so's I could become a policeman, too."

"Lay off'a the kid, Mickey," Van Dreelan said. "He can't help what his grandpop is. An' at one time or another we all did a little rear-end kissin' to get a job."

"John," said Corbbo.

"What?"

"Go suck a fig."

At the front desk, the clock inched on. McShayne tried the telephone again. Again there was no response to the call. He was about to step in back to conduct the roll call when the door flung open and the Chinaman Charlie Wong blew in for the first of his tri-nightly visits. Normally Charlie wouldn't come in with anything but his inborn peppy brightness, but this time he was carrying an overly large wok pot.

Dressed in his usual severely-pressed white suit with polished brown and white wing-tipped shoes on tiny feet, by Elton Head's standards, Charlie was dapper. But more than anything, he was a non-stop, snappy-moving, half-stoned irrepressible nut.

Close to the age of 40, Charlie had been born in China and hadn't stopped smiling since he was seen holding his behind while outrunning the tips of a squad of Japanese bayonets during the rape of Nanking in 1937.

Charlie loved America. One of Elton Head's happiest people, he owned a dismal little restaurant only a few doors down from the station. But the short, moon-faced man was best known for spending the nights scouring the streets, looking for anything that wore a skirt. It was said that if it didn't wear a skirt, he would lower his sights. Anything with hair would do.

Arming the big pot to the desk, he beamed, "Sargento, Sargento, what a fantasti-co night, Sargento! *Walla:* It is Chinese New Year. You not Chinese. Big surprise. Wong Chinese. Ho, ho, ho. Wong do very special for friend-o of Chinese. *Walla:* a wok pot for the Sargento! Happy New Year! Or, as they say in the old country: Gung Ho Fat Choy!! Nice night. Beee-u-tee-ful moon. *Walla:* Wong go New Year party, but Wong no forget favorite Sargento."

Snappily, he came around to the side of the brass-railed desk and slopped the pot down for the formal, but solemn, pronouncement. "In honor of Year Of The Pig: Wong presento to favorite Sargento a Wong special. *Walla!* Seaweed soup. But not justa seaweed soup, Sargento! *Bamboooo* anda seaweed, prepared with sautéed egg yolk, sweet tea, steamed sake, Peking gin, Hong Kong scotch, Far East rum, anda from ice of the great Kai River, north of the China Sea, flozen lice wine!! *Walla!"* He said a little blessing over the pot, and chipped in, "Enjoy, enjoy, enjoy!" He turned and headed for the door. "Now, I go anda get lucky. *Walla!* Plenty pletty girls. As they say in old country, I'm off to follow yellow blick load. Ha, ha, ha. Ho, ho, ho. Gung Ho Fat Choy! Happy New Year!"

Out Charlie went. Into the tin waste container went the soup. McShayne swiveled back to the telephone.

The call went unanswered again.

Back in the patrol room Spagg adjusted his sunglasses, crossed his feet on the table and said to Tetrollini: "Hey, Georgie-Porgie, what's with you? Why so glum?"

Tetrollini didn't want to go into it and dismissed him with a quiet, "Nothing."

Spagg had a point. Tetrollini was glum. In fact, he had been literally dragging for the past few weeks or so.

Georgiovone Tetrollini was quiet by nature, but now he was down and uncomfortably withdrawn. Of late, he never wanted to look anyone directly in the eyes. It created concern because, if Elton Head wanted to show a model policeman, Tetrollini could have easily been the one. Deeply religious, he was married, and it was well known that he was dedicated to both

home and job, and his wife was an auburn-haired beauty who could have —
and often had been — mistaken for a cover-girl. But Marge was not a cover-
girl, and in fact, had no interest in anything close to the profession. What she
was, she enjoyed. She enjoyed being Mrs. Tetrollini, and she enjoyed the
reputation of being the best nurse at the hospital in nearby Maywood. At 26
there was only one thing missing in her life, and that was a baby. It was
something she and Georgie were working on.

Spagg swung his attention across the table to Frank Pippilo. "Hey, Pip,
how many Beech Street calls did you get from Miss America last night, Pip?"

"Mrs. Ina? Three."

"The ol' bag's gettin' worse, huh?"

"Umhuh."

Corbbo yawned, and sniggered, "Maybe Mrs. Ina wants you to give
her a li'l poke, Pip."

"Why don't you set your face out with the garbage?"

"Good idea. It'll give your mom somethin' else to lick on."

Pippilo grabbed his nightstick and sprang across the table. "I'll murder ya. I'll murder ya."

"C'mon! C'mon," Corbbo said. He was on his feet, his baton poised
for action. "I'll cream ya. I'll cream ya! C'mon. I dare ya. I dare ya." They
stood there like two home-run-hitting baseball players, ready to swing for the
fences. No one was concerned; nothing was going to happen. Interrupting
the non-flow of action was the I've-seen-it-all-before McShayne. He had
sauntered back to the patrol room to call the roll. "Cut it out," he said, casually laying his clipboard on the table. "How many times I gotta tell you guys,
you wanna fight, go outside!"

Pippilo and Corbbo backed off and, as usual, harmlessly jawed at each
other, then followed the rest of the men in picking up their notebooks, pens
and pencils, and automatically falling into a careless line for inspection.

"Sarge, you see the moon, t'night, Sarge?" Spagg asked.

"I'll moon *you* if you don't fall in," McShayne answered.

Bucky dug for his dentures again and said to anyone who was listening,
"Did it stop snowin' yet?"

"Put'cha teeth in, Bucky. And the next time you come to work, you'd better have a clean shave," McShayne said, moving to the front of the sad-sack formation.

"Yeah, put'cha chop-chops in," Corbbo said.

"An' have you been upstairs in the chief's bourbon again?" McShayne said.

"Me?" said Bucky, "I never touch the stuff."

Before anyone could say anything, Pippilo said, "An' what difference do it make to you if it's snowin' out there, Bucky? You ain't gotta be out there in it."

"You're gonna be in here where it's warm an' cozy, kissy-kissin'," Corbbo added, which drew a stern response from McShayne.

"Hey, Sarge, did'ja hear?" Bucky said, fingering his dentures, in worse condition now because he had been sitting on them. "Ike's gonna go over to that there Korea an' visit th' troops."

"Put'cha teeth in, Bucky."

"Yeah. An' who cares where Eisenhower's goin'?" Pippilo said. "He ain't been elected no president yet, an' that ain't no real war over there, anyhow. He ain't doin' nuttin' by going over there but wastin' gas."

Bucky held the dentures up for another look.

"Put the teeth *inside* the mouth, Bucky," McShayne ordered.

"Would'ja like to hear a li'l Mario Lanza, Sarge?" Corbbo said.

"No," McShayne said firmly.

It didn't stop Corbbo from belting out: *"Beeeeee muy loooove.....!"*

"Quiet, Mickey!" the desk sergeant ordered. He switched his attention to Spagg. "Spagg, it's minutes before midnight. It *should* be dark outside. Take the damn sunglasses off!"

"Wha...? No freedom in this country?"

"I'll show you freedom, all right. An' what in the blazes are you doing with that motorcycle outfit on? What do you think you're doing, working traffic?"

"S'th' only thing I got left, Sarge. Lately everything else's been shrinkin'."

"How'n hell do you go about getting a blue serge uniform to shrink?"

"By puttin' it in a washin' machine."

Before McShayne could fire off his response, Bucky complained, "Did

I tell you, Sarge? These new teeth hurt."

"More than your teeth is gonna be hurtin' if you don't put 'em in!" McShayne said.

"Did I tell you what I paid for 'em?"

"I don't give a damn how much you paid for the teeth, Bucky," said the sergeant. "Just clam up an' put 'em in your mouth!"

Hurt, Bucky did as ordered.

"Beeeeee muy loooove.....!"

"I said: *Shut. Up. Mickey!"* McShayne yelled, then routinely called for the showing of notebooks, pens and flashlights. When it came to displaying the pistols, the procedure was to empty the cartridges into the palm of their hands, hold them out in the left hand, and hold the pistol-butts up with the thumb and forefinger of the right hand for the sergeant's inspection. It was rare that McShayne would look at a weapon, but every night since being there he would have a comment to the always quiet but observing rookie. Normally it was: "When was the last time you've cleaned that thing?"

"Just before coming to work, sir."

"Clean it again," McShayne ordered, then picked up the clipboard from the table. Before starting to read it aloud, he said to the rookie, "By the way, Carlsson, what time did you report in?"

"2340. I spoke and saluted when I came in, sir. "

"Lineup for the midnight shift is 2345. 2330 is the required time of arrival."

"Yes, sir."

Corbbo again: "Hey, Sarge...?"

"Shut up, Mickey," McShayne ordered. He began reading from the clipboard. "Bucky Simmons — assisting on the desk."

It sent the shaky policeman peeling off to go back up to the bathroom. After another drink, he came back down and went to the front desk.

Pippilo groaned, "How come I never get to work the desk?"

"How come nonna us don't?" echoed Spagg.

"Shut up," McShayne said bluntly. "If you don't like your assignment, you know what you can do."

"What's that, Sarge?" Corbbo asked, needling.

McShayne stabbed him with a look and went back to the clipboard. "Car 101 — Frank Pippilo. 102 — Curley Spagg. 103 — Mickey Corbbo; 104 — Georgiovone Tetrollini; 105 — Johnny Van Dreelan. Danny Carlsson: post 1-A, walking."

Corbbo sniggered, and said, "Think we gonna need the snow chains on the cars t'night, Sarge? Because I'm really gonna rack up the ol' miley-miles. I'm gonna knock 'em dead."

"I'll bet," Pippilo grumbled.

"Chains for what?" McShayne asked, negatively. "There ain't that much snow out there."

Spagg leaned over to Van Dreelan. "Whaddaya say we change posts t'night?"

"Hell no," the Dutchman said with uncommon firmness. "I ain't changin' with nobody. An' don't *nobody* forget it."

"Cheez," retorted Spagg, "it was just a suggestion t'break the monot'ny for a night. You don't have to get so hot under the collar over it."

"I just want you to know, I ain't changin'. I ain't changin', one night or no night," Van Dreelan said flatly.

"Nobody's changin' anything," McShayne said. "You've got your assignments. And that's it."

Corbbo tee-heed, then lipped a reminder to McShayne.

"Oh, yes," said the sergeant. "Don't forget, Carlsson: Make sure you check all your doors. You missed one last night, and the chief heard about it."

"Howz he hear about anythin'?" Pippilo said.

"How *can* he hear?" Spagg added.

"If you guys got a problem with the chief, come in during the day, and take it up with him," McShayne retorted.

"How?" Spagg blurted. "He ain't never here."

"He can't even find the station," Pippilo continued.

"Bet his wife could," Van Dreelan said. "Specially if she knew there was a coupla full bottles in the office up there."

"I'm tellin' you guys for the last time," McShayne said. "Cut it out."

"Yeah, sure," Pippilo said without conviction.

"Like I said, Carlsson," McShayne continued, "When the chief hears about something, I hear about it. And I don't like hearin' from the chief. Clear?"

"Clear, sir."

"An' I want you to pull your rear doors first, then hit your fronts. You got that?"

"Yes, sir," answered the rookie.

Corbbo, two men down, teased: "Could'ja have him say it a li'l louder, Sarge? I can't hear him down this end."

"Shut up, Mickey," McShayne said, and checked his watch: "Synchronize — 2353." When the watches supposedly were synchronized, he said, "Now, I want no goofin' off in them cars tonight. You've got a good clear night out there, an' things are liable to happen…"

"It's a heavenly night out there, Sarge," Corbbo said, spreading hot air. "An' you can count on me to do my share to protect the good and decent people of this great city."

"Mickey, shut up," McShayne said, knowing Mickey was full of crap. "Now, I want this town covered like a blanket. I want mileage on them cars. That means no sleeping. No excuses. I want *mileage*, you got that? *Mileage.*"

There were a few mumbled "um-hums" along with a "what a crock" comment from Pippilo.

"You can grumble all you want," McShayne warned. "But the mileage reports will be thoroughly checked in the morning."

Mileage was *the* important thing as far as the department was concerned. It meant that the patrol cars were covering the city and that the men were not — as inelegant as it might have sounded — goofing off.

The department had a point. On the graveyard shift, the night had a way of taking its toll. It would start with monotony and work its way to the eyes. Eyelids would become heavy, and more often than not the patrolmen would start by dozing mentally, or thinking about grabbing a little shuteye here or there, or planning on spending the night parked behind a building or some out-of-the-way place.

Many were the mornings when the shift ended and the patrolman was still asleep.

McShayne was about to dismiss the formation when Mickey Corbbo sliced a hand in the air. "Er...Sarge...?"

"What is it now, Corbbo?!"

"You wanna tell 'em about that other thing?"

"What other thing?"

"The reservoir?"

As if remembering, the sergeant said, "Van Dreelan, you're in 105. Keep an eye out on the reservoir."

"Why?"

"Corbbo thinks something suspicious has been going on out there."

"Like what?" Van Dreelan asked. "What would anybody be doing at a water reservoir?"

Said the adolescent Mickey Corbbo in a tiny, innocent voice: *"Pee'n in it."*

"Pee'n?" Van Dreelan lifted his voice. "Somebody's been peein' in the reservoir??"

"Umhuh."

"How would you know something like that, Mickey?" Van Dreelan pumped.

"Yeah," said McShayne. "Come to think of it, how *would* you know?"

"A li'l birdie told me," Corbbo said. "A little water-tastin' birdie who was very upset because he doesn't like the taste of human tinkle." He started laughing.

"You're gonna try me just once too often, Mickey," McShayne said, crumbling the sad-sack formation and stalking up front. "Just once too often!"

The sergeant arrived behind the desk just in time to catch Bucky responding to the buzzing switchboard. It was a call for Frank Pippilo.

Bucky covered the mouthpiece and hollered to the patrol room in back. "Hey, Pippy? Frank? Telephone."

"Who'zit? The wife?" Pippilo called back.

"S'a male's voice," said Bucky.

"Then it must be the wife, Pip," Corbbo snorted.

Apparently Pippilo didn't hear him. He yelled up front. "Plug the phone in tickets, Bucky."

At about that time, the rest of the men were sauntering past the front desk. Corbbo went back to teasing Carlsson. Spagg took a moment out to make a comment to McShayne and Bucky. "Don't you girls hurt each other tonight," he said.

"Another crack like that, Spagg, an' I'll have you down in the cemetery, patrollin' headstones," the sergeant responded.

In the ticket room, Pippilo picked up the telephone. "Yeah? Oh, Doc Conforti, how we doin'?" It took but a fraction of a second. The cop's face sagged, his body drooped: *"Whaaaaat?"* The bad news had him putting the phone down and slipping over to close the door. He came back to the phone. "Oh, geezus, Doc, please, whatever you do, don't tell me that. Y'gotta be wrong."

At the desk, the switchboard buzzed again. En route to answering it, Bucky said to McShayne: "Oh, that r'minds me, Sarge; we've already got two missing cat calls. An' Mrs. Ina, she called again."

The moment he ended the call, the switchboard sounded again.

Bucky got it. "EHPD...? Righto." He turned to McShayne. "It's Charlie Wong, Sarge. Somethin' about how you enjoyed the soup? An' he says, *Walla* — whatever that means. An' don't forget this is the Year of the Pig, he said."

"Pull the plug, Bucky," McShayne said, already showing the initial stages of wear and tear.

Outside, the gentle snow had stopped falling and the midnight air had gotten warmer. It felt almost balmy. Corbbo hadn't noticed. Once outside, he had stopped talking and hadn't noticed anything. He wasn't even paying teasing attention to Carlsson. He was too busy sneaking something that looked like a blanket and a sack from his personal car to the trunk of the patrol car.

What had not been noticed, either, was that Johnny Van Dreelan in car 105 had, with great care, taken the strange move to stash a garment bag into the trunk of the patrol car before driving off. In the bag was a spanking-white tuxedo.

Giggling, and pleased that his work had been done, Corbbo swung a look to Carlsson, who was about to saunter off for the three-block walk to his post on Main Street. Corbbo couldn't let him leave before giving him a final shot. Exaggerating an ape-like walk, he hooted: "Git along, li'l dogie: *walk,*

walk, walk. An' when you get to them doors: *pull, pull, pull."*

Carlsson turned, gave the teasing patrolman a noncommittal look and moved up the street.

The quietly troubled Tetrollini in car 104 had been the first to pull out of the yard. Like the girl who had passed the station earlier, he was on his way to the park. He hadn't said anything to anyone; no one paid attention to him as he drove his Hudson deliberately away. It was not unusual for Tetrollini to be the first to leave when going on patrol. He was never apt to remain in the yard longer than necessary. He was there to do a job, and he was known to do it in the best way he knew how. His post — 104 — was closer to the station than the other four, and the responsibilities were to cover the city's easternmost section, bounded by Main Street, the cemetery, the adjacent park, and the river.

It was nice to say that Elton Head had a river. New York had a river. But, factually, Elton Head's river was a betrayal. They should have just called it *sludge* and let it go at that. But no. Back in the Twenties, no doubt touched by the fever that prohibition had created, somebody was saddled with the idea that a good Northern city wasn't really a good Northern city unless it had a river — and since Elton Head had *some* water running through it, a river it should be called. What the wags of the day forgot to consider was that, generally speaking, a river was defined as a large body of water that fed into the ocean at some point. Of course rivers flowed into lakes and other rivers, but, in this case, the operative word was *large.* Elton Head did not have a "large" body of water. At one time — probably around about the time Mr. Elton's head was being claimed by the Indians he had duped — the city had something that *resembled* a river, but in the latter years, the years of progress and modernization, it became filled with so much dirt and debris that the traffic department could have pretended it was another street and painted lines on it.

"Friggin' guys on the evening shift."

That was the beefy and empty-headed Spagg talking. He was still in the yard conducting a sloppy but mandatory inspection of his patrol car before pulling out for the night. Angered at seeing something he didn't like, he slid his cap over an eye and hollered up to the second-floor window. "Hey, Mariscalco! *Mariscalco*!!"

A partly undressed patrolman from the evening shift raised the window and stuck his head out. "Wha...wha...wha?!"

Spagg put on his sunglasses, tossed the butt of a cigar into his mouth, and silently jabbed at the vehicle's right front wheel, indicating something was wrong.

"Whaddya pointin' at?! I can't see nothin' from up here!"

"I'm pointin' at where the hubcap is supposed to be, you ape," Spagg said. "You lost a hubcap. You know that? You lost the last hubcap that was on the car. Whaddaya think I'm gonna look like ridin' around all night without a hubcap on the car?! How come you lost it?!"

"I didn't do nothin'," Mariscalco fired back. "It was lost on the day shift. Mike Greenfield did it."

"Oh, he did, did he?"

"I sure as hell didn't do it."

Spagg clamped down hard on the butt of the cigar, looked back at the wheel again. "Figgers," he crudely muttered, "two Hebes on the department an' one of 'ems gotta be a thief. He prob'ly sold the friggin' thing." He hollered back up, asking if Greenfield had filled out a report.

"How should I know?" Mariscalco responded.

"Because you're s'posed to know!" Spagg hollered back. "You just got finished from usin' it! An' I ain't gonna be r'sponsible! They ain't gonna tack no missin' hubcap on me, you got that?! This ain't gonna be like the fender last week! An' the bumper an' lights the week before that! An' the grille the week before that! Y'hear me?!"

"Up yours, ya kraut!!" Mariscalco hollered back down.

Spagg ripped off his sunglasses. "Hey! I'll '*up yours*' all right. Come down here, I dare ya. I dare ya to come down! I'll show you who's gonna do the uppin', you goddamn dago!"

"Get lost," Mariscalco said. He ended it by giving the rough-edged patrolman the finger and slamming the window back down.

Spagg responded with a clenched fist and a rousing "Ah, bahfahgoola, you Mish!" He eared his sunglasses and slid into the car. Before driving off, he spotted Pippilo dragging to car 101. The short policeman's head was hanging and he was muttering under his breath.

Spagg pulled the vehicle closer. "S'matter, pal-o?"

Pippilo slammed his emergency kit and eight-cell flashlight onto the passenger's seat, got into the patrol car and almost broke the key trying to jam it into the ignition.

"Hey, hey, hey," Spagg said, trying to console him. "What gives, ol' bud-bud? Me an' you don't keep nuthin' from each other. We're a team. Wha's up?"

Pippilo finally blurted, "The damn'd test came back positive!"

Spagg whistled, "You're kiddin'!"

"The hell I am. I'm a goner, Spagg."

"Mama Mia!" said Spagg, putting his car into neutral gear for a chat.

"Y'know what it means? Know what it means? Huh?" Pippilo said. "I'll tell you what it means. It means I gave it to Helen."

"Oh, she'll kill ya," Spagg said. "Th li'l lady'll kill ya."

"She'll murder me."

"She'll do both," Spagg said agreeably. "'Cause that's the one thing you never wanna do, give the missus the ol' Social Disease. 'Specially one who works on a tugboat. I mean we ain't talkin' about no Rosie the Riveter. Your wife was a Marine drill instructor during the war."

It didn't sound right, but Pippilo's wife did serve in the Marines during the war, and was now a four-year veteran of the docks of New York's harbor. She was not a delicate woman. She packed a pistol, her mouth was coarse, her attitude worse, and her hands were knotty and callused. Pippilo was quite right in thinking that he would be a "goner" if she ever came close to finding out he had been untrue.

The dreary-faced cop banged on the steering wheel. "I gave my wife a dose! Can you b'lieve it? As good as I've been!"

"You've been a prince, ol' buddy," Spagg said. "Hell, you're one of the best hub-hubbies on the department. Who'd you get it from, li'l hum-hum-hum?"

"No, whoozis. The redhead that works in the city clerk's office."

Spagg slapped his forehead. "Oh, geezus. Of all people. I hear she's as hot as a firecracker. You didn't use protection — a raincoat — when you two's was doin' it?"

"I couldn't find any," Pippilo lamented. "The store we use was closed."

"Why didn' you call me? I had one. You know I keep a spare."

"You was usin' it," Pippilo said, putting the car in gear and backing out. "R'member last week when I radioed you for one?"

"But'cha still could'a come on over an' got it," said Spagg. "Should'a asked. I woulda saved it for you. Hell, it was almost new when I found it."

Overlooking car 104, and with Carlsson as the stem, looking down from a high-up distance, the four Hudson patrol cars formed what was nearly a cloverleaf in their patterns of departure. 101 would go east. 102 would go west. 103 would go north. 105 would go south — and thus the good city of Elton Head, New Jersey, was covered like a blanket. Everyone and everything could rest well. With that hint, that pinch — *that smidge* — of change dangling in the air, the boys in blue were on the job.

3

Main Street; Post 1-A.

In some ways it lay there like a collapsed vein, spiritless under a row of dust-baked neon lights that sputtered erratically from an array of stores and dallied with tired street lamps. With a few trees here and there, the street was a mile and three-quarters long, and served the needs of the town's almost 15,000 inhabitants. A long line of low-clinging wood, brick and asbestos-shingled shops dressed each side of uneven curbs and promoted the feeling of Tiny Town trying to spring into the big time while still trying to maintain an isolation and aloofness from tomorrow.

Elton Head's Main Street had always sent out mixed and troubling signals. There was an unwillingness to settle for yesterday, yet there would be no satisfaction with the future. A new shop, for instance, seemed out of place; a long line of old shops meant progress had failed to stop by; but then a new shop would fight character and destroy tradition. But despite the conditions there was a kind of coziness there; a certain kind of "I remember that" quality, even though it was hard to remember where or when. Like Anytown, USA, Elton Head's Main Street zeroed in on life. The stores offered their wares via poised and coiffured mannequins, dreamily announcing what was — and what was to be. But there was also the gradual decline to the low end. There were the marked-up bus stops, a forlorn tavern, a three-ball pawn shop, a flophouse, a few more stores, and two seamy alleyways with grease-stained gutters that ran down to a glutinous sewer that fed the *river*.

Danny Carlsson, on post, was on the other side of the street, which was still coated with snow. He returned a resigned, unenthusiastic wave that was delivered by the drudging patrolman he was relieving and watched as the 4-to-12 man melted into the night. He then went around to the rear of the stores and started on the required procedure of door-pulling. As McShayne had said, the fronts would be checked after the rears.

In addition to not liking the police station and the department itself, the rookie policeman disliked going from door to door, pulling and yanking on them to make certain they were locked. It was an asinine idea, and he quite rightly reasoned that common sense alone should have told the department that if a store owner or manager was careless enough to forget to lock his doors, he should suffer the consequences.

Carlsson was at the start of pulling when he saw Mickey Corbbo speeding by the alley in car 103. Severely off post and heading in the wrong direction, Mickey was taking a tour of the city before settling in for the night.

With red light flashing, and him singing out the window, *"Hi Hoooo, hi hoooo. It's off to work I gooo,"* the jolly policeman nursed the vehicle around the corner of Main Street, where he saw the rookie. Mickey tooted his horn, hit the siren, stuck more of his head out the window, waved, giggled heartily, and sped on.

Zipping out of Carlsson's sight, the patrol car spun down Railroad Avenue, cornered Berdan Place, and zoomed down River Street. As luck would have it, there was an accident at the intersection of River and Moonachie. It involved a '49 Ford and a '47 DeSoto. The two cars had smacked into each other with such getting-to-know-you thoroughness, that they looked like two giant accordions engaged in something immoral.

Apparently no one was hurt in the accident, but the two drivers, feeling no pain after a hard night of drinking in Jess Brown's Flamingo, were in the middle of the street, sleeves rolled up, slipping and sliding in the snow and looking as if they were about to kill each other. They were so into it that they did not see the policeman's car. But the policeman saw them. Instantly Mickey hit the siren, tooted his horn, put both hands on the steering wheel — and executed one of the swiftest U-turns the car had ever made. When the two about-to-be-combatants stopped long enough to see the departing patrol car, they hollered and whistled for assistance. It was all for naught. Mickey was heading for the other side of town.

Corbbo loved speeding with the siren on. A lot of times he would have it blasting for no reason at all, and with no concern about waking anybody from a midnight sleep.

Mickey loved flashing the red light on top of the car as well, but he couldn't see it from the inside and sometimes he would be speeding without it. Sometimes, too, he'd stick his head out to check. When he did, no tree, pole, gutter or curb was safe.

Unnecessarily, in leaving the two drivers who were involved in the accident, but with a mission in mind, Mickey had skidded around Rudd Street, sped down Walker, crossed Davis, picked up speed on Clay and had given it all she had when he passed JoMo's, the town's only black nightclub. He didn't see Johnny Van Dreelan parked on the side of the club, but Van Dreelan saw him. He had heard the siren, and now he saw the flashing red light.

The Dutchman, who himself should have been patrolling rather than being fixed at the black nightclub, was curious. He picked up the mike. "105 to headquarters…"

"Come in, Five," McShayne's voice answered.

"You give any signal eighty-eights yet?"

"No."

"An' ain't no emergencies nowhere?"

"None."

Van Dreelan thoughtfully returned the mike back into the cradle. Although Corbbo was off post again, and driving as though somebody's life was hanging in the balance, Van Dreelan had a hunch where the elfish cop was going. He cranked up and drove off, making a beeline to Daisy Lane.

Van Dreelan had correctly anticipated where Mickey Corbbo would eventually end up, and so when he arrived on Daisy Lane, he simply pulled in front of a house that was midway up the block. He put his headlights out and waited. He wasn't there long before Corbbo ended his tour by skidding around the corner and speeding directly to the third house down. It was 190 Daisy Lane, and car 103 zipped down the driveway and slid to a stop inches away from the garage door with amusing familiarity.

190 Daisy Lane was a charming, two-story, out-of-the-way, hard-to-see house with a back staircase running up to the second floor. Though it was hard to see from the street, it was still nicely framed with winking blue and white Christmas lights. Corbbo didn't live there, but he acted as if he did.

By now Van Dreelan had moved his car up and was eyeing his every move. He was a long way from being surprised when he saw the dumpy little policeman working with the double-door garage.

"Aw, Mickey," the Dutchman said to himself, "You slick little devil, you. I know what you're up to. I *know* what you're up to!" He chuckled to himself and pulled away, knowing he would be back in an hour or two.

Getting set for the night, Mickey Corbbo was working as though he had just moved into a new home. Even though it was not his house — and certainly it was one that he would *never* have been invited to — Mickey was a paragon of odd efficiency.

He chuckled, smiled at the moon, opened the garage doors and drove car 103 inside. He quickly got out, turned on the garage lights, closed the doors, and went to another level of work. He got two jacks from the trunk, and a couple of blocks from the sack he had secreted in the car earlier. Obviously, this was not a new act.

Diligently and routinely, the cop placed the blocks in front of the front tires, and the jacks under the rear axle of the vehicle. He jacked both sides of the car up to a point where the wheels were barely clearing the garage floor, then removed a hose from the sack and attached one end to the Hudson's exhaust pipe and slipped the other end outside just above the snow. He secured the hose by wedging it between the two garage doors. With a quick, admiring eye on his handiwork, he got back into the vehicle, started the engine and hopped back out to check the wheels. They were rotating beautifully. Satisfied, he dug into the sack and came out with a pillow. For good measure, he grabbed the blanket and lantern. The lantern added a homey atmosphere. He tossed the blanket and pillow into the back seat, lit the lantern, hung it on the antenna, and secured it with tape. Next, he re-checked the odometer on the speedometer. The mileage was on the move. He congratulated himself; he shook hands with himself. Then the grinning, busy-as-a-bee patrolman cut the garage lights off, hopped into the back seat, reached over and grabbed the mike from its cradle. He pressed the side button a few times and allowed the mike to remain up front. He was testing for "squawks" and the proper volume. Everything ship-shape, he slid under the blanket and started singing, *"Hi Hoooo, hi hoooo.   It's Off To Work I Gooo!"*

Mickey really loved the next level. He bolted upright, grabbed the mike from the receiver, stretched the loosely curled coil all the way to the back seat, and adjusted to transmit. "Er...patrol car 103 to headquarters, come in."

It irritated the sergeant of the desk just to hear Mickey Corbbo's voice on the radio. "What?"

"Er, Sarge, could you give me a test, please?"

McShayne fumed, "What do you need a test for, Mickey?"

"I'm trav'lin' in a static area, Sarge, an' I'm gettin' squawks an' static on my radio. Particularly up here on this hill."

"What hill?"

"This big one."

"This is Elton Head, New Jersey. There ain't no big hills in this city."

"High Street."

McShayne fired into the mike. "That ain't a goddamn hill! That's an incline!"

"Maybe that's why my radio ain't *'inclined'* to be workin'."

"If it ain't working, how can you hear me?!"

"That's just the point, Sarge. I can't hear you."

"If you can't hear me, Mickey, how'n hell can you be answerin' me?!"

"Oh, have you been sayin' something?"

"Corbbo, you sonofa..." The sergeant was too miffed to get it out. "Corbbo, what are you up to?!"

"Out here on the road gettin' mileage, kind sir," Corbbo said, still resting easily. "I'm doin' just like you said, an' all I want the test for is, I wanna make sure we keep in touch. S'gonna be a busy-busy night. You can call B.F. Goodrich an' have 'em stand by with some more tires, 'cause I'm gonna be peelin' lots an' lots of rubber. So let's stay in touch."

"We're gonna keep in touch, Mickey," the sergeant said. "We're gonna keep in *very* close touch." Then in an official voice, he delivered, "This is the Elton Head Police Department, badge 71, on a test to patrol car 103. How do you read, Three?"

Corbbo slid all the way under the blanket for a more accurate reading.

McShayne, not getting a response to the first transmission, repeated, "Elton Head PD, badge, 71, on a test to car 103, how do you read, Three?"

Corbbo lifted himself from under the blanket and tilted over the front seat to adjust the volume knob.

"Come in, Three!" McShayne demanded.

The pudgy cop flipped back with the mike.

"Dammit! Squad car 103!!"

With the mike stretched under the cover, Corbbo said, "Er, Sarge...?"

"What?!"

"How far're you away from the mike?"

"How far am I *what*?!"

"Away from the mike. In other words, are you in your regular position an' speakin' in your regular tone?"

"Corbbo!" McShayne said through gnashed teeth, "What in the hell are you doing?!"

Corbbo quickly sent an arm into the sack. He started digging for something he had forgotten, leaving the voice on the other end hanging.

"Three!!!" McShayne demanded.

Corbbo continued looking.

"Damn you, Three! ...*Three!!*"

After extracting a loud-ticking alarm clock from the sack, Corbbo grabbed the mike. "Sorry, couldn't read you on that last transmission, Sarge. Will you repeat? I say again, will you repeat?"

"I said," blustered the sergeant. "I said, what in the hell are you doing?!"

"Just burnin' the ol' midnight oil, Sarge," Corbbo said, then held the ticking clock to the mike. "You hear them miles click-click-clickin'?"

The sergeant hauled off and fired, *"That's a goddamn clock!!"*

"No, no, no, Sargeroni. What you are hearin' are smiles an' miles addin' up."

"Miles?! You call what I'm hearin' *miles*?!"

"Yessir, O'great and wise leader. An' that means that once again your Mickey Corbbo will be your mileage leader. *Calling all cars, calling all cars, be on the lookout for Mickey Corbbo, your mileage leader.* How do you read, baby blue?"

"CORBBO?!!"

"That's good, Sarge! That's it! Now you've got it! That's just grrreeaaat!! Try an' keep that same volume all night." The cop pulled the blanket up snugly, then stuck his head back up with the mike. "Oh, an' Sarge, if Bucky's gonna be on the mike, tell him to do the same. This is your mileage leader, over an' out."

McShayne could have killed him. He knew Corbbo was up to something, but he didn't know what.

"Give the time-check, Bucky," the sergeant said before stalking off to the rear.

"Wha'ja say, Sarge?"

"The time-check, Bucky! The time-check!" McShayne answered, his nostrils ready to flare. "I'm going up to the female cell to take a look at the one lone prisoner we have up there. Shortly, I would like for you to do the same. Because she's been coughing and hacking all night, sounding like she's about to succumb to pneumonia. But I ask you now to give the time-check because it is a regulation; a *time-honored* regulation — a standard police procedure — a standard *operating* police procedure that we give the time-check — with our badge number — every hour on the hour and every half-hour on the half-hour! And the reason *why* we give the time-check every hour on the hour and every half-hour on the half-hour is to ascertain the location and safety of our patrol cars. And that is *why* I ask you to give the goddamn time-check — as you have been doing for the years you have been assisting on the desk! Going back to before Pearl Harbor!"

"Oh," said Bucky, as if struck by newness. He then moved to carry out the order. Before he could start, Corbbo's voice came through the speaker again.

"Hey, Bucky, y'near the mike?"

"Yeah."

"Is the sarge? 'Cause I want him to be sure an' here this."

"He just went upstairs. Wha'cha got?"

"Some new static. Wanna hear?"

"New static? Y'got some?"

"Lean in close, Buckeroooo," Corbbo giggled.

"I'm leanin'," Bucky said.

"...Okay, here we go, Buck-Buck."

What crackled through the speaker was the most screwed-up static ever heard. Bucky loved it. So did Corbbo.

The jolly and fat little policeman should have. There he was, parked, with the patrol car's rear wheels spinning freely in somebody's garage there at quaint 190 Daisy Lane — a lantern taped to the antennae, a cereal bowl close to him, a mike at his lips, and happily munching on dry Wheaties. And to awaken him in time for the off-duty report-in time, the alarm clock was perched in the back window. It was set for 7:55 a.m. The shift changed at 8 a.m.

"H'ya like the static, Bucky-boy?"

Bucky was tickled. "S'great. Y'got some more?"

"Plenty," Corbbo laughed. "Hey, Buck...?"

"Yeah?"

"Be sure an' tell the sarge, it's *tuffff* duty out here." He filled his mouth with another handful of dry Wheaties, gave Bucky another shot of static and laughed himself off mike.

When McShayne came back to the desk he looked at Bucky and started to say something to him about the prisoner. He was thinking of the approach when Bucky said, "Boy, Sarge, you shudda heard Corbbo's static."

"His what?"

"His static. His radio is really messed up."

McShayne, forgoing what he was going say about the prisoner and valiantly suppressing the urge to kill — but not knowing whom he wanted to kill first, Bucky or Corbbo — gritted his teeth and said, "Did you give the time-check?"

Bucky looked up at the big clock that hung over the door, and reached for the microphone. He was stopped by another switchboard call. "Yeah,

yeah, yeah, Mrs. Ina," he said, without waiting to hear the voice on the other end. "I'm sending a car over there right away." He turned to the sergeant. "Sarge, Miss America…"

McShayne wouldn't let him finish. He jabbed at the mike.

Getting the message to make the time-check, Bucky miked, "Elton Head PD. Badge one-one. Time o-one-twelve-hundred-hours. Car 101, your location?"

Pippilo was east on the narrow, dead-end street called Polk. "Near the station; just passin' the Chink's joint," he said. Obviously he was nowhere near the station or Charlie Wong's restaurant. He was parked and ready for sleep.

"102?"

Spagg was stopped in the middle of Clay Street. He was busy beaming his spotlight up to a second-story window. Preoccupied, he picked up the mike. "Yuh?"

"Where you at, Curley?"

Spagg was too busy with the window.

"102?"

As Spagg was about to absently answer, a woman in curlers appeared in the window, looked down and attempted to wave him away from the front of the house.

"Two, what's your location?"

"Hold it a sec, Buck," Spagg said, trying to read the woman's signal. She silently lipped, *"My husband's not asleep yet. Come back later."*

"Got'cha," Spagg lipped in return. He drove off.

"Your location, Two?"

"The library," said Spagg.

"'Kay, Two. 103? Three?"

Corbbo didn't respond.

McShayne almost knocked Bucky to the other side of the desk getting to the mike. "Corbbo! One more time! Just <u>one</u> more time and you've had it! You got that?!"

Corbbo sent an arm scrambling for the mike, which had gotten lost in the blanket.

"Corbbo, goddammit, do you hear me?! <u>Corbbo!!</u>"

"Got'cha, Sargeroni," Mickey finally said. "Er...Sarge...?"

"What?!"

"I like that volume."

"Don't keep trying me, Mickey!!"

"Er...Sarge, just one more thing..."

"What is it now, Corbbo?!!"

"A small request, sir," Corbbo said, comfortable under the blanket. "Is it possible for you to patch me in to the chief's house? The thought just occur'd to me that I never did pass that driver's license test — so, I figger if I can get a few days off a week from Tuesday..."

"Get off the damn mike!!!"

"But, Sarge..."

"Get off the damn mike before I come out there and personally strangle you with the goddamn cord!!"

Corbbo's radio fell silent. McShayne remained at the mike. "104, what's your location?!"

Lights out, his eye on the lonely little Henry J, Tetrollini was parked motionless in the park.

"What's your location, Four!" McShayne repeated.

"Four. Present location Elm and Huyler."

From under the blanket, Corbbo sang devilishly into the mike, "Blink ya lights, Georgie-boy, I don't see you-u-u."

"What's your location, Three?"

"Same as 104. Elm and Huyler," said Corbbo. "Headin' south."

McShayne gave it a thought. Somebody was wrong. "An' what's your location, Four?"

Tetrollini didn't respond.

"104," said McShayne. "What is your location?"

Misrepresenting his location again, Tetrollini came with the change: "The courthouse."

"You'd better straighten up, Tetrollini."

Corbbo giggled and slipped the blanket more snugly around him.

McShayne was still on the mike. "105, what's your location?"

Van Dreelan had returned to his favorite spot on Central Avenue. He was back at JoMo's, the black nightclub. "105, present location er…at the reservoir."

Corbbo couldn't resist. "An' howz the water taste, John-John?"

Van Dreelan transmitted in return, "You better cool it, Mickey, before I blow your cover. 'Cause I know something you don't know I know."

"Whas'zit you know that I don't know you know that you know I don't know you know, John-John?"

"You want a clue?"

"Whip it on me, Johnny-boooy-y-y."

"Let's put it this way," the Dutchman miked in return, and making direct reference to Corbbo's 190 Daisy Lane location. "If I mention *Daisy*, you know I ain't meanin' *'fresh as a.'*"

Corbbo laughed and slid farther underneath the blanket.

Bucky swung back from the switchboard and said to McShayne, "Mrs. Ina again, Sarge."

McShayne grabbed the mike. "H'quarters to 101."

"Yeah?" Pippilo responded, his head tilted sleepily against the window.

"What *yeah*? Answer the mike like you're supposed to."

"I did," Pippilo retorted and replaced the mike.

"The hell you did! Now get over to Beech Street."

Pippilo snatched the mike back from the cradle. "F'chrisakes, how come you can't send somebody else?! How come it's gotta be me all the time?! Why can't that rubber-mouth Corbbo roll sometime?!"

Corbbo heard his name, giggled, and sent a hand from under the blanket to the mike. "Anything I can do, Sarge?"

McShayne yelled in return, "Shut up, Corbbo!"

Pippilo continued to jaw into his mike. "Every night it's Pippilo, Pippilo, Pippilo."

Corbbo, borrowing the melody from *The Marriage of Figaro*, sang: "*Pippilo, Pippilo, Pippilooooo....*"

"Shut up, Mickey!" McShayne hollered.

Pippilo continued, "I'm gettin' just a little bit sick and tired of this."

"*Pippilo, Pippilo, Pippilooooo....*"

"Beech Street and shut up! And you shut up, too, Mickey!!"

"An' drive carefully, Pipperoni," added Corbbo. "I might be needing your license t'morrow. Tee, hee, hee."

"Screw you, Mickey," Pippilo radioed back.

"Oh, an' when you get there, Pippo," Corbbo transmitted, "if you find you gotta arrest the li'l lady, try not to blow your breath in her face. We can't afford to lose anybody on a technicality."

McShayne didn't know it, and obviously Mickey didn't care, but there was truth to what he said about the driver's license. Mickey Corbbo didn't have a license, which was why he didn't mind hiding out on the graveyard shift. Quite some time ago the Department of Motor Vehicles in Trenton had taken his license. Some said they threatened to sue him if he even thought about re-applying.

Exactly why the DMV had taken such a hard stance against Mickey wasn't difficult to understand. With eight years on the department, behind the wheel, he was a one-man wrecking crew. Police Officer Mickey Corbbo was so bad in operating a motor vehicle that years before, after he had taken the original road test for his license, the examiner wrote on the application: *"Training wheels needed."*

Back when he was partly ambitious and was working on the day shift, Mickey used to park the patrol car up on Prospect Avenue to try to catch the speeders who whizzed by. Most of them were from New York and worked at the Wright Aeronautical plant in Wood-Ridge. Most of the time they had gotten held up coming off the crowded George Washington Bridge and Route 17. They felt they could make up time speeding through Elton Head on Summit Avenue. Frequently they did. The good men of the Elton Head Police Department were usually away doing something else, mainly taking coffee breaks that could sometimes last an entire day.

Feeling especially frisky one sunny June morning, Mickey Corbbo made history. In pursuit of a speeder, he ran red lights, railroad crossing lights, stop signs and proceed-with-caution warnings, and scared any number of pedestrians half to death. Shifting gears, he created enough damage to place the city budget in jeopardy for the rest of the year. Mickey ran into a milk truck, a bakery truck, and an ice truck — all at the same time. And this was at the start of the pursuit — and at one intersection. One wag swore that when the cop shifted gears and went into third, he came so close to crashing into a hearse that the corpse got up and walked to the cemetery. It was never verified, but the upshot was that Mickey never caught the speeder. If the truth be told, he didn't have to go quite as far as he did in chasing the offender. A few feet would have done it. The motorist had stopped as soon as the cop turned on the siren. It was the cop who kept going.

4

Beech Street was one of Elton Head's oldest. It was a beautiful but dark and non-active street with huge, curiously armed trees hiding wealth and mystery. Mrs. Ina — or Mss America, as she was often called by the midnight shift — had been widowed since before the war. She lived alone in the largest house on Beech Street, and from it she kept a large American flag flying 24 hours a day. The tiny woman was frighteningly old, and she had a pasty and striking face that was home to a series of wrinkles so many in number that they criss-crossed each other from every angle imaginable. But still there was a grandmotherly sweetness about her.

When 101's headlights came to a stop in front, Pippilo, as he did every night, secured the big flashlight. He got his nightstick, readjusted his gun belt and slowly made his way to the white-gated estate. He didn't ring the bell. He never did. As usual, he came to the door, and tapped on it lightly. Without waiting for a response, he spun around and headed back to the car. As usual, he didn't get far.

"Hellluuuu, I'm back here."

Mrs. Ina's voice came from out of the darkness. Her rattishly white hair was rolled under an erect black plume, and she was dressed in a somber black crepe dress. She was standing a few feet forward of the guesthouse, which was surrounded by trees, and was located deep in the back of the main house.

Moping back to her, Pippilo said, "You called, Mrs. Ina?"

Mrs. Ina waited until he was closer and said, as she said every night, "Oh, it's you? You dear, sweet thing, I haven't seen you in ages."

The cop deadpanned, "I was here last night, Mrs. Ina."

"Well, it really has been a long time, hasn't it? How have you been?"

"No change since last night, Mrs. Ina."

"And your health? You look a bit fragile. Would you like some soup?"

"No to the soup, and my health is fine, Mrs. Ina. Same as I said last night."

"And your family?"

"Fine. Same as last night, Mrs. Ina."

"And your wife?"

"Fine, Mrs. Ina. Same as last night."

"And your children?"

"Same as last night. Don't got none, Mrs. Ina."

"Well, you should marry and get some."

"Will do, Mrs. Ina. Same as I said last night."

"That was the mistake Louis and I made."

"Same as I said last night. Sorry to hear that, Mrs. Ina."

"— So was he."

The last remark stumped Pippilo. It always did. He never understood most of her conversations anyway. Mrs. Ina would say a lot of strange things, but in talking about her husband, there was a little something added to the tone and manner. It would sometimes cause Pippilo to think back to the time when word surfaced that the gentleman had vanished. No one knew how, where, or when. One day, after she had announced that he had come home from the war, word had circulated that Mr. Ina was gone again. When she was asked about it, she never gave a straight answer, and nothing else was said or done.

"Well, nice seein' you again, Mrs. Ina; same as I said last night," Pippilo said, mission not accomplished and anxious to leave. "If anything else comes up, be sure an' give us a call, same as I said last night. And the night before. And the night before. And on and on and on, Mrs. Ina," the cop said, then turned for the departure.

"But wait. You haven't looked."

"Mrs. Ina, I been up in that attic ten dozen times already. Ain't nobody up there. An' if you'd have some of that stuff up there towed out, you'd see for yourself."

"But this time it's not the attic."

"Then wha'cha callin' for this time?"

"The nursery."

Pippilo frowned. "You keepin' children or sumthin'?"

"No, the *nursery*."

"Yeah, that's what you just said. A nursery. S'where they keep little kids."

"I'm talking about the arboretum."

"Hey, now, Mrs. Ina," the cop tried to say delicately, "you're a little old for one of them things."

"For an arboretum?"

"Yeah. An arbor'tum. It's one'a of them operations to get rid of babies or sumthin', ain't it?"

"Not that I know of," she said, puzzled, then dropping it. "I've had the guesthouse converted, and I need help with a little something I picked up on sale. Come, let me show you."

Pippilo didn't want to go in back to the darkened area, but he finally surrendered.

Leading the way, Mrs. Ina was chatting amiably. "Actually, it is slightly used. But they had it crated so nicely when they brought it in. You don't find bargains like this often, you know. Especially for Christmas."

"Wha'zit, some kinda piano or organ or somethin'?"

"In an arboretum?"

"Sorry. "

"Oh, no. This is much different."

"Makes sense," Pippilo said, trailing behind her. "'Cause if I r'member, you already got an organ. In fact, you've got two."

"I'm going to have a third. I'm going to put a Wurlitzer in the attic."

"Three? S'great, if you like organ music."

"I detest organ music."

"Oh?" said Pippilo. "Don't wanna pry, Mrs. Ina, but if you don't like organ music, why do you want three organs?"

"Louis."

"S'cuse me for soundin' dumb, but do you mean *Mister* Ina?"

"Yes."

"S'cuse me for soundin' dumb again, Mrs. Ina, but didn't Mr. Ina pass away some years ago? In the war?"

"Dear boy," Mrs. Ina said soberly, "We've all passed away." And with that, the dear little lady broke out in song. *"Tis the season to be jolly. Tra la la la la, la-la-la-la."* She continued to sing until they entered the deep-set, platformed guesthouse, which had been converted into an arboretum.

Inside, and with the reluctant Pippilo showing more fearful signs, she put a whispering finger to her lips and then stepped back for him to see. She snapped on the lights and said, "There."

It was a mounted coffin. The lid was closed.

"Mrs. Ina…"

"Sssshhhh," she cautioned with the same finger. "What's nice about this one is, it's only been used once. My Henry never had one."

"Henry? Mrs. Ina, I thought your husband's name was somethin' different? I mean, one time it was Conrad. Then it was Courtney; Then is was Louis. Another time it was somethin' else."

"He changed all his names shortly after he was buried."

The cop gave her a look. He had to get out of there, but at least he would give the courtesy of appearing to be interested.

Mrs. Ina was crouching over him and he was feeling the weight of her frail body.

"Mrs. Ina, I'd kinda like to get outta here," Pippilo said, moving back.

Mrs. Ina was still fixed on the coffin. "What I need is a warm body. You see, this won't work. Watch."

The cop, now near the door, stopped and turned.

With that, she pressed a button, the coffin lid flew open, and a skeletonized version of World War II's Uncle Sam popped up.

He was smiling a bizarre *I Want You.*

🔲

Back at the station, gesturing and sweating, Pippilo was pacing back and forth in front of the desk.

"I'm tellin' you, that woman is outta her mind! She's nuts!"

Bucky asked if it was a real coffin.

"You dumb jerk," Pippilo fired back, "what kinda coffin do you think it was Of course it was real!"

"All right," McShayne said, "Settle down."

"'Settle down?!' That fruitcake tries to get me to lay down in a coffin — in a greenhouse — with an Uncle Sam in it, an' you're telling me to settle down?!"

"Should'a arrested her," Bucky said.

"On what charge?" said McShayne. "Ain't no law against having a coffin in a house if it ain't got a body in it."

"In that case, Frank, you ought to go back an' lay down in it. That way you can put the pinch on her."

"Why don't you send your mother," Pippilo snorted.

Bucky came from around the desk, fuming an obscenity.

"Cut it out," McShayne said, causing Bucky to back off. "Get back behind this desk or get out an' find yourself a post!"

"He'd better learn how to watch his mouth!"

"Shut up!" McShayne said. "And you, Frank, hit the road."

Pippilo grumbled something, and moved to the door. "I ain't going back to that house, so don't call me."

"You'll go where you're told," McShayne responded.

"Oh, yeah?" said Pippilo. "Watch me."

"Out!"

Pippilo drearily exited.

"Check it, Bucky," McShayne said.

"Huh?"

"Give the damn time-check!"

Bucky looked up at the big clock over the door, and grabbed the mike. "Badge one-one. Elton Head PD, Time o-one-thirty-thirty hundred hours, come in, One? ...*One?*" No response. He looked at the desk sergeant. "I can't get One, Sarge."

"Who's in 101, Bucky?"

"...Who's in 101?"

"That's what I just asked, Bucky. Who's supposed to be in radio car 101?"

Bucky had forgotten. He needed a drink.

"You don't know who's in 101?"

"I can't think at the moment, Sarge. There's just too much on my mind."

"You idiot! Ain't Frank Pippilo assigned to 101?!"

"S'right!"

"Then tell me how in the hell can you get him, if he just walked out of the damned door?!"

"Oh," said Bucky. Back on the mike: "102, where are you?"

"102," Curley Spagg answered, "Rogan and Francis."

"Roger, Two," Bucky said. "Three?"

"Doin' good on Shipley and Blake," came Corbbo's response from the garage. But he was not doing as good as he had reported. The pudgy little policeman was not very comfy. As the transmissions continued, back into the sack he went.

"104, your location?"

"Four," said Tetrollini from the park. "The Parker Avenue School."

"Roger, Four," said Bucky. "Five, your location?"

Johnny Van Dreelan picked up his mike. "The city dump."

Corbbo grabbed his mike. "No fair workin' at home, John-John."

"Screw you, Mickey," was the response.

Corbbo laughed. But he was still a mite uncomfortable. Back into the sack he went. After digging around, he extracted a long cotton nightgown, complete with a peaked sleeping cap. It had all the comforts of home. And it was large enough to fit over the uniform. On it went.

He slipped back under the blanket with the mike. "Hey, Buck-Buck, when you call me for lunch, make sure it's loud an' strong."

"'Kay," said Bucky. "Wha'cha gonna be doin', Mick?"

Corbbo munched on the Wheaties again, "Static, Buckerooo. Static."

With that, the policeman prepared to go to sleep.

5

Danny Carlsson had completed about two-thirds of his checking of doors on the north side of the street when he discovered an unlocked door at the rear of 279 Main. It was just another tacky, second-hand dress store in a long line of cheapies. The young policeman dug for his flashlight and entered, setting the little inside bell above the door tinkling. Inside, he looked around, saw that there were no signs of wrong doing, found a telephone and dialed headquarters. Getting the desk sergeant, he said: "Post 1-A reporting an opened door: The rear of Wilson's, 279 Main. Nothing disturbed."

"Can the door be secured?" McShayne asked.

"No, sir. A key is required and I've been unable to find an alarm."

"Wait there," ordered McShayne. The desk sergeant turned to Bucky. "Find ol' man Wilson's number. Have him go down there an' lock that junk pile of his up."

"His real name's Hymie Wyberg. He had it changed to be like us."

"Find the number, Bucky. Leave the editorializing alone," McShayne retorted, then grabbed the mike. "'Quarters to 104, come in." Getting no response, he tried it again.

Tetrollini was still in the park.

Seeing car 104 in the park was strange, because normally the outlying stores and the few small factories that sparsely dotted the post were the first to be checked. The park was last on the list, if checked at all. Certainly it wasn't covered in winter. No one was ever there, especially at midnight. It was even more strange, because 104 had pulled into the park with lights out. For a moment it looked as though the patrol car was going to close in on the quiet and dilapidated Henry J that Carol, the all-American teenager, had parked after cruising past the station earlier. Instead, the cop brought the vehicle to a stop to the rear and far out of view of the girl's car. He had turned the radio down and again made certain that the Hudson's lights were off. Like the girl in the little Henry J, he, too, waited.

But, unlike the girl, he didn't have all night.

Although it was dark, the policeman's face was showing deep worry and it is doubtful he even heard the call.

The teenager's face, on the other hand, was noncommittal. Although when she first pulled into the park, well before the patrol car arrived, it did appear that she was putting her face and voice through a series of weird spasms and grimaces. It was as if she were rehearsing an act.

The all-American teenager loved movies. The back seat of her car was littered with what looked like a ton of romance novels and movie magazines. After putting herself through another series of contortions, she plowed the back seat, grabbed a handful of both the novels and magazines, and tried reading in the dark. Unable to read a book, she spent the next half hour running her fingers across the pages of several magazines as if practicing the skills of the blind. Frustrated in the effort, she popped out of the car, went to her trunk and retrieved a small record player.

Trouble was, there was no place to put the cord.

The all-American teenager spent the next hour looking for a plug.

"Headquarters to car 104! Come in, Four!"

Tetrollini turned the radio's volume up and responded, "Four."

"Stay on the mike, Four!"

"Yes, sir."

"Take a confirmation run down to Wilson's on Main."

"'Wilson's on Main.'"

"Right. An', Georgie, stay there 'til ol' man Wilson shows up with the key. Have Danny Carlsson resume his post."

"Four. Roger."

Tetrollini placed the mike back in the receiver and fought with the decision as to whether to approach the Henry J or not. He backed away, deciding to answer the call first.

The park was only a few minutes away from the store on Main Street, and so only a few minutes had passed when Tetrollini drove up. Being the conscientious policeman that he was, he first sent the vehicle's spotlight searching the building and made certain there were no obvious signs of illegal activity. He got his flashlight and entered with normal caution. He was relieved to see Carlsson, and Carlsson was relieved to see him, although, as he had observed earlier at the station during lineup, Tetrollini definitely hadn't been the same lately.

Carlsson had taken notice of Tetrollini's apparently worried state, because since joining the department he had always kept an eye on the policeman who he thought was the best of the lot. Of all the policemen in the department, the dark and curly-haired quiet one had shown promise. He was certainly unlike the rest of the cops, to include the guys on the day and evening shifts. Most on them were on the job simply because, like the 23-man fire department, for the average man it was the most secure and prestigious job in town.

Being an Elton Head policeman did have status, and, again like the fire department, it was not an easy job to get. To work for the city required connections. One didn't just apply for an opening. One applied to someone with influence. Often the connection would be political; other times it would be through the financial route. *Greased palms* was the term. Whatever, it was always the City Manager who had the major say when it came to police and fire department appointments. In Elton Head, the City Manager was the morally and politically corrupt Ernest R. Mulkey.

"Everything secure?" Tetrollini said, coming into the cramped store and looking around.

"Seems so," said Carlsson.

"Did you check the cellar?"

"Gosh, I forgot to do that. I'll go down and check it out now," the younger policeman said, getting up.

"No, no. That's okay," Tetrollini said. "I'll do it while waiting for the old man to show up. But next time, don't forget to do that. It's important."

"Right."

"Better call in, then resume your post," Tetrollini advised, and went back to inspecting.

Carlsson went back to the telephone and reported in, essentially saying to Bucky what he had said to the sergeant earlier. He hung up and started to saunter out. "Thanks, Georgie," he said.

Tetrollini looked at him. "You've got what it takes to be a good cop, Danny."

It surprised the rookie. "Thanks, Georgie. Coming from you, that's a real compliment," Carlsson responded. He took a moment and said, "If I weren't thinking about re-enlisting in the service, I'd kinda like to talk to you. Talk cop talk."

"No," said Tetrollini, quickly. "No. You don't want to do that. Not with me, you don't."

There was relinquishment in the way he said it, not harshness. Carlsson didn't understand it. He walked away wondering. He had gotten as far as the door when Tetrollini said something else. "Sorry to hear you're thinking about going back into service." He paused and advised, "This job is what you make it."

Carlsson thought about it, thanked him, and walked away, still wondering.

Seconds after the departure, Tetrollini's flashlight was leading down the cellar steps. The light bounced on three or four live-looking, out-of-use mannequins and continued down to a number of boxes and piles of rubbish. The light went on to explore a discarded jewelry display case that still contained an old watch, some trinkets, and a few more cheap items. The probing light searched on, then it hit an old, discarded Yale safe. Tetrollini beamed the light closer. Judging from its condition, the safe shouldn't have aroused an inner interest, but it did. The cop looked back at the stairs and then tried the handle. With effort, the door swung open. The safe was empty. There shouldn't have been, but there was a small show of disappointment on the policeman's face. The search continued. With everything seemingly in place, and not seeing anything of apparent value, he went back upstairs.

But the cop wasn't satisfied. He came back down and went over to the four concrete steps that led to the two big metal halves horizontally forming the sidewalk cellar door. Staring at it for a minute, he reached up and slid the locking lever back. He was about to change his mind and slide the lever back to the original locked position when he heard the little bell over the door musically tinkling.

The policeman didn't know it at the time, but it was the store owner entering. He was huffing hard after having exercised much effort in getting out of his much-too-tiny vehicle.

Mr. Wilson was a sloppy, unshaven man, weighing close to four hundred and twelve pounds. He was unable to drive, had difficulty breathing, and whenever he went someplace, his wife would have to drive. It was she who had driven him to the store. But one couldn't have much confidence in the wife's driving, either. Her belly touched and slowed the steering wheel almost as much as his would have done.

"Hello-o-o," Mr. Wilson called out.

Tetrollini had moved down from the metal halves and was near the regular cellar steps when he heard the voice.

"'H'looo," the obese man called out again.

"Down here, Mr. Wilson."

Mr. Wilson took more time and breathlessly tried for the stairs. He couldn't make it and decided to rest up first. "Knew one of you boys was here," he said from upstairs. "Saw the car."

He tried coming down the stairs again, and when the policeman was in view, he stopped and said, "Oh, you're that nice boy."

"Just checking things out down here."

"Everything all right?"

"Seems so," Tetrollini said, looking around. "Everything look in place to you?"

From part way up, Mr. Wilson took a cursory look around. "Seems okay." He looked at the safe's opened door. "Now, let's see, did I leave that open?"

"Oh, er...I opened it," Tetrollini stumbled. "We have to check everything out, y'know."

"Of course," Mr. Wilson said, and started to make the laborious climb back to the top. "It's a good thing you boys are on the job."

"We try to do our best."

"And it's a good thing you boys check these doors at night. Makes an old absent-minded fool like me sleep better."

"It'd be better if you merchants securely locked up, though. And you always want to keep your safe locked."

"You're right," Mr. Wilson struggled to say. "But you never have to worry about me keeping anything in it."

They had reached the top. Mr. Wilson was huffing so badly that Tetrollini slid a chair underneath him.

"Why wouldn't you keep anything in the safe, Mr. Wilson? That's what they're for."

"Ah, but, my boy, if some of them big-time crooks is gonna nail you, the safe's the first thing they'll blow. Like they do in New York."

"You got a point there," Tetrollini said, with interest. "But if you carry your receipts home with you every night, somebody'll figure out your pattern and your route and waylay you."

"I know," Mr. Wilson said, smartly. "That's why I don't take nothin' home with me."

"What do you do? When you close up, the bank is closed. Or maybe you've found a way to make deposits after three o'clock?"

"Wouldn't interest me," Mr. Wilson said dismissively. "I don't trust banks. I always say, 'Keep your money where you can get your hands on it.' Take it from me, that's the only way to do it. And you've got to be clever, my boy. You've got to be clever. Now, I keep my money down there, but in a safe place." He dropped the subject and reached into his pocket for his change purse. "Here, lemme give you a few pennies for your troubles."

"Thanks, but we're not allowed to accept money."

"Must be a new policy," Mr. Wilson said.

"No, it's always been that way," Tetrollini said, fully understanding what the man meant. "But thanks anyway. You just make sure you lock that door every night."

"First time it's ever happened to me. I always check my doors before leaving."

"Well, anyway, you take care," Tetrollini said, leaving.

"Thanks much. And you have a good night."

Out front, in coat, bathrobe and curlers, an almost equally obese Mrs. Wilson was behind the wheel of the car.

The cop gave her a thoughtful wave. As he was about to climb in his car, far down the street he saw Carlsson. Tetrollini held for a second, gave the rookie a wave and climbed into his car. On the mike: "104 to headquarters."

"Come in, Four."

"Wilson's is secure."

6

Curley Spagg leisurely rolled the nub of the cigar in his mouth, hocked a good spit, forgot the window was up, stained it with a dark blotch, casually lowered it and said to the always glum-looking Pippilo, "So, Frank, whaddaya think about that new civil service thing they're talkin' about down at City Hall, Frank?"

Cars 101 and 102 were on the same street, but headed in opposite directions. Spagg had been idly cruising, and Frank Pippilo was on his way to break boredom by capturing a full night's sleep, but they had stopped dead center on the railroad tracks that crossed Essex Street. It was interesting, because Bucky had just given the 0230 time-check, which was late by 15 minutes, and both cars had reported the same street but different directions.

Stopping their cars and talking between the two was a nightly occurrence. The conversation was always banal and hackneyed, but why they liked to park on the railroad tracks was never known. It could only be hoped that they both didn't fall asleep before moving. The train generally came thundering through town at 0302.

Sometimes they would shoot at it.

"Y'know what I think abut that civil service?" Pippilo sleepily answered.
"Wha'cha think?"

"It stinks," Pippilo answered, still burdened by the doctor's report. He was morose but talkative, and was back with the theme that he and all the rest of the department had been hammering on for the last two years.

"Y'know Sergeant McShayne is for it. So's Lieutenant Murphy," Spagg said. "An' the chief. They're all for it."

"Sure. Along with Zemora and a coupla others," Pippilo said, his mind now slipping back to the days when the Irish were ill-treated and the country tried to stop the stream of famine-starved immigrants, which had turned into a flood. "But what's it mean to them? They don't gotta be out here on patrol like us. Nonna them ain't gotta be out here with the crud. An' anyhow, they're Irish."

"Micks," added Spagg.

"Right," Pippilo said with emphasis. "What do Micks know?"

"Nuttin'."

"I'll tell ya, Spaggy, that whole thing is gotta be a Communist plot. The Commies do things like that to screw up the system. I tell ya, if they let that civil service crap in, *anybody* can join the force."

"Hey, palsy, with the testin' and all'a that, this department won't be nothin' but a bunch of smart-alecky screw-offs."

"It'll be a bunch of 'em, all right," Pippilo said with certainty. "The flood gates'll be wide open — to anybody, and anything. They might even start ballyhooin' them minority whatchamacallits."

"And *foreigners*."

"Foreigners. Ugh. What a drag," dragged Pippilo.

"The rookie Danny Carlsson is a foreigner, ain't he?"

"Yuh."

"Where'd he say he was from?"

"Whatchamacallit. Same place they make them rolls that go with the coffee."

"Doughnut?"

"No, the other one. The thing with the jelly on top of it."

"Pastry? He's from Pastry?"

"No, it's got another name," said Pippilo. "It's round, but don't got no hole in it."

"…Cupcake?"

"…Danish, that's it."

"Danish? I didn't know them things was foreign. Geez, I might have to start dunkin' somethin' else in my coffee," said Spagg. "Good thing the rook ain't no real cop, yet. But so that's where he's from, huh? Danish."

"Yeah, but that ain't really, really foreign. I mean, it ain't like the spicks, the micks, the Commies an' Russians an' all. Real foreigners."

"All of 'em, they hurtin' the country and the department, Pip."

"You damn tootin'. An' what gets me is that ain't nothin' wrong with this department the way it is. You wanna know what's wrong with it? Nuttin'."

"Nobody's usin' the ol' bean, Pip," Spagg said, tapping his head, indicating there was brainpower under that thinning head of hair.

"They ain't usin' the ol' bean, is right."

"I tell you, Spaggy, if they let them sissified bums in just because they pass some nitwit faggo test, you wanna know what this department'll be like? Huh? Y'wanna know? I'll tell you. It'll be just like across the Hudson River over there."

"Or any of them crummy, big-city places," Spagg agreed.

"I can't see why people don't leave well enough alone. That's what's wrong with this country now. What's wrong with appointments? Look at us."

"Hey, we could be the last of a dyin' breed."

"We very well could be, Spaggy. We very well could be."

"Y'right."

"If a guy is good — an' got a little pull…"

"Connection an' pull is the thing."

"A few connections, he gets appointed…"

"…He gets appointed. If he don't got no pull, he don't get appointed. Simple. No fuss, no muss."

"That's the way it should be, Pippy. It's the ol' American way. That's what we fought the big one for," said the short cop who had avoided the draft by faking illness and claiming 4F status.

"We fought it, an' we won it," said the beefy cop who, like the short cop, hadn't contributed a thing to the war effort. "We put our shoulders to the wheel an' did what we had to do."

"The whole world is safe because of us."

"But Civil Service, what a crock," Pippilo said. "Y'wanna know what I think?"

"Wha'cha think?"

"It stinks. I tell ya, the whole country's goin' pinko. Pinko, Spaggy, Pinko."

"Pinko, pinko, pinko. We're headin' straight down the ol' tubee-woobees."

"S'gotta be a Commie plot."

"A Commie plot *and* un-American."

The conversation ended for a second. Spagg brought it back to life. "So whaddaya gonna do about that other thing? The dose."

"Oh, geezus. Don't r'mind me."

"Why don'cha tell the li'l lady the ol' flu-buggy is here, an' she's gotta get some shots to protect herself. S'what I used to tell Myrtle."

"The flu just left, Spaggy."

"Well, tell her it's comin' back. She's only a wife. What the hell's she know? 'Cept yours is got a job. Nice one, too. She's usin' the ol' bean."

"She looks good on that tug, huh?"

"For an ex-Marine, she looks great, Pip."

"My little honey, stannin' on that thing with a rope in hand, keepin' up with the big boys."

"Wish my Myrtle had a job."

"Myrt's too good of a housewife."

"Yeah, she is," Spagg said. "An' I appreciate you sayin' it, Pip. She's a house-fry. The best kind. A cooker an' a cleaner. Cook n' clean; clean 'n cook. She might be a little chunky and long in the tooth, but she's a honey."

"You got lucky with Myrt."

"Yeah, I did, buddy. Yeah, I did."

"How minny years is it, now?"

"I'm over twenty."

"Married for over twenty, an' she still looks good," Pippilo said of the woman who, not only was long in the tooth but, as someone said, her feet were so lengthy that she should shop for skis instead of shoes.

"She looks as good now as when she walked down the ol' aisle. 'Member the day, Pip?"

"Hey, palsy. I was best man. An' your sister-in-law gave the bride away."

"An' that ain't all she gave away," Spagg said, salaciously.

Pippilo picked up on it. "Did'ja, really?"

"Yep," Spagg said, contentedly.

"You nailed Penelope?"

"Same night. *Va-va-va-vooom,*" boasted Spagg. "Had to keep it in the family, ol' bud-bud."

It ended for a moment. Pippilo groaned over his predicament again and reached behind the passenger's seat to pry at a lump of used bubble gum.

"Hey, I got an idea, Pip," said Spagg. "Why don'cha tell the li'l lady you've been handlin' a TB case, an' Doc Glendenhall says the both of you gotta get the shots. He'll be glad to fix yous up."

Pippilo tossed the wad of used gum into his mouth. "Say, now, that's not a bad idea. *That's* usin' the ol' bean, Spaggy. She might go for somethin' like that."

"She's gotta," Spagg said. "That's good stuff you'll be layin' on her."

"I'll just go to the ol' phone booth an' do a signal sixteen." The short cop threw a hand out, "Lemme have a nickel. I'll call 'im now."

"Call 'im collect. He's only a coupla blocks away."

"Good thinkin'. I'll just do that."

"Sure," Spagg said. "That's what doctors are for, to help out cops in a jam."

"S'right."

"Look how minny times we've tossed business his way. You ever have even an accident case you didn't give to him?"

"Not a one," Pippilo agreed.

"He gets all the fights. Everythin'. We're always doin' somethin' for him."

"Hey, an' don't forget; he did a li'l number for Hutchins up in traffic," said Spagg. "An' his dose wasn't no better'n your dose."

"Skinny had it, too?"

Caught the li'l lady jay-walkin'. Gave her the ol' *put out or pay up* routine. Nailed her on his motorcycle, behind Woolworth's."

⌛

Spagg and Pippilo's mentioning of Dr. Drew Glendenhall and what he would do for the police could have also tied in to an incident that had happened back in January 1945, one that had undoubtedly been forgotten minutes after it happened.

McShayne was off that night. Sergeant Dominic Arati was on the desk. Tootie Camarini, now working in traffic, was the post 1-A man. He was walking the beat one night when he came across a curled figure sleeping in the doorway of a store. Before even rolling the figure over, the post 1-A man knew that it was Robbie Smalls.

Robbie was a town fixture; an unquestionable drunk. Every night he would go into Kelly's, a tavern just off Main Street, buy a half-pint with money he had hustled elsewhere, and would go into Kelly's about an hour before closing. It would be his last stop of the evening before ending up in a doorway on Main Street. Everyone was used to Robbie Smalls. Certainly the police were.

At night when Main Street's post 1-A would change, the man working the midnight shift could count on beating the chill of winter by searching the doorways and finding Robbie. Most of the time the liver-infected little ruddy-faced man would be shivering, not so much from the cold as from the toll the alcohol had taken on him over the years. Robbie was a sure arrest, hence a sure way for the 1-A man to get back to the warm confines of the police station. Sometimes the post 1-A man would be a little too aggressive in handling Robbie, but he was not one to resist. Robbie was a drunkard, not a resister. It didn't matter to a policeman seeking refuge from the onslaught of the bitter cold. With the drunk in tow, the post 1-A man would call the station and a car would be dispatched to the scene. Together they would ride to the old building in silence, although the post 1-A man would already be feeling better by virtue of riding in the warm car.

Filling out the record-of-arrest form at the station could have been done in a matter of minutes. If it happened to be really cold outside, the procedure would be stretched into an hour or more. Normally, upon seeing Robbie, the desk sergeant would dig into the bottom desk drawer and give Robbie a teaspoon of the sobering paraldehyde, and the post 1-A man would escort him back to one of the cells to sleep it off. It was another procedure that should have been over in ten or fifteen minutes — which, again, amounted to ten or fifteen minutes of additional warmth to the blue-coated and silver-shielded man who had to spend long hours trudging and fighting the long winter nights.

But one night it didn't happen that way. The procedure was the same, but the results were not.

Desk sergeant Dominic Arati was a gruff and bitter man who, ironically, wasn't much larger than Robbie. But to Robbie's everlasting misfortune, the small desk sergeant had had a bad night. The worst he had ever had. In addition to his not being able to keep in touch with the cars in a timely way, the chief and his wife had gotten into a fight and she had called the station for his arrest. It should have been shocking, but it was not the first time such a thing had happened. It had happened several times, in fact. Each time, though, cooler heads had prevailed and the matter was settled by the wife's withdrawing the demand. It didn't seem likely that she would this time.

As now, they had no protecting Civil Service in Elton Head, and it was for certain Arati wasn't going to put his job in jeopardy by arresting the chief. He called the city manager. Mulkey laid him out for calling him at that hour of the morning, and called the mayor demanding that he start preparing papers, getting rid of both Arati and the chief. Intimidated, the mayor called Judge Harkavey. He was supposed to have authority in that area. Actually, the judge didn't know if he had authority or not, but as far as he was concerned it was a case of opportunity knocking. The judge, known for having lusted after the chief's wife for years, slipped on his robe and threw his coat around his shoulders, grabbed his gavel, and sailed around to the chief's house, sans underwear. Not wearing any underwear was by design. It was the judge's hope that in breaking up the melee his bathrobe would fly open, the wife would see what he had to offer, and matters could take off from there. The judge was so happy with the prospects of finally getting the chief's wife that, before leaving home, his last act was to call the Notell Motel in Englewood to book a room.

Matters, however, didn't quite happen the way the judge wanted. Thirty minutes later, the mayor was calling the city manager, and the city manager had called the station. The problem was that the wife had beaten up the chief, and had cracked the judge in the head with his own gavel.

Sergeant Arati spent the night worrying about arresting the wife.

He never did. He didn't fall out of favor with the chief, but the judge hauled him into court, sued the mayor, and tried to arrest Mulkey for dereliction of duty.

Robbie Smalls wouldn't get the usual teaspoon full of paraldehyde that troubled night. He got the whole bottle.

Even before the post 1-A man had armed Robbie up to the desk, Sergeant Arati saw how badly the alcoholic man was shaking, and instead of getting a spoon he dug into the bottom drawer and sat the small bottle on the desk. Robbie was in a haze. But haze or not, he still had an alcoholic's awareness, and anything in a bottle looked good to him. The weak and thin little man picked up the bottle, and, in one swoop drank the contents dry. It took but a second. His face contorted for a moment, then settled back into normalcy. The shaking subsided, but it didn't disappear. Sergeant Arati was not concerned. Showing no emotion, he flicked an eye on the post 1-A man and ordered the drunk to the cell. Tootie Camarini did as ordered, then left the station. He returned exactly three hours and fifteen minutes later. It was 0400 — lunch time for the post 1-A patrolman. One of the three all-night restaurants was down the street from the station, but before going to lunch it was necessary to check with the desk. Arati was still there, and in checking the cells in back, he discovered a very sick Robbie Smalls. Robbie was stretched out on the metal cot with his eyes closed. He was breathing hard for a thin man. Occasionally he would manage a cough and the effort would send the saliva dribbling uncontrollably down his chin and the corners of his mouth. Robbie was a sick man. The post 1-A man knew it. He studied the prisoner for a bit longer then went back up front and informed the desk of his impressions. Without even raising his head from the blotter, the desk sergeant said, "Go eat, an' let me worry about the station."

Tootie Camarini did just that. He returned to the cell twenty-one minutes later. It had not been a good lunch. Four a.m. lunches never are. But on this occasion it was particularly bad. So was Robbie Smalls' condition. His breathing was all the way down to that murky and awful-sounding bottom. Camarini could feel the dry and saliva-less rattle of the esophagus. Robbie the drunk didn't have far to go. Camarini went back up front to tell the sergeant. His words fell on deaf ears. Said Arati in no uncertain terms: "Get back on post."

Camarini, the post 1-A man, did as ordered.

0800 did not come with speed, but it came, and brought with it post 1-A's relief man. The midnighter walked in slowly.

Desk sergeants usually leave about twenty minutes before the change of shifts, but, oddly, Arati was still at the station. He was complaining because there were forms to be filled out — forms that delayed his departure.

The police physician was there. He had to fill out forms, also. And when the midnighter arrived he, too, had forms to fill out. But Tootie Camarini, the post 1-A man, did not have to think. The sergeant and the physician had it all worked out. Robbie Smalls, they said, died of natural causes.

Dr. Glendenhall had been the physician that night.

7.

On a December night that was gloriously atmospheric, yet one that seemed tinged with the vagaries of whimsy, hurt low-quarter shoes covered by tattered Army-issued leggings found themselves tapping happily in the snow at the far end of Main Street's eastern alley shortly before Danny Carlsson's call-in time. The alley had that forlorn look, and there was nothing moving except the leggings, the low-quarter shoes, and a man's hands. They were keeping time to an impoverished tune being hummed and sung by a voice that ignored all the rules of melody. But it was a happy voice. And the garbage cans were happy too. They were out for commercial pickup, and Soldier Boy, owner of the unstructured melody, was using the tops for rhythm.

Rich with self-entertainment, Soldier Boy was a cactus-looking, warm, black wino in the strongest tradition. Except for a soiled bandanna he wore under an equally soiled Army overseas cap, his entire outfit was an abusive reminder of long-ago Military days. But he was a fun-loving, happy drunk. He was hard to understand, but easy to love. When the heart of the entertainment was over, he waved a weaving goodbye to his friends — the garbage cans — and left the alley saying, *"Shoot low, boys, they might be crawlin'."*

He rounded the corner, marching to the bar.

The newly-named Flamingo was a small, misnamed, loud and smelly hole-in-the-wall tavern that catered to the down-and-out country-and-western set. Down at the moment, there was a time when, as an upscale club, it was the place to be seen and showed promise of being even better. But no longer. It became roach infested, and the kitchen stoves, no longer in use, were still dark and thick with grease.

The Flamingo was a place Soldier Boy would normally avoid. After marching past a few stores, he squinted down the street and saw Danny Carlsson pulling on doors that were fairly close to old man Wilson's store.

The old black man flashed a long-distance smile and crept up on the young policeman. When he was close enough, he hollered: *"Sandy Boy!"*

Danny Carlsson recognized the voice. He smiled and instantly turned. "Soldier Boy, hi'ya doing, pal?"

The man with the bloodshot eyes grew serious and wandered in closer. They were now close to the Flamingo's front door. The soldier became anxious. "Sandy, listen' to this. Y'gotta hear this. Sssshhh. Listen, Sandy, listen."

Carlsson stood attentively. The soldier cleared his voice and stood as though he were in concert. He began to sing — wrongly, but he was singing nonetheless.

Oh, Sandeee Buoyeee....
The Pipe — The Pipe
Just called meee...
from Tree to Tree —
Yes, I'll be there when
Sunshine is a Shaaadoo-o-ow
Oh, Sand-y Boy —
Oh, Sand-y Boy —
I love you — soooooo."

"Ain't that great, Sandy?!" Soldier Boy said excitedly. "Ain't that just great?"

Carlsson grinned. "It was beautiful, Soldier. The way you sing, almost puts a tear in the eye. But, Soldier..."

"An' did'ja like the way I hit that: *'sooooo'?*"

"I'm telling you, Soldier, I was almost crying."

"An' this is really gonna s'prise you. Wanna hear?"

"I wanna hear."

"I just learn'd that li'l ditty yesterday. I learn'd it yestoooday. An' I learn'd it for y.o.u. Nobody else."

"Thanks, Soldier, but my name is…"

Soldier Boy interrupted and confidentially said, "An', Sandy, that song is for me an' you. *Only.* I ain't gonna never let anybody else hear it. Got me?"

"I got'cha, Soldier Boy," the rookie policeman said, still wanting to make a correction of his name.

Soldier Boy made a move and braced for something else. This time he stood erect, like a polished Army field sergeant. Danny Carlsson knew what was coming.

"Tennnn-huttt!"

The junior policeman snappily responded to the command, playfully going along with his ancient-appearing friend.

"Present…Harms! Right…Face!"

Carlsson faced south. He waited for the next command.

"Forward…Harch!" barked the Soldier. *"Column Left, Ho!…Hup, Two-Three-Four. Hup, Two-Three-Four…"*

With that, the two men filled the minutes marching down the street and through the dark alley and around the corner. Soldier Boy was in his glory. Patrolman Danny Carlsson was marching proudly.

After a nice tour that lasted far longer than it should have, they finally returned to the original spot. Soldier Boy gave the appropriate command and broke formation. "Y'sonovagun," he laughed. "You soldier like a nat'ral champ. Kin you imagine what would'a happen'd to you if they'd a let you soldier under me, instead'a them fools you was with?"

"It would have been great. But…"

"Great?" Soldier Boy interrupted, "It'd been sensational! Under my leadership, you'd a'been a general by now. A full-fledged general, with chickens and stars an' bars runnin' all over your shoulders an' any other place you want'd 'em to run. You'da made MacArthur look like a cadet."

"Why, thank you, Soldier. But the only thing is, I wasn't a soldier. I was in the Navy."

"I ain't gonna hold that against you. We still vets, so you still all right with me. Dig?"

"I dig."

"Now, back to the issue of the day. Hear what I said, Sandy? I said: 'The *issue of the day...*'"

"I heard you, Soldier. That's military talk."

"There you go, Sandy; there you go. See, you got it. An' if we was still in the military, I'da had you so well trained they wouldn'a let Eisenhower in the Army. You hear me, Sandy Boy?"

Carlsson was now able to make the gentle correction. "But Soldier, I gotta tell you, the name is *Danny*."

"Sandy...Dandy...what's the diff? A name's a name. It's the position of the troops that wins the wars."

"You're right, Soldier," Carlsson said, then took a moment to ask a sensitive question. "How's the head, Soldier?"

The old black man switched gears. He leaned against the building, removed his overseas cap and tugged at the soiled, loosely-tied bandanna. He rubbed his head and looked away. "It's okay now, but it hurts me sometimes, Sandy Boy. It hurts me..."

"I can imagine how you feel, Soldier. Any battlefield wound must be tough. But to suffer a head wound..."

"You know what it is, Sandy? I'll tell you what it is with me: The daylight ain't no friend, an' the night ain't nothin' but a natural born enemy. You hear me, Sandy? *The daylight ain't no friend, an' the night ain't nothin' but a natural born enemy...* Sometimes I wish I could just reach up an' rip this sonovagun right from outta my head. Know what I mean, Sandy?"

"I know what you mean," Carlsson said with care. "But don't do anything to hurt yourself. You've lived with it this long. You can live with it longer."

The old black thought for a long while, his mind recreating the hardships of battle. "Y'right," he said, distantly. "A lot of men's gonna be suffering a long time because of that war."

"War is hell," Carlsson said sympathetically. "I don't know who said it first, but he was right. War is hell. And now it seems we've got another one starting: Korea."

"Well, they gonna have to do without me on this one, Sandy. The old Soldier can't cut it no more. I done give 'em all I got, Sandy. All I got. I know they gonna miss me, but I ain't got no more to give, Sandy."

"You've done your best, Soldier."

The Soldier's mind drifted away for a bit; his eyes became deep and moody. It was unusual. Terribly unusual. He came back, and the subject was changed. "Howz your Grandpop?"

"He's fine," answered the policeman, at first a little concerned because of a strange look that had covered the man's face. "My Pop's doing okay."

"He still on the job?"

"Yep. He's still there."

"I was s'pose to have that job. Did'ja know that? They wouldn't give it to me. I'da been great."

"You'd be great in anything, Soldier. But I never knew you wanted to be the station janitor."

"Hey, I 'plied for it b'fore your Gramps."

"I didn't know that."

"Well, I did. Long time ago. I bet you won't even born then."

"Sorry you didn't get it," Carlsson said, sincerely. "But after all these years, my Pop's still there."

"You didn't think I'd remember him, did'ja? He don't remember me, but I remember him. Wanna know why?"

"And why is that, Soldier?"

"He got me with his mop one time, you know?"

"His mop? How'd that happen?"

"He mopped me, that's how. He sho' did. I was stretched out on the floor in the cell up there, an' suddenly I felt all'a this water seepin' through me, so I looked up. Damn if it wasn't your old man an' his mop. I said, 'You want me to move a li'l taste, Cuzz?' He didn't say nothin'; wouldn't talk to me. Wouldn't say 'S'cuse me 'or 'Kiss my potatoes,' or nothin'. He just kept on moppin'."

"I'm sure he didn't mean anything by it."

"Y'never know 'bout people, Sandy. Y'never know."

"True, Soldier. But I know my Gramps."

The Soldier looked away again, rubbed his head in pain for a bit and came back. "Them sonsabitches still got'cha walkin', huh?"

"Yep."

"You're too good for them people, Sandy Boy. Listen to me. I been in this town forever, an' I'm tellin' you right here an' now, you is too good for them people. The cops in this town is so dumb they couldn't catch a train, let alone a crook. Like that fool who had the nerve to arrest me — officer Hoag. And that other creep, Hutchinson. That skinny one that rides on that motorcycle. He arrest'd me for drinkin' somethin' God grew. If I'd been drinkin' whiskey, I could understand it. I was drinkin' wine. I'm an honorable, wine-drinkin' Baptist. What's wrong with that? If you gonna arrest people for drinkin' wine, start with Jesus. An' when they have Communion in church, call out the reserves, 'cause there's enough wine bein' drunk in there to drown a vineyard. You hear me, Sandy Boy?"

"I hear you, Soldier."

"Glad you do. Now, like I was sayin', Hoag an' Hutchinson an' all the rest of 'em up there is dumb. I mean, *Dumb*. If a big-time crook was to come to town, they'd get so excited they'd end up directin' traffic for 'em. An' them two or three detectives you got up there, they couldn't detect daylight. They couldn't crack a suitcase. That department is hurtin', Sandy. 'Specially this night shift. The only thing's gonna save it is an infusion of new blood; a complete changin' of the guard. And it's comin'. Soon. Real soon. I done seen it. An' I'm gonna let you in on a little secret, Sandy: You gonna be the last man standin', Sandy. You hear me?"

"I hear you, Soldier," said Carlsson, thinking it not worthwhile pursuing.

"Now let's let that part lay, 'cause I'm gonna tell you 'bout somebody else who needs workin' on. He is got a *serious* problem. I mean *real* serious. Want me to tell you who it is?"

"Who?"

"Your chief. I'm tellin' you, Sandy Boy, that is one man who won't be remembered for what he's got upstairs. Y'know what he did? That whiskey-drinkin' fool looked up an' saw the moon one night. Not like this moon. Nobody knows it, but this moon is sayin' somethin'. It's got two faces in it; masks. It's a beautiful moon, pal. But it's deceptive. A deceptive moon means strange things is gonna happen. Any good Gypsy will tell that. So watch it. Check with me in the mornin'. I won't be around, but gimme some thought. 'Cause you gonna be standin'. But a lotta somebodies ain't. In fact, none of 'em. So gimme a thought in the a.m., lemme know you're all right."

"Whatever you say, Soldier."

"Anyhow, the moon that night was dull. The chief looked up an' said, 'Who's that shinin' that light up there?' The moon moved two inches. The chief reached for his ticket book. I said, 'Wha'cha doin', Home-boy?' He said, 'I made a mistake.' I said, 'A slight one.' He said, 'Yeah. It's some S.O.B drivin' with his high-beams on.' I ain't lyin', Sandy Boy. A reporter was writin' this book about some of the all-time baddies, an' he asked the chief what he thought about Al Capone. The chief said, 'Don't talk to me about religion.' The reporter said, 'Can I hit you with John Dillinger?' The chief said, 'Don't get nasty.' The reporter said, 'Jack the Ripper!' The chief said, 'I didn't know it was open.' The reporter said, 'Let's try Baby Face Nelson!' The chief said, 'I got him up in juvenile hall.' The reporter said, 'Maybe we ought'a dig a little deeper in the pages of history.' The chief said, 'Shoot. — Just kiddin'.' The reporter said, 'Attila the Hun!' The chief said, 'Watch out — I don't play that.' The reporter said, 'But, chief, Attila the Hun was the scourge of Europe!' 'The chief said, that proves my point. Any man walkin' around with a skirt on, an' you call him *hun,* somethin's gotta be wrong somewhere.' The reporter took his time an' said, 'Chief, let me hit you with this last biggie.' The chief said, *'Shoot'* — just kiddin'.' The reporter said, 'Genghis Khan!' The chief said, 'Boy, you'd better be careful who you're runnin' around with. The reporter said, 'But, Chief, Genghis Khan was the ruthless ruler of the medieval world.' 'The chief said, 'See.' The reporter said, 'He was born on the Onon River in the year 1162 A.D.' The chief said, 'A.c., d.c. — ha, ha, ha.' The reporter said, 'Genghis Khan was a Mongolian.' The chief said, 'See.' The reporter said, 'Chief, we're talkin' about a race of people.' The chief said, 'Now I got'cha. Tell me a li'l more about this boy, I might find a spot for 'im.' The reporter said, 'Chief,

Genghis Khan conquered Mongolia, consolidated all China, and led a growing confederacy westward.' The chief said, 'Oh, so he's a local boy.' The
reporter said, 'Chief, Khan rode through rivers, thundered across mountains,
and tiptoed across the Gobi Desert. He left his mark in Persia, cut through
Russia, and set up shop in Afghanistan. He defeated the Turks, destroyed the
Bulgarians, and laid claim to the Caspian Sea. He was the son of Yekusai,
father of Hulagu, an' granddaddy to the Lord High Kublai Khan'.' The chief
said, 'They puttin' pressure on me. Sign him up! I got a quota to fill. Sign
the boy up!' The reporter said, 'But, Chief…?' The chief said, 'Hurry up,
boy. 'Cause to be truthful, I don't like any of 'em, but better a Jew than a
colored man.'

"The reporter got up an' slowly walked away. He knew what I've been
tryin' to tell you, Sandy Boy: Your chief is not a very bright man."

There was laughter during the slurred, drunken speech, and the Soldier
had talked himself into a deeper thirst. "Howz about a drink?"

"No, thanks," Carlsson said, almost absently. He had little voice because he was taken by the man's breadth of knowledge, and how he was able
to fabricate and jubilantly weave his way to wherever he wanted to go. There
was art in that, thought the rookie who was still questioning and missing
something in life. Maybe it was for kicks, maybe it was to learn something;
maybe it was simply to sit and listen to the rhythm and fervor of an old mind
that rambled in strange and distant areas; an off-centered old black mind that
emerged from the shadows and broke the boredom of night, but whatever it
was, he wanted to get to know the man better. He should have done it before,
he thought. Maybe in a week or so he'd invite him out for a bite.

For the moment, the young policeman said, "So, Soldier, what are you
doing down in this area on such a beautiful night?"

"Nuttin'," Soldier Boy said, rubbing his head again. "Know what I
feel like, Sandy? I feel like I been touched by the moon."

"Must be a good feelin', Soldier. Don't lose it."

"It's a strange feelin', I can tell you that. Whenever you're facin' the
end, it's always a strange feelin'," Soldier Boy responded portentiously, and
then changed. "Howz about a toddy?"

"Can't," said Carlsson. He very much would have liked to quiz the

Soldier on the last statement — and the one about being the last man standing — but he was running late.

"S'matter?" said the Soldier. "Don't wanna drink with your ol' pal?"

"How about next week? Christmas. We'll spend some time together, do some talking. We'll have a few, and something to eat."

"An' we'll talk about where you was born, Sandy. Denmark."

"You know about Denmark??"

"I know a li'l something about it."

"Do you know where Denmark is, Soldier?"

"Northern Europe. An' not only that, Sandy, I can tell you *what* it is: It's an archipelago between the North and Baltic seas. Unified in the 10th century by the Viking king Harold Bluetooth. Died in 985. Made the people Christians before he left. Danske. Briefly controlled England in the 11th century. United with Sweden 'til 1523; Norway 'til 1814. I could go on an' bring you up to date — talk about some of your queens. But my thirst rules, Sandy. Time for us to go in an' have a quick one."

"Soldier…what you know…what you just said was amazing. Incredible."

"See, we got a lot to talk about, Sandy."

"But, how…??"

"We'll get to all'a that, Sandy. But, now, howz 'bout us goin' inside, an' havin' that toddy?"

"I really wish I could, Soldier," Carlsson said earnestly, and still trying to control his astonishment. "You don't know how much I'd like for us to talk. But I can't now. I really can't. 'Specially while I'm on duty. And besides, I gotta call in on that box down there every hour, and on the half hour, I gotta call in on the box at the other end of the post. I'm already late."

"Well, that's where you got one on the old soldier, Sandy. My tour of duty is over. Finito. It's over, Sandy Boy," Soldier Boy said. "'*God and soldier all men adore — in time of strife and no more; for when the war is over — and all things righted — God is neglected — and the soldier is slighted.'*"

"That's a hell of a quote, Soldier," said Carlsson, again overtaken by something the Soldier had said. "That's really a hell of a nice quote."

"An' damned true. So true, my ol' pal, that I'm gonna go in the bar an' have a drink for the both of us, Sandy Boy. I shall have a drink for me an' you — for *us,* the slighted."

"Okay, but only one. Remember, we've got to have our quality time together. An' I want to ask you about some of the other things you said."

"Right. We'll talk. But in memory of you, I'm gonna go inside here and have a tod. I'll have only one, my combat buddy. Only one."

"And take it easy in there, Soldier. The place changed hands quite a while ago, and the new owner is not the kind of a person you or I can stand."

The Soldier moved to the Flamingo's doors "It's graveyard time, but I can handle him if I want to," he said in a strange manner, and for an instant his bloodshot eyes became meditative. There was an aura around him. He thought about his own words, then stumbled back to the young policeman. He became sad for a moment, then hesitant but proud. "Sandy Boy, you wouldn't want to help an old soldier out, would you? An old soldier whose end is near; an old soldier who is beyond the cocktail hour of a brilliant career..."

Carlsson, though dazzled, got the deeper message and reached into his pocket. He separated about three or four singles from his billfold and held them out for the old black man to take. Soldier Boy looked at the bills, then at his benefactor. He gently selected a single dollar. "A man's gotta have some pride," he said.

The young man smiled. He wanted to tell the man to take them all, but he understood. Pride was at stake here.

The Soldier returned the smile and carefully folded the single. "We'll talk about Mozart, Debussy, Shakespeare, Byron, Carver, Tubman, Robeson. Then if we got time, Sandy, we'll talk about some of the great philosophers, then we'll slide into the higher tiers of mathematics. Trig an' all that stuff. I'll show you how it all ties in."

The old black turned and moved unsteadily to the tavern's Western-type doors. He turned back to his stunned, open-mouthed friend. "Sandy, if you should see any of my old comrades in arms, tell 'em you saw the Soldier. Tell 'em that you saw the Soldier Boy. An' when you tell 'em, they're gonna automatically stop doin' what they're doin' an' hop to *attention*. Then look 'em straight in the eye, Sandy, an' tell 'em that the old Soldier want 'em to always be true to the cause. Tell 'em I want 'em to hold their positions; to soldier to the very end. Go down fightin'. An' tell em' to shoot low, the enemy might be crawlin'. An', Sandy, tell 'em that the old Soldier said we may no longer be on the field of battle; I won't be here to lead them anymore, but duty, honor, and valor are still the dimensions of one's soul. And tell em' this, Sandy — leave 'em with this quote: *Our yesterdays I shall leave to their keeping, and I shall smile farewell with eyes too sad for weeping.* Will you tell 'em that, Sandy?"

"I'll tell 'em, Soldier."

"Do that, Sandy. Tell 'em'. Then dismiss 'em, Sandy. — Dismiss the troops."

Carlsson saluted and said: "I will dismiss the troops in your honor, sir."

It got to him. It was a moment of moments for the old soldier. He thought about the duty and the words that accompanied the duty: *"I will dismiss the troops in your honor, sir."* He visualized the act, and grinned beyond measure. He was not talking to his friend. He was talking to himself, his body taut, his tired, maroon eyes far away. *What an honor. What a God-given, dignified, magnificent, fit-for-a-king, honor for an old soldier! There ain't nothin' in the whole wide world to beat that! It ain't even worth tryin'! To hell with Eisenhower, MacArthur, Patton, Marshall, Rommel, Grant, Robert E. Lee and any other son-of-a-bitch who called himself a soldier.* His young friend had said: *"I will dismiss the troops in your honor, sir."*

And he said it with a salute. It was something worth carrying to the grave.

The Soldier wanted to call his young friend to attention and return the salute. He couldn't do it. He was too mesmerized by the honor.

And Danny Carlsson was mesmerized by him.

⌛

"My fello' Americans!"

Those were the words that heralded the tattered and red-eyed old black man's entrance into the mustiness of the new Flamingo. It was late, and by law, the place should have been closed. But the Flamingo didn't operate by law.

A fully bagged, cigarette-dangling, hefty female customer took one look and tried her best to deflate the man. "We don't want no niggers in here."

"Then you better call your momma an' tell her to stay at home," Soldier Boy countered. He ignored the drunks spaced between a faded under-new-ownership sign, the *Drinks for 50 cents* sign, and, under a patch of dried mistletoe, a couple on the dance floor, gyrating to a Hank Snow oldie.

The old black man took a seat at the bar, looked at the burly, Southern-talking owner/bartender, Jesse Brown, and waited. The two exchanged looks. Soldier Boy cleared his throat. He spoke regally. "As the Earl of Essex said shortly before he was beheaded: *'If it wasn't for the honor, I wouldn't go through with it.'* I shall have a bit of the berries."

Nothing he said or did was appreciated by Jess. "Did you hear what the lady down there said?"

"I heard what that tub said."

"Who you callin' a tub, you black sonovabitch?!" shouted the woman, whose name was Bertha, and who, before Soldier Boy's entrance, was barely able to lift her head up from her drink.

The Soldier kept talking. "If I recall correctly, *it* said *it* didn't want no niggers in here. And I heartily agree. So if you should happen to see one, have him to call my office."

Jess resisted the impulse to throw the old black man out. Instead, he glared at the man, grabbed a glass, partly filled it with wine and slid it just past the unwanted man's reach.

"Wha' the hell you doin' that for, Jesse?" the big woman said, her voice heavier than a long-distance truck driver's. "Throw the nigger out."

"Shut up, Bertha, I'll handle this," Jess said, his eyes not leaving the black man.

Undaunted, the Soldier got the glass, lifted it, and stabbed at eloquence. "Here's to colored folks and connoisseurs. And in that order." He downed the contents with one swallow.

Jess answered by shattering the glass into the garbage can that was next to several kegs of beer.

"Now you cookin', Jesse," said the woman, now receiving vocal support from two other patrons who had been silently looking on.

"Now give 'im the boot, Jess," said a man with a pitted face and short arms.

"I'll have another," ordered Soldier Boy.

"If you give 'im another one, Jesse, spit in it," hollered Bertha. "Hark an' spit innit!"

Jess poured another and Soldier Boy drank it. Jess sent the emptied glass shattering again.

"Let's keep 'em rollin'," Soldier Boy said.

Jess didn't move.

The old black confidently reached into his pocket and splattered some change on the counter. "I *said* I'll have another."

"I wouldn' give that nigger nuttin' else," egged the chain-smoking Bertha.

"Berth's right," supported another voice. "Don't give 'im nothin' else, Jesse."

Jess ignored them both and angrily poured another. He watched the man drink it and again sent the glass crashing into the garbage can.

"The bigger they are, the harder they break. This time, I'll have a double."

"Kick his ass out, Jesse!" said the woman.

"Toss 'im, Jess. Toss 'im," said another man who had thus far been silent because he was too drunk to realize what was going on.

"You're out of funds," Jess said without looking at the change on the bar.

"That's where you wrong," Soldier Boy said. "I got money John D. Rockyfeller ain't seen." He dug into his pocket, came out with Danny Carlsson's crushed dollar, and flattened it on the bar.

"Don't take it, Jess," said the man with the pitted face and short arms.

"Don't even touch it, Jesse," Bertha cried. "Niggers is germy."

The two men starred at each other. They were eye to eye. Finally Jess had had enough. "Get your ass outta here."

"Whooo-ray," said the woman. "Now you're smokin', Jesse. You smokin'."

"Why don't you shut up, cow," Soldier Boy hollered down to the woman, then turned back to Jess. "To begin with, that hag ain't no woman."

"You sonovabitch!" Bertha shouted, and stood to come to where the Soldier was seated.

"Siddown, cow," Soldier Boy said, not at all threatened.

Jess motioned for Bertha to sit back down. His attention returned to the black man. "Now, I've had it with you, boy. I want you to apologize to that woman, then get your ass outta here."

"I wouldn't apologize to that fat, blubbery tub o' lard sittin' down there if my life depended on it. She ought to be apologizin' to me for mistaken identity. An' if I don't get it, both you an *it* can go an' tap-dance on a watermelon."

Jess replied, as threateningly as he could: "Get your ass out of here."

"Why don't you make me get outta here, you Juggie. That's what I call all white folks I don't like: Juggie. *Juggie, juggie, juggie!*"

"He done gone too far now," said the pitted faced man with the short arms.

"Don't take that from no nigger, Jessie," egged the woman. "Let 'im have it! Don't ever take nothin' from a nigger! I wish it was even colder out there so's when you kick his ass out, he'd freeze to death 'fore he hits the ground."

"Boy, I'm tellin' you to move!" Jess said.

"An' I'm tellin' you to make me," countered Soldier Boy.

"For the last time, boy, I'm tellin' you to get your ass outta this here bar."

"For the last time' nuttin'! I was born in this town. I fought in *two* world wars for this town, an' I was comin' in this bar when you was back in Alabama pickin' cotton, you redneck gorilla."

Soldier Boy had turned his head, starting to say something to Bertha. But he hadn't gotten a word out of his mouth before Jess hauled off and whacked the turned head with a bottle, splattering wine everywhere. The hit had been so hard that the bandanna, soaked with wine, started dripping blood. All but the dancing couple joined the heavy-throated woman as she whooped and applauded. The bottle had a strange clanking sound when it shattered, and Soldier Boy — his eyes transfixed — was frozen in place. Feeling that the bottle had not done the job, the big man hopped across the bar and, scissor-squeezing the neck, knocked the older man to the floor and began pummeling him. The bartender was ruthless in his attack. Seething and mouthing obscenities, he pressed his thumb inside the old black's man's mouth and sent his fingers digging into his cheeks. Bertha, leading the others, was shouting support. Jess slid the head over and began pounding it against the metal base that ran the length of the bar. With the customers looking on, and with one lending an assist by kicking at Soldier Boy and another trying to stop the melee, the struggle continued. The restraining customer finally gained success by separating the two. Soldier Boy, bleeding profusely, made an agonizing crawl for the door. Breaking away from the customer, Jess flew over and delivered a final, booted kick directly to the old man's head.

"Good job, Jesse," said Bertha. "Good job." She hocked, emptied her glass of beer and lit another cigarette. Ordering another beer, she was joined by the pitted-faced man. The too-drunk-to-care man nodded back to sleep.

Danny Carlsson was down the street on the police callbox reporting in when he saw the three or four customers looking at the figure crawling for the gutter from the door. Frantically, he dropped the phone and ran as fast as he could to the scene. It left an angered McShayne hanging on the other end.

On the run and making a quick assessment that it was Soldier Boy, Carlsson called for someone to call an ambulance.

"Already did," said the man who had tried to help earlier.

At the station, McShayne swung around in the chair and leaned into the mike: "Headquarters to 103." After getting no response, he yelled, "GAWDAMMIT, Three! Headquarters to patrol car One-Zero-Three!!" Still getting nothing, the sergeant shouted: "Headquarters to 103!!"

"Three," Corbbo sleepily responded.

"Corbbo, you sonovabitch!" the desk sergeant blasted into the mike. "Get down to post 1-A and see why that idiot left the callbox, and then report to the desk!"

"'Kay," Corbbo responded. He moved the blanket more snugly around his head and went back to sleep.

McShayne pressed the button on the mike again: "Headquarters to 102."

"Two."

"Spagg, take a run to 190 Main and back up Corbbo."

"Two. Rolling."

At the switchboard, Bucky capped his hand over the telephone. "Sarge...? Ambulance rolling to Main Street."

McShayne bent back into the mike. "And put some speed on it, Two; there's been an 88 in the area."

Carlsson removed his jacket and was now at Soldier Boy's side. He placed it under the bleeding head and removed the bandanna. The injury was far more serious than he had believed. It was not necessary to ask who caused it, but he did anyway. None of the bystanders said anything. Jess, having remained behind the bar, called everybody back inside. The drinks were on the house.

Coughing and heaving blood, the old soldier squeezed the young patrolman's hand. "This is a heck of a way for an ol' soldier to go, ain't it, Sandy?"

"You're going to live, Soldier. I'm going to see to it. You're not going anywhere. You're *not* going to die. Help is on the way."

"Yeah, I am, Sandy. I told you the end was here. You didn't believe me, huh?" the Soldier coughed. "But I ain't scared of dyin', Sandy Boy. I ain't. I'm gonna be soldiering in God's army."

"Stop talkin' like that," Carlsson said, urgently. "You're not going anywhere. You're going to be all right. I've got an ambulance coming."

"Think they'll give the old soldier a good going-away, Sandy? Y'think I'll have drums an' bugles an' flags, an' all'a that? Will you be there, Sandy Boy?"

"Sure, sure, Soldier," Carlsson said, still talking fast, comforting, all while trying to stop the bleeding. "But you gotta stop talkin'. You're gonna be alright. We still gotta have our talk."

"He wouldn'a done that awhile back, Sandy, he wouldn'a. I'da taken him, huh? Wouldn't I, Sandy Boy? Wouldn't I'da taken 'im?"

"Sure, sure, Soldier. But don't talk any more. You're gonna pull through."

"Will you get him for me, Sandy Boy? Will you get him for me, huh?"

Carlsson, holding his head with utmost care, and knowing the old man was fading fast, pledged, "...I'll get him. I'll get him for you. I promise you, Soldier Boy, I will get him. You can bet on that. I will get Jess Brown, if it's the last thing I do. Justice will be done."

"An', Sandy, don't forget our song."

"I won't. I won't ever forget it. And I won't ever forget you, Soldier."

"Want me to sing the song for you again, Sandy?"

"No, Soldier, don't. You gotta save your strength."

"...*Oh, Sandeee Buoyeee.... The Pipe — the Pipe...is...*"

"Please, Soldier. Don't, please. You sound great, but save your breath. I'll hear the song again. Soon. Real soon. You'll do it alone or we'll sing it together — for Christmas. Whatever way you want, but it'll be done. Just hold on. Hold on, my friend. Hold on."

"When I see you next time, I'll do it. You may not be able to hear it, Sandy, but I'm gonna be singing it real good for you, Sandy. An' I'm gonna know all the words."

"You did fine, Soldier. Great. I like the way you did it. And it's the meaning that counts. But lay still; just hold on for the ambulance."

"An' next time I'll talk to you some more about Denmark."

"Sure you will, Soldier. But don't talk any more. We'll do it later. Please save your breath. The bleeding is slowing, and you're gonna pull through."

"An' do me one more favor, Sandy. Can I count on you to do it? It means a lot to me."

"Just tell me what it is, Soldier, and it's done. We're buddies."

"Check the trailer. Y'gotta do that, 'Kay?"

"Okay," said Carlsson, not knowing what he was saying *okay* to. He wanted to ask, but didn't. "Just lay quiet. Don't talk. Save your strength."

"An' you ain't gotta worry about that Gypsy moon, or the faces in it, Sandy, 'cause you ain't a regular on that department, an' you got a good heart. Now, lean down a li'l bit closer, 'cause I wanna tell you somethin'." And when the policeman's ear was close to the stricken man's lips, the stricken man whispered. "You ain't a believer, is you?"

"A believer?"

"In the hereafter; the eternal."

"I think I know what you're sayin', Soldier. But I don't know what I believe. I have a grandfather who brought me up thinking one thing, and things that happen tell me another. I don't know. I just don't know. I wish I did know."

"Soon you will, Sandy. Soon you'll know," the Soldier whispered knowingly. "An', like I said, ain't nothin' gonna bother you. You're the future. You got work to do. A lot of it. You're gonna start off with a hard one. You're gonna *do* wrong, but you're gonna *be* right. An' you're gonna be on the edge. But, like I done told you, you're gonna be the last man standin'. The rest of these fools?...Say goodnight to 'em. Say goodnight to your boys in blue, Sandy. — This is a night of inevitable fates. You hear me, Sandy? *A night of inevitable fates.* The hits, they gonna be slow at first, but, Sandy Boy, they gonna keep on a'comin'. You might end up doin' a little pleadin'. It's gonna be strange, but it's done been decreed, you're gonna be alright."

Then the soldier stiffened a little, as though something had shot through the very core of the body. Even he was startled. "Sandy Boy...Sandy Boy..." The tired, old maroon eyes widened and the legs started moving in place, like they were scrambling. Suddenly they stopped.

"What is it, Soldier?" Carlsson asked anxiously. Now he wanted him to talk. It was the look on his face that did it. He was holding the man as tight as he could. "Soldier Boy, talk to me. What is it, Soldier? What is it?"

"....Sandy Boy — the p-p-pain — the pain — the pain in my head is going away, Sandy." He said it with newness, liberation, and wonderment. "It's gone, Sandy — for the first time in my life...An'...Ooooh, Sandy Boy, there, up ahead, I c-c-can...I'm s-s-seein' somebody. He's risin' up through all the pages of history, walkin' through all the great faces of history! An' the great people of history! But they're all children, Sandy. Every person that's ever lived an' done somethin', every person that's done made a mark on Earth — they babies, Sandy! Every single person! *Babies!* Oh, Lord. Now, I'm seein'...I'm seein'...He's comin' this way, Sandy! He's comin'!...I — I can almost see clear through Him! Sandy, I can — Sandy, I can! Ohmilord, milord, milord! — Ohmilord, God A'mighty — I see Himmmmm! It's got to be Him! He's real! He's *real,* Sandy Boy! He's *real*!!! He's glory. Pure glory! *Nothin' but eminence.* Ain't no other way to say it! *God!* It's God, Sandy Boy. *God!* Oooh-oooh, He's gonna touch me, Sandy! He's reachin' out for me...He's gonna do it! He's gonna touch meeee!"

Then, with his body stiffened, the old black laughed. It was a laugh of utter gladness. Then with more rapture, more joy, more reverence than any earthly man had ever known, he yelled. *"Sannnndy Booooyyyy!!!"*

No longer bloodshot; no longer tired and maroon, the cleared eyes rolled back into a damply stained head. The body became still.

The Soldier was dead.

8

When car 102 arrived in front of the Flamingo, after having taken much longer than it should, the first thing Curley Spagg wanted to do was to unload on the timid-appearing ambulance driver because he had beaten the patrol car to the scene. Not that he had been in any hurry to begin with, but the cop had been delayed because the car's battery had gone down and the Hudson had to get a push from a passing bus that made a nightly chug to the nearby cities of Lodi, Garfield, and Passaic. But it was the ambulance driver who had gotten his goat. Spagg simply did not like the man.

"Hey," Spagg said to the driver, his cap tilted over one eye, and continuing to ignore Carlsson, still kneeling with the body. "Don't you zeroes know you ain't supposed to buzz that thing after midnight?!"

"Buzz what thing?"

"The siren, you ignorant pimple on a boar's butt! You don't blow it after midnight! There's a city ordinance against that kinda stuff. You screw up the community; you wake up the people; an' the people pay taxes — an' the taxes pay us. If you do it again, I ain't gonna just give you a ticket. I'm gonna haul you in. You got that?!"

"Hey, cop…" the puny driver said, and went on to say something unintelligible.

Spagg didn't get it all. Moreover, he hadn't liked the way he had been addressed. Now he was really mad. Snorting. The big cop tugged at his motorcycle trousers with man-devouring ferocity. But he felt undressed. He went back to the car, put his sunglasses on, came back and narrowed his eyes for action. He was towering over the man.

"Now, what was that you said?" snorted the cop, his hands jammed tightly into each rib cage.

"I can't remember what I said," said the ambulance driver, casually looking up at the moon. "But I can tell you what I shudda said."

Now Spagg's face was less than a tenth of an inch away from the short man's face. His voice was low and was designed to conquer. "Well, then, you pasty-faced imp. Tell this here cop what you 'shudda' said."

"I shudda said: Kiss my siren-blowin' ass."

Startled, Spagg gave the little man a look, tripped over the sheet-covered dead man, bounced off the bar's doors and did everything but fall inside.

The way Curley Spagg's belligerence led him to tug menacingly on his motorcycle trousers and adjust his sunglasses was reminiscent of the time about four or five years earlier when he had been ordered to make a routine run over to New York's 22nd Precinct to bring back Wee Willie Wilonoski, a bookish and owlish-looking writer of bad checks.

Wee Willie was an unmitigated, phthisis-scarred gnat. He was so weak he needed help blowing dust off a book, and he wore eyeglasses that were bullet-proof thick. When the New Yorkers released him into Spagg's custody, the man had actually grown weaker. But the first thing Spagg did when they got outside the precinct station was to set the ground rules for the less than 22-minute trip back to Elton Head. The big cop circled the man, and took a stance by the patrol car. He tilted his cap, adjusted his sunglasses, spread his legs and jammed both hands deep into his hips. He was biting hard on the nub of a cigar and looking mean. *Formidable.*

"Now, Willie," the big cop said threateningly, "you're a felon. I'm the law. I'm takin' you back to the big Head. We got a long ride ahead' a us, and we won't be makin' many stops. Our route will be the George Washington Bridge. I don't like bridges. And I *don't* like anybody talkin' while I'm ridin' on bridges. You got that, you insignificant, potty-trained piece of turd?"

Willie coughed. Unable to say anything, he nodded weakly.

"An' another thing," said the cop. "They sent me all the way over here from the big Head in NJ to pick you up. They don't assign just anybody to do that. They picked me. They picked me because I am the baddest of the bad; the meanest of the mean. I've been known to eat people like you. Do yourself a favor an' don't let my rep as a *jenn-u-wine* ass-kicker scare you."

"I won't, sir," said Wee Willie, cooperatively gasping. Then the poor man with the owlish face and weak lungs coughed and accidentally spit. In the effort to wipe his mouth, he raised a bony arm. It scared Spagg half to death. He got so scared that he ran and hid behind the patrol car. Willie, gasping, choking and stumbling around for dear life, raised the other arm, fighting for air. The cop, thinking he was under an even bigger assault, threw the man the keys and caught a bus back to Jersey.

Spagg liked the interior of the Flamingo. He particularly liked the way the liquid-looking lights from the juke box danced along the red-flocked walls and hit home with the Ballantine's beer sign and the pictures of the Rheingold beer girls. Still not thinking about Carlsson or the dead man, the big cop temporarily removed his sunglasses, gave the cruddy place a quick once-over, and brushed his way to the bar where Jess was.

"Jess Brown, me boy."

"Hi, Spaggy, wha's doin'?"

"Aw, nuttin' much. Samee-samee," Spagg said, pulling his motorcycle trousers up with enviable masculinity. "Had to get a li'l rough on some creep out there."

"Did'ja handle it all right?" Jess asked, automatically sliding a full shot glass in front of him, which Spagg quickly gulped down.

"Let's put it this way," Spagg said, dusting off his hands. "It'll be another charge of police brutality."

"You gotta lot of them agin' you, huh?"

"A file this thick," Spagg boasted, indicating a file that was as thick as a New York phone book. "I hate to get rough with people, Jess. But some of 'ems got it comin'."

"Well, you're the type to handle 'em, all right. How 'bout another shooter? Wet the ol' whistle an' relax a little."

"Yeah. Lemme have another quickie."

Jess poured another.

Spagg emptied the glass. "What'd the drunk do? Come in here an' start somethin'?"

"Yeah," Jess said, pouring another.

Bertha volunteered, "The slob."

"Ain't had no business down here, anyway," said the cop, overlooking the woman. "Who nailed 'im?"

"I did," said Jess without concern.

"Did it good, too," said the man who had been too drunk to notice.

Spagg emptied another glass, and again admired the surroundings. "Y'gettin' it fixed up pretty nice in here, Jesse."

"Yeah," said Jess, refilling the glass, "I never did like that uppity look it had before. An' you notice I closed the kitchen. This is a place for drinkin', not eatin'. I got some more stuff I wanna do. Like puttin' in a popcorn machine, some pink lights, cuppla new chairs. Maybe a booth."

"Booth would be nice."

Jess slid the bottle on the bar. "I'm thinkin' about changing the name of the place to La Flaminko and puttin' the booth in the center, so people can dance around it. Then when they get tired, they can just plop down."

"Good thinkin'." The big cop didn't waste any more time with the little glass. He took a healthy swig from the bottle. Then, thinking he heard the ambulance departing, he gulped: "Might as well get the ol' wheels of justice spinnin'."

"Might as well," Jess said. He removed his apron and announced to the few customers: "Y'all hold on. Bertha'll handle the bar. I'll be back in about 20 mins. Don't let nobody steal nuthin', Bertha."

Bertha rolled off the stool to go behind the bar. She looked at Spagg. Spagg returned the look. "Wha'chu lookin' at?" Bertha said, roughly.

"Don't start nothin' with me, woman," said the cop.

"Shut up," said Bertha.

Spagg looked at her arms and at a face that almost matched his in hardship and strength, and thought about sailing for the door. He swung a look to Jess. "What time you closing 'er up, Jess?"

"Beautiful night like this? Whenever. Need sumthin'?"

"After we fill out the report, I might want to come back for a li'l kicker."

"No prob. Better yet, let's just take this little goody with us," said Jess, grabbing the bottle.

Before going fully out, and making certain he didn't have to face the ambulance driver again, Spagg asked Jess if he had heard the ambulance departing. Jess said no. Too intimidated to look, Spagg went back to the bar for another drink. "Take a look out there, Jess, and call me if the thing is gone," he said. "I don't wanna have to go back out there an' kick some butt again."

The coast was clear, and when the two finally came out a distraught Carlsson was leaning on the parking meter. He was outwardly calm, but his insides were on fire. In his usual quiet manner he said to Jess, "Why'd you do it?"

"Why'd I do *what*?"

"You killed Soldier Boy. Why did you do it?"

"'Cause he was a bum an' had diarrhea of the mouth."

"He had a plate in his head. You knew he was a sick man."

"Then he was a *sick* bum. A *colored* sick bum with a plate in his head, so what?" The point made, Spagg led the man to the car. Fortunately, the Hudson kicked over.

Carlsson stood there, soaking in anger.

Ready to pull out, Spagg said to the rookie, "You walkin' in? You got a report to fill out."

Carlsson didn't say anything. He remained draped over the meter.

Spagg put the car into gear and drove off.

A block away, his radio popped, "Hey, Spaggaroni...? 102, come in."

Spagg picked up the mike. It was Frank Pippilo. "Yuh, Pip."

"I called Doc Glendenhall an' got an okay for me an' the you-know-who to see 'im about the you-know-what when I get off in the you-know-when."

"Good show, Pip. Good show. That's usin' the ol' bean, kid."

"I like ol' Pippo," said the passenger. "He comes in an' turns a few."

"An', Jess, m'boy, me an' you is gonna come back an' turn a few soon's we get this li'l thing squared away."

"Lovvit."

"Hey, I like the new name you're comin' up with. *La Flaminko,*" Spagg complimented. "S'gotta good ring to it. S'got class."

"Snazzy."

"S'like that new car comin' from Detroit...The...?"

"Tucker," Jess said, knowledgeably.

"Yeah. S'got style. It'll be here forever."

When car 102 pulled into the yard, Spagg wasn't feeling any pain. Neither was Jess, for that matter — mainly because en route to the station they both took more comfort in the bottle they had carried with them. Going inside, Spagg said, "Don't tell the boss in here, but, Jess, ain't nuttin' like good whiskey to keep the ol' heart pumpin'."

"An' ain't nuttin' like good people to drink good whiskey to keep the ol' ticker hummin'," Jess said, wrapping a friendly arm around the policeman's neck.

McShayne was just returning from upstairs when the two came in.

"Hi'ya, Demo," Jess said brightly.

Without enthusiasm, the desk sergeant mumbled something.

Jess turned to look at the sparse Christmas tree, lonely in the corner, and dug for his wallet. Got a spare envelope, Bucky? I wanna sweeten the tree a li'l bit."

"Don't bother," said McShayne, who, incidentally, was the only sergeant not in favor of having a tree. He thought it was a form of bribery. Pure and simple, McShayne couldn't be bought.

"'Kay," said Jess. "I'll sweeten 'er up tomorrow. So, Dem, no more probs with the ol' ticker?"

"My heart's beating fine, Jess." McShayne said.

The desk sergeant, however, had not been truthful. Not that he would have shared truth with Jess, but shortly after his the death of his wife, he had undergone a heart operation and, against doctor's orders, had returned to work. Earlier that week, pale and not feeling well, he had to go to the doctor's office again. Trouble was brewing. So much trouble, in fact, that the doctor scheduled an appointment with a specialist in Englewood the very next day. McShayne never showed up.

"So the ol' tick-ticks doin' better, huh, Dem?"

"To repeat, Jess, the heart's fine," the sergeant answered, disinterestedly.

"Glad to hear it; glad to hear it," Jess said, and looked at Bucky. "Bucky-Buck. See you made it here all right. Listen, if you run dry, I've got another pint out there in…"

Bucky quickly put his fingers to his lips to silence him and looked at the sergeant. "We need some more EPRD-21 forms, Sarge. I'll get 'em." He quickly stepped into the other room.

McShayne turned his attention to Spagg. "Have you been drinking? You smell like a still."

"That's b'cause I was handlin' a drunk."

"Did you answer that 88?"

"Jess had a little trouble down at his place."

"Yeah," said Jess, "some bum tried to come in there an' start somethin'. His mouth had the runs."

"It was that wino, what'sisname. You know, the sick-in-the-head colored one. The soldier one."

"Zachariah Hill," Bucky called out from the other room. "The one that's got a plate in the head?"

"Yeah," said Spagg. "That's the one. Good thing I didn't get to 'im first."

Jess said, "Come into my joint insultin' the customers, cussin' an' carryin' on. Even took a swing at me with a barstool. But I bet'cha he won't do it no more."

"Jess had to wipe 'im out," said Spagg.

McShayne asked, "'Wiping him out,' meaning…?"

"Took 'im out," answered Spagg. "Killed him."

"*Killed* him?" McShayne asked.

"Had to," Jess said, casually. "He was going for his knife."

The sergeant was disturbed, but didn't comment. He leaned back in his chair, tilted forward again and pulled out a form. "Make out a report on it."

"Boy, you oughta see Jess's new place, Sarge. New juke box an' everything. Really swings. No more of that hifalutin' stuff," Spagg said, bringing the form closer to him. He produced a pen and got set to start writing. "To begin with, what we got here is a case of self-defense." He muttered to himself, "self: *s-e-f-f. Defense: d-e-e-f-e-n-z-e.*" Then aloud he said, "How'ya spell your name, Jess? — G...?"

"*J*-e-s-s. Yeah, I got some real cuties comin' in there now."

"Sure do," said Spagg. "Brown? — B...?"

"...r-o-w-n," Jess said. "An' the li'l honeys put out, too, Dem. I can get you fixed up with any of 'em. Fact, there's a li'l honey in there now, named Bertha."

"She ain't exactly a li'l honey, Jess," Spagg said.

"Yeah, but she puts out."

"Then she's a li'l honey. A sweetie," Spagg agreed. "I go down there a lot, don't I, Jess?"

"An' you get straight, too, don't you?"

"Sure do," Spagg said, still struggling with the writing and spelling — a defect that was not caused by the alcohol he had consumed. "Some good stuff, too, Sarge."

"Speakin' o' that," Jess said, "you know what had the nerve to come into my place t'night an' tried to pick up somethin? A damn Chinaman."

"Musta been Charley Wong. Sarge, you said he was out t'night," Spagg said. "Was he stoned?"

"Plastered," said Jess. "Smellin' like a case of homemade rye. An' stumbled in there just as big an' bold, just like he was white or somethin'."

"The nerve," said Spagg. "It had to be Wong. He should stay in his own crummy joint. Did he do anything?"

"Nuttin' like that colored bum. He was just tryin' to get lucky with one of the li'l honeys. He had his eye on Bertha. Didn' happen, though. I kicked him out in a hurry. 'Course, as drunk as he was, he could'a grabbed a rattlesnake, he wouldn'a known the difference."

"'Course, bein' a chink."

"Y'got a point there," said Jess. "Y'know, that's somethin' I just can't picture — a Chinaman with a white woman."

"S'gotta be the pits."

"The bottom of the barrel," agreed Jess.

"Sicko time."

The talkative Jess belched and picked up with: "Say, I hear Father Cribbs, the ol' priest at St. Agnes, is on his last leg. The poor man is about to croak. He's in that iron lung thing. Got pneumonia and TB."

"Really?" mumbled Spagg.

"Yep. Kidneys shot, legs gone, weak heart, can't eat, and don't recognize nobody. They're ready to give 'im last rites an' call in the wagon."

"So, how's he feeling?" asked Spagg.

The desk sergeant couldn't hack it any more. His first inclination was to kick both of them away from the desk, but as though allowing steam to pass through a valve, he held off and swung around in the chair and to the other room. "How long's it take to find the forms, Bucky?"

Bucky was in the room, sitting down, having a smoke and enjoying a drink from the bottle he had stashed when he first came to work. "Got 'em right here, Sarge," he responded, and departed empty-handed.

Spagg was still writing his report. He was secure on the line requiring date and time. But now he had gotten to the second line, the one calling for the description of what happened. "A-t-t-k is still the way to spell *attack*, ain't it?"

"A-t-t-a-k-k," Jess said knowledgeably. "Two t's, two a's, two k's."

"An' you say he was hit in the head, Jess?"

"Yup."

"Head. H-e-d-d."

"One *d*," corrected Jess. "Yep, hated to do it, but I had to use the ol' deadly force on 'im."

Spagg looked puzzled for a moment. "Did'ja say 'deadly force,' Jess?"

"Had to. He was actin' like a caged gorilla."

"How'ya spell gorilla?"

"G-u-r-r-i-l-l-u-h," spelled Bucky.

Spagg wrote it down and followed up with a blunt "Deadly?"

"D-e-dd. L-e-e." Bucky spelled.

Spagg stopped writing. He had a better idea. "Actually, he fell an' hit his head, didn' he, Jess?"

At first Jess didn't get it. He thought Spagg was making a mistake. He started to say, "No, I whacked him in the head." Then he got the message. On paper, falling would look better than hitting. "Good point, Spaggaroni. Good point. He fell an' hit his head."

"'Cause he was drunk an' stumblin'?" Spagg winked.

"Drunk as a skunk," the big man said.

"An' going for his knife?"

"Knife?? Oh, yeah. Right, right. He was goin' for his knife."

"Knife. N-y-y-f-e," spelled the cop. "An' after abusin' the customers, what'd he do, Jess? Slip?"

"On a banana peel."

"How'ya spell banana?"

"B-u-n-n-a-n-n-o."

Jess unconsciously broke off what he started to say, took the cop's report and began filling it out for him. "So, howz the little pride an' joy — your li'l niece, Dem?"

McShayne didn't appreciate being called "Dem," but didn't say anything.

"She still in school?"

"Yes. And I know a few other people who should be there as well, starting at kindergarten," McShayne said, quietly taking the report from the bartender and sliding it back before the cop's unhappy eyes.

"Bright kid," Jess said, not offended. "Shouldn't be no problem there. So they say she's with you because she needs a li'l discipline, huh? It's the same ol' story, one you hear everywhere you go. Your nearest an' dearest dumping their kids on you."

McShayne didn't say anything. Jess continued to prattle.

"Yep, today kids need the ol' firm hand — an' who's got a better one than the ol' top cop. An'a relative, at that. But I'll tell you somethin', Dem. Top cop or no, it's tough raisin' a 16-year-old kid by yourself. It's tough doin' anything alone, 'specially without the guidin' light of a good missus. That's why I'm gonna tie the ol' knot again. You ought'a think about doin' the same. 'Member what the father of our country said."

"Wha' was that?" Spagg asked.

"Said there's a chicken for every pot."

"I thought Truman said that."

"Nope," said, Jess. "T'was ol' Abe. Abe Lincoln himself. Said it to Miss Maggie right after he crossed the Fotomat."

"I 'member that. He said it on Valentine's Day," said Spagg. He swung back to Bucky. "What'd you say the bum's real name was, Bucky?"

"Zachariah Hill," Bucky answered.

"Hill. One L or two, Buck?"

"One," said Bucky confidently.

Spagg mumbled something to himself and came to a stop. The name Zachariah was a tough one. Said he to the desk sergeant: "Just the last name'll do it, won't it, Sarge?"

McShayne continued to look at the cop dressed in motorcycle gear and sun glasses and struggling with a form he knew his 16-year-old niece could fill out blindfolded. It was no longer a look of disgust or anger. It was one of wonder.

Not even taking into account that he was a policeman with almost 12 years of service under his belt, the desk sergeant was trying to wonder how a person Spagg's age could have *possibly* survived being human as crudely dumb as he was. Then he remembered the old saying about an apple not falling far from the tree. Spagg stayed so close to the tree, he could have been part of the trunk. He didn't know Spagg's father — nothing new there, Spagg never knew him, either. But McShayne did know his mother. She was a lot like Spagg's wife, salty, and the way she kept house it looked like a cyclone had hit it. And the sergeant could understand why the uniform had been put in a washing machine. Neither Spagg nor the wife knew any better. The only surprise was that they even had a machine.

The desk sergeant was still thinking about Spagg's home life when Carlsson drifted into the station. McShayne got right on him.

"Why'd you leave that call-box phone off the hook?"

Without responding, the young patrolman walked directly up to Jess. He was coldly somber and quiet. "I'm not going to let you get away with this."

"Why aren't you in uniform?" McShayne said. "An' where's your jacket?"

"He was too busy nursin' the drunk," Spagg said.

McShayne fired another verbal shot and reached for another form. "Get in back and make out a report on what happened."

There was an exchange of looks, not between the rookie and the desk sergeant, but between the rookie and Jess. If looks could kill, Carlsson would have been tried for murder. McShayne took note of it, and watched as the young policeman took the form and sauntered off to the patrol room.

McShayne hollered after him. "You got a change in your locker?"

"No, sir," Carlsson called back from the corridor.

The desk sergeant gave another unhappy reaction and reached for the mike: "Headquarters to 103, come in....Three?" He got no response, and called again.

The second call blasted Corbbo from a modest sleep. He couldn't answer, because the mike had gotten lost in the cover. With McShayne's voice still blasting, it took almost a full minute before Corbbo was able to find the instrument.

"Corbbo, you goddamn Kentucky-fried Bohemian!" McShayne hollered, again violating the FCC's ruling against using profanity over the airwaves, and again violating a promise he had made to his church-going wife. "What'n the hell do you think I'm runnin'?! Now, if you don't stay on that damn mike, I'm gonna personally see to it that you walk a post for the rest of your sorry life! Do you hear me?!"

"Yessir."

"Now, get in here!"

"If you bringin' him in to see if he's got a spare in his locker, he don't got one," Bucky advised.

"What the hell is this department comin' to?!" McShayne said, heatedly spinning back to the mike. "Stay put, Three."

"'Kay," said a delighted Corbbo. Now it was time for serious sleep. He tilted over the rear seat, saw that the odometer was continuing to rack up the mileage, and waved "nighty-night" at the squawk box.

McShayne grabbed the mike again. "By the way, Three, what's your mileage count?"

Nothing.

"CORBBO!"

"Yes, my friend?"

"What's your mileage count?"

"Howz that, Sarge?"

"*I said:* I wanna know how many miles you got on that thing?!"

"A hunnert."

McShayne exploded. "A hunnert?! There ain't a hundred miles in this city and the three hundred next to it! Now, *what* in the hell are you doing?!"

"It's such a clear an' beautiful night, Sarge, I've decided I'd spend the night chasin' speeders. I'll be backin' off 'round about lunch time."

"Chasin' speeders, huh?"

"Yessir."

"How many speeding tickets have you given out, Corbbo?"

"None yet, Sarge."

"Why not, Corbbo?"

"See," said the patrolman, snuggling under cover in the back seat of the patrol vehicle, "there's some pretty swift traffic up here. Lotta automatic stick shifts."

"Up here — *where*, Corbbo?"

"Come again, Sarge?"

"What's your location, Corbbo!?"

"Old Summers Road."

"What in God's name are you doing — off post — on Old Summers Road?"

"Gettin' mileage, Sarge. Doin' just what you said. An' I'm really puttin' out tonight, rackin' up miles an' miles, an' chasin' dozens an' dozens of out-of-town speeders. I even let Bucky hear the miles goin' up earlier. I'm almost down to ridin' on my inner tubes. Did'ja ever call B. F. Goodrich?"

"Tell me one thing. Just <u>one</u> thing, Corbbo!"

"What's that, Sarge-Sarge?"

"There ain't two out-of-town cars passing through this entire city at night! But even if there was a ton of 'em, how do you go about chasing speeders on a one-block, dead-end street called Old Summers Road?!"

"By usin' the ol' double clutch an' really puttin' out. An' guess what, Sarge? So far only six of 'em have out gunned me, and I was juusssst about to call in an APB on the seventh."

"You sonovabitch!" McShayne said. "Report to the desk!"

Corbbo popped upright, put a sleeping pill into his mouth, turned the radio's volume down, checked the alarm on the clock, and lay back down to sleep.

Back in the patrol room, Carlsson had been in agony. He left the form McShayne had given him untouched on the table and slipped out the back door. He was now sitting in his pickup truck. He had started off immersed in anger, but then he thought about Soldier Boy. He stayed with the memory for a long while, then came back to his own life. Returning to college slipped back into his mind, but re-enlisting won out. Re-enlistment was a simple thing, and if all went as planned — now that he had sorted it all out, he'd resign from the department within a day or so, hang around long enough to see that his grandfather was okay, then, the week after Christmas, back into service he'd go. A few months later he'd probably be in Korea.

The Air Force was a good choice, he thought. But even if he had to settle for going back into the Navy, it would be all right. The Navy didn't see much action, but he was sure he'd see enough to make him feel as though he had made some contribution to the country, and at least he would be able to talk about war on a first-hand basis. With Soldier Boy he hadn't been able to do that. It meant that he really couldn't appreciate his pain.

The rookie policeman couldn't readily shake the thoughts of the old black veteran. That led him to thinking of blacks in general. He felt somewhat remiss that he had not gotten to know at least some of them. There they were, across the tracks, away from the mainstream of the city, and, as they were in just about every place he had seen, tucked behind the shades of a country he had adopted, a country that had accepted him without question. Why? he wondered. What was it about the American psyche that caused them to treat the foreign-born, such as he, better than the native-born?

The young Dane was not pleased at what he was thinking. He switched off by readdressing a deeper concern.

Soldier Boy. Who was he? Who was this likable, outlandish old veteran who, just about every night, would emerge from the shadows and add a few minutes of brightness to an otherwise dull and dreary night? Lunch or some kind of get-together would have answered a lot of questions, but that opportunity was gone now. And so the question remained: Who was he?

Who was the man behind the mask? What was he? How had he lived? He simply could not have been just a banged-up veteran with no life, no past. There was something about the old black man that told the young policeman there was too much tragedy in all that humor of his. What was it? What was *he?* Where did the mind that had been encased by a metal plate come from? The mind had been without organization; it had been, at times, comically free-wheeling and tragically unstructured. But yet here was a discarded old black drunk in Elton Head who spouted philosophy and talked about European history. Genghis Khan. He knew about *Genghis Khan?* Mongolia? Bulgaria? The Caspian Sea? The Onon River in 1162 A.D.? Yekusai? The Lord High Kublai Khan? And, after mentioning Mozart, Debussy, Shakespeare, Byron, and others who just didn't roll off the tongue — he had said something about *"the higher tiers of mathematics? Trig and all that stuff?"* He had to have meant trigonometry — and he called it "stuff." And he wanted to talk about *philosophers?* Amazing. Then, equally startling, he knew something about Danish history — *10th and 11th century history? That Denmark had actually controlled England?* It was too much. In a town where the police could hardly spell the word *hello,* and helmed by a mayor who was as empty as a sheet of paper, and a part-time city council who only met as an excuse to get out of the house, and a chief of police who was as dumb and as thick as a stone, and was chief in name only — and here was a disheveled old black veteran talking about the Gobi Desert, the Caspian Sea? And then be able to talk about the Viking king Harold Bluetooth? *Incredible.* He language wasn't pure. But he *knew* things. He *really* knew things.

The young policeman's Danish roots surfaced briefly, and he made a comparison with the American schools. It would have been different had Soldier Boy been schooled in Europe. But not so. Soldier Boy was a pure, pure American. He grew up here, he was schooled here. He was a black man who had gone to war, suffered an irreparable injury then became a wino. How did he become a wino? *Why?* And why wasn't he given help by the government or some of the veterans' organizations? In pondering the questions, Carlsson recalled something the Soldier had said the first night they had encountered each other. The Soldier quoted something from an old Danish play: *Everybody says Jeppa drinks. But nobody says why Jeppa drinks.*

There again, the disheveled old vet had stunned him. Not that there was the need, but Americans didn't know anything about Denmark — let alone being able to quote something from a Danish play.

And then there was that totally amazing ending. Without question — or *questioning* — it was something he would carry with him for the rest of his life.

It would stand alone.

Now to be deciphered were the strange things that the Soldier had said about being "the last man standing. *And say goodnight to the boys in blue?"* What was that all about? And there was that look he had.

Who was this man? What was he?

9

While dying, his friend had said *Check the trailer.* Danny Carlsson hadn't understood what the Soldier meant at the time. But in thinking it over, he could only have been talking about a residence. There was only one trailer in that out-of-the-way section of town. The young policeman cranked his vehicle up and backed out of the yard.

Bucky had just returned from relieving his alcohol-hardened kidneys and was back in the little ticket office for a follow-up swig of rum when he spotted the pickup's lights through the window. "Hey, get back here! *Carlssuuun!!*" It was too late. The pickup was gone.

Bucky dashed back to the desk, knocking Spagg and Jesse Brown out of the way to get to the one step leading up to the desk. "Carlsson's takin' off!"

"That ding-a-ling!" McShayne said, and swung around to the mike — only to be interrupted by the buzzing phone. It was Mrs. Ina. This time she wanted to talk about the moon's rays and flying saucers.

The sergeant of the desk responded by saying something harsh and slamming the phone down before she could get fully started. "That woman's going to drive me straight out of my cotton-pickin' mind!" On the mike:

"'Quarters to 103, come in, Three."

Corbbo was fast asleep, dreaming his response.

"Three!" the radio crackled again.

Corbbo was too far gone.

"Dammit, Three!" the radio blistered again. "Three! *Corbbo, will you answer the goddamned mike!!! Squad Car 103!!!*"

It was useless.

"That's it! That's it!" the fired-up sergeant said. "He's gone too far this time! He's had it! That sonovabitch has had it! I'm swearin' out a warrant for his arrest! I'm throwin' that wasted bag of bacteria in jail!"

"Can you do that, Sarge?"

"Whaddaya mean, *can I!?* I'm doin' it!" McShayne thundered. He snatched the mike up. "Headquarters to 104, come in, Four!"

"Four, go ahead," Tetrollini responded. He was back in the park, eyeing the lonely little dumpy car.

"Boy, it sure gets busy in here," said Jess.

"Shut up, Jess, and stay out of the department's business," McShayne said. He got back on the mike. "Tetrollini, take a run by the park an' see if you can find Corbbo. If you can't find him there, take a look behind the warehouses. If you don't find him there, try the bus terminal storeroom or behind the trestle..."

"Might be sleepin' in the cemetery," Spagg overlapped; he had still not completed the first page of his report.

"I don't give a damn where he is, find him, Four! I don't care if you have to spend the rest of your eight lookin' for him. Find him! And when you do, handcuff the sonovabitch an' bring him in!"

Tetrollini's transmission was slow. "Did you say *handcuff* him, Sergeant?"

"That is precisely what I said," McShayne shot back. He turned to his assistant. "And log it in the blotter, Bucky."

"That's gonna look funny," Bucky snickered, as the switchboard buzzed again. "A cop in handcuffs."

"Log it, and shut up!"

"Boy, that Carlsson is somethin' else," Jess chipped in.

"A nut," Spagg said. "H'ya spell report, Buck?"

Jess confidently spelled, "R-u-p-p-o-r-t."

Bucky went to the big book, then over to answer the buzzing switchboard. "EHPD."

The voice said something.

"Another missin'-cat call, Sarge," Bucky said, handing the instrument with the long curled cord to McShayne. "The guy said it was a woman who snatched it. He followed her an' got a good look at her. He said she had electric-socket hair and a face to match, an' she's been patrollin' the streets and alleyways with a net an' a burlap sack. He also says she's been leavin' a string of toy mice around the garbage cans. You wanna talk to 'im?"

"Get the phone out of my face with that nonsense, Bucky!" said the sergeant. "Spagg, fill that thing out later. Drop Jess off, then go by that idiot's place and drag him back here."

"Which one?" Spagg wanted to know.

"Which one *what*?!"

"Bring who back?"

"Carlsson! You flea-brain!"

"You don't have to get so touchy about it," said Spagg, miffed.

"Get the hell out of here!"

"See, y'later, Demo," Jess said, leaving with Spagg. "An' watch that ticker."

McShayne sent Bucky to the mike. "Have Pippilo cover 1-A."

Bucky pressed, "'Quarters to 101. Come in, Pip."

Pippilo was busy catching his nightly shut-eye behind another gas station. He responded to the third call. "One, standin' by."

With Bucky holding the mike, McShayne hollered in the background, "I told you to stay on the mike, One!"

"I've been on it."

"The hell you have. Now, cover 1-A."

"Cover what?"

"1-A."

"Why?" Pippilo demanded. "Why should *I* cover a walkin' beat?"

McShayne pushed his way to the mike. "Whaddiya mean *why*? You cover the post because the sergeant of the desk *said* for you to cover it! That's why!"

"How come somebody else don't do it?"

"Because I said for <u>you</u> to do it! And if you can't do it, turn in your badge! And turn it in *now! Right now!*"

Pippilo swung an angry fist at the mike, slammed it back into the cradle — and didn't move.

⌛

Carlsson's pickup led to a far-back area in a field, adjacent to where a large concrete structure stood. During the war it had been designated as an air-raid shelter. Since then it had fallen out of use. The moon provided help, but it was still dark and the trailer the policeman was looking for was a lonely, tragic-appearing, rounded little thing with a single lamp shedding dull light through the rearmost window.

When Carlsson pulled up front he still didn't have a jacket on, but he wasn't cold. He sat thoughtfully behind the wheel and did nothing but stare out at the dark that surrounded the place. After more thoughts he climbed out of the pickup and went to the door and gave it a tap or two. Getting no response, he tried the handle. It worked. He put his flashlight to work, and entered slowly. Greeted by clutter, he smiled when he saw some of Soldier Boy's belongings scattered throughout. For the first time he felt the cold, and noticed that there was no stove. He wondered how his friend had managed without a stove. True, he spent most of his time wandering the streets, but he still needed a stove.

Looking around, the cop saw a lone Sterno can that, whether for cooking or warmth, couldn't have been of much help. Even at that, the can looked as though the wax had burned out long ago. Moving to the side window, he peered outside. With the help of the flashlight he was able to see a small snow-covered picnic table that held what looked like a pot of food and grocery-store bag that was being chilled in the snow. Next to it was a clothesline and an empty doghouse. There was nothing else out there.

Pulled by a muffled, sermonizing voice on the radio, the young cop took the few steps that had him peeping behind a faded quilt that had been hung to separate the trailer into two sections. Carlsson thought the bathroom was there. Not so.

The rearward side of the quilt told more stories of poverty. The dull light was there, but to his surprise there was a tragically weak and feeble, ebony-black old lady who lay pensively beneath the bed covers. To his surprise, too, in a strange unknown way, she looked almost as if she had been expecting him.

When the radio preacher's voice was replaced by a choir, the old woman rolled her head over to face the stranger who was angelic-looking to her, and who had come in and stood wordlessly next to the dresser.

Not knowing what to say, for a long while Carlsson simply stood there, leaning against the dresser, which was covered by a long doily. On the dresser stood a photograph of his old friend. It was next to a hand-sized aluminum Christmas tree that was under-served by three or four oversized bulbs, a few strands of tinsel, a tiny black angel, and nothing else.

The old lady was not afraid of the intrusion. She stretched a feeble arm out to turn down the radio that was on the tiny table next to the bed.

She was a terribly ill woman, and her voice, constantly on the verge of coughing, was soft, barely above a whisper. She spoke slowly. "My boy is dead, ain't he?"

And so, as the policeman had surmised, the old woman was Soldier Boy's mother. He was surprised that she immediately went to her son's death. But then again, he thought he shouldn't have been surprised at all. For a long time he had known there was wisdom with age. He knew, too, that a mother's natural instincts were without end.

He shifted and said it gently: "Yes, ma'am, the Soldier Boy is dead."

She thought about it, coughed, and quietly asked, "Had he been drinking?"

"No, ma'am," Carlsson said, being charitable.

"He'd been doin' that a lot lately," she said, as if she knew better. "Did you know him?"

"I think everybody knew the Soldier. They loved him; respected him. We were going to have lunch or something next week. Mostly I was just going to listen to him."

"How did he die?"

"Well, he was..." The young patrolman didn't quite know what to say.

"Your son was killed by a system that doesn't understand a man and his rights."

The old woman accepted it slowly and turned her head away to look at a window that, because of height, revealed only the moon and stars. "It's such a beautiful night out there tonight, ain't it?"

"Yes, ma'am."

"The moon is shinin' almost like the night he was born. Big and bright, lots of rays. Strange, because his life ended up bein' so tragic. There was nothing fair about it at all — and when life is unfair at the outset, I guess there ain't nothin' much can be done about it. I always wondered why life treated him so bad, why everything went wrong. It was wrong even before he was born," the feeble woman said, distantly. "As his mother, I guess I can be faulted."

"How is that, ma'am?"

"It was me who gave birth to 'im." She coughed again, then with effort, she moved a little and became even more reflective. "'Soldier Boy'. You called him that?"

"Yes, ma'am," Carlsson said. "Everybody did."

"He used to love that name," she said warmly. "Zachariah was his real name. "Did you know that?"

"No, ma'am," the young policeman said. "I imagine some of the boys down at the station knew it, but I didn't."

"I took the name from the Bible. But even when he was a little boy growing up, people used to call him the Soldier Boy. They was the days when his daddy was alive an' we had a little somethin'. An' they was the days when he used to get that ol' broom handle an' put it on his shoulder an' go an' find that ol' pot an' put it on his head, and strut his stuff like he was some big ol' gener'l or somethin'. 'Look, Maw,' he used to say. Then off he'd go around and around the house, an' then he'd march down to the railroad tracks. He used to like the railroad tracks 'cause he said the tracks helped him with his rhythm, an' the railroad ties, he said, would keep him in step. I think the Army was in that child's blood the day he was born. Then when the war came, it really had him goin'. It was like somethin' he'd been waitin' on all his life." She smiled and faced the young policeman as she thought about her son's one and only desire. She added, "He would'a made such a good soldier."

Carlsson who had been leaning on the dresser, shifted noticeably. He wasn't sure he had heard correctly. "...Ma'am — you said he *would* have made a good soldier?"

"Yes," she said, quietly thinking it over. "If they'd only wanted him. He would'a been a real good one."

His mouth was wide. He shifted more noticeably. "Are you saying...??"

Danny Carlsson was too stunned to speak. For the want of something to distract him for what he was thinking, he looked at the black angel on the tiny tree, and then at her again. He wanted to get it right. Delicately he asked, "Are you saying, ma'am, that Soldier Boy was never in the Army of the United States?"

She was matter-of-fact. "No, child. He was never in any army. This Army or nobody else's. Didn' you know that? The Army didn't want him. Even if they did, I s'pect he would'a been too old. But he tried to get in there. Lord knows he tried. Bless his heart. He'd get all slicked up and be down to that place where they signed 'em up 'fore the place ever opened. He was always down there. Waitin'. He was down there so many times they threw him out an' told him never to come back. But that didn't stop him. He'd still go down there. I used to cry every time he come back. I still get sad just thinking about it. He even tried the Salvation Army. No coloreds, they said. Then he tried the Red Cross. The same thing happened. Then when the war was over, he tried to march in the Victory parade they had on Main Street. They locked him up. When he got out, he wanted to go New York an' march, but he didn't have no money. I s'pect all'a that is what started him to drinking. But I'll say this for him...in all his drinkin', he never forgot to look after me; he was always tryin' to get me to go to see some doctor, or go to some hospital. He had that much presence about him." Her mind drifted away, then returned. "But that Army. Lord, you'll never know nobody who tried to get in that thing any harder that he did. An' then when the Salvation Army an' Red Cross wouldn't take him, it really got bad. He just went to pieces..."

A feather could have knocked the young policeman over. There was something almost too unbelievable in hearing that Soldier Boy had never been in the Army of the United States.

"Ma'am, how…?" he started to say, but was stopped by bafflement. He finally said, "The plate in Soldier Boy's head, ma'am…I guess what I'm trying to ask is, how did Soldier Boy hurt his head?"

"On a plow."

"A *plow*… ??"

"Umhum. He was growin' a Victory Garden out back. What was so sad about it, he was growin' it after the war. But his real troubles started long before then."

Now Carlsson was almost talking to himself. "Soldier Boy was never in the Army…*And he hurt his head on a plow? After the war?*"

"While he was out there plowin', he fell an' did somethin' like crack his skull," she said quietly. "They had a doctor over near Maywood who was s'posed to be specialists. But he won't. He an' a bunch of 'em put a plate in it, but they didn't do it right. An' they didn' care. Chile, you don't know how they used to treat us. I 'spect they still doin' it. That's why I don't go to no hospitals."

It was almost too much for the young policeman. He tried to find words, but they wouldn't come. But the old woman knew. It was her understanding face that put him somewhat at ease. She coughed and said, "But he didn't lie. In his mind; in his heart; in his soul, he'd been a soldier."

"And one of the best," Danny Carlsson said. He looked at the picture of his old friend, held it for a moment, then placed it back down. It was time to leave. "Ma'am…if…I…if I can ever be of help…"

It wasn't necessary to finish.

"You already have," she said. "You cared."

There was appreciation on both sides. He went to her bedside, and despite her coughing and deathly sick appearance, he leaned down and pecked her softly on the cheek.

And so in a darkened trailer, the flushed face of a young Scandinavian met the dark, drained skin of the very old. It said a lot. "I'll stop around from time to time," he said. "Starting tomorrow."

Her eyes widened with delight. "Tomorrow? You'd come back and see me tomorrow?"

"And the tomorrow after that, if I can."

"Really?"

"Yes, ma'am. And maybe, if you don't mind, I can even take you to see that doctor the Soldier wanted you to see."

"That's kind of you, son, but, like the hospitals, I don't believe in them neither. 'Specially now."

"Well, you're going to need some care. I'd like to help, if nothing more than coming around to talk. I may be gone for awhile. But I'll be back."

"You are God's blessing," she said. "What can an old woman do to repay you, son?"

"A *nice* woman don't have to."

She understood. "You say you might be gone for awhile? Where you goin'?"

"I was in service once before, and I'm going back in. But don't worry, they still give furloughs. I can always come back and see you. I'll even see you before I leave. Maybe Christmas day."

"My God, you are wonderful," said the old woman, gratefully. As if wanting to delay his departure, she asked, "Do you have family?"

"There's just my grandpop and me here."

"No mother and father?"

"They're in Denmark?"

"Denmark. Is that near here?"

"Oh, no, ma'am. Soldier Boy knew where it was, strange to say. But Denmark is a little country, thousands of miles from here. It's in Europe."

"Oh, I see," she said, sheepishly. "What's the people like?"

He smiled. "They're like you, warm and wonderful. And a lot like Soldier Boy. Very dedicated."

"Yes, he was that way, wasn't he? He was such a good son," she said reflectively. "Will you be bringing your family here, to this country?"

"They've been here to visit."

"How'd they like it?"

"They didn't fall in love with it. But they thought it was okay."

"Only 'okay?' How come they didn't like it?"

"America was too fast for them. They loved the power of the country, though. But they thought everything here was a little too massive, too powerful.

I think they were a little overwhelmed. I think America's freedom scared them, too. They didn't understand it. And I think they thought America preached one thing and did another."

"And that ain't good, is it?"

"I don't believe so."

"You say you have a grandfather here?"

"Yes, ma'am."

"He like it here?"

"Some."

"Why only 'some'?"

Carlsson didn't quite know how to explain it. He smiled. "I'll have to ask him."

"You do that," she said. "Always learn as much about your family as you can."

"Yes, ma'am."

"And when you come back, you cover yourself up. Wear somethin' warm. Your heart is too good to lose."

He smiled and turned to leave.

"Son," she said, momentarily stopping him.

"Yes, ma'am?"

"You mustn't worry. My boy didn't die tonight. He died a long time ago."

"Yes, ma'am," Carlsson acknowledged. "He might have died a long time ago. But tonight he was still a victim of the system."

He started to leave, then hesitated. "May I ask you something, ma'am?"

She nodded.

"How did Soldier Boy know so much? I mean, he knew an awful lot. Things that anybody else wouldn't even come close to knowing."

"In some ways he was a lot like his daddy. After he died, when my son was young, and I was able to work — cleanin' houses an' all, all the money would go to the teachers I hired for him. Some of 'em was real good an' tried real hard. One of 'em thought he could've had kinda like a genius streak in him. But they all thought he was smart. When he put his mind to it, he could talk about anything. He even know'd somethin' about that opera stuff. An' did you ever hear him do any 'rithmetic?"

"No, ma'am," Carlsson said. "But I think he did say he wanted to talk about it."

"That's what he was really good at. He could do all'a that hifalutin' stuff; calcium, an' algebah, an' the one that starts with a 'T'."

"A 'T'? — You mean trigonometry?"

"If that's what they call it."

"He really knew it?"

"He could do all of it. That's what his teachers said. One of 'em was real interest'd at what-all he could do at the start. She was the one we sold the house for. Then the money ran out. She did, too. I guess deep down, she knew it won't gonna do no good, nohow. 'Specially livin' here. But you see, son, my boy was sick, an' I didn't want him to walk around town like he was a veg'table."

"Well you can feel good that he didn't," Carlsson said. "The Soldier walked around being proud. Very proud. And he made me proud. I was really glad to know him, and I'm proud to say he was my friend. And, ma'am, I can tell you, the one thing the Soldier Boy was not: He was not a vegetable."

"I'm glad to hear you say that," she said.

Carlsson smiled, said goodnight and left. He was hesitant and didn't get far. He remained by the pickup, thinking. With something on his mind, he went back inside to see the woman.

He was inwardly searching for something. He resumed his position by the dresser, looked around the room for a quiet moment, then hesitantly asked, "Mrs. Hill...was Soldier Boy very religious?"

"'Very' religious?" she asked. "No; he won't religious a'tall. I wish he was. I wish it for you. That's somethin' I wish for everybody. Why do you ask?"

"No, reason," Carlsson said, starting to leave.

She stopped him. "Why did you ask, son?"

The policeman started uncomfortably. "I was just outside thinking that, going back, the Soldier said some things that were kind of...kind of mystical. He even seemed to look that way sometimes. Well, maybe not mystical, but...something different. I mean, the strange things he said, the way his eyes moved, and the way he could be funny and loud, yet bring a calm to everything...then...it sounds kinda weird...but at the end...in the end...I know it seems kind of odd to tie the two together, but…well, to go back, he said something about 'the last man standing'…"

"And you will be," she injected. "It's God's clock, son."

Carlsson was even more baffled.

She knew he was struggling. "But you started to tell me about the end."

"Well, in the end, the Soldier was trying to describe the face of a…a…Su… A S-s-s-upreme Being."

"A 'Supreme Bein'?' You mean God?"

"Yes, ma'am."

She studied him, then the old woman asked wisely, "Is that a hard thing for you to say? Or to believe in?"

"It used to be," Carlsson said.

"But no more," she answered for him.

Carlsson thought about it; Carlsson confirmed it. "But no more."

"Which means if you ain't seen the light, you gettin' close to the light?"

"Very close."

"That's good, son," she said wisely. "That's very good."

But it had been a statement long in coming from a young man who, under his grandfather's influence, had been straddling the fence of faith for as long as he could remember. Feeling secure in a new direction, he smiled at her and started to leave.

"Son," she said, "You said my son was a victim of the system?"

"Yes, ma'am, he was."

"And he was your friend?"

"You bet. And he deserved a hell of lot more than he got."

"He didn't receive justice?"

"No, ma'am. But he will."

"Thank you," she said. "The higher good, I'm glad to know you're gonna be servin' it."

When the policeman came out to the pickup, he stood there not feeling the cold but tossing a thousand and one thoughts around in mind. The "higher good" and the words that followed stayed in his mind, and he never could get over the "last man standing" idea, and how, as it had been with Soldier Boy, a strange religiosity had invaded the conversations. It was unnerving to continue thinking about all that was said, and all that had been implied. Feeling comforted, he settled on the more immediate, his warmth and concern for the old woman. He wondered what was going to happen to her. It was obvious that she needed medical care, and he could tell by her condition that time was running out. Perhaps, before going back into service, on one of his visits he could try to get her to change her mind about doctors, or coax her into going to the hospital. She was worth fighting for; worth doing anything he could to help her.

If a store had been open at that hour in the morning, Danny Carlsson would have gone grocery shopping. That, too, would have been in the interest of the higher good.

Sad to say, though, even if it had been the proper hour to shop, he wouldn't have found a neighborhood store. They no longer existed there in that part of town that, like the old woman herself, was dying by degrees.

⧗

Pulling out of the yard and away from the broken-down, metallic trailer that night, Carlsson allowed himself to think about one of the questions Soldier Boy's mother had asked — the one he hadn't fully answered. It was the one having to do with whether his grandfather liked being in this country. He didn't answer fully because he really didn't know. He loved his grandfather and he would always be grateful to him for bringing him to the States and supporting him during the earlier years. But Danny Carlsson never really understood him; he really didn't *know* him. The grandfather never liked talking about family history. What Carlsson had been able to learn came from his mother and father the time or two they came to visit. The visits were supposed to be exciting, but, owing to the grandfather, they weren't. It was probable that he was embarrassed because he was not even close to living the life he had written home about.

Wilhovthen Carlsson, Danny Carlsson learned, was much too restless and much too dissatisfied with the Nordic way of living to remain in Denmark when he was a younger man. He took it upon himself to leave family and friends to come to America, landing at New York's Ellis Island in October 1910. To Wil, the new country was a disappointment. The streets were not paved with the proverbial gold, and democracy had a price. Still, to prove himself right — as he always had to be — he always wrote home that he was doing well in the green pastures of the new country. He was wrong. In truth, Danny learned, the grandfather had a tough row to hoe and, if he had had the money, he would more than likely have returned home. But he couldn't return home, and eventually wandered to Elton Head because he had difficulty with the language and the New York pace was too fast. During that time, back in Denmark, his son had a son. Close on the birth of that son, Hitler's Germany reared its ugly head. No place in Europe was safe, particularly a country that was so small it didn't even have an army. To be on the safe side, Wil Carlsson's son thought it wise to send his son abroad until the threat of war was over.

Danny Carlsson arrived in the United States on March 17, 1938. He was 10 years old. At the age of 22, he was a Navy veteran.

⧗

Curley Spagg had pulled his patrol car in front of the shabby duplex on Amsterdam Street and had already washed it with the spotlight before deciding to climb out. He was impatiently banging on the door when the old man inside was heard to say, "Cahming, Hi'm cahming."

The voice didn't stop the cop. He gave the door another series of whacks.

The old Dane was a stooped, lonely-appearing man with a thick accent that hadn't managed to lessen over the years. He had a deeply creased face. It was foreign and narrow. Hunched because of age and a combination of back and leg affliction, he was nonetheless resolute and had none of his grandson's patience.

He shuffled to the door, saw Spagg, and showed alertness out of a deep sleep.

"Vhy, ovicer Spagg. Cahm in, cahm in. I'm good to see you," Wilhovthen Carlsson said, standing protectively in the doorway and never looking at the man directly. The accent was not from Copenhagen or from one of the larger Danish cities. It was from Jutland.

"'I'm good to see you'," Spagg mocked. "I wish you'd say that to them johns you ain't been cleanin' lately."

"What john? What you talk?"

"You know what a john is. Ain't you the station janitor?"

"Every morning at five o'clock I am there. For thirty-two year I am there. You know that. You see me all the time."

"I see you ain't been doin' such a hot job on them toilets. There's enough crud around them things to take fingerprints," the cop inaccurately said. Wil Carlsson, if nothing else, took exceptional pride in his work. He never missed a day, was never a second late, and, except for the front desk where they usually didn't want him around, he never missed cleaning a corner or a toilet.

"What you talk?!"

"You know what I talk. But I didn't come here to talk about that. I'm lookin' for that nut grandkid of yours."

"My grandson no nut!"

"Yeah. Sure," tossed Spagg. "Now that we got that straight, where is he?"

"Him verk."

"Him not *verk*. Him took off from *verk*."

"He no mit you?"

"Do you see him *mit* me?"

"He no patroli?"

"If he was *patroli* do you think I'd be stannin' out here in this cold askin' you where he's at?!"

"His vroom?"

"I already tried his *vroom*. He ain't in it."

"Vhy he no verk??"

"'Cause he's a nut!"

"My son no nut. He good police."

"He can't prove it by walkin' off the job."

Troubled, the old man anxiously pushed the policeman aside and moved off the porch. "Ve find him."

"Hey, get back here!"

"Ve go," said the old man, moving down the pathway that was covered with a light snow.

"*Ve* ain't doin' nuttin'," Spagg said, coming down after him.

"Ve go, I said!"

"And I said *ve* ain't goin' nowhere!"

"S'my son! You no tell me no'ting!"

Spagg decided he couldn't fight the determination. "All right," he surrendered. "Get'cha coat. It's cold in the car. The heater's out."

To please the policeman, Wil Carlsson went back inside and rummaged for his hat and coat and rushed back out. He could have taken his time.

Curley Spagg had already driven off.

The old man stood pathetically at the door, then pushed his collar up and braced himself for a long limp in the snow.

⧗

Back at the station, McShayne had placed another fruitless call to the number he had been trying to reach since he came on duty. Still there was no answer. Bucky Simmons, dentures removed, slipped from the ticket room after having taken another quick one, and joined the sergeant behind the desk. Bugged by the unanswered call, and now by Bucky's toothless presence, McShayne directed his attention to the mike. "H'quarters to Four, come in."

"Four."

"Did you find Mickey Corbbo yet?"

"No," Tetrollini responded. He had not looked. In deep worry, he was still in the park, still eyeing the Henry J.

"Keep looking 'til you find him. And when you do, don't forget to cuff 'im."

"'Kay."

"Headquarters to 102."

Spagg was in his car, engine off but lights on, and wasting time with the driver who made the nightly run to the cities of Lodi, Garfield, and Passaic. He excused himself for a moment and got the mike. "Yuh?"

"Did you locate Danny Carlsson?"

"No," replied Spagg. "I checked his place an' the old man's place. Ain't at neither one."

"Well, keep looking," ordered the desk sergeant.

"Yeah, sure," Spagg said, and unconcernedly resumed talking with the driver. "...But like I said, she had some knockers. I mean they were huge. Whoppers. Mountains! Bazoooms!"

"Bet'cha got lost in 'em, huh?" asked the driver lustfully.

"Did I get lost — ho, ho, ho..." The cop stopped, his eyes widened.

"Wha's up?"

"Omigod, I forgot somethin'!" Spagg exclaimed.

"What?"

"Dammit to hell!"

"Wha', wha', wha'?"

Spagg wanted to burn rubber getting away, but the car wouldn't start. The bus had to give him a push, all while the driver was behind the wheel, still asking what was up. When the Hudson kicked over, the cop hit the red light and sped away. "Top secret," he yelled back to the driver.

The emergency took the policeman back to the "Come back later, he's home" woman. In front of her house, he hit the window with the spotlight. The husband, a dense plant manager who normally worked the midnight shift at International Paper Company in Hoboken, was taking the night off. Earlier, after Spagg's first signal, the woman had managed to convince her husband that he was needed at the plant. He was there within the hour.

The woman responded to the patrol car's spotlight by flicking her bedroom light on and off twice. The coast was clear; the back door had been unlocked.

Spagg picked up the mike. "102 to headquarters."

"Come in, Two."

"....Going out of service on a traffic violation. If I'm late callin' back in, it's because I'm havin' battery trouble."

"Roger, Two."

Spagg's waywardness was by no means exclusive. A case that sprang to mind was that of another patrolman, Terry Gillingham. He was even more notorious with his midnight trysts — that is, until he was caught by a husband who faked his wife out with a sleepwalking act. Since the husband was a used car salesman, accustomed to being on his feet, the wife thought the sleepwalking condition was brought about by the man being immersed in his work.

Unknown to the wife and Terry, the first few times were rehearsals, but for about a month or so the woman's husband, eyes closed and arms straight out, would rise up, stiff-walk downstairs, and continue on out the door, sometimes passing Terry, who would generally be hiding in the car down the street from the house. Looking like a refugee from a bad Boris Karloff movie, and always leaving through the front door, the husband would walk precisely three blocks, consuming twenty-seven and three-quarter minutes in the process. He wanted to make it more, but it was cold outside, and in researching the subject, he learned that sleep-walkers usually didn't take the time to put on boots, gloves and coat. Not to be outdone, the next night he came up with the idea of lining his pajamas and padding his feet. It was at least better than going to bed with his galoshes on — as he had done on the second rehearsal. That was the night when he forgot to keep his arms out and almost walked through the plate-glass window. The error corrected, he resumed the act, stretching it for another twelve and one-quarter minutes. Terry and the wife found benefit in the additional minutes. Moving like jackrabbits in heat, they resumed the tryst. They weren't caught, but they came close.

The time Terry and the wife were caught, they made history. It was that cold night of November 8, 1948 — a night when the sleepwalker was alighting at the front of the house, heard the wind rustling and the sleet whistling, turned around and headed for the back door. Less wind, he thought. Three minutes later, arms out, freezing, and now looking like a zombie on the hunt, he made it to the corner. He stuck a damp finger in the air. The wind was the same. Time to cut the act short, he thought. Arms still out, eyes closed, walking stiff-legged, he turned around, circled the house and zombied through the rear door. Neither Terry nor the wife heard the re-entry.

Neither could Terry and the wife hear anything thereafter. But they did make history.

November 8, 1948, was the only time Elton Head, New Jersey, had hosted a double homicide.

10

While Elton Head's uniquely splendid moonlit night — a night that proffered just a hint — a pinch; a *smidge* — of change, and a night that followed a weird series of 1949-like winds that pranced into town, sucked up what little bit of cheer there was, left an impolite deposit in the air and danced away like the clown prince of black comedy, the hours droned on with telling familiarity.

And familiar it was. McShayne and Bucky were manning the station, and the rest of the boys in blue — the guardians of night — were doing everything else but policing the city. The troubled Danny Carlsson of Post 1-A was at home, Frank Pippilo in car 101 was grabbing his nightly shuteye behind the Esso gas station, and sleeping in somebody's garage at 190 Daisy Lane was Mickey Corbbo in car 103. Georgie Tetrollini in 104 was secretly in the park, worrying about the all-American girl in the pink Henry J, and Curley Spagg, the only one not in his patrol car, was in a house on Beech Street, getting ready to service, and be serviced by, some husband's wife.

The Dutchman, in car 105, was back at JoMo's, the black nightclub on Central Avenue.

Central Avenue centered the city of Elton Head, but it did so in principle only. Heading west for about a quarter mile, rude and oppressive rail-road tracks cut across what amounted to a main thoroughfare and became the point of racial demarcation. The blacks nested for about a four-block stretch, thinned out for another block, gave up, then surrendered the remaining two and three quarter miles to the whites.

But the cop in car 105 loved the little spot that was two blocks west of the tracks. All night long he had been sitting in the car with a hungered, anticipatory look. Coinciding with the look, he had already changed into the white tuxedo he had placed in the trunk earlier. He was now seated in the patrol car waiting to again fulfill a dream that had lived with him since childhood.

It had been interesting.

Johnny Van Dreelan had been a cute little underweight boy. Nature, however, played a trick on him and he grew to be a giant of a man who was saddled with a face that nested somewhere between that of a failed pugilist and a rock that had been crushed in an avalanche. His teeth were spaced, sturdy and powerful. But he had a voice that belied his looks. It was tinny and squeaky. Additionally, Van Dreelan had no rhythm — top or bottom, meaning in either voice or feet. It was a severe problem, because all his life, although it was held in high secrecy, he yearned to be on stage — singing and dancing the way the coloreds did. In that one lone regard the cop would have given his life to be one of them. But, ironically, his love for the limelight had started because of Shirley Temple, the very symbol of America's innocence, purity, sweetness, light, and hope.

Before being tucked away in a home for the mentally deficient, the big Dutchman's mother, Muriel Van Dreelan, had never missed a Shirley Temple movie. She was so in love with the little tyke that she often dressed her little man in curls and look-alike clothing and waltzed him off to the movies with her every chance she could.

Sometimes mother and child would spend an entire day watching the same movie over and over. Always it would be one with Bill "Bojangles" Robinson. He had been featured in three Temple movies and the favorite was the one with Shirley and the grinning old black tap-dancing up and down the stairs. The mother loved it. She would follow up at home by having her little darling sing and dance for hours more.

The desire to be like, or rather, the desire to *do* what the old Shirley Temple black man did had become so firmly rooted that years later the spongy-haired boy who grew into a hard-faced man with a tin voice was still reverberating.

Something else was having an effect, too. Johnny Van Dreelan, with 12 years on the job, was not quite as virile and masculine as one would have believed. Inwardly he was struggling. But with that aside, and now on the post where the coloreds did their thing, the big cop with the long-held desire in entertainment was at home. And being home explained why the cop wanted to remain on the midnight shift — and on this post. It also explained why, when Spagg had suggested changing posts with him during lineup, he was so adamantly against it.

Every working night — though sometimes to a lesser extent and not with the white tuxedo on — the cop would park the patrol car near the blacks' only nightclub. He would wait quietly in the dark until it closed. On a good night, his pulse would quicken when the doors opened and he saw the old-time musicians strolling away. With the mike already in hand, he'd wait for the stragglers to leave and the owner to come out and lock up. The Dutchman would wait a little longer, making certain that all was clear, then he would give an *Out of service* call to headquarters. As soon as it was *rogered,* he'd sneak across the street to the rear of the club and, using a master key for the lock, he would go inside and feed the juke box.

At first the cop in the spanking white tuxedo would stand facing the colorfully gaudy machine, totally transfixed. Then, when the music swelled, snapping his fingers and tapping with the rhythm, he would let the feeling grow. Soon his body would blossom into an easy sway. Although there would be no selections on the juke box by Bill "Bojangles" Robinson, Shirley's masterly dancing partner, eventually one of the blacks on a record would put him in mind of the old soft shoe-er. Still swaying with an easy motion, off the cop would go to the stage. He wouldn't rush it, though. He'd maintain the ease — confident, with an entertainer's swagger. En route, the big man with the thinning light hair and hard, spaced teeth would weave in and around the tiny round tables, glad-handing imaginary patrons. At some of the tables he would recognize an imaginary face or two, beam his greetings and wrap it up with a nod over to the supposed bartender. "Set 'em up, Hoss," he'd say with a star's panache. "The drinks are on me." Then up on stage he would go. To the heavy plaudits of the ebonized crowd, he would tug at his bow tie, then caress the mike. With great, self-effacing modesty, he would thank everyone for being there to see him. He would follow up with a few words about finally accepting a long-standing offer to appear at the place across the Hudson River — Harlem's Apollo Theater. In his mind, the crowd would roar their approval. He would bow modestly, rise up and clasp his hands in victory. Then, settling everyone — which was no easy task for a demanding crowd, he would offer solemn acknowledgment of the great entertainers who had inspired him. Always, he would end the acknowledgments with a toast to the great Bill "Bojangles" Robinson. *My brother, my friend, my soul-mate.*

Showtime.

Now the cop would begin. A Robinson routine was always first. It would bring down a wildly cheering house that could only be silenced by the introduction of other greats. On they would come. Getting carried away, the big club-footed cop would start emulating the acts of some of the best colored entertainers who had ever lived. He'd start *Hi-dee-hi-dee-hi-dee-ho-ing* like Cab Calloway, do *Ain't Nobody Here But Us Chickens* with Louis Jordan, grab a mop and sing with Nellie Lutcher. Then he'd get sassy with Sarah Vaughan, cute with Lena Horne, kittenish with Eartha Kitt, soulful with Dinah Washington, and growl with Satchmo. Next he'd tickle the ivories with Oscar Peterson, tinkle the keys with Erroll Garner, roll with the Count, get down with the Duke, smooth it out with the syrupy-voiced Nat "King" Cole, go deep with Billy Eckstein, then stay there with the newcomer, O. C. Smith and soon-to-be-great sax altoist, Jackie McLean. The big cop would then bring it back up with Billy Daniels, drive harder with the blues-rocking Wynonie Harris, then hit with big Jimmy Rushing. On a roll, he'd join Lionel Hampton and the boys, groove with Ivory Joe Hunter, back it with Herb Jeffries, "the Bronze Buckaroo," — and on and on and on. Any of them would do.

But his was not all an imaginary act. Not only could the Dutchman mix riffs with the big names on stage, he could name every single black entertainer of the day. No one would ever know it — no one would ever know him — but Johnny Van Dreelan was no Johnny-come-lately. He *knew* "race music"; had anyone challenged him, he could drop names with the best of experts — black or white. The big Dutchman could go all the way back to Eubie Blake, Fats, Noble Sissle, Joplin, W. C. Handy, etc. He could even throw in the gospel groups — groups like the Dixie Hummingbirds, the Four Blind Boys, the Davis Sisters, Sister Rosetta Tharpe, and the like. And he could name them in rapid succession. He didn't have to wait or think. *Zap!* he could go, snapping off names of black entertainers so rapidly and accurately that one would almost feel like checking his birth certificate. Ask him about the white entertainers — about Fred and Ginger, Burns and Allen, Haymes or Lombardo, or about the likes of Dorsey, Miller, or Waring; or Harry, Bing, Bob, or Piaf, Kay, or Frank — the big Dutchman was at a loss. But make no mistake, Johnny Van Dreelan was as white as the law allowed and his love of the music should not have been interpreted as a love for the people.

Daylight was avoidance time.

In daylight, the coloreds went their way; the Dutchman went his. Save for Clink Jefferson, there was not one colored person in the entire city of Elton Head that he could call a friend; there was not one he could call by name.

Finishing up on stage, the big cop would bow to the imagined whoops and hollers, and modestly beg off from an encore. With outstretched arms the bedazzled blacks would insist — pleading, pulling, and begging for one more go-around from the master entertainer. To settle them, he would give them just a hint more; a pinch — a *smidge* more — then he would bound from the stage, grinning, bowing and mopping his brow around circles of little squared tables, the exuberant arms pawing and grabbing at him as he moved.

Winter or summer, the cop would leave the cabaret as he had come — out the back door, amid the rapt adulation of a glistening crowd of coloreds. He knew he would return with something even more special.

Back in the patrol car, Johnny Van Dreelan would sit. He was mesmerized. Minutes would go by, then, as if reentering the world of the ordinary, he would remove the tuxedo and put his uniform back on. But he wouldn't do it hurriedly. Every waning moment in the apparel had to be savored. And when it was removed, it was done with a reverence, and without concern for the cold. With great care the sweaty ensemble would be placed in the garment bag to lay flat in the trunk of the Hudson. He would pat it and look at it longingly. Then slowly he would close the trunk, mop his brow and slip behind the wheel again. There he would sit quietly, not a muscle would move. What the man had done in the club would build again, as would the perspiration. It would trickle down his face and neck. Breathing hard, a look of utter seriousness would mold his face. It would hold for a moment. Then, suddenly, the cop would burst out in one joyous, ear-shattering scream. Pounding on the steering wheel, stomping and kicking his feet on the floorboard, he'd whoop and holler uncontrollably, then up would go his arms in victory. *YESSSS!!! YESSZZ!!! YEESSSSSZZZ!!!* Heart pumping, he'd take a breather. Then his face would go back to the mold of seriousness. He'd let it ride for a moment or two, then he would say to himself — ever so quietly: *Yes.*

He was not a smoker, but he would dig for a cigarette. Time would pass, then, settled, the cop would reach for his handkerchief, and then the mike. He'd hold onto both for awhile — thinking the deepest of thoughts, then, personality totally changed, he would press the microphone's button and transmit in an official voice, *"105 — back in service."*

Another moment of triumph would come; the cop would drive away. On this night he drove away feeling particularly good. *Fantastic.* The Dutchman had reached a new high. He had neither voice nor rhythm, but the cop had come close to cresting. The next time would do it. Better yet, he would postpone everything until the night of December 25. It was only a week away. He would come clean with the truth and give the coloreds something really special. *Shirley*, he thought. He would get a little bit closer to Shirley.

On Christmas night he would perform the act in a dress.

⌛

The little club with the peeling, Art-Deco face that remained alone after the crowd, the musicians, and Johnny Van Dreelan had gone away was sad. Under the glow of a bounteous, silvery-blue moon it was easy to see that it was in ruin. It sat there on Central Avenue financially strapped.

But JoMo's had not always been that way.

The coloreds' only nightclub had been the dream of JoBeth Monohan, a middle-aged, ultra-sophisticated, wealthy white woman who lived in nearby all-white Tenafly. The club had been a dream of her's since 1941. When the war was over in 1945, she sought to do something about the dream.

With a love of music, particularly black music, JoBeth thought it was deplorable that other than going across the bridge to chancy New York, there wasn't a place close by where one could go to hear some of the better entertainers of the day. She became obsessed with the idea of opening a place in her home town. Business-wise, it was a terrible idea. Politically it was worse. To begin with, Tenafly was not ideally situated. More important, there was no way the ultra-conservative city with its old-line money was going to allow anything that came even close to a nightclub within its borders — particularly since it would attract coloreds. None lived there; none should be given cause to visit there. It was the law unspoken.

But at war's end, feeling that the jubilation of victory would cause a change in attitudes, JoBeth put forth a plan before a group that amounted to a zoning commission. Whether they had the authority or not, the plan was roundly rejected. Undaunted, JoBeth made any number of appearances before the city council, all to no avail. She tried other approaches as well, but the determined lady was rebuffed at every turn. Finally giving up hope for the tucked-away little New York suburb, she set her sights on nearby Elton Head. With its sleepy, but thought-to-be anything-goes philosophy, she met with Mulkey and the council, and was eventually given permission to open the club. It occurred after a modest bit of wrangling with the council, and after warding off several detestable advances from Ernest Mulkey, the city manager. For resisting him, she was steered to Central Avenue, the black section of town. Unknown to Mulkey, it was just what the woman wanted.

JoBeth immediately went to work. She spared no expense in building a club that, as far as looks were concerned, was second to none. It was small, and as classy and elegant as anything seen in New York's Harlem. And she cared for her workers. They were the best paid; the entertainers received top dollar. But in the long run, Elton Head proved to be more problematic than Tenafly would have been. First, just being in the city of Elton Head meant the club would be a logistical disaster. It was away from the circuit; off the beaten track. Next, beyond local apathy, and being in a neighborhood where the average income came close to being less than what she paid in income tax, there was the problem with the three black churches. They fought the woman at every turn. In the end, after much effort and spending a tremendous amount of money, JoBeth couldn't fight it any more. She walked away.

Asked what she wanted to do with the building, the beautiful lady was most magnanimous in defeat. "Give it to charity," she said.

Charity never got JoMo's. One of the local hustlers did.

He ran it into the ground.

11

"Headquarters to 101, come in," squawked the radio, breaking the silence of a night that had grown a wee bit chillier but had lost none of its zip, zest, or flavor.

The snow continued to add a cleansing look to the city. The moon still hung low with an all-encompassing resplendence. It seemed peculiarly imaged with a face or two now, but on a night that had cut deep into the hours, it still hadn't come forth with that hint, that pinch, that *smidge* of change it had omened; that change that was supposed to come by way of, or because of, a dalliance and fraternization with hours of uncertainty; a change that said that by morning there would be room for a changing of the guard; a *complete* changing of the guard — the one that was supposed to be in Elton Head's favor.

"H'quarters to 101. Come in, One," the sergeant of the desk transmitted again.

Pippilo was still parked at the Esso station, grabbing shuteye. All night long he had been trying to stay ahead of the curve.

In an inactive police department, as Elton Head's surely was, the approach of serious sleeping on duty would generally start around 3 a.m. Winter or summer, it was the same: Sleep would come. Winter, however, had its own special flavor. It was helped by the sheer protectiveness of the vehicle's artificial heat, which warded off the natural cold that nipped and licked at the windows but couldn't get in. Even in cracking the window the artificial heat still rose to the occasion and established supremacy over a natural occurrence. The cold came in, but the heat won. The cold came in and momentarily re-alerted the eyes and the senses, but the artificial heat droned on with such consistency and baby-in-the-belly comfort that it would gain all confidence of the eyes and senses and, without knowing it, the driver would simply drift away.

Frank Pippilo was still drifting.

"H'quarters to car 101, come in, One," McShayne's voice said with much more force.

"....One, standing by."

"Frank — ?"

"I said, 'standing by.'"

"Stay on the mike!" said the desk sergeant. "Have you seen Mickey Corbbo in 103 yet?"

"Nope."

"And you're still searching?"

"Still searchin'," Pippilo said. He put the mike down and went back to sleep.

Johnny Van Dreelan in car 105 was back cruising his post after having completed his smashing success in the black nightclub. It was incredible. Never had that good-good feeling carried over for as long as it had done this night. The Dutchman was still reeling. He had exceeded the "show-bizz" high. He was feeling good — so good, in fact, that when he was slipping out of the white tuxedo and putting his uniform back on — all within the confines of the car — he actually said to himself that if, by chance, he never got the opportunity to be on the Central Avenue stage again after Christmas night, he could live with it.

The only thing that concerned him now was whether to make the appearance in a dress or gown. And the makeup? What kind of makeup should he wear? Something simple, thought the entertainer.

The cop had heard the desk sergeant's transmissions to car 101 regarding 103. Since Corbbo was a perennial jokester, he thought this would be a pretty good time to turn the tables. Still elated, he drove the Hudson back around to 190 Daisy Lane. Once there, he slid out of the car and tiptoed back to the garage where Mickey Corbbo was sleeping. He threw a quick eye through the iced window. Van Dreelan couldn't actually see Corbbo, but he could hear him snoring and he could partly see the elevated patrol car, and one of the jacks that held it up. Most of all, he could see the spinning wheels.

Tiptoeing back around to the front of the garage, he spotted the free end of the hose that was attached to the exhaust pipe and was peeping from under the garage door.

It was too tempting. He had to do it. Van Dreelan picked up the loose end of the hose and gave it a gentle tug. Already loose, it came off with ease. Knowing he would come back later to awaken Mickey — probably during lunch — he allowed the hose to clear from under the garage door and land in the snow. He chuckled to himself and went back to his car. On the mike he used a playfully fake voice, singing, *"I know where Mickey Corbbo is. I know where Mickey Corbbo is. I know where Mickey Corbbo is..."* He laughed and drove off.

McShayne shot for the mike. "Who is it? Who's on the mike?! *Who the hell is it?!"* The sergeant's beet-red face was looking drained again, and he backed off. Still, he wanted to let loose. Indeed, he started to. But Bucky turned from the switchboard with phone in hand.

"Sarge, a neighbor's callin' about some more screamin' cats and weird noises comin' from that French lady's house. Every night it's the same-same. She must have a ton of cats. Sarge, I think we'd better get..."

"Yeah, yeah, yeah, Bucky. I'll get somebody over there! Now, unplug the phone jack." The sergeant reached for the mike. "'Quarters to 105.'"

"Five. Go ahead."

"What the hell do you mean, 'go ahead'!?" McShayne said, unable to hold his ire. "Answer the mike like you're supposed to!"

"Whaddya want from me?!" Van Dreelan blistered back, having put his entertainer's high on hold.

"You insubordinate slob! Get over to that French freako's house and then report to the desk. I'll show you what I want with you!"

Fuming, Van Dreelan spun the car around and zoomed off.

Over the buzzing switchboard, Bucky tried to make a contribution. "Did'ja know that French lady used to be an actress on the stage in New York, Sarge? An' they say she used to work for a museum or somethin' like that. An' they say she's openin' up her own zoo."

"Answer the phone, Bucky," said a weary McShayne. "Just answer the phone."

⌛

Charlie Wong's night had not gone exactly as Charlie Wong had desired. The beautiful night had done nothing for the beaming, moon-faced man. His prowling had been fruitless. There were no women about, it didn't appear that he was going to get lucky, and, at that hour of the morning, typically, the lonely streets of Elton Head were not sending out the best of signals to a hunter who would almost walk to Alaska for action. And so the effervescent little white-suited man with the wing-tip shoes decided to temporarily cut his losses. He was not through for the night, however. He merely had to reassess matters, and was now back in his restaurant, which was a suffering little place with red, white and green Chinese beaded curtains running everywhere. He thought the Italian colors added zip to the place.

It was not actually a bar, but at the entrance of the restaurant there was something that pretended to be a bar that was sectioned off by more beaded curtains. Most times Charlie didn't lock the door until he was leaving for the night — and even then he didn't feel it was necessary.

The Chinaman was in the kitchen thinking about concocting more "Year of the Pig" soup for his friend, the desk sergeant, when he heard the sound of the glass curtains parting with a tinkle. A customer at that hour in the morning was highly unusual. Charlie slipped up front to take a look.

Walla! The gods had smiled on Charlie Wong.

Sliding up on a stool and slit-skirting the early morning hour was a Chinese woman so beautiful that it looked as if Charlie didn't know whether to attack or call the hospital. At high noon a beautiful female customer alone could cause palpitations. At night she was apt to create apoplexy. This one was a stunner and was there in the middle of the morning, when everybody and every*thing* should have been in bed hours ago. The gods had indeed smiled on Charley Wong. *Walla. Walla! Walla!!*

The short and snappy Chinaman made a swift decision. Except for the woman, the restaurant was empty; and in a place that had not seen business in ages, Charlie announced: "So solly, but last call, ever-ree-bod-dee." For efficacy he did it again, then slipped his face fully into the room. He smiled, then marched all the way in. Still smiling, he slipped behind the bar and leaned into the woman's face. "I was give 'last call' call. But you no hear. But okay. Charlie go out on limb. You Chinese. I Chinese. It is Chinese New Year. Oh, ho-ho-ho. Gung Ho Fat Choy. *Walla!* Happy New Year."

The lady sat quietly. Undaunted, Charlie pulled back, grabbed two glasses, blew the first layer of dust off, and didn't worry about the second. He sat the glasses on the bar and waited for a sign from the woman. None came. He waited a little longer. None came. Progress made, he grabbed two champagne bottles from underneath a lower shelf, coated them with soy sauce, turned back to the woman and began pouring.

He smiled. "Cham'pagny for a lovi-lee lady. And'a for Year of Push-Push."

The lady remained quiet. She watched the bubbles through olive eyes.

"You have lovi-lee eyes," said Charlie Wong, romantically. "Wha'chu name?"

The lady didn't say anything.

"You sweetie-pie. What sweetie-pie name?"

"Way," said the lady, quietly, and after Charley had asked her the third time.

"Oh-ho. *Walla!* I Wong, you Way. Oh, ho-ho-ho," said Charley, clearly overdoing it. "I Wong, you Way. *Wong-Way.* Ho, ho, ho. *Walla. Walla! Walla!!* Miss Way was not amused. She took a modest sip from her glass and slipped back into silence.

Charlie, not known for tact, moved in for the kill. "You flool aroun'?

Hanky panky?"

The lady maintained her silence.

He followed up by giving the woman a fingered demonstration. "Hanky panky? *Push-push?"*

He shouldn't have said it; he shouldn't have done it.

The beautiful woman with the brocaded skirt with the thigh-length slit gulped the drink down and used her index finger to "*come here"* him. Charlie was excited. The smile grew brighter, and when his moon face beamed all the way into hers, she threw a delicate arm out and yanked him clear over the bar. She hauled off and belted him with a left hook, collared him across the room, body-chopped him against the wall, threw a half-nelson around his neck, pounced on him with a Gorgeous George slam, powered him with a step-over toe-hold, zapped him with a whirlybird body-spin, threw him back over the bar, one-armed him back, knee-lifted his head to an upright position, socked him again, and finalized part one with a karate chop, landing him against the other wall. For part two, she sent his short peppy, frame sailing through the beaded glass curtains.

Breathless and slumped like a wet noodle, Charlie was down but not out. "S-s-so," he prompted, "what's you ansa???"

⧗

In response to the call McShayne had made about the cat calls, car 105 had pulled in front of the tri-storied monstrosity that loomed up eerily on Arbor Street. Van Dreelan had been there once before, but he had never been inside. He reported to the desk that he had been inside, but it was not the truth. The big cop had never gotten beyond the porch, reasoning that the house was in Mickey Corbbo's territory and not his. More accurately, he was scared.

Matching the description Bucky had used earlier, the woman was tall and her hair sprouted out like she had gotten a finger stuck in a socket. Wide-eyed, with a long, slender face coated with makeup and false, misplaced dimples, she came close to looking like a turn-of-the-century vampire.

Her name was Pilar. The name was Hispanic, but she adopted it because she though it had strength and would look good on a marquee.

Pilar was a supposed Shakespearean actress. She had been born in Bulgaria, but since no one ever heard of a Bulgarian actress, she hijacked the French language and had been destroying it ever since. But Bulgarian or not, French or not, the woman was a disaster on stage. One critic wrote that her acting was so bad that he was switching to writing obituaries. In Azerbajan.

Bounced from just about every stage on the European continent, Pilar made her way to the United States. She arrived by freighter, having convinced the management of a traveling troupe of club-footed midgets that she could teach them the fine art of ballet. It was an interesting idea, but the woman could hardly walk a straight line without help. Management couldn't wait for the ship to dock. They were going to have her arrested, but she beat them to the punch by jumping ship when it got close to the New York docks. Rescued by a tug, she landed a job with the zoo, got bounced within the hour, did a stint at a Coney Island creep show, got fired from there, found Elton Head by accident, returned to the zoo two days later with a U-Haul truck and beast-napped the main attraction. He was prone to get upset at times, and worked under the name of Sassy — short for Sasquatch. A Bigfoot look-alike, he was a sad-eyed, gigantopithecus-descended, bipedal hominid that had been discovered roaming the unexplored jungles of Peru.

She renamed the brute the *big O* — short for Oscar — and kept him chained in the attic. The chains were about the size of mini anchors.

The cop had heard that something strange could be heard in the house at night and that the woman dabbled in the occult — or, more accurately, animal sacrifice. Whatever it was, the house on Arbor Street was the place to do it. The bold, miserable-looking place hadn't been painted in years and was boarded up in the oddest of places. As with the chimney and cellar door, there wasn't an exposed window anywhere.

The house was located at the edge of car 103's territory, and the Dutchman had a point regarding jurisdiction. The only problem was that when Mickey Corbbo was given the nightly call to go to the house, he would never show up. He would report that all was well, but he didn't know if it was or not. Of the many calls that had been logged and given to him in the past, Mickey had actually been to the house only three times. It was not that he was afraid. Mickey didn't know any better. One time he was there because, awakened out of a deep sleep in somebody's garage, he had gotten lost trying to answer a cardiac-arrest call. He never made it to the correct address. He had skidded to a stop at Pilar's house because it had a light on, and didn't leave until three hours later. That was the night he learned that the woman had been on stage.

Corbbo was over-the-moon about meeting a real live performer who had been on a New York stage — which was all right, but the appearance was not quite the way she had said. Pilar's appearance had been limited, to say the least. It had occurred a few days after she arrived in the country. On her way to the zoo, and pushed by a personal need, she hopped out of a cab, barged into Carnegie Hall, ran down the aisle and up on the stage, interrupting a performance. She was looking for the bathroom.

But Mickey was impressed with the woman. The woman was impressed that he was impressed. She was so impressed that he was impressed that she kicked in with an impromptu performance of what was supposed to be "Medea" on the front porch. Barely knowing the difference between Shakespeare and a spear from the jungle, Mickey thought he was being treated to a scene from "Beauty and the Beast." Her acting didn't do much to change things, but he nonetheless stomped and applauded royally — making it a first for the woman. When she was through, she took a stage bow so low and long that she looked like a question mark frozen in place. Mickey had to help her regain the upright position.

Thrilled by the applause, Pilar offered her admirer a post-midnight snack, which was easy to do because she had just returned from another of her street-scrounging, cat-napping escapades, and the meowing and clawing sack was still on the counter in the kitchen.

With the nicely entertained Mickey sucking his teeth in the living room, Pilar went about hammering the sack into a suffering silence and throwing it into a pot. After letting it stew for less time than one would spend cooking one-minute rice, she dumped the sack's contents onto a plate and invited the cop into the dining room.

"Steamed rabeet. Smothered in cheese," said the woman, sliding the plate on the dining table.

It made no difference to the cop that the "rabeet" — still kicking and obviously disappointed at the failure of the nine-lives theory — was making one final gesture at meowing. It made no difference to the cop, either, that the "rabeet" had short ears, feline hair, and an even longer tail. Mickey ate heartily. When he finished, he picked his teeth with the claw of a paw, and couldn't have been more complimentary when he left.

The second time Mickey Corbbo had aimed patrol car 103 to the house on Arbor Street he had a trunkload of pots and silverware that, as added income, he was selling on the side. He felt that the great cook and exotic lady of the stage would be a good customer. He knew she stayed up all night; better still, he still hadn't gotten over the steamed "rabeet" taste. Again he was invited inside; again Pilar went through the routine; again the cop ate heartily.

Mickey had stopped by the house on another occasion, but Pilar wasn't in. When she did show up, around 3:20 a.m., Mickey was waiting on the porch swing. Besides having an appetite and needing warmth, he had a business proposition he wanted to talk over with her.

Huffing and puffing after another fence-hopping night, Pilar arrived and happily invited him inside. She was carrying a huge net and several mousetraps — three of which were occupied. Because it was the weekend, she also had two sacks tucked under her arm. Both sacks had nice bulges to them. But again the occupied traps and meowing sacks didn't tap the cop's concern.

What did arrest Mickey was the woman's excitement over a new play she had in the works. She invited the cop inside, sat him in the living room, and had him witnessing a scene from "Richard III" — something she had been working on since they last saw each other.

Hard to do, but Pilar's acting had actually gotten worse. The woman's acting exceeded all bounds of horror — legitimate or otherwise. It was enough to make the long-dead Shakespeare suicidal, but Mickey was on his feet: "*Bravo, bravo, bravo.* One of my all-time favorites," said the cop, who should have stopped there, but went on to leave the woman cross-eyed and snorting. "Beauty and the Beast! And you, little lady, did it without the beauty!"

Nostrils flaring, when Pilar went into the kitchen she was still snorting. She started hacking at the meat with a vengeance.

Mickey was lucky that the woman wasn't using the cleaver on him.

Untroubled by the meowing sounds that escaped from under the meat cleaver's final thud, the cop had moved into the dining room, and was again waiting at the long, splintered, knotty-pine table with fork in hand. When it was time to eat, and still untroubled by the final meow, the short ears, the long hair and even longer tail, and the slight movement that came from the plate, Mickey dined for forty minutes — this time enjoying new bits of spice the woman had inserted into the meat. The spice wowed the cop. He praised the woman for ten minutes, again picked his teeth with the animal's claw for five, promoted his proposition for ten, took a nap for another forty, praised the hostess again when he awoke, and left with a good-sized burlap sack of meat under his arm. He wanted McShayne to enjoy the spongy taste.

Still standing cross-eyed by the door, Pilar heard neither the final compliments nor the final sales pitch. The only thing she kept hearing over and over was: *"Beauty and the Beast. And you, little lady, did it without the beauty!"*

The woman had heard the same when, she spiked the meat he was carrying with a goodly amount of spice.

To the naked eye, the spice looked suspiciously like rodent droppings.

"Here y'go, Sarge. You might find the little dark egg-shaped things a bit dry and chewy for your regular herbs, but everything else is nice and moist. Strictly Grade-A. You're in for some mighty good eats," said Mickey, late for report-in time, but trying to make up for it by tossing the sack on the desk — and before the sergeant could get on him for being out of service all night. With his uniform matted with cat hair that he had picked up while sleeping on the sofa, he said, breezily, "It might look a little furry, but that's the quality of meat I'm gonna be servin' in my new restaurant when me an' my new partner opens up."

That was another time Dempsey O. McShayne wanted to kill Mickey Corbbo.

⧗

Van Dreelan tapped on the woman's door with his flashlight beaming, which he really didn't need to do, since the porch light was on. Even if the light had not been on, his way had been brightened by thoughts of his performance at JoMo's.

The door was answered by Pilar. She was ready to fire off at any minute because, while she initially liked Mickey Corbbo — that is until he came up with that *Beauty and the Beast* comment — it was apparent she didn't like any of the other cops from the start.

"You called?" Van Dreelan asked, in a hurry to leave.

"Why I call you? Pilar do not like zee people like you. Pilar ees not stupeed."

Without saying another word, Van Dreelan returned to his car. The woman remained silhouetted in the doorway, her arms coolly folded.

On the mike, Van Dreelan reported, "Five to h'quarters. I'm over here with this cat-lady dame. She says she didn't call."

Bucky was at the mike. McShayne, hearing the transmission and breaking his one-fingered typing effort, yelled over to Bucky, and, as though making a child-like explanation, said: "Tell that dummy *we know* that ding-a-ling didn't call! It was a neighbor! We got *complaints* from the neighbors! We are always getting complaints from the neighbors! Now, can he understand that?!"

"You got that, Dutch?" Bucky said into the mike, after having held it open for his sergeant.

"Yeah," said Van Dreelan.

Not satisfied, the desk sergeant moved to the mike. "And would you be good enough to inform the lady that not only are the neighbors bitchin' about all'a that crying and meowing that's going on around there every night, but they would also like her to do something about all'a that stinkin' that's going on. And there's also been some strange howlin' an' groaning goin' on around there every night. And I want it stopped."

Going back up the stairs at the front door, Van Dreelan said, "Listen here, Miss French-fry..."

"Eet ees <u>Mademoiselle</u> Pilar! *Star!*"

"Well, Madummummsel Pee-lar — *Star*; the neighbors is been complainin' about you. Y'got some cats that's been disturbin' 'em; that's number one. Number two — there's been some oddball moanin' an' groanin' goin' on 'round here. An' it's been goin' on for a lotta nights. Number three, the place stinks. I can smell that, stannin' right here."

The inflammable lady answered the charges by slamming the door in his face. Van Dreelan, without moving, took a moment and coolly rapped on the door again. Pilar yanked it open.

"Now, li'l lady, you do that again an' I'll toss you so far in the pokey it'll take an act of Congress for you to see daylight."

Pilar was not to be intimidated. She proved it by attempting to slam the door again. It was blocked by the policeman's foot.

"All right. All right," he said. "That's it. That's it. Get'cha coat. An' be quick about it. I gotta get back to wake somebody up."

The woman didn't move.

"G'wan, get your coat, I'm takin' you in." Van Dreelan persisted. "G'wan! I told you I was in a hurry. And don't start with that cryin' or woman stuff that some of you women like to go through when you're about to be arrested, 'cause I *ain't* interested in nothin' you've got to offer."

"You want my coat, you geet my coat."

The cop brushed past her, went inside and swung a quick eye around. Not seeing the coat, he stood in the middle of the living room. The odor bothered him. "It smells like somebody died in here."

She was still standing by the open door, her eyes unmoving. "Maybee zomebody ought to die-ee here."

"What'd you say?"

"Eet waz very clear."

The policeman tossed it off and looked around the room again. Suddenly he furrowed his brow. "Say, correct me if I'm wrong. Ain't you supposed to be some kind'a New York actress or somethin'?"

"I am star! I am Europeen star! I am stage legeen!!"

"You're talkin' to a star and a stage legend lady," Van Dreelan boasted. "But I ain't gonna waste my time talkin' to you about it. Now where's all'a these cats you're suppos'd to have? Every night we're missin' a ton of 'em, an' I personally think you know a helluva lot more than meets the eye."

Pilar didn't say anything.

"C'mon, where you keep 'em?" the big cop demanded.

Pilar maintained her silence and watched him as he sniffed at the air and continued to move around.

Finally the cop wandered to the other side of the room. He pointed to one of the two doors that was just off to the left of the living room. "Is that the closet for this dump?"

Knowing she wasn't going to answer, he turned on his flashlight. His flattened nose pulled by a smell, he moved over to the first closet door and cracked it open.

To the patrolman's surprise, the door did not lead to a closet. It hid a staircase that stretched to the attic. On the side were several large nets — used to snag animals. The stairs were covered with fur and bones. They were not rabbit remnants. Cat carcasses came to mind.

"Holy smokes…" the policeman started to say, and looked back at the woman. She was unruffled; her eyes remained directly on him. He swallowed a bit, and decided to investigate further. Climbing up, his suspicions were confirmed. Leftovers from skinned, headless cats became thicker and thicker. It was much too heavy for the Dutchman. He started to back down.

Back on the bottom step, he turned to look at the woman, her presence reminding him that he was a cop and that cops were supposed to investigate *all* things suspicious. The investigation should take place at some other time, thought the giant policeman with the face of a pugilist. After a noncommittal moment, it became clear: The investigation would definitely be better at some other time — with someone else. As his hand went pawing to close the door, a wee sound was heard coming from the landing. Pilar folded her arms and smiled faintly. Van Dreelan looked at her. The two eyed each other for much longer than the policeman had intended. She was standing as though she were on a stage, her eyes maintaining the hard look of challenge.

"You are afreed. You are scaredy-cat."

"Lady, I ain't scared of nothin'," Van Dreelan said, more to comfort himself. "I've entertained in places worse than you've got up there."

"Prove eet."

She was quiet when she said it. The non-singer was equally quiet. He was scared. Thoughts of her being involved with the occult came to mind.

He wasn't sure about what one did in the practice, but this wasn't the time to find out. Again he started to leave. She was still challenging him, not batting an eye. It was probable that he didn't want to be laughed at, which was sure to be the case if anyone back at the department had found out he had been too chicken to check out an attic. Still scared, he thought about using the excuse of going back to awaken Mickey Corbbo from the deadly fumes.

Thinking about Mickey and deciding to do the job hurriedly, the cop accepted the challenge. He started going all the way up for the investigation. Then he slowed down and took it step by step. He was nervous, very nervous. With his feet trying to negotiate the creaking stairs without squashing the littered, furred bodies, he started to perspire. More than once he almost stopped and come back down. But with Pilar's eyes on him, he continued to inch frightfully upwards.

Perhaps it was on cue from the lady, perhaps it was the sight or smell of a warm-blooded human — maybe it was the sight of the brass buttons on the uniform, but the moment, the very instant the policeman put his foot on the top step, the fierce, hollow-eyed, sub-human-looking creature with the prehistoric tendencies sprang his heavily-chained and cat-bloodied body down on the man. Like a lion on the Serengeti plains, with one holding bite on his neck, the giant of a beast bit the cop into a silent, gasping death.

And then he went to work on the rest of the body.

12.

It had taken a long while but old man Wil Carlsson finally reached his grandson's apartment. It was a comfortable place, set on a wooded street, and it was a lot more upscale than what Elton Head normally offered. It was certainly better than where the rookie policeman had been living before going into service.

In fairness to the young man, however, at the time he had just moved from his grandfather's place, had little money, and was not sure he would remain in Elton Head. The latter thought was still with him, but owing to some serious thinking and the recent turn of events, the idea of re-enlisting was on the wane. Certainly his growing disappointment with the department had to be considered. Maybe the answer was in making a simple move to nearby Teaneck or Tenafly. Several times before he had been nudged by the idea of packing it up and leaving Elton Head. In fact, even though he couldn't see himself leaving the beautiful, green Garden State altogether, when he was leaving the Navy he had thought about not returning to anywhere near the area.

But Elton Head was Danny's home town. He had never investigated living anywhere else, and it didn't seem right to leave his aging grandfather, his only living relative in this country. He owed him something because, after all, the old man was responsible for bringing him to the country, and he had seen him through school.

Obligated or not, young Carlsson did love the old, traditional man, and never would have forgiven himself if something happened to him and he wasn't around to help. The old Dane was a stickler to deal with, and he had not been an easy one to grow up with. His European ways were hard, and he was always on his charge about something. There were the constant attempts at manipulating the young man's life; the incessant talk about how much better things were in the old country; and the unending mistrust about what he was going to do with his future. Then, every time he would come up with something solid, something he thought he might like to take a shot at in the future, the grandfather would strongly object. When he became of age, fell in love and talked of marriage and raising a family, the grandfather objected. Even before that, in high school, when the subject of college, a career, or different jobs came up, the grandfather objected. Wil Carlsson objected to everything, stubbornly saying only that he would tell him what was right for him to do when the time was right. Without revealing anything, he would conclude by saying: "In H'America, there is only one thing to be." Danny thought he knew what it was. He wasn't impressed.

Although born in Denmark, Danny Carlsson considered himself a full-fledged American. The idea of being a foreigner never crossed his mind. He was so tuned to the idea that he was an American that the *Where were you born* question that was a must on a lot of documents would often find him writing USA. In making the correction, he'd think to himself that it didn't make any difference where he was born. He was an American, and that was that. He was here to stay — not that he liked the country all that much when he first got here. But there was a reason why. Like a lot of young immigrants unable to speak the language, he felt himself estranged, and the strong, clinging European influence cast by his grandfather didn't help. He would even go so far as to insist that they speak in Danish, something Danny refused to do. Nor would he read anything in Danish. It was not that he was against the culture. Although he had collected them for only 10 years, he loved yesterday's memories. His mother and father were Danish, and he loved them. They were still in Denmark, but he was in America. And if he wanted to *be* an American, he had to do everything the Americans did. He knew, inside, that he would be getting back to his culture at some point in his life, but in small-town America, an accented person was an outsider — something he never wanted to be. Accents invited cruelty. So, then, the best thing he could do was to put the old country on hold and learn the new language as best he could, and go on from there — which he did. The method was simple. He learned structure from books and picked up the nuances of the language by listening to the radio, learning mostly from the comedy shows and serials. By the time he entered high school, he had little or no accent.

After high school, which was a breeze for him, having benefited from Denmark's strict and more well-rounded methods and techniques, he tried college — spending slightly over two years at Rutgers University, the fine and diversified state college, in New Brunswick. He considered the first year an orientation period, and he probably would have drifted over to the Newark College of Arts and Sciences had he not fallen in love with an attractive young miss from nearby Hackensack, who went on to become a schoolteacher. Ruth Denson was her name.

At about the time the two were getting serious and discussing the future, a certain faction in the country had begun hinting about another force on the horizon that it considered more deadly than Nazism. It was Communism. Two years later the country was still hinting. Along with the hint came the belief that the country was not going to disband its draft. In love and set to marry, he and the young lady decided they could kill the two birds with the same stone by his volunteering for service. In doing so, the military obligation could be satisfied on their terms and they would not have to face it later, particularly since they were planning on having a family. They also reasoned that he would be learning, getting hands-on experience and saving money at the same time. In investigating the service, he discovered that recruiting promised electrical engineering. It sparked an interest, although there was a time when he had been leaning on something in the area of human resources or social services.

On August 9, 1946, Danny Carlsson found himself in the Navy for the customary four-year stint. In the Navy, however, he ended up as a torpedoman on a submarine. No loss, he thought, and as he wrote to the young miss, he would pursue the studies under the GI bill and take it from there.

She agreed. Her letter was slow in coming, however.

When the nice-looking young Dane with the slightly undernourished look and quiet demeanor was discharged in June 1950, the young miss from Hackensack was not there to greet him. Ruth was committed to another.

It took time, but Danny got over it.

Too late to enroll for the fall semester, he was told that he had to wait a few months. When he told his grandfather what had happened, the old man felt relieved. It would have been nice to think that the relief and the course of action taken by the grandfather thereafter stemmed from altruistic reasons. It did not.

The station janitor who, for almost 30 years, had been cleaning the building that once was the home of horse auctions but was now an ill-functioning police station wanted his grandson to become a policeman in the worst way. He never said it directly, but it was always in him. All the earlier talk about the various occupations and the more recent talk about college, grades, semesters, social studies, electrical engineering and all that was attached to it, was wasted. It meant nothing to an old man who had lived the latter part of his life wanting his grandson to become a symbol of authority: a cop. From the day the grandson got off the boat, the grandfather had uniformed him in the brass buttons and midnight-blue uniform of the Elton Head Police Department. He envisioned nothing else, not even seeing him moving up and becoming a detective.

Detectives didn't wear the brass buttons and blue coats; they weren't seen by the people.

Danny Carlsson didn't know it, but when he told the grandfather about the delay in going back to college, the old man played it with sadness, but he couldn't have been happier. Seizing the moment that second week in October, he left work early, shuffled home and put on his Sunday best. From there he went directly to the office of the man who wielded the power and signed his checks — Ernest Mulkey, the city manager.

Mulkey was a slob of a human being. He made no bones about his power. He controlled everything from the city dump to the highest city hall appointee. The part-time mayor and city council meant nothing. They were only pawns of whatever political group that was in power. Interestingly, Mulkey was never troubled by elections. How he was able to do it is not known, but the sometimes-gruff-sometimes-slick operator managed to escape both Republican and Democratic tentacles and, through several political changes, steered the city on his course, and his course alone — although the last primary had been unusually rough. One of the issues, ironically, involved employing a certain doctor as a part-time coroner. Mulkey was against him from the start. As the election date grew nearer, so did Mulkey's opposition. In November the doctor won. But he would not live to enjoy the fruits of victory. His body was discovered in a dumpster the night after the election. His head had been bashed in and a bloodied baseball bat was next to it. The fingerprints on the bat were art-gallery clean. But the detectives never saw the prints, and the cause of death still mystified them. They weren't sure, and they didn't have a qualified coroner to make the determination.

Wil Carlsson knew this. In being around the station he picked up a lot of information, and Mulkey's name struck as much terror in him as it did with anyone else. But the old man wouldn't let anything stop him. He didn't care about politics, corruption, murder — nothing. He cared about one thing and one thing only: Mulkey was the city manger; and the city manager could make his grandson a cop. Nothing else mattered.

He feared power and was sensitive about his accent and low status as a janitor, but he was dressed in his Sunday-best when the day finally came for Wilthoven Carlsson to see the city manager. He didn't go there empty-handed. Every pocket in his suit was stuffed with envelopes containing money — money he had been scrimping and saving for as long as he could remember. He thought it was going to be a long meeting. He was wrong. Three minutes later the old man found himself heading home to get his grandson. Shortly after, Danny found himself in the city manager's office. He was being harangued by the gruff-talking man who was unwilling to accept "no" for an answer.

Mulkey played it well. His theme was civic duty — which obviously would register with a young man fresh from the military. Along with civic duty and the lack of qualified young men to make Elton Head a better place, the boss-man made it appear that there was one position *and one position only* open on the Elton Head PD. He wanted the young veteran to fill it — and he wanted it filled right then and there. True to what he wanted, the position was filled right then and there.

Danny Carlsson was sworn in as an Elton Head policeman before he left the city manager's office that day in October.

Carlsson never knew what it took to get into Ernest Mulkey's office. He had always believed that his grandfather had more to do with it than was said. Had he known for certain that his grandfather was involved — and had he known just how much — the grandfather would have been in more trouble than he could ever have imagined.

But it must be said that, despite his doubts and misgivings, the rookie approached his first two months on the job with commendable zeal, and it was not solely to please his grandfather. It was simply a matter of a young man searching for answers and trying to do his best in any given situation. Pride and hope could have been at play, as well.

There was no such thing as police training, and so the rookie spent most of his off-hours at the library, devouring everything he could on the subject of law enforcement. He was so conscientious he even spent time in one of New York's better libraries in Manhattan. But the rookie's disillusionment came swift. When he first came on the department he was working on the day shift. Often he brought books to work with him and kept them in his locker so that he could read them on his lunch hour, but the men teased and rode him so hard, he switched to the evening shift. There he encountered the same difficulty. Making matters worse, the chiding was led by Sergeant Zemora, the desk sergeant. Although Carlsson never raised his voice to counter the ribbing, Zemora thought he was thin-skinned and had him switched to the midnight shift. One night with that bunch and the rookie knew for certain: Nothing was going to work. This was a department without hope.

⧗

Danny Carlsson's apartment was devoid of decoration and bric-a-brac. A combination radio and record player was on one side of the room, a built-in bed on the other side. He was on the bed drinking from a carton of milk, thinking about re-enlisting and a little about college, when his grandfather arrived.

The milk wasn't very enjoyable, because it was in the carton. Like most people, he felt that something was lost the day the milk companies abandoned bottles. He didn't appreciate the idea that the cream was no longer on top, either. Those were two of the small surprises that greeted him when he returned from the Navy. The big one was that Ruth, his girlfriend, had married. She had added insult to injury by marrying a cop from Hackensack, the nearby city that lay low on the scale of progress but deemed itself the jewel of the Bergen County crown, partly because it was the county seat. Carlton didn't fall apart over the loss. He took it in stride, feeling that if he had to lose her, at least it was at a time when he could bounce back without irreparable harm.

"Wvhy you here?" the grandfather asked, his shoulders stooped and his face showing more concern than the grandson thought necessary.

He didn't want to ignore the old man, but he allowed the question to pass without comment.

The grandfather was persistent. "Wvhy you here?"

Carlsson sat upright on the bed. "C'mon, Gramps. It's almost four in the morning. It's almost time for you to go to work. I'll take you back home, so you can get ready."

"But wvhy you here? Wvhy you no wverk? You sick?"

"No, Gramps, I'm not sick. And I don't feel like going through a lot of stuff."

"No. You here. You not sick. You no wverk. This is not *stuff*."

"Let's go," Carlsson said, standing. "I'll take you back home."

"You take me home. And you go wvere?"

"I'm coming back here."

"No! You go wverk!"

"Pops, let's go. I don't feel like talking."

"You not can talk to me, your own grandfather. I spend my life cleaning and cleaning and cleaning for you. I do everything for you to become police, and you not can talk?"

"That's something I've been a little troubled by, Gramps. Tell me, what did you do for me to become a policeman? What happened in Mr.

Mulkey's office that day when we went down there?"

"What I do not important. You have job. Not everyone be police here."

"I'm a vet, Pop," Carlsson said, without wanting to hurt the old man's feelings beyond what he was already feeling. "I'm a 22-year-old veteran of the United States Navy. And even in this lousy, one-horse town, vets have a preference. Now, it might have been difficult, but I could've cracked this crummy department if I'd wanted to."

"But you must wverk."

"I don't have to work here."

"Yes, here! Everybody must wverk! You have best job!"

"No, Gramps. If I go back to college, I will *get* the best job. If I go back to the Navy I will *have* the better job. If I join the Air Force, I will have the *best* job."

"You not can do that!"

"Why can't I?" Thinking it more acceptable to say that he was going to school, rather than back in service, he eased into: "Gramps, I've saved enough money to last me through school. I was going to get married, remember? And if I re-enlist, I won't need any money. And besides, over in a place called Korea there's a war going on. I don't mind being a part of it. In fact, I *want* to be a part of it. I never wanted this job. I never asked for this job. I don't like this job. I don't like these people."

"Now, you listen to me — !"

"Listening to you and the shenanigans with city manager Mulkey is what got me into this mess. Now, c'mon, let's go before I say something I really don't want to say."

"No," said the grandfather, heatedly. "You wvait a minute!"

"I said, let's go, Gramps!"

Sorry that he had spoken harshly to his grandfather, Carlsson went to the cot, sat for a moment, then stood again.

Wilhovthen Carlsson knew there was something deep stirring in his grandson. "Wvat is it? Talk to me, boy."

Carlsson sighed heavily. "I saw a man get killed tonight. And just like these sorry people on the department, I didn't do a thing about it. Nothing."

The grandfather took it to heart. He limped around for a moment, and said, "You are taking too hard."

"I should take it hard, Gramps. Tonight I was a coward."

"Never you coward. You police. You good police."

Carlsson went back to the cot and sat. He sent his mind back to the old black and smiled a bit. "I bet I'm the only one he ever sang a song to."

"The man killed, he singer?"

Carlsson started to say, no, Gramps, he wasn't a singer, he was a soldier. But then he thought, how could he say that? The man was never in the Army and never could have made it into the Army. He thought about what the man's mother had said, that the Army didn't want him. And then he thought about how the Soldier Boy had called cadence and marched him up and down the street, giving the right commands without ever having been in the military. He thought about how the old black, before going into the bar, had not asked directly for money, but had asked him if he didn't mind helping an old soldier who was past the cocktail hour of a brilliant career. How classy. How nicely stated. Then he remembered how, when offered the bills, the Soldier would take only one, saying, *A man's gotta have some pride.*

Those were the words of a soldier.

In further evidence, the last thing the man said before losing his life in that diseased place called the Flamingo was, *Our yesterdays I shall leave to your keeping, and I will smile farewell with eyes too sad for weeping.* If that act and those words weren't the traits of a great soldier, none would ever be.

"No, Gramps," Carlsson finally answered. "He was not a singer. He didn't even know the words to our favorite song, but a singer couldn't touch him. My friend was a soldier. And he was a brilliant man."

The young cop smiled inwardly at the memory again, got up, and moved to put the half-empty carton back into the tiny Frigidaire. He held there in thought. "He was great. And you know something else, Pop? I was there when he saw God."

"God? There is no *God."*

"Pops," Carlsson said slowly, "when I was a kid and you told me that, I believed you." It was at this point that he wanted to say to the old man: Sit down, I want to tell you something. Pops, I want to tell you how you've steered me wrong. I want to tell you how you're doing yourself a terrible disservice by not opening up your mind and believing in something higher. I want to tell you how good and solid I feel about certain things now. And I want you to feel as good and solid as I do. But he didn't say anything. He simply gave his grandfather a look. "Gramps, I'm gonna have to talk to you about that one day. Soon."

The grandfather sloughed it off. "On that, there is no'ting to talk. Now, you friend. Wvat happened to him?"

"A slob killed him. But it doesn't mean anything. And what gets me is that it's not *going* to mean anything. *That's* the problem."

"You don't know wvat you talk. Everything mean something."

"Not this man's death."

"You listen me. Everything mean something."

"No, Pops," Carlsson said. "I love you, and I've learned a lot from you. And I'm grateful for all the things you've done for me. But there are some things you don't know. There are a lot of things you don't know. And one of them has me worried. I'm worried about it for you, but we'll get to it sometime later because it is important. *Very* important. But, now, this department..." He broke it off. "Look, Pops, you've been around a long time, but you don't know this department."

"Enough about department!" the old man flared. "If something wvrong you make it better. You stay and make better. You in this country to be something."

"And what about the 'something' who was killed? What can I do to make it better for him? He was killed because of a stupid racial squabble."

"Oh, he colored?"

"Yes. He was 'colored.'"

"Then he wvas not a something."

"Then what was he?"

"He wvas a no'ting."

Carlsson was stunned. "Pop; we're immigrants. *Immigrants. Foreigners.* You're saying that and you can hardly speak the English language?"

"This is H'America," said the old man. "Wvat has language got to do wvith color?"

13

The night was moving on.

"102, back in service," Spagg transmitted, having returned to patrolling after an extended stay with the window-woman.

McShayne transmitted in return, "You were out of the car a long time, Two, what were you doing?"

"Tol'ja. I was havin' battery trouble."

Bucky looked up at the big clock. "You want I should give the time-check now, Sarge?"

McShayne resumed sitting in the swivel chair and listened to the clattering teletype unit. He rubbed wearily at his temples for a bit and answered "No" to the question. "Give Van Dreelan a buzz an' find out what happened at that cat-lady's house."

"H'quarters to 105, come in. Five, your location?"

There was no answer.

"Gimme a location, John-John."

But John-John could not respond. At that moment his bloodied torso was wrapped in a blanket and the head was leaning limply against the passenger's window of his patrol car. He was being driven erratically through the streets. Pilar was at the wheel.

"Can't get Five, Sarge," Bucky reported.

The desk sergeant's mind was beginning to slip.

"Sarge, I can't reach 105."

"And I didn't give him a lunch call?"

"Not yet," said Bucky, peering at the log.

"That r'minds me," McShayne mused, turning to the mike: "H'quarters to 102."

"Yeah?"

"You find Mickey Corbbo yet, Spagg?"

"No."

"And you haven't seen 'im drive by?"

"Nope."

"Well, keep lookin'."

"Will do," Spagg said, lazily.

McShayne spun around in the chair aimlessly. "That sonovabitchin' Corbbo. He's had it this time. His butt has had it."

No sooner had the jowl-faced sergeant gotten the words out of his mouth than Carlsson walked through the front door. He was quiet. Uniform changed, he was back to being spit-and-polish. He looked at the desk sergeant as if ready to accept any and all punishment.

"Now, just where'n hell have you been?"

"Home."

"Well, isn't that lovely," McShayne said corrosively. "Maybe we should all go home. Now you listen to me — and you listen good. If I ever catch you — or if I ever hear talk of you walkin' off your post again, or away from this department without authorization, I'm gonna personally escort you down to the county jail. Do you hear me?"

"Yes, sir."

Carlsson had been so simple and amenable in both presence and delivery that the desk Sergeant was not positive about unleashing more. He flicked the rookie a concluding look, and said, "Now, get back out on post. And make *damn* sure you do your job."

"Sergeant, that is the only reason I came back. To do my job. And the department's job," he said significantly. He walked out the door, leaving McShayne and Bucky exchanging *What'd-he-mean-by-that?* looks.

McShayne turned his attention to the phone. Should he try to place that personal call one more time? "Later," he said to himself. He looked up at the clock that topped the doorway and said to Bucky, "Tell 101 to go to lunch."

"Signal 10, One."

Pippilo was stretched out as far as he could get on the front seat of his patrol car. He sent a lazy arm out for the mike. "What was that, Buck?"

"Signal 10. Lunch."

"I switched off with Van Dreelan," Pippilo said, knowing full well that he and Van Dreelan hadn't changed anything.

McShayne yelled into the mike: "Who gave you permission to switch?"

"Nobody."

"Well, eat now or starve!"

"But it ain't my time."

"Eat <u>now</u> or <u>starve!</u>"

As the flustered sergeant withdrew from the mike, his eye slipped to the door. Poking a bandaged head in was the irrepressible Charlie Wong. "Gung Ho Fat Choy. Good New Year news, Sargento," he beamed. "After I find nice pletty girl who no fight, I go back anda open my place anda make more New Year soup."

"You over-baked fortune cookie, get the hell outta here!"

"*Walla!*" The head ducked back out.

Bucky slid over to answer another call. Before answering, he asked, "Is this really the Chinese New Year, Sarge?"

"Do you believe that nut?"

"No reason why I shouldn't."

"It's <u>December!</u> If you believe this is a Chinese New Year, you'd be-lieve this is the season for the Pope's Bar Mitzvah!" McShayne fumed. "Who's on the line?"

"Mrs. Ina."

The sergeant went back to the mike. "H'quarters to 102!" he said, then held up. "Wait a minute, Spagg. Frank, where're you gonna eat?"

"I ain't eatin'," Pippilo said.

"Then get over to Mrs. Ina's."

"...I'll be lunchin' at McLauren's Diner." He went back to sleep.

"Roger, One. 'Quarters to 102."

"Two," answered Spagg, who was now beaming his spotlight up into another second-floor window.

"You haven't seen Corbbo yet?"

"Nope. Lookin' all over for 'im. Ain't seen 'im. An' I'm lookin' right at this very moment." What Spagg was really looking at was a hairy-chested man who suddenly appeared in the window and caused him to burn rubber getting away.

"Roger, Two. 'Quarters to 104, cover for 101. Take a run by old lady Ina's."

No answer.

"Headquarters to 104!"

Tetrollini's response was delayed. "Four, standing by."

"Did you get my last transmission regarding Mrs. Ina?"

"Yes, sir."

"Then move it."

"Four. Roger."

But the nice-looking policeman, who wore a rosary under his uniform and who, most would say, had been saddled with the wrong job by not pursuing something more related to religion, did not move the vehicle out of the park. Instead, he put on his parking lights and slowly closed in on the Henry J. The girl, Carol, had been watching the Hudson's parking lights through the rear-view mirror. She withdrew the look when the car stopped alongside. With no signs of the facial expressions she had used before, she waited for a moment, and slid out of her car. She held herself as though touched by a minor pain, then joined the policeman in patrol car 104.

There was a slight protrusion to her midriff, but at 16 she was nicely developed and her blonde hair looked beautiful under the moonlight. But mainly she was soft. Wholesomely soft.

Tetrollini hadn't looked at her when she slid into the car. By way of welcoming her, the only thing he did was to remove his clipboard and flashlight from the passenger's side of the car. He had already touched his rosary.

The deeply worried policeman's gaze remained fixed elsewhere and there were long, uncomfortable moments between them. The seriousness of the situation was evident. She took more time and broke the awkward silence by sniffing gently in a disordered Kleenex and saying, kitten-like, "I've been waiting out here in the cold and snow since before 12, Georgie."

He was distant. "I'm sorry you had to wait, Carol."

"That's okay, Georgie. I had my romantic books with me. But it's too dark to read."

"Carol, I told you, you should stop reading those things. They aren't good for you. It's like those movies you go to, they're too trashy."

"I was just going to read a page or two. I also brought my record player to keep me company, but it didn't work."

"That's because a record player requires an electrical power source, Carol. In a car you don't have an electrical power source that you can plug into."

"Oh," she said, "Can I get it and plug it in here?"

"No, Carol. It won't work in here, either. But even if it could, a police vehicle is not quite the place for playing records."

"Oh."

Nothing was said for another minute, then the teenager picked at the paint that was caked on and under her fingernails. She looked out the window. "Do you like the way I painted the car, Georgie? Can you see it?"

"I saw it when I drove up. You did a great job," the cop said sullenly — and most inaccurately. "You still have a little paint on your face."

"Oh," she said, "Is it a lot?"

"No, its just a smudge."

Rubbing and picking at a face that was delicate with youth, she said, "I wanted to make the car nice and bright for you."

"Thank you, Carol," he said without enthusiasm. "But you really didn't have to go through all of that. And, to repeat, I'm sorry if I held you up. But it's been a busy night."

"You didn't use to be so busy."

"I don't mean to be," Tetrollini fumbled. "It just happens that way. And tonight — well, tonight just happens to be one of those nights. It's been so weird, I can't even begin to think straight."

She sat with her head low, her hands clasped innocently in her lap, alternately pulling on the Kleenex and picking and rubbing at her nails and face. Searching for something to say, she said: "It's a lovely, moonlit night, isn't it?"

"Yes, it is," he said slowly.

"I really think it's the best we've ever seen together in the park. And with the light snow on the ground, it makes everything look so peaceful and clean. Doesn't it, Georgie?"

"Yes, it does, Carol," he responded, tediously.

Needing something else to say, she asked, "Are you finished with your Christmas shopping?"

"No," he said, without presence in his voice. "I'm late. I haven't even started."

They lost it by lapsing into another long, uncomfortable silence. She looked up at the moon again and sighed. Over the radio Bucky's voice started with another time-check, but something happened and it was suspended.

Forgetting about the Kleenex and the paint under her nails, the teen-ager finally said, "So, did you get the money?"

"No," said Tetrollini quietly.

"Why not, Georgie?"

Flustered, he said, "I just couldn't get it."

She had a tear in her voice. "But, Georgie, you promised."

"I know I promised I'd get it, Carol, but...I'm sorry…"

"How can you say you're sorry at a time like this, Georgie? Do you realize what I have to go through? Or do you really care about what I'm going through, Georgie?"

"Of course, I care, Carol. You know I care. I'd do anything in the world for you. You know that."

"No, I don't, Georgie. I don't know it. I used to think it. I used to believe it. I used to believe in you. I had reason to — then. But now something has changed between us," she said with more tears and hurt in her voice. "Georgie, has it ever occurred to you, everything I know about love — and *loving* — I learned from you? I never knew anything before you,

Georgie. I never *wanted* anything until you. Sometimes I find myself in tears thinking about what we did — when I gave my all to you; when I surrendered my everything…"

"Carol, you don't have to go through it again. Your forget it was only the one time."

"Once, yes. But think about the times that led up to that one time, Georgie. And think about what happened, and the condition it left me in." She sniffed again and tried for pacing. With dialogue fit for a home movie, she said, "But I don't choose to think about the bad things. I choose to think about what we used to be, about the many moonlit nights we spent together — talking — wanting to give each other our all — wanting to let the rest of the world go by; us; you and I — wanting to love; to trust — to belong. And then the talking turned into something else — and we were about to do something else — right in this very same car. Georgie, I was about to lose my virginity in this thing. Me, Carol — in the back seat of a Hudson! But then, Georgie, what we had for each other was real, so true, we couldn't fight it any longer — we couldn't hold back the fire. With wild, passionate abandonment, we took off all our clothes and ran down to the river — in the cold — and we let nature take its course. Do you remember that magic moment, Georgie?"

"Yes, Carol, I do," he said, glumly and apologetically, and wanting to get away from the subject.

"And now you want to throw it all away."

"No, I don't. I don't want to throw anything away," he answered in confused earnestness. "Look, Carol, I don't want to hurt you. I've never wanted to hurt anyone."

"But that's exactly what you're doing to me."

"I don't intend to."

"But you are, Georgie. That's exactly what you're doing."

"Okay, you're right. You're right, you're right. But this isn't going to get us anywhere. If I had the money I'd give it to you. But the simple fact is, I don't have it. I didn't get it."

"But, you see, Georgie, that goes back to trust again. You said — *you promised* — you'd have the money tonight. And I believed you. I trusted you, Georgie."

"Carol, I know, I know, I know," Tetrollini said, again more out of disgust with himself than her. "I just couldn't get it."

"Why not?"

"Because the guy I was supposed to get it from didn't have it."

"Couldn't you have borrowed it?"

"From who?"

"From a bank, a loan company…"

"Carol, I've told you before. I told you when this thing first came up that I couldn't borrow anything from a bank or a loan company."

"Why not?"

"Because my wife would have to co-sign."

"Well, then, couldn't you have gotten it from one of the guys you work with?"

"Like I said when this thing came up, as much as the guys on this job talk, they are the last people in the world I'd go to."

The soft, vulnerable-looking all-American teenager pulled at her blonde tresses, dabbed at her nose again and pleaded, "Tell me, Georgie, what am I supposed to do? Keep delaying, and have the baby?"

"That would be a disaster for the both of us, Carol. You know it. We've talked about it over and over."

"As we should have, Georgie. This is serious."

"I know how serious it is, Carol. Believe me, I know."

"Now that you say you know, what do we do? What steps should I take?"

The cop tinkered with the steering wheel, looked out at the river that the moon was partly highlighting and said, "Give me a little more time, give me until tomorrow."

"'Til tomorrow?" Carol said, now in tearful dismay. "And then after that another tomorrow? Georgie, I originally came to you because I needed counseling…"

"And I did try to help you, Carol."

"Yes. We talked. I talked out all my problems. But it didn't stop there. It didn't stop with talking. Look at what happened. Wait, give me your hand…" she said, reaching for it.

"What? What are you doing?"

"I want you to feel my stomach, Georgie. I want you to realize that we did more than talk. My parents were always afraid I'd end up like this. That's why they sent me away from Hackensack — to be away from the bad elements; they wanted me to be away from the bad influences, where the boys only have one thing on their minds. That's why they sent me here to Elton Head. To live with Uncle. And now look at me. I'm not the pure little girl I used to be. Even my classmates won't want to have anything to do with me now." She dabbed at her nose and eyes again. She clutched herself as if to ward off an added cold. She was a girl alone. "I said all that, Georgie, because I can't afford to wait for any more tomorrows."

"But Carol, you have to wait. You *have* to."

"I can't wait any longer, Georgie. *It* can't wait any longer. The doctor said that if I'm going to have the operation, I have to have it done now. It's now or never." The girl moved her body closer to him, and pleaded. "Feel, Georgie. Feel this. Feel my stomach."

Tetrollini, to placate her, touched her slightly protruding abdomen lightly. It felt a little soft — unusually fluffy and uneven — but his mind was much too troubled for anything to register. It was a desperate and delicate situation. Common sense had completely abandoned him. Silence came again. It remained until the radio crackled with urgency.

"'Quarters to 104!"

"Four."

"Signal 88, Flo-Control's warehouse."

"Four, Roger," Tetrollini said. He absently started to re-cradle the mike, and remembered. "But you gave me Mrs. Ina's a few minutes ago. I'm almost there."

"There's a <u>fire</u> at Flo! Now, turn around and get over there!"

Tetrollini hurriedly replaced the mike and tugged at the gear. "Listen, I gotta go. Will you wait for me?"

"Wait for what, Georgie?"

"I'll think of something, I promise. I'll think of something."

"Don't trouble yourself," said the young miss, "I've already thought of a solution."

"What do you mean?"

There was serious threat in her voice. "...There's always the river."

"Aw, Carol," he pleaded heavily, "you don't mean that. You *can't* mean that."

The all-American teenager didn't skip a beat. "I mean it from the bottom of my heart, Georgie. I can't go on living like this," she said, adding more threat. "And there's something else to consider. Christmas is less than a week away?"

Tetrollini hesitated. "Yes." He'd been so troubled that he wasn't even sure about that. He sighed. "Yes, Christmas is only a week away."

"It doesn't make any difference. Even if Christmas was tomorrow, it wouldn't make any difference." She lowered her baby-blue eyes. "I won't be here, Georgie."

"What??"

She said it simply. "I said, I won't be alive."

"But...but..." Tetrollini struggled. "You can't think like that. You can't do it, Carol. You *can't*."

"Why shouldn't I think about ending it all, Georgie? My life is in ruin. I first came to you because I was in trouble. And now I'm in more trouble. Deep trouble. The worst a girl can get."

"Carol, I made the one mistake. I did wrong. I was wrong, very wrong. And so help me, I'm sorry."

"Being sorry isn't going to do it, Georgie."

"I know that, Carol. All I'm trying to do...all I'm trying to say is..."

"Headquarters to 104," McShayne's voice interrupted with pressure. "Acknowledge that you're rolling on the 88, Four."

"Carol, I can't go into it now. All I'm asking you to do is to hold on — wait."

"Four!" Are you rolling on the Flo-Control fire, Four?!"

Ignoring the radio, her desperation was matching his. "And I'm asking you, wait for what, Georgie? Are you going to marry me? You can't. We can't even go to the movies together. You have a wife. Georgie, I'm in trouble — desperate trouble. What else can I do? Who can I turn to? Where can I go? Who's going to help me? You? Your wife, Georgie? My parents over in

Hackensack? I've already told you what they thought. And now that what they were scared of has come true, they'll kill me if they ever found out that I'm pregnant. They'll put me away. Maybe I should turn around, go back and wait 'til Uncle comes home...and tell him..."

"FOUR!!!"

"Carol, no. Oh, God, no," Tetrollini froze. "Carol, please. Don't even *think* like that."

"But something has to happen, Georgie."

McShayne's voice cut through the speaker again, *"Dammit, are you rollin' on the 88, Four?"*

"Yes, I'm rolling," the cop said, so disturbed that he hadn't keyed the mike. "Carol, do me this one favor. That's all I ask. Wait until after I answer this call?"

"Tetrollini!!!" blasted the radio.

"Carol, listen — "

"TETROLLINI!!"

Tetrollini, on the mike: "Four. Rolling on the 88." Tetrollini, back to Carol: "Honey, listen to me. Please. All I ask is that you wait until I get back. I'll have the money. I swear to you, I'll get it. I'll have all of it."

Carol looked at him softly, her troubled baby blue eyes pleading. "Will you really, Georgie? Georgie, will you really have the money?"

"I swear to you, I'll have it when I come back. Whatever you need, I'll have. Every penny; every cent."

"And you'll give it all to me?"

"Every dime."

"Oh, Georgie, you're wonderful. *Wonderful!* Say it one more time. Say you'll have the money."

"I will have the money, Carol," he said, exasperated.

"And what are you going to do with it?"

"Give it to you, Carol. You'll have all the money you need for the operation."

"Oh, how wonderful, wonderful, wonderful. You are so sweet, Georgie..."

"I gotta go, Carol. I've *got* to answer this call."

"Will it take long? Because if Uncle…"

"Carol, please <u>don't</u> mention him again."

"It's just that…"

"Carol, *please*, I gotta go."

"And you'll be right back?"

"Yes, Carol. Yes."

"With the money?"

"With the money. *All the money.*"

She became bubbly. "Oh, Georgie. I love you, I love you, I love you. You're such a nice, sweet man. When I was in trouble and I first came to you, I knew I was right. I just knew it. And when we did it, I knew that was right, too. Kiss me. Gimme kissy-kiss."

He briskly kissed her on the cheek and started to speed away.

"A movie kissy-kiss," she said, closing her eyes and pushing her lips forward.

He kissed her with pursed lips. She shrieked happily, slid out of the car, and ran around to the driver's side. She motioned for him to roll the window down. Quickly, it was done. She leaned in and asked him to kiss her again — which he did hastily. "Can we do it when you come back?" she asked.

"It??"

"You know. *It.*"

The policeman lowered his head guiltily and brought it back up. "I'll think about it, Carol, I'll think about it."

"Promise you will."

"Carol…"

"Say *Promise*."

Clutch in, gear ready: "I promise, Carol. *I promise.*"

"Cross your fingers and hope to die?"

"Carol, I've *got* to go. *I've got to.*"

"Cross your fingers and hope to die?"

"Yes!"

"Say it, Georgie. Say: 'Cross my fingers and hope to die.'"

"Cross my fingers and hope to die," said the cop, squeezing the wheel in frustration.

"Say, cross my finger and hope to die, if we don't do it."

"Crossmyfingerandhopetodieifwedon'tdoit, Carol!!"

She squealed delightedly, took two steps back, clutched her stomach, then groaned. "Oooooh," she cried. "Hurry, Georgie, hurry...It's starting to kick, Georgie! It's starting to kick!"

She was so young; so vulnerable; so troubled. He hated to leave her in pain. But he had to. Duty called.

The cop flicked on the red light and skidded away.

She watched the patrol car cut a new path through the snow. She waved and called out: *"And don't forget the money, Georgie!!"*

With red light flashing, minutes later Tetrollini's 104 was crossing Balanta Street, heading for Main. There, instead of remaining on the street, he drove hurriedly to the rear of the alley that led to the back of Mr. Wilson's store. For an emergency warehouse call, his route from the park was unusual and deserved to be called into question. But the policeman had his reasons, and it was of high interest to him that the Wilson car wasn't where he had last seen it. Slowing for a bit, he came to the conclusion that the old man had obviously completed doing what he had to do, and Mrs. Wilson had no doubt driven them both home.

The patrol car sped out of the area.

When the desk sergeant returned downstairs, fresh from relieving himself, Bucky was at the switchboard. He had already received a call from another irate cat-lover saying that his favorite Persian cat had just been kidnapped by a shadowy figure who lured the feline away with a toy wind-up mouse. He could tell it was a toy by the tracks in the snow. Since the call had been over three minutes ago, it had already been forgotten by Bucky — but he had logged it, and was now on another call. Before that, he had already stepped into the ticket office and had another quick nip from a bottle that was getting low. His face was molded in surprise at what the caller was saying. "Huh?" he said. "You're kiddin'! I can't believe it!"

"'Tis the season to be jolly," the other voice sang in conclusion.

"Well, sure," the stringbean of a policeman agreeably said. "Anything you say, Mrs. Ina. Of course. Absolutely. An' what you said before, we think the same of you. An' we were glad to be of service. Call back any time. An' thank you for calling. Huh? Yes, ma'am, it is a gorgeous night. An' you're right, that is one beautiful moon. The best I've ever seen....Beg y'pardon?...Yes, ma'am, I saw the rays, an' I know what people say about 'em. I didn't see the faces in the moon, but I'll be careful...You, too. Nighty-night." Bucky hung up and said to the sergeant, "Sarge, I just got the damnedest call we've ever had. Mrs. Ina. That was her. She said, thanks to a rekindled friendship, she wouldn't be needin' our services any more. We don't ever have to send no more patrol cars out to the house. Can you beat that?"

McShayne knitted his brow. "Are you sure it was her?"

"Positive."

"'Rekindled friendship.' What the hell is that supposed to mean?"

"I dunno," Bucky gummed, "but it seems that this ex-friend of hers wanted to make up, so she dropped by with this *hunk*. He was unconscious, and so they had to carry him in the house. Seems he sweats so much they had to keep his head wrapped in a blanket. Anywho, Mrs. Ina, bein' the kind sport that she is, helped put him in the nursery of hers. Later on, soon's he dries up an' comes to, she's gonna put 'im in the attic. Sweet of her, huh? Oh. She also said that her re-kindled friend has another friend waitin' at her house, and that he was gonna be a *major* star someday. She's gonna send us some tickets to a play if she changes her mind about directin' it. S'gonna be called 'Dracula With a Dress On.'"

It was more kookiness. McShayne dismissed it. "Did you check on the prisoner up in the loft yet?"

"I didn't know we had any," said a surprised Bucky. "I thought there wasn't nothin' but storage up there."

"Obviously, the storage has been removed, Bucky. The storage was removed to make room for the one female prisoner up there in the cell. I thought I'd mentioned it once or twice before. But even if I didn't, it seems that you would have heard her, since her whooping-cough hacking sounds like she's going to kick off at any minute, and since you've already started on your customary one dozen trips to the john up there — and to the chief's office. But forgive me if I was in error. And forgive me, too, Bucky, because you, of all people, should know about this prisoner in particular. Now forget that the arrest is on the blotter for the entire world to see, let me explain who we have housed in the loft: One female, Protestant, white, Anglo-Saxon. Age 81; blood type pending. Prior arrests too numerous to count. However, today she was booked by the day shift at 1120 hundred hours. Charges: disorderly conduct, public drunkenness, excessive use of foul language, urinating on parking meters, resisting arrest, and panhandling from a police officer — and mind you, this was all before noon."

"Gee," said Bucky, going over to answer the phone, which had buzzed again, "an 81 year-old panhandlin' female drunk who pees on parkin' meters. We sure don't get too many of them. No siree, bob. I'll get to her in a sec, Sarge."

"Please do, Bucky. For your sake, please do," the sergeant advised with uncommon concern, and rarely using the term *please*. "And, incidentally, I talked to that cat lady on the phone one time, she didn't sound French to me."

"Oh, she's French all right."

"Maybe she is," McShayne said of the woman who had never seen so much as the Eiffel Tower. "But how do you know she's French?"

"She said so. An' to prove it, a coupla nights ago she belched on the phone and she sounded like General Charles de Gaulle."

"Answer the switchboard, Bucky. Answer the phone."

"EHPD?"

Charlie Wong was on the line. He was bright and upbeat. "Gung Ho Fat Choy. Tonight I am happy man. Two times. I am little tipsy, but I am getting plenty lucky. Soon we go beddy-bye. *Walla!*"

"That was fast work, Charlie."

"I was a smoothie," said the Chinaman. "Tell Sargento, Wong going to let it all hand out."

"You mean *hang* out," Bucky corrected.

"Whatever," Charlie laughed. "As long as I get push-push."

"Hit a lick for me, Charlie," Bucky said, and hung up. "That was Charlie Wong, Sarge. He says it looks like he found a live one."

Tetrollini's voice came through, "104 to headquarters?"

"Go ahead, Four," McShayne responded, mercifully ignoring Bucky and all thoughts of the Chinese man.

Tetrollini was in the area where the few warehouses stood, circling and spotlighting a building. "Hey, I'm out here at the Flo-Control warehouse on the signal 88, and there's nothing happening."

"You mean those fire engines didn't show up?"

"No."

"An' you don't see any signs of a fire?"

"Negative."

"Hold on, Four." McShayne said. He plugged a jack into the switchboard.

"Elton Head Fire," answered the voice.

"Listen here, you brainless idiot: the next time you jerks have a false alarm and don't notify us, I'll have my men ringing every box in the city!" He yanked the jack from the switchboard and went back to the mike. "Go to lunch, Four."

"Four, Roger," Georgie Tetrollini said, driving off with more than eating on his mind.

"Hate to bring this up, Sarge," Bucky said, turning from the phone, "but we ain't heard from Mickey Corbbo or Johnny Van Dreelan in quite some time. 'Specially Mickey."

"Did you call 'em at home?"

"Yeah. Both of 'em. I called Dutch's place twice."

"Corbbo's screwin' off someplace, I can feel that. But Van Dreelan, what was his last log?"

"The cat call at the French lady's," Bucky said, checking the blotter. "But we figgered he took off for lunch from there."

"Lemme see that blotter," McShayne said, moving over to take a look. After a quick run down, he said, "Van Dreelan never called in."

"That's what I'm sayin'."

"You wouldn't have taken the call and didn't log it?" McShayne asked, confirming.

"No. But I did hear Frank Pippilo say he changed lunch hours with 'im."

"I said there were to be no lunch-hour changes or any other kind of change. Anyhow, he didn't call in," McShayne said. "Do you remember taking a lunch-call from Five?"

"No, sir. If I had, it would've been in the book. I woulda logged it. That's the one thing that I do do right. I always log the calls."

On that score Bucky was right. He could be as drunk as a skunk, but he'd never miss logging a call.

"Strange," McShayne mused. "That ain't like Van Dreelan. He's got his problems, but not callin' in ain't one of 'em." He turned to the mike, "'Quarters to 102, come in."

"Two, standing by."

"H'quarters to 101, come in, One."

"One," Pippilo sleepily answered. "I'm still on lunch, y'know."

"Shut up an' listen," McShayne said with a serious tone to his voice. "I want both of you guys to get on your high horses and get over to that nut's dump, Pilar, or whatever the hell she calls herself, and check it out thoroughly. Gimme a signal 16 on her phone when you get there, clear?"

"Two. Roger," Spagg said.

Pippilo inquired, "Two cars on a neighbor's complaint? What gives?"

"Johnny Van Dreelan."

⧗

When Georgie Tetrollini arrived at home, 12 minutes away from the warehouse and less than 15 from Main Street, he was moving swiftly. He went inside, went directly for the telephone in the kitchen and quietly dialed the station. As usual, Marge, his wife, had prepared a sandwich and soup and had left it on the kitchen table along with the customary note saying, "I love you."

"It's me. Lunch at home," the policeman whispered into the mouthpiece when Bucky answered. He hung up and tiptoed upstairs, eased the bedroom door open and looked inside. He smiled warmly at his sleeping wife and quietly closed the door. He moved away quietly, but then came back. He couldn't leave without looking at her again. He cracked open the door and studied the auburn-haired beauty with the fawn-like neck and rich textured skin who lay so graceful beneath the covers. How he loved her hair; her skin.

How he loved her. She was so elegant; so delicate, so calm. She had class and character, and with her cover-girl looks that meant nothing to her, all she wanted to complete life — all that was needed to round out a wonderful marriage, was a baby. That would come, too. She had already purchased the crib.

Georgie Tetrollini thought about his affair with Carol, the girl he had left in the park, and lowered his head in guilt. *Why?* he asked himself in torment. *How could I? How, in God's name, could I have done such a cruel, senseless thing? Why, as men, do we do such things? How sinful; how so much against the teachings of Christ.*

The husband collected himself and whispered to his beautiful, sleeping wife, "I love you," he said. "I will love you forever." He begged for forgiveness, and said something else; softer this time — and left.

The day that they had gotten married came to the policeman's mind as he quietly descended the stairs. He remembered the ceremony and how beautiful the love of his life had looked, and how marvelously everything had gone. He remembered her father and how he had expressed joy over the fact that his daughter had married the *"nicest guy in town."* Before marriage, it was the father to whom the dilemma-laden, curly-haired boy from the deeply religious family had gone when he needed advice. There were two loves in his life, Christ and Margie. The young man didn't know which road to take, priesthood or marriage.

"Christ will love you, no matter what. He will always be there," counseled Marge's father at the time. "My daughter is young and beautiful. She will not be here forever. If she marries another, you cannot expect her to love you, no matter what."

Georgie Tetrollini never regretted the choice.

He had been blessed.

But the cop was in need of more than a blessing that night. He was about to commit a wrong. It was not right to commit a wrong in the uniform, and so from the closet in the hallway he removed a knitted cap and hunting jacket and very quietly came back downstairs and hurried out to the car. The moon hovering over his driveway was as bright as it had been in the park, but he hadn't noticed it there. Here, he did. He stopped for a moment. His wife would have looked even more beautiful under that moon. And that creamy-textured skin and lovely auburn hair of hers would have looked even more radiant. If the moon was that bright and the rays that sobering, the next time he had a night off he would take advantage of it. He and his wife would take advantage of it.

Even if he had to take an extra night off from work, he and his wife would enjoy that moon. It was something they had enjoyed immensely during courtship. It was time to reconnect.

The policeman hurriedly placed the cap and jacket in the trunk and quietly drove off.

In good time car 104 was back on Main Street, at first cruising the 200 block to make certain Mr. Wilson hadn't returned, and that his wife hadn't moved to the front of their dress store. The policeman's next concern was Carlsson.

At first Tetrollini didn't see Carlsson walking the post. He checked his watch and realized that it was shortly after the half-hour, which meant that the rookie was due to be near one of the two callboxes that served each end of the post.

The post 1-A man was at the north end when he was spotted. It was a good distance away from Wilson's store.

"Hi, Danny," Tetrollini said when he pulled up in the patrol car.

"How's it goin', Georgie?" Carlsson said, leaning on the Hudson for a chat.

"Listen," Tetrollini said, "Sergeant McShayne has got everybody out looking for Mickey Corbbo. I got a hunch he might be passing this way pretty soon, so why don't you kinda hang down on this end, just in case. I'll be circling around the other end. If you do spot him, call the desk right away, because McShayne is furious. Got it?"

"Got it."

Before driving away, he added, "And, Danny, I hope we get a chance to have that talk you wanted to have. But in case we don't...whatever happens, I hope you decide to stay with the department. It needs new blood; it needs better blood." The dark, curly-haired policeman wanted to say something else, but he didn't. He held there for a moment, then drove off purposefully.

Carlsson felt a strange chill in evaluating what the other policeman had to say. He appreciated the thought, but still he felt a chill. He watched the patrol car's lights disappear in the darkness. He resumed walking his post.

Three blocks away car 104 made the turn to come back to the Main Street alley. The coast clear, Tetrollini sandwiched the vehicle between two buildings, got out, went into the trunk, and removed the cap and jacket. He was not worried about the tracks in the snow. The real burglar would have made them, or to be sure, under the pretense of double-checking the unlocked door, he would come back later and park in the same spot.

Looking around, the cop replaced his police jacket with his hunting jacket, pulled the cap low over his head and slipped around to the front of the store. He checked the street again, cleared the snow and began working with the two metal halves that formed the cellar door. At first they seemed stuck, or locked, but he remembered sliding the locking lever back when he was inside earlier. He remembered the precise moment. It was seconds before the grossly obese, heavy-breathing man showed up. But what if Mr. Wilson had locked it again? He couldn't have. There was no way a man of his weight and condition could have positioned himself to work the sliding lever. Struggling with the two stubborn sidewalk metal doors, which hadn't been used for years and had been rusted and iced together, Tetrollini was nervous and had begun to sweat. The whole operation wreaked havoc with his mind. In panic, he pulled, yanked and stomped. The halves wouldn't budge. Equally bad, he was making too much noise. A thought hit him. He hurried back to the car, went into the trunk, searched and found what he was looking for — the crowbar-like lug wrench. Back around to the front, he put the tool in motion and chipped away at the ice. With the seam cleared, he was able to insert the tool under one of the halves and pry with leverage. Slowly the snowy and rusted doors began to loosen. Seconds later, he was able to slip through one side and struggle down to the inside concrete steps.

He beamed the light around. There was something about the manne-quins tossed carelessly in the corner that arrested his attention. Making his way around a clutter of boxes, he took note that the mannequins were not just "carelessly" tossed into the corner as he had thought when he was down there earlier. In moving some of them, he noticed that one of them had a metal rod running from the body. Nothing unusual about that, except that it was cemented to the floor. Why would a mannequin be cemented to the floor if it was needed for upstairs? he asked himself. It didn't make sense, especially to a cop who had already been told by the owner that he kept his money in the cellar. *And you've got to be clever,* the man had said.

On a hunch, the policeman rubbed a hand over and around the form. There was nothing unusual about it. He sent a hand crawling under the form's bottom. He felt a bump. No, it was a button. He gave it a twist, but nothing happened. He went to a knee, threw light on the button and pressed it. It snapped, and from it dropped a hanging metal box. It was attached by a small chain, and swung from side to side.

Money was inside; the cop knew it. He wouldn't take it all, though. It was not the gluttony of greed; it was a matter of need. This was an emergency — an emergency loan, really. He had every intention of paying the man back, and he would take — rather, *borrow* — just enough of the loan to satisfy Carol, enough to satisfy a quick and mind-freeing abortion. And at that moment, as he had done while waiting in the park, he promised his God that for as long as he lived — for as long as he was on this Earth, he would never do wrong again. Georgiovone R. Tetrollini would never — *ever, ever, ever* — get involved in another situation that amounted to an unforgivable tragedy. And *tragedy* was not an overuse of the word. A spotless young girl had come to him wanting counseling because of a minor problem in adjusting to her new school. Georgiovone R. Tetrollini had taken advantage of her; ruined her. Worse, he had broken faith with his wife. He stopped for a moment, thought about what he had done, and shook his head in disgust. Then he thought about life's cruel irony. Here, all his wife ever wanted, all she had ever asked him for, was a baby; a baby they were still trying hard to conceive. Conversely, all the faultless young girl had asked him for was help. Something happened — one time — and he had impregnated her.

Enveloped in failure, he remained motionless. Thinking. What he had done was unbelievable, unforgivable, and even if he were never caught, some way, somehow, he deserved to be punished without end. He was willing to accept it.

The cop stopped the small swaying motion created by the little box and took another moment out to ask his God for that which he felt should not be granted: Forgiveness. Then, slowly, he started to pry open the lid. It gave a bit. It gave a little more, and, suddenly, like a thunderbolt, came the shattering sound that stunned him: *BANG!!*

It was a strange sensation. The flashlight went one way and he went another.

At first the policeman was so startled and his body became so numb that he didn't realize that he had been shot. At first he felt dizzy and light-headed, like his feet no longer touched the floor. Then there was the burning in his chest. It was like fire. He became weak and disoriented. His strength gone, he backed up and stumbled over a series of mannequins and fell to the floor. In trying to get up, he clutched himself, and his hands became wet. They were blood-soaked. Now he knew. He'd been shot. *Don't panic*, was the first thing his mind told him. He rested for a moment and tried to clear his head. Now he became dizzy; he felt faint, but he had to get up. If he could just get to his feet he could make it to the metal halves — to leave the cellar. But the money. *What about the money?* Carol needs the money. Carol is having a baby. She shouldn't have to go through with it. It wasn't her fault. It was his — and his alone. He had been recklessly irresponsible; he had been untrue.

Carol *has* to have the money.

From the stairs came another shot. Apparently, it missed the policeman and hit the mannequin. It didn't stop him; he didn't flinch. His mind wayward and knotted, he reversed his course. He was moving for the money again. The policeman wouldn't take it all. He didn't want the girl to have it all. She needed some — not all — not much. How much? Just enough for a quick abortion. As wrong as it was; as wrong, sinful, amoral — and so very, very much against the will of God and everything he, as man and husband, had ever believed in — Carol had to have the money. After that, everything would be okay. *How much? Not much.* Just enough to save a young girl; enough to save a marriage. *How much? Not much.* And he would pay the man back.

Georgie Tetrollini was still moving for the box that swung from the mannequin's bottom, his mind cinched on the one thought when another shot came from the stairs. He was hit again, but he didn't stop. He had to have the money.

The policeman wouldn't take it all, just enough to save a young girl; enough to save a marriage. *How much? Not much.* His hand pawed for the flashlight. He had no choice but to try for the box, which had started swaying again. This time he had to be more careful. He would approach the main mannequin with the cemented rod running from its torso from a different angle; from the side, perhaps. If he could get to it from the side, he would be away from the mannequin's line of fire. Surely it couldn't turn. It was life-like in appearance, and it had been rigged to fire, thought the policeman, but it wasn't human. It could only fire in the one, unmoving direction.

Now the blood was seeping from the policeman's mouth. He was becoming disoriented and the mind started wavering again, and the mannequin was no longer cold and aloof. It seemed to be taking on a life of its own.

The cop looked at the figure again, sending the eight-cell light searching every inch of a face that was becoming all-too familiar now. Even the torso had a familiar look to it. Perhaps that was why he couldn't get angry when it fired. He had seen it before. Georgie Tetrollini had seen that very same face before. Where was it? Where had he seen that wonderful, calm, creamy-rich face before? *Where was it? When was it?* And then, like now, she was poised so gracefully; she was so elegant — angelic. And her hair was auburn, a special kind of auburn. Who was it that he knew that had that unique auburn hair? Who could it have been? Who was she? And that face — that face with the cover-girl looks? Where had he seen it? Where had he seen that fawn-like neck before? Who was the woman? She was so nice. She had decency, character; goodness. She didn't belong in a cellar. She was too good to be mixed in with the dark, dank, and uncaring. And she was so quiet. And her eyes — transfixed...silent; looking directly at him...

His mind tried to move on, but it wouldn't budge. It was stuck on the woman. He wanted to tell her not to look at him like that — that he was there only because he needed money — to help someone. *How much? Not much; just enough to save a young girl who first came to him because she was in trouble.*

"*BANG!*"

With more blood dripping, the cop tried to move forward again. He was not stable, and he fell back on the discarded boxes next to the broken mannequins. Again he sent the light searching the face of the woman standing amid the cold and the inanimate. Something was wrong. This was somebody he knew; somebody who needed help. That's why she was looking at him. She was in trouble. He had helped people before; he would do it again. His life had been dedicated to helping people. That is why he became a policeman. That's why he was good cop, a decent and honorable man. He had made one mistake. But, never again would he make the same mistake; there would never be another Carol.

"*BANG-BANG!!*"

Knocked to his knees, the cop stumbled and tried to scrambled forward again. He had to talk to the woman. Mainly he wanted to say, Get out. *Get out, now. Get out while there is still time; go, leave. Please leave. You don't belong here. Whatever — whoever you are looking for is not here.*

Closer to the mannequin, and something bolted through a cob-webbed mind. The bleeding, curly-haired policeman panted and sobbed, *Oh, my God, Oh, my God. This is not just somebody who needs help! This is...this is...Oh, my God, Oh, my God..."*

From the stairs came yet another shot. It was followed by a series of *click-clicks*. The gun was empty. One could hear the old man panting and digging into his pockets for more rounds.

The cop, hit again, remained oblivious. He never even turned his head in the direction of the stairs. Bleeding and struggling to get to his feet, he stumbled and went down again. But he had to get up. He was hurt — fatally, he believed — but had to get to her. He knew her, and there were thousands of things he had to say. He would start by apologizing and begging for forgiveness, saying that had wronged her, that she could no longer depend on fidelity; that there could be no future; that there was no loyalty there; that if there was no loyalty to the most sacred of sacred vows, there could be no union. No union; no baby; no nothing. He had to tell her the truth; that he had cheated on her; that *he* was wrong — *one time*; that he had lost control — *one time;* that he had shown weakness — *one time;* that in that one weak, reckless and unforgivable moment — *one time* — he had broken trust in the worst way, and he had caused her irreparable harm and all he could do now was apologize, apologize, apologize.

If he could only get to his wife, he would do exactly that. Then he would cradle her in his arms and carry her away, and together they would try to reconnect at a better place...at a better time.

The policeman struggled dizzily to his feet again and reached out for the auburn-haired mannequin. He had almost touched it when another shot rang out. He went down again. Rolling over, he still did not look at the staircase that slanted down from the store. He did not see the fat man; he didn't see Mr. Wilson standing midway up the stairs with the reloaded old gun in his hand, still spiraling a small whiff of smoke. The policeman was still trying to touch the mannequin that had shot him. He had to talk to her.

The severely overweight Mr. Wilson didn't know that it was a policeman who had been his target. But he could tell from the way he fell that whoever it was still had life in him.

Closer came the man with the gun. Disoriented and bleeding badly from several places now, Tetrollini slid along to another spot. He thought he was closing in on the mannequin from a different direction. But he was not. Mr. Wilson completed coming down the stairs and moved to where the burglar had fallen. Unable to see, he fired off two more shots and leaned in for a closer look. Tetrollini, thinking he was under assault by yet another person, realized his misdirection, made the adjustment and quietly circled the man. Still not knowing that it was Mr. Wilson, he held his breath and watched as the fat, adipose body struggled for his breath while trying to get closer to the box.

It was ever so evident that the policeman did not want to do it, but as the face and pistol led closer to where the mannequin stood, the cop managed to grab hold of a metal dress-form base. With all the strength he could muster, he sent the base crashing into the fat man's skull.

Blood gushing, Mr. Wilson was dead before he hit the floor.

Feeling as bad as it was humanly possible to feel, Tetrollini slumped down at the head of the dead man's body. His mind gone, he still didn't know it was Mr. Wilson. All he knew was that it was a human being — one of God's own — and that, again, he had done something that he shouldn't have done. The cop was tortured. He tried to stop the bleeding, but it was a flood. It couldn't be stopped. He wanted to breathe life into the man, and so he tried mouth-to-mouth resuscitation. Defeated in the effort, the only thing he could do now, he did. He made the Sign of the Cross and closed the man's soggy eyelids. They refused to remain closed. The lids popped back open. The orbs were cementing. Eye to eye the two stared at each other. The dead and the almost dead. Finally, in sorrowful relinquishment, the policeman folded the man's arms across his obese body. He couldn't look him in the eyes any more, but he stayed there for a while, sobbing apology after apology. Then, with life ebbing away, he picked up the gun and flashlight and struggled back to his feet.

As he started to leave, his mind asked about the money: *How much? ...Nothing,* he said to himself.

The policeman sent a beam back to the dangling metal box, then up to the woman's face. He hesitated for a moment, then the weakened body went down again. He struggled back to his knees and tried for the woman again. He reached her, then pulled himself up, and, putting a silencing finger to her lips, he told her not to say anything there; not to scold him there; that he knew he had committed yet another wrong — a wrong that they would talk about elsewhere...at a better time; in a better place.

The policeman held the mannequin tightly and kissed her. Then, with care, he tried coaxing her away, but she wouldn't budge. He tried using more effort, saying that he would tell all once they were home. She resisted. She didn't want to go home. Then with all of his weakened might he tried, squeezing and pulling and pleading, but still she wouldn't budge. With no more energy, he was forced to stop.

The policeman was not angry with her; she had every right to refuse him. He understood.

He was fading even more. Carol came to mind, as did the need for money. Georgiovone R. Tetrollini couldn't bring himself to take anything. At least he would show some measure of honesty.

The dangling box would remain as is.

Coughing and bleeding more from several places, the patrolman again made the Sign of the Cross and again looked at the eyes of the woman he had married. The eyes remained hard and unforgiving; they had not been affected by his honesty.

Maybe when he came back later, after they both had had a chance to think, together they could go home and try for a new start.

In momentary defeat, the policeman allowed the flashlight to drop to the concrete floor. His eyes dampened, his body limp, he struggled up the stairs and out to his patrol car. It looked strange under the light of that peculiar moon. Before turning the engine over, he stopped to wonder if he and his wife would ever share another moon together — any kind of moon. It was something they had enjoyed immensely during courtship. Magic was in the air then. He drove away thinking that they enjoyed each other much too much for the magic not to return.

From four doors down, quiet Danny Carlsson watched the Hudson as it got lost in the dark.

The rookie didn't move.

14

Patrol car 104's drive from the rear of the store on Main Street to the park that was quiet and detached in the night was erratic, deranged, and seemingly interminable. The policeman had the presence of mind to toss the gun into the sewer en route to the park, but that was about all the mental acuity he had. Vision blurred, a blood-soaked handkerchief at his upper torso, several times he almost blanked out. It appeared that he would not make it back to Carol, but he did.

Totally different now, the cute, all-American teenager was bright and perky. She showed no trace of the graveness or somberness — or even the gladness — that she had displayed before her cop had driven off. During the wait, she sat in the powder-pink car she had spent the afternoon painting with the heater blasting, whacking on a wad of bubble gum, finger-snapping and joyously listening to the radio as it cranked out the hits of the day. With one tune, the Andrews Sisters singing a lively *boogie-woogie,* she actually popped out of the car with a travel brochure and rolled-up movie magazine under her arm and danced a Hawaiian *hula* in the snow.

She was a tad off kilter.

When Carol saw the headlights of the patrol car creeping back in her direction after what she considered an interminably long wait, she quickly ditched the gum, and cut off both radio and heater. By the time the Hudson pulled alongside her paint-smeared, muffler-hanging, powder-pink car, she was back looking like a frozen little forlorn waif.

Painfully, pitifully, holding her stomach as if the baby were due any moment, and as if she were emerging from a cold cocoon, she consumed a full three and three-quarter minutes getting out the vehicle. She took an almost equal amount of time opening his door. Before climbing into the patrol car, she swallowed in anticipation, coughed softly, and looked at him with those soft, pleading, baby-blue eyes.

Bleeding from the mouth, the policeman rolled his head over to face her. He, too, was coughing easily.

Her eyes spoke in quiet hopefulness. "Well?"

The almost-dead policeman coughed and gasped, "...I...I...I didn't get it."

The teenager was stung. The baby-blues widened, "You didn't *what*???"

The cop's breath was fading. "...I...I...I didn't get the money."

"....Come again?" sputtered the young miss. "You didn't...No. I didn't hear that...Carol, you did not hear this man say he didn't get the money. Now, cool down. Take it slow. Think. Repeat what you *thought* you heard him say. Okay, startin' slow, he said: ...No, he didn't...No. He couldn'a..." She broke off the thought and came back to him. *"Did I hear you say, you didn't get the money?!"*

All the policeman could do at that moment was barely tilt his head in agreement.

Carol was fit to be tied. She stormed around to the driver's side of the vehicle and demanded that the policeman roll the window down — which he struggled to do, making it the last act he would carry out alive.

With the window down, she wanted more confirmation. "Did I hear you say...?" she gulped, unable to get to the words. But the thought was burning. She changed rhythm. "Hey, cop!" she demanded, "You didn't...? No, Carol, don't lose it. Cool it, Little Cee. Easy. He didn't say that. You're hearing things." It didn't work. She backed off and charged again. "Hey, cop!" she fired, "You didn't get the money???" She thought he said *no*. It was only a thought, because he was no longer able to say anything. It must have been an echo from before. It didn't matter. She hauled off and called him a rotten, low-down, dirty, good-for-nothing sonovabitch, kicked the door, and backed off. For the occasion, she was wearing a smock under her coat. She reached under it, yanked off a crudely tied-on pillow she had lifted from her uncle's sofa, and whacked him over the head. She called him another series of names, then angrily went back to her car, grabbed an armload of movie magazines and romance books from the back seat and threw them at the Hudson. She hopped back into the Henry J, cranked up, and skidded all the way out of the park, cursing as she drove. She was headed for a phone booth.

The policeman was not angry. He was not surprised, he was not anything. Georgie Tetrollini was dead.

⧗

At the moment Tetrollini was drifting down the corridor of the dead, back at the station the plump and chunky Mickey Corbbo had seeped through the desk sergeant's mind. The sergeant was a little more deliberate and thoughtful when he picked up the mike to call his errant cop this time. He felt something.

"Headquarters to 103," McShayne said, his voice having lost some of the earlier anger. Not that he wasn't holding heat, but the more low-key approach was in keeping with what he felt. It was also better for his heart. But the desk sergeant could have shouted in the mike at the top of his lungs for his patrolman. In the end it wouldn't have made any difference what the sergeant did. From under the cover in the back seat of the patrol car, Corbbo tried to respond. The will to live was supreme. There was an imperceptible move from the eyelids and there was an automatic, though energy-less attempt to reach the mike. But the arms, the hands, the fingers were much too heavy; much too weighted down with carbon monoxide. Supremacy was not enough.

Now, Mickey Corbbo was dead.

And the night slipped on.

⧗

And the night slipped on for the remaining boys in blue.

Responding as ordered, radio cars 101 and 102 had arrived at Pilar's house at about the same time, and both Pippilo and Spagg caught a glimpse of the woman as she was coming in. Before going inside, looking for Johnny Van Dreelan's 105, they checked the front and side of the house and gave a quick glance around the surrounding areas, seeing only tire tracks and dragging marks. They didn't check the rear of the house. Since Pilar had moved the car quite some time ago they wouldn't have found it anyway, but still they didn't check. But the roaming around allowed the woman enough time to dash upstairs and quickly change into a nightgown before they entered.

Inside, Pippilo, on a signal 16, used the phone to check in with the station. The two patrolmen then began to conduct a modest search and quiz. Spagg had started off by asking the woman about some scuffling or dragging marks that had been embedded in the snow — marks that carried from her porch to the street. They also inquired about the tire tracks that had been left in the snow in front of the house. Silencing them, she said that the dragging marks didn't lead from her house to the street, but from the street to the house. She said they came from dragging a Christmas tree inside. The fact that there wasn't a stitch of greenery on the premises didn't bother the cops. As to the tire tracks that were left, the woman quite rightly stated that if the policeman had been there and left, there *had* to be tire tracks. That silenced the two policemen until they thought they could come up with something more indicting.

Darting the big flashlight into corners and around the room, Spagg came up with: "Smells mighty ana'septic in this place. You make it a habit of cleaning up this time of night?"

Dressed in the flimsy nightgown with enough hair showing through the lower part to make one think of a baby bear in hibernation, the failed actress with the fake French accent, who came from Bulgaria and looked like an escapee from a dark castle in Transylvania, was standing in the middle of the room. She was steaming over the policemen's intrusion and stood there with her arms folded, eyeing their every move.

"I said, lady," emphasized Spagg, putting on his sunglasses to check the hair and look more official. "Do you make it a habit cleanin' up this time of mornin'?"

"Eet would be weell if you did zee same," said the woman, sounding like a tourist from Tijuana, Mexico and Hamburg, Germany.

Spagg gave her a hard look and wandered into the dining room, where he accidentally spotted a net that, had it been any larger, could have snared a baby whale. "Hey," he called. "Wha'cha use this net for?"

"My hair."

The cop looked at her socket-like hair, and the other hair that was peeping through the nightgown. He tried to maintain his composure, but it didn't work. He started rapidly lifting his eyebrows up and down.

Pippilo withdrew from nosing around in a closet that produced a vacuum cleaner, a mop, a bucket, scouring powder, and various cleaning items. Then he spotted a box of mechanical toy mice stuck in the corner. "What'cha use these toy mice for?"

"I am zee cook. Zay are zee tastiers."

It made sense to the cop.

He couldn't see the second door, the one that produced the stairs to the attic where Van Dreelan had met his demise — and where Oscar was still waiting. But not seeing the second door wasn't fully the cops' fault, although they wouldn't have wanted to leave the room because of the parted nightgown. But the door leading up to the lair-like hideaway was hidden by a crudely hung, Persian rug that Pilar had tacked up before dragging Van Dreelan's body to the car. Close by the hanging rug there was a tiny box of thumbtacks, some small nails, a ruler, a hammer, and a leveler.

"How long did'ja say he stayed?" Pippilo asked, not attaching any significance to the rug, the ruler, the leveler, the hammer and the thumbtacks. To get a better look at what was under the nightgown — and what Spagg was still staring at, he stepped over them and repeated, "Hey, did'ja hear me? I said, how long did the officer of the law stay, lady?"

Occupied with the thought of another meal for her charge, the lady withdrew from studying the bigger man's neck and said, "I haff already told you zat."

"Well, tell me *zat* again," Pippilo said. "I'm hard o' hearin'."

"He come zee door, he tell me keep zee dumb cats quieet — which I repeet, I do not haff — now, how long zat take?"

"With your understandin' of the English language, it could take a week."

"You don't talk my Engleesh like zat."

"Just cool it, lady, an' ansa the question."

"I told you what I know," responded the fiery woman. "I am ti-eed of zee stupeed questions. I am ti-eed of you. I weel not answer more off zee stupeed questions. No'ting else. Now, *goh!*"

Spagg, in the interest of the nightgown, and not in the interest of duty, said, "We ain't in no hurry. An' we'll 'go' when we get good an' ready. Not one minnit before."

"What more you want?" responded Pilar, that hot theatrical temper rising higher, and continuing to massacre the English language. "You talk, talk, talk, talk, talk-talk. You look outside zee houze. You look inside zee houze. You go zee bazemeent. You go zee rooms. You search zee kitcheen, zee closeets, zee beethroom. You go zee ateek…" She stopped; she gave it a thought: "Noh, I do not have zee ateek. I will beeld zee ateek. You look all over zee houze. You come back, you talk-talk-talk some more. You ask zee stupeed questions about zee stupeed policemeen. You theenk I keednap him? You theenk I shack up him?!"

"Shack up with you?" Pippilo said. "He ain't *that* hard up."

Pilar sailed for the door and flung it open. "Goh!"

"I toldja we ain't leavin'!"

"You will leef my houze!"

"An' I said we *ain't* leavin'!"

Spagg, taking the role of peace-maker, gently interceded. "Okay, okay. We'll get outta this dump. Ain't nothin' here, anyway."

They made their way out to the porch and breezily flashed the lights around again. Pilar was still fuming by the door.

The two patrolmen gave the immediate area another quick shot and started to leave the porch.

"Oh, before we go, I wanna ask you somethin'," Pippilo said. "Because I got the feelin' you're tryin' to pull a fast one. We ain't stupid, lady. You said you was gonna build an attic?"

"I beeld tomorrow."

"This house's already got an attic. Whaddiya need another one for?"

"To geet to zee ateek."

"Oh," Pippilo said, peering back inside to look at the tiny box of thumb-tacks, the small nails, the ruler, the hammer, and the leveler that was near the part-falling rug. "Is that what them nails an' tools is for? In other words, you gotta build an attic to get to the attic?"

"Oui. Oui."

Not understanding the *oui-oui,* Spagg said, "If you gotta go, you gotta go, lady. Just don't be doin' no *wee-wee'n* out here."

The remark left the woman crossed-eyed.

The point made, and with the explanation of having to build an attic to get to the attic satisfying the two cops, they started to leave.

Pippilo had a final question. "Oh, before we go, when we first got here, you was just comin' in. Where were you?"

"Yeah," said Spagg, "who do you know t'be floatin' around the streets this time o'morning?"

"On zee bee-yew-tiful night like zees, what you expect star to bee do'ink? Never before zee bee-yew-tiful night like zees."

"That ain't answerin' the question, lady. Now, where were you?"

"An' what were you doin'?" added Spagg.

"It ees none off you bizz-a-nezz what I do."

"Whaddiya mean 'none of our 'bizz-a-nizz?!'" Spagg flared. "Any-thing that happens in this town is our *bizz-a-nizz!* An' as much as I hate t'say it, keepin' our eyes on creeps like you is our *bizz-a-nizz!* Now, can you parley-voo that?"

Pilar parley-vood it, all right — so much so that she slammed the door and came close to cracking Pippilo's foot in the process.

He hollered out: "You almost cracked my foot! Now, open that door and apologize or I'll cave it in."

The door didn't open. Pippilo waited. Mainly to capture another look at the parted nightgown, Spagg banged on the door again. A moment later Pilar opened the door, slowly. The hair-revealing nightgown swung with even more freedom, and she spoke with a remarkably nice change in attitude.

"You come back zee later. I will show you zee good time. I weel even cook zee breakfeest for zee two off you."

"Oh, really?" inquired Spagg, his eyes not leaving the lower part of the nightgown. "Breakfast — *and...*??"

"Oooh-la-la."

"Yum-yum-yum," said Spagg, who usually breakfasted on Royal Crown Cola and Fig Newtons, "Anything else on zee menu-ee?"

"Zee steamed rabeets," said the lady. "And whatever elze strike zee fan-cee."

Flashlighting their way down the walkway, and with neither of them wanting to reveal what was really on their minds, the short cop said, "Weird broad, huh?"

"A friggin' nut, if there ever was one," agreed the big cop. "Weird."

"Talkin' about wee-wee'n on her porch. What a sicko. She's worse than ol' lady Ina, with her talk about needin' a warm body for a used coffin."

"Didn't they used to be kinda palsy-walsy?"

"Yep," answered Pippilo. "One night when I was up to Mrs. Ina's, I think I heard her on the phone agreein' to sponsor some kind'a play or somethin' this nut was writin'."

They stopped curbside, leaned against car 101 and got set for another nightly chat under a still beautiful moon that captured neither man's concern. Spagg removed the nub of a cigar from his pocket and lit it.

"Y'know what that dame's trouble is? Huh?" Pippilo started, unwrapping another wad of used bubble gum from the glove compartment. "She could use a little. Notice how a li'l leg was showin' through that nightgown?"

"She looked like a bearskin rug underneath. But we showed her we wasn't interested, didn't we, Pip? We used restraint. An' nobody'll believe we did it."

"Not a soul."

"Pippo, I wouldn't touch that if you offered me that moon up there."

"Me neither," emphasized Pippilo, and lying with the same ease as the other cop. "But she could use a little. Ain't nothin' wrong with her that a li'l action couldn't straighten out."

"Hey, maybe...kno' what I mean?"

"Hey, we showed restraint. But, Spaggy..."

"Yuh?"

"Maybe we ought'a take her up on that offer. For breakfast, I mean."

"Yeah, breakfast only," said Spagg. "I mean, we're cops. We do gotta eat. An' ain't nothin' wrong with havin' a li'l breaky-poo with one'a the customers, is it, Pip?"

"We're the boys in blue. We're here to protect and serve."

"And that's all we do, Pippo. Serve the people."

"Duty, duty, duty."

"But I can tell she wants us, palsy. She *wants* us."

"She was practically beggin us, Spaggy."

"We didn't break, though."

"An' we won't," Pippilo reemphasized.

"Noooo way. No weakenin' of the flesh here, boobala," Spagg said, pulling at the nub of the cigar with emphasis. "But then again, Pippo, treat her nice and...va-voom-m-mmm. Y'know what I mean? Not that me an' you would do anything."

"Not with her we wouldn't."

"No way, Pippso. No way."

"But, hey, seriously, some of them old kooks'll give you a better run than some of the younger ones."

"I heard," Spagg said. "I heard."

"'Specially one of them old-time French stars," Pippilo said knowledgeably. "France is where that French-kissin' comes from, y'know."

"Y'kiddin'?" said a surprised Spagg.

"Naw. Straight stuff. I heard it on the radio. I mean, the women over there open up the ol' mouth, an' let'cha have it with the tongue. Imagine that."

"Ugh," Spagg said, frowning as if to gag. "That's about as distasteful as discoverin' two roaches in a Coke bottle."

"An' I heard it can get worse than that," said Pippilo. "They call it yodelin' in the canyon. You know, chop-chop."

"Ugh!"

"I don't know what the world is comin' to, Spaggy."

"I don't either, Pip. I just don't know."

"Clean livin' is out. Guys like us don't stand a chance any more."

"Y'right," said Spagg. "The whole American way is changin'. Things sure ain't what they used to be."

"We're at the end of the first year of the '50s, Spaggo."

"The future is here, Palsy."

"This is it," confirmed Pippilo. "Everything that needed to be invented is done been invented. The only thing left is for the people to go crazy."

"An' if you ask me, that's exactly what they're doin'. Not slowin' down, an' goin' crazy." Spagg bit on the nub of the cigar and spit the loose end onto the windshield of the car. "So, you're off'a all the young stuff?"

"I'm off'a *all* of it — young and old," said Pippilo, tugging his collar up to ward off an imagined chill and not necessarily appreciating the beauty of the night. "'Specially all outside stuff. I'm through. I've been doin' a lotta thinkin', Spaggy. Do you realize how much trouble you can get into foolin' around? I mean, forgettin' the home — with the wife and all'a that. F'instance, y'know what would happen if Mulkey, or the chief, or a councilman — or anybody, for that matter — even some crumbum from off the streets came around an' caught you nailin' somebody in the back seat, like we always do? You know what would happen? Huh? It'd be your throat, an' 10 or 15 years on the job would be down the tubes, just like that."

"Hey, an' so will 69 smacks a week."

"Sixty-nine smacks, an' change — an' all the benefits. An' it could happen, too. We could lose it all."

"Easily."

With more time on the force than any of the patrolmen, Pippilo said, "Sure. Think about it. Think'a how many times you've stopped a female on a simple traffic violation, an' she offers you a little to get off."

Spagg topped him. "Think'a how many times you've accepted."

"Sure," agreed Pippilo. "Think'a all the barhoppers who didn't get lucky — an' after the joints close, she sees you..."

"In your pretty midnight-blues," the policeman in the motorcycle uniform proudly added.

"Right. Lookin' good in your pretty blue uni's."

"An' all the power that goes with the uni's," Spagg agreed.

"It's somethin', ain't it? The power behind the badge. We can do anything with it. An' we got guns to back us up. That's what I like."

"Me too," said Spagg. "Guns an' authority, you can't beat it."

"What more can anyone ask for? — Guns, authority, and the law."

"But there's a price we gotta pay, pal," Spagg said. "There's always a price for the boys in blue."

"Yep. There's the drunks an' all the others we gotta deal with. The lonelies, the sickies, the crazies, the Commies..."

"Hey, an' don't forget them you-know-who's from across the tracks."

Pippilo agreed. "An' y'never can tell when they might go off. Thank heavens we don't got none on the department."

"We got a colored," said Spagg. "Clink Jefferson."

"Oh, him. I stay so far away from him, I almost forgot he was on the job."

"Same here," Spagg said. "I've been on the department what? — almost 14 years. One year less than you, an' I still ain't spoken to 'im."

"I don't speak to none of 'em. But, Spagg, let's be real. Jefferson ain't really no cop. He can't come across the tracks an' and make no arrests. He'd go to the clink or get kicked off the force, if he did anything like that."

"As he should," Spagg agreed.

"Right. But he sure ain't like us."

"Can't be. He's too dumb; ain't got nothin' upstairs, Pippo."

"Nothin'. As I said, he sure ain't like us," said Pippilo. "An' I'm gonna tell you somethin', Spaggy: It ain't easy bein' us."

"Never was, Pip. Never was — anyway you look at it. An' as cops, we're the last line of defense. We're the last of the good guys."

"An' from here on, this good guy is walkin' slow. I ain't sacrificin' my all no more."

"Same here, buddy-boy."

"You're talkin' to a changed man, Spaggo. I'm just gonna hang on for the twenty. Can't let that pension get away."

"Hey, the pension's the thing, all right. That's what it's all about. What is it we say? *Do the twenty an' collect the plenty.*"

"Yep. No more horsin' around from this boobala."

There was a moment or two more; Pippilo blew a small bubble from his gum, and they both slid into their respective cars.

Spagg stuck his head out the window. "So…about the dose, the Doc's gonna fix you an' the wife up, huh? Gonna give you's two's the shots?"

"Yeah."

"S'great," Spagg said. "So wha'cha gonna get the li'l lady for Xmas? Only a few more days left."

"I was thinkin' the shot would do it."

"Should."

"Wha'cha givin' Myrt?"

"My li'l sweetie? She likes antiques. I got an old nightstick in the cellar I was thinkin' about fixin' up for her...put a li'l polish on it, shine it up. Maybe I'll go over to the in-laws, find a card they got last year, an' give it to her. I might even wait 'til after Xmas, go over and find a newer one. Keep it modern."

"Sounds great," Pippilo said. "Boy, that TB yarn sure did the trick. Takes a load off my mind. It's great. Can't wait to tell the wife."

"Told'ja. Couple of the boys used it."

"What a lifesaver."

"Yep. Givin' her the shots for Xmas should really put you over."

"Big time. But I tell you, Spaggy, I've learned my lesson. From now on, it's the ol' straight an' narrow. I'm usin' the ol' bean from now on. From now on, you can call me Mr. Clean."

"Samee-samee."

"I am now Mr. Clean."

"You're usin' the ol' bean, kid. You're usin' th' ol' bean. An' like we said before, tonight we didn't weaken. We showed the ol' restraint."

"Yeah, we did," said Pippilo. "Yeah, we did."

Under a quiet, appreciative mood, the two cops drove off. Spagg delivered the transmission. "101 and 102 to headquarters: Regardin' Pilar, the cat lady, the situation is negative. Johnny Van Dreelan was there, but he departed the premises."

"Roger," said the radio. A moment later it followed up with Bucky giving the time-check.

15

The strength of being "Mr. Clean" didn't hold with Pippilo, nor did anything hold with Spagg. The new image had lasted all of seven minutes. Both men were crusing the streets with nothing but visions of what lay beneath the hair-revealing nightgown sponsored by the woman on Arbor Street — the woman neither of them would touch if offered the moon.

It was in the forefront of both minds to circle a few blocks, fake each other out, come back, and have a solo shot at the woman. But no sooner had Pippilo gotten to the intersection a few blocks north of the Greyhound bus terminal when, at the signal light, he looked over at a heavy-riding 1948 Packard that had pulled up in the next lane. In it was a woman in bathrobe and curlers who had just dropped someone off at the terminal. It didn't appear that she was a woman of easy virtue, but it was worth a shot. Pippilo leaned over and winked. The woman winked in return. He rolled the window down and motioned for the woman to do the same. She did.

Said the droopy-faced cop, stabbing at sweetness, "Hi."

"Hi," smiled the woman in return.

Connection made, the light changed, and the two cars rounded the corner in matchmaking unison and headed to the rear of the bus terminal.

Parked, Pippilo picked up the mike. "101 to Headquarters: I'm goin' out of service to check on a possible four-eight."

Spagg, on a slow cruise in his car, heard the transmission. He didn't pay it much attention, but the call did register a little something because a four-eight was either a robbery or a B&E, and ordinarily a robbery or a B&E — a *breaking and entering* — would necessitate a second car.

Not that the call had set off any bells and whistles, and not that he was looking for car 101, but driving by the bus terminal a few minutes later and thinking that, perhaps, there could have been a whiff of female action there before sneaking back to the Arbor Street address, Spagg happened to approach the terminal from the rear. Much to his delighted surprise, there was patrol car 101. Seeing it meant that he could now return to Arbor Street and take a solo shot at the woman without Pippilo's ever being the wiser.

But what slowed Spagg was the Packard parked next to the patrol car. The patrol car was rocking and squeaking, and knowing that Pippilo was up to something, Spagg parked, got out and crept up to the vehicle. Because the windows were steamed, it was difficult to get a good look, but the voices inside said it all.

Pippilo and the li'l lady were just about ready to go at it in the back seat.

"Pull 'em down just a li'l bit more, honey," nursed the cop.

"I'm trying to," said the woman, struggling. "But it's so close in here."

"Darlin', this ain't exactly the Waldorf-Astoria. Ain't you ever been in the back seat of a car before?"

"I've never done anything like this before," she said innocently. "Lift that leg up."

"Sure," said Pippilo. "What's your name, sweets?"

"Lydia," said the woman. Then she squeaked that something was wrong. "You've got bubble gum stuck all over the seat!" She shifted, then hollered, "Ouch! What's that thing sticking me?!"

Pippilo gave it a feel. "Sorry, darlin', it's my badge."

During the struggle, Spagg, laughing, had moved back to his vehicle. He laughed some more, because he was up to something. He got his first aid kit, took out a roll of tape, tore off a strip and tiptoed back to car 101.

The windows were still steamy, and the two lovers were still too engrossed in the back seat to notice, but, chuckling to himself, Spagg eased open the car's fly window, slipped an arm inside and got the mike. Quietly, he taped the talk button down, then slung it as close to the back seat as he could get it and tiptoed back to his car.

Pippilo and Lydia were moving in for the final turn.

"Ummm, it's kinda long," she said.

"Long?? Hold up a sec. Lemme feel," said the cop. "Lydia, that's my gun."

"And this other little round thing I'm feeling? Is this you?"

"It's a bullet, babycakes."

"Good grief! Don't you ever take any of that stuff off?"

"Not while I'm on duty, Sweet Lumps."

Back at the station, McShayne had been outside taking a much needed breather. His eyes were absently scanning the quiet streets.

Since the sergeant of the desk was outside, he was missing what was coming over the speaker, but not Bucky. When the first sounds came crackling through, he sneaked into the ticket room, polished off the first pint of rum, and started working on the second. When he came back out, he found the little emergency speaker and hooked it up so that he could be closer to the action. It was all joy. He had gotten so excited and was laughing so hard that he dropped his dentures and was banging on the desk.

Through the door McShayne saw Bucky slapping at the desk and laughing. Moderately curious, but unable to hear what was taking place, the sergeant resumed starring at the empty streets.

On a roll, Pippilo was moaning in ecstasy, touching nerves that had been dormant for years. Not wanting to miss anything, Bucky turned the speaker up.

"Oooooweee, baby, ooooooh-oooooohhh."

"Hey, cop," Lydia said, dryly.

"W-w-w-what?"

"It ain't in."

Going faster than a rabbit, Pippilo said, "Y-y-y-yes it is!"

"Ugh," said an unmoved Lydia.

"W-w-wha's the matter, baby?" Pippilo vibrated. "Can'cha feel it?

The Earth is crumblin'!"

"I thought that was your thumb."

Bucky rocked with more laughter. McShayne, hearing him, broke off his thoughts, turned to see what was going on and headed back inside. The voices snapped at him. Then there was the one long groan that leaped through both the big speaker above the door and the little emergency speaker that Bucky had placed behind the desk. With the sounds bouncing off the walls, the Sergeant stormed behind the desk, grabbed the mike and almost broke a blood vessel. He wanted to get on Bucky about his rummy breath, but he shouted into the mike.

"Who is it?! Dammit, who is it?! Dammit to hell, I wanna know who the hell is on the goddamn mike! 101! Two? Three? It's gotta be you, Mickey! It's gotta be you! Damn your hide!" He broke it off and then found himself screaming louder. "SPAGG! PIPPILO! — JOHNNY VAN DREE…"

"Er, Sarge," Bucky tried to interrupt, gently.

The sergeant continued to yell into the mike.

Bucky tried it again. McShayne still wouldn't listen. Fearing that the sergeant was going to break a blood vessel, the stringbean policeman yelled at the top of his lungs: "SAAARGGGE!"

"WHAT THE HELL DO YOU WANT!?"

"Er…er…Sarge, if one of the mikes in the cars is open, we can't transmit," said Bucky, discreetly unplugging the emergency speaker and cutting the main speaker off. "An' the other cars can't transmit, either. Everything is blocked, 'cept for the one car."

Bucky was absolutely right.

The beet-red desk sergeant almost broke his neck kicking at the cold, dead microphone.

The only sound to be heard in the station after that was the old teletype unit that sputtered to life for a second.

It, too, then died.

Spagg had laughed himself hoarse. He was now miles away from the bus terminal. He knew that when Pippilo was through, and could see that his mike had been taped open, and knowing that everything that had happened in the car had been aired in the station, he was likely to shoot the offender. At first the big cop decided to drive to the station to get a reaction — but no, that wouldn't do. McShayne was apt to be on fire.

But Spagg was wrong. The desk sergeant was not on fire. He was whipped. The grandfatherly/Santa Claus look had given way to serious wear and tear, and he had slumped down into the big swivel chair. He was looking like a hogtied chicken. Here it was 0420 in the morning — with almost four more hours to go, and on a shift where absolutely nothing ever happened — and it seemed that the world was caving in on him.

The sergeant of the desk couldn't take much more.

Bucky gently uprighted the mike and tried to bring the sergeant back. "Er...what about Van Dreelan, Sarge?"

McShayne didn't hear him. Even if he had, he couldn't say anything at that moment.

Bucky took advantage of the lull to slip into the ticket office to swipe another quick nip from the second bottle. Once in there, he had a change of heart and decided to take two. He came back out and waited for a minute. Feeling that the time was right, he bent down into the sergeant's ear with the same question. "Sarge...what about Dutch?"

Apparently the whiff of alcohol worked its magic. But the mind was slipping. "Who?" the sergeant asked.

"Johnny Van Dreelan. 'Member, we was tryin' to track him down?"

"Put in a call to Lillian McLauren's Diner," McShayne said, trying to snap out of the lapse.

"Already did. He ain't been in."

"Did you try him at home?"

"Uh-huh."

"And, Bucky, and...?!"

"An' no word, Sarge. An' 104 had to pass by his house in order to get to the 88 at the Flo-Control warehouse. Georgie didn't see the car. I asked him."

"Did Georgie check his garage?"

"Don't you r'member, Sarge? He ain't got one."

McShayne, depleted, said, "And you said Georgie Tetrollini in 104 had to pass by the house?"

"Yessir."

"Get 'im."

"He ain't reported back from lunch yet."

"He hasn't?"

"Nope."

"How long's he been out?"

Bucky checked the log. "The better part of an hour."

"What?!" said McShayne, his temper rising again, and, as he had promised his beloved wife, trying to stay from using coarse language, "Get on the phone an' tell Georgiovone Tetrollini to get his rear end down to this station right now! And I mean: *Right now!*"

Bucky flipped through the card box, found the home number and dialed. While waiting for the phone to be answered, he turned the stationhouse speaker back up.

Marge answered her telephone with the sleepiest of hellos.

"Hi, Margie-Marge," Bucky said alertly. "Hi'ya feelin' this mornin'? Same here. Listen, li'l darlin', is Georgie there?"

"No, Bucky, he's with you, working."

"What I mean is, has he been there for lunch?"

Marge said she didn't know, and asked Bucky to hold on while she went down and checked — which she did. She came back upstairs and said to Bucky, "He hasn't been here, because the soup and sandwich I made for him is still on the table. If he comes in, shall I have him call?"

"Have him to get in touch right away."

"Is anything wrong, Bucky?" she inquired with a trace of disquiet in her voice.

"Yeah," Bucky said tactlessly. "We wanna know where he's been all night."

Bucky hung up. His statement, of course, worried the hell out of Tetrollini's sensitive wife, and it was for sure she wouldn't sleep for the rest of the night. He turned to the sergeant, and, as he did, with both men too absorbed to register, the speaker said, "101 — back in service. Time 0438."

"Marge said Georgie ain't there, Sarge," Bucky said. "An' she don't think he's been there, 'cause the soup an' sandwich she made for him is still on the table."

McShayne automatically reached for the mike. "Headquarters to 104, come in, Four?!"

The patrol car was in the quiet park, and the patrolman's body was slowly icing behind the wheel. The radio remained loud and clear. "Come in, Four," the sergeant's voice continued. "This is the Elton Head Police Department, Badge 71 to car 104; come in, Four! Tetrollini!!"

Getting no response, and now not knowing exactly what to do, McShayne rose from the desk, pushed his stiff fingers through his silver hair, rubbed his chest around the heart area and began to wonder. He reached for the mike again. "Headquarters to 103, come in."

With Mickey Corbbo it was useless to continue the call. There was no doubt in the sergeant's mind he was off someplace sleeping. Corbbo was going to have hell to pay when he came in. His job was in jeopardy.

The sergeant's mind shifted to Johnny Van Dreelan. Again he rubbed his chest in the heart area and reached for the mike. "H'quarters to 105, come in. Come in, Five."

As it had been with Corbbo in car 103 and Tetrollini in car 104, the radios were working but the men were not. Johnny Van Dreelan's radio was working fine as well, but unlike Corbbo and Tetrollini, his body was not in the car.

"What in the hell is going on, around here?" said the sergeant.

McShayne had not gotten a single response from either of the three cars. It was more than troubling. Bucky was now in the background, with his back turned to the sergeant. He was on the telephone carrying on a muffled conversation with someone and was mentioning something about a key being under a mat. And so basically the desk sergeant was talking to himself.

"I can't understand it," said the sergeant — not overly harsh, but through a disappointing befuddlement that, had it been anyone else, would have brought tears. "I simply cannot understand what'n the hell's going on. I don't understand what's gotten into these guys. This shift is treated better than any shift on the department and look what happens. I protect 'em, I go to bat for 'em, I do everything in the world for 'em, and now look at this. Three cars out, an' on shift, where *nothing* ever happens. I don't believe it. I simply don't believe it. I can't explain it. Three cars, out. I can't reach a single one of them. Corbbo. Van Dreelan. Tetrollini — all screwin' off some place. I can't reach not *one* of them. Three radio patrol cars out. *Three cars on my watch — gone!* I can't believe this night! It's been enough to turn me into a full fledged cadaver. It's got to be something in the air. There's no other way to explain it! Nothing has gone right. Everything: *wrong!* I can't even reach my own goddamned house. My *house*, I can't reach!" The sad man didn't know what else to say. He sat and leaned a weary head on the back of the chair. He tried to rest his mind. But the cars came back. "103, 104, 105. Three cars — out! The way things are going I wouldn't be surprised if every goddamn car on the shift goes out. And the drivers, too!"

The sergeant muttered something to the effect that this station is a goddamn killer, and continued: "Over 40 years on the force — *40* years — half of 'em on this desk, and I've never had anything like this to happen. And it's happening on a shift where *nothing* ever happens. *Nothing!* But I'll bet one thing. I'll bet my life it'll never happen again, because some heads are gonna roll. I mean every blasted word of it! — Heads are gonna *roll!"*

Bucky, having finished with his muffled telephone conversation had tiptoed upstairs to the bathroom, eased back down, and now he went into the ticket room again. This time he took a hard swallow from a bottle that was getting uncomfortably low. Putting on his cap and coat, he took another jolt, almost cornering the bottle, and stepped from the room.

"Er...Sarge?"

"What is it, Bucky?"

Coming to the desk, he eased into: "Er...speakin' of *roll*, can I go to lunch now? It's already later than I usually go."

McShayne was set to fire a response. He thought about his heart and took the low approach. It was not, however, too low. "With all'a these problems I've got here, and you're talking about lunch?! And you usually bring a Thermos!"

"But I didn't put the right kinda soup in it, Sarge. An' I gotta eat."

"And so has that parking-meter peein', panhandling, drunk upstairs you haven't checked on yet."

"I'll get to 'er, Sarge."

"You said that *four hours* ago!"

"I've been busy, Sarge. You said it yourself, this is been a night of nights. Maybe the moon…"

"Don't say another word to me about that goddamn moon! It's enough to make me sick!"

Bucky gave him a moment to settle down, then again asked permission to go to lunch.

"All right," McShayne unhappily surrendered. "Go to Mac's Diner. Be back in a half hour."

"But, Sarge, I can't do that. I'm expected at home."

"Who in the hell's expectin' you? You ain't married, and your only livin' relative is…"

Bucky interrupted. "But I'm still expected at my apartment, Sarge."

Again McShayne was about to explode. Wisely, he held up. "Then go home. An' hurry back."

Bucky buttoned up hurriedly and hopped to the door. Before going out, he turned and asked, "Er…Sarge. 'Til I pay a visit to my maw's house sometime in the mornin', can I put the touch on you for a small loan?"

McShayne picked up the county telephone book and sent it sailing for the skinny man's head.

Fortunately the thick book missed the head, but it hit the wall with such force that it knocked the picture of the old-time cops askew and seemed to have awakened Charlie Wong, who was all the way on the other side of town.

The switchboard buzzed again. McShayne slid along the desk to answer it. It was Charlie Wong. The desk sergeant was too miffed to speak. Charlie did the talking. He was in trouble. He didn't know where he was. The only thing he remembered was that he had been walking the streets, somebody had approached him, and he ended up in that same somebody's house where he was having the time of his life. At the height of the party, shortly after he had called Bucky saying that he was a happy man — tipsy, and feeling no pain — Charlie was invited to bed. Not being one to turn any bed action down, he lovingly complied. In fact, he was still in bed. Nothing wrong with that — except that Charlie, his back turned, couldn't see his undercover companion who was snoring loudly and happily.

He couldn't see, but he had his suspicions.

In one of the rare times when he wasn't smiling, Charlie was lying stiff on the other side of the bed. He had sent an arm out to quietly dial the phone on the nightstand. His body language was tight, and his worried eyes were riveted on the two pairs of footwear that were parked part-way under the bed.

Charlie had a very good reason to worry. The small, wing-tipped shoes were his. The other pair obviously were not. Worse, they were combat boots — size 16, triple-E.

His voice weighted with the terror of error, his eyes still glued to the triple-Es, Charlie's mind was shooting back to '37 when he was outrunning the tips of the Japanese bayonets during the rape of Nanking. His rear end was tender and there was no *walla* in his voice. He said to the sergeant, "Sargentoooo…I thin-n-n-k Wong no get luck-e-e-ee, Sargentooo."

"You sack of fried rice!" McShayne shouted on the other end. "*Get off* — and *stay* off'a my back!!"

Beyond Charlie Wong, there was another annoyance on the surface of the sergeant's mind. All night long, as he did every night, Bucky had been spending too much time in the ticket office. The sergeant knew why. Tonight it called for action. With Bucky gone, and without missing a beat, he stepped away and went into the small room that was just off the desk. He looked in the bottom drawer and found one of the bottles Bucky had been sipping on all night. It was exactly what he was looking for. The sergeant held the bottle up to the light, looked at the color of the light rum that was almost down to the corner of the bottle and marched it upstairs.

⌛

About 20 minutes after the desk sergeant had marched back to the ticket room with the bottle, Bucky was pulling up in front of his apartment. It was on a narrow street with deep gutters. The place was less than two steps above a Skid Row dwelling, but to Bucky it was home. He was jovial, whistling, and feeling no pain when he pressed the elevator button and waited as it slowly creaked down.

When the elevator arrived, strong and damp with the odor of urine, he merrily went up to the third floor and, if a bit wobbly, continued whistling down the long corridor to the door marked 3-B. It was his room; there was romantic music coming from his room. That was something that had never happened. In all his years on the department, Bucky Simmons had never had a romantic visitor.

With sparks in his eyes and getting set for what was to be a historic night, the unshaven, bean-pole policeman spit-patted his few strands of hair and reached for his dentures. They were bent and uncomfortable, but he stuck with them and leaned a confirming ear to the door. He chuckled to himself and looked under the mat for the key. "Oh-oh," he said, lightly teasing himself, and remembering that there was no key under the mat because when he had gotten the call at the station shortly before leaving, he had told the visitor to use the key to get in. And as he had told her during that muffled conversation, she was to "go right on in and make yourself at home."

She did.

When Bucky entered his apartment, the bouncing young miss was popping her fingers near the portable record player she had brought with her. With her back to him, he waltzed over to where she was and grabbed her playfully around the waist. Coat off, she was still wearing the smock. He planted a distilled smooch on her neck and uttered a dove-like "My li'l coochie-poo. What would I have done if you hadn't called me, you li'l poochi-poo? And you dress so nicely. I like dresses when there's a lot of room in 'em."

She wiggled her behind playfully. "Only for you, Buck-poo. An' I had to call you, because I could tell you are all man."

"Yup," giggled, Bucky, weaving.

"I knew that everything I've wanted to know about love — and *loving* — I knew I could learn from you. And you know what?"

"What, my li'l moo-moo?"

"You sound just as cute in person as you do on the phone, Bucky-poo-poo. You sound just like a movie star."

"Yup, an' I didn't know you'd fit into my arms so nicely, you li'l moochi-moo," Bucky smooched. "You li'l kissy-face, ever since you came to town I've been waitin' to get my hands on you."

"Ummmhummm, well now is the time," she coochie-poo'd, and turned. Her body was still in his arms. "Like I asked on the phone, Bucky-poo-poo, did you get the money for my car, dumplin's? Your li'l shugie-shug really needs the money."

"There's something I gotta tell you, Smoochie-moo."

"What, Hon-bun?" The teenager's voice had gotten a little stronger.

"I didn't get the money."

"What?!" Carol said, as if suffering from a bad case of audio deficiency. "Come again? You didn't...No. I didn't hear that...Carol, you did not hear this man say he didn't get the money. He could not have said that. He couldn'a..." She broke it off, came back, "Did I hear you say...no, watch it Carol, he didn't say that." She charged with full force. *"Did I hear you say you didn't get the money?!!"*

"But I'm workin' on it, Coochie-poo."

"And so am I, Bucky-boy."

It was the second time that night that Carol had heard the words. She didn't take it lightly. She hauled off and belted the cop — smack in the eye. She picked up her portable record player and started for the door. She changed her mind. She looked at the bent-over Bucky, lifted the record player and tried to cream him over the head with it. She left in a huff. She had to. Daylight was coming and she hadn't picked up a dime.

16

By law and by reason the Flamingo should have been closed hours before it did. It was not an issue of great concern, because Jess had Ernest Mulkey on his side and neither closing the five or six bars in town nor checking liquor licenses was high on the list of priorities in Elton Head. Even so, there were one or two private houses that illegally functioned as bars and never closed. Before purchasing and renaming the Flamingo, Jess Brown had opened such a place shortly after he had arrived in town.

With an extended gut that pressed hard against a too-tight belt, Jess came from Roanoke, Virginia. He ended up in Elton Head because he had a sister there whom he had temporarily moved in with after having been run out of Roanoke because of too many run-ins with the law. The sister's husband never liked him, but lay low because Jess was the wife's younger brother.

A gambler, a former drunk and part-time preacher, Jess had always operated on the other side of the law, but vowed that he was going to change his ways once he had settled in Elton Head. The first thing he did was to open an after-hours place. One of his customers was Ernest Mulkey, the city manager.

Mulkey was a former habitué of the old place, but he and management had fallen out of favor with each other when they bounced him for non-payment of bills.

Not paying tabs was not an uncommon occurrence for the Elton Head city officials. Similar to the police sponging coffee and doughnuts in restaurants, they often went into various places, ordered, ate, and departed, leaving behind nothing more than their good wishes. In some cases they didn't take time to leave their good wishes. Certainly Ernest Mulkey wouldn't. The big-shot city manager would dine, go into the bar area after dining and spend the evening ordering rounds for the house. If the bartender was slow in pouring, Mulkey would let him have it in no uncertain terms. Once he made the mistake of cursing out the owner while a roomful of customers looked on. Embarrassed, the owner ordered Mulkey to pay up and get out. Mulkey didn't pay, but he did leave — taking neither the demand for payment nor the embarrassing ejection lightly.

In his office the next day, the city manager moved fast. When he had finished moving, the Flamingo was up for sale. The liquor license was being yanked because management had, quote, violated too many city ordinances. *City ordinances,* interestingly. Not state laws. It didn't matter. Ernest Mulkey had won another one. He wanted the club for himself, but suffered a cash-flow problem. With something up his sleeve, he went to Jess, telling him that the Flamingo was up for sale and, better still, that it could be bought for a can't-miss price. Neither the license nor the hours of operation would ever be a problem. His status elevated by even talking to Mulkey on a business deal, Jess immediately went to his brother-in-law for funding. In less than 90 days after the Mulkey ejection, Jess Brown was in business. In business with him was Ernest Mulkey. The city manager was his silent partner.

But anyone with good sense should have known it wasn't a partnership that was designed to last. Mulkey never liked partners — silent or not. He liked the boisterous, country-talking Jess even less. And when Jess turned the club into a dive, Mulkey became furious. He was working on gaining sole ownership shortly after the first of the year.

When the man from Roanoke, Virginia, finally turned out the Flamingo's lights and locked up for the night, he came out the rear door, stretched, and got into the garish old Cadillac, which was complete with mud flaps and two fox tails that hung from the antenna. As he had done in front, for some reason Jess took a brief look for Danny Carlsson. He didn't see him. But he had seen him earlier. That was when the rookie patrolman had come back on post and had sauntered past the Flamingo's front window. Pretending not to see him, Jess had grabbed a pail of water and aimed it out the door, almost splashing the policeman. Jess then popped out the door, laughed, apologized insincerely and tried to get the young man's goat even more by chuckling: "Glad to see you back on the job, li'l boy blue."

Carlsson said nothing in return.

"Say, that r'minds me. Didn't I hear you tell that ol' smoky — ol' Smoky Joe that you was gonna get me?"

The young cop said: "I did. And I will, Mr. Brown."

Jess laughed; the rookie walked away quietly.

The reason Jess didn't see the rookie policeman now was that when he left earlier, he had gone around to the rear and positioned himself in a darkened doorway just a few doors down and across from where the Caddy was parked. His final words to Jess were still on his mind.

Carlsson was still holding the position when the Caddy backed away from the Flamingo's rear door and pulled slowly forward down the alley. His eyes remained on the taillights as they narrowed and eventually faded out of sight. Knowing that the car would eventually go around to Main Street, the rookie moved for the first time.

Without even checking, he coolly sauntered off to the callbox, swinging easy with the nightstick.

Both halves of the big metal cellar door to Mr. Wilson's dress shop were upright. They were not supposed to be open, but they were. Jess was not supposed to stop, but he did. As Carlsson had presumed, the Caddy came to a stop on Main Street. It had to. The upright cellar doors were simply too inviting for a greedy man to pass up.

Avarice had the man rolling the window down and staring at the metal halves. Knowing that this was the policeman's beat and that it was possible he might be checking the area again, Jess pulled the vehicle around to the rear, almost to the exact spot where Tetrollini had earlier parked car 104 when he returned to make the illegal entry. The owner of the Flamingo looked around again, got his flashlight and quietly got out of the Caddy and crept back around to the front. To the upright doors he went, checking and looking all the way. He had no way of knowing, since he and the old man had never talked to each other, but it was almost as if he knew Mr. Wilson kept his money in the cellar. Even if he didn't know money was down there, surely he would find some fixture or something he could make use of.

Jess spotlighted his way down to the bottom step. He was surprised at how much junk the old man kept down there, but what frightened him were the mannequins. There were so many of them, and they were so eerie, too spooky and lifelike in a darkened cellar — and, interestingly, a cellar now devoid of Tetrollini's dropped flashlight.

As he continued to uncomfortably flashlight his way around, the beam hit the old display case. Surely, Jess thought, there had to be something in the case worthwhile taking. Looking closer, he saw that there wasn't much he could use. Scattered about was old costume jewelry, one or two broken trinkets, and a broken watch. There was nothing else. Without wanting to waste the effort, the big man pocketed the watch and the trinkets and pushed the light forward. It hit another set of mannequins. They glowed with more eeriness. The eyes were cold, blank — penetrating. The most frightening one was the one with the unusual auburn hair and cover-girl looks. Jess stared at it curiously and darted the light on it.

Moving over, he saw the dress form with the metal box hanging from underneath. Interesting, he thought. He crept closer. And closer. Something *had* to be in the box he concluded, still inching in. Suddenly his toe hit something. A mannequin, he thought. No. The pawing foot said that it was something else. Without looking down, he kicked at it. It was heavy, but it rolled a little. And it made a noise. Jess sent the beam down. It was a metal base. It had to be moved out of the way. Touching it, the big man discovered that it was damp. A little of the dampness rubbed off on the hand. It was red and sticky. He put it to his nose. It smelled. Clothing dye, it had to be. Dismissing the thought, he moved forward to the box that hung loosely from the dress form with the rod cemented in the floor. Trying to inch closer, the big man stubbed his foot on something that felt like another mannequin. He kicked at it. It wouldn't move. He kicked at it again. Still it wouldn't move. It was kind of soft — pliant-like; there was nothing about it that had the hardness of a metal base. This time he toed at it. There was no movement, but, using the foot, he felt there was a frightening familiarity to the form. He toed at what felt like arms, then legs.

Moving on, the big man's foot touched a bigger lump. It had a rise to it; and on the rise, it felt like a belly. It was far-fetched, but it felt like a human belly. The big man started sweating. He sent the beam down; he looked down. The dead man's eyes were transfixed. They were staring directly up at him. Jess, frozen, started sweating like a madman. *Help!* he wanted to scream. *"He-l-l-l-p-p-p m-e-e-e-e!!!"* His lips moved, but there was no sound in his throat. The legs helped him now. They started to move back. Soon they were ready to do more. Breathing hard, the Flamingo man back-pedaled for the cellar doors, knocking over mannequins and boxes. He stumbled for the hard concrete stairs, and as he fought to scramble up, he ran smack into pairs of police legs. Gripping two of the legs, barely able to speak, he sputtered, "Th — th...the man...down...down there; he's...he's d-d-dead. Mr...Mr. WWWilson is dead..."

The rookie policeman, standing quietly at the top of the cellar stairs with patrolmen Pippilo and Spagg by his side, said, "And who killed him, Jesse?"

It was not so much a question as it was an indictment.

⧖

Jess didn't like being in the patrol room, or squad room, as it was called in the old days, and for a man who had done nothing to cause a man's death and was strongly tied to the city manger, he was getting a little testy. He also didn't like the idea that the three policemen had brought the dress form with the metal base along with them. Of course he had touched it. But the idea, fed by the rookie, that he had used it on old man Wilson was preposterous.

McShayne, adding to what Carlsson had said, figured that Mr. Wilson, having been called down to his store earlier, probably had some work to do and sent the wife home with the intention of calling her later. It was likely, McShayne further figured, that the old man didn't want to disturb her at the later hour in the morning, and so he decided to sleep in the store and was awakened by the burglar.

But the desk sergeant was not convinced of Jess's guilt or innocence. He did explain that if Jess were anyone else, he would have been upstairs in the interrogation room waiting for the examining detectives to arrive at the station, and not sitting in the patrol room, answering easy questions and sipping coffee.

Jess countered that if they were being that courteous, he should have been home.

There was a different kind of tightness in the room. Both Pippilo and Spagg were seated at the corners of the patrol room's linoleum-covered table with the man who was now a suspect. McShayne was standing. Bucky, semi-sobered by the bang on the head, was also standing, only he was near the narrow corridor that led to the desk up front. He was keeping an ear out for the phone and at the same time trying to hide a black eye and two criss-crossing Band-Aids that topped his nearly bald head.

The most relaxed person in the room was Danny Carlsson. Jacket open, he was standing next to the water cooler, generally acting as though the world couldn't have been a better place.

What had slowed the procedure and made the tightness different was that Jess had spent most of the time talking about his under-the-table partner-ship with City Manager Mulkey.

To be accurate, mentioning Ernest Mulkey's name to any city employee struck terror in the hearts of most, and if it didn't do that, certainly it elicited a certain amount of fear, or at least a respectful ear. McShayne was not worried, because his days on the department were few. Even if his days were not numbered, it is doubtful that the sergeant would have buckled on hearing the man's name, as did everyone else on the department. But even at that hour in the morning, Pippilo, Spagg, and Bucky were impressed with Jess's association with the man. They tiptoed around the issue as though trying to prevent egg yolks from breaking.

Carlsson, of course, couldn't have cared less.

The silence held for a while, then McShayne, again not certain of the man's guilt, asked, "All, I'm askin', Jess is what did you go down in the cellar for?"

"Dem, I told you. I went down there 'cause the doors was open, an' I thought, maybe somebody was robbin' the place."

"But that's what bothers me, Jess," McShayne said. "You said you had just seen Carlsson on the corner. Why didn't you report what you saw to him?"

"Because," Jess said, having answered the question before, "I didn't see him when I was leavin'. I looked for 'im."

"Okay, then. Why were you looking for him?"

"I just was."

Carlsson broke his silence. "Do you make it a habit of looking for a patrolman when you close up, Jess? I've seen you close the bar before — several times. You've never wanted anything. You never said anything. It never looked like you were looking for me."

"Nobody's talkin' to you," Jess responded.

"It was a pretty fair question, Jess," McShayne said. "Why would you be looking for a cop?"

"Like I said, l just was," Jess said glumly.

"And you didn't see him?"

"No."

Now McShayne was getting a bit more serious. If Jess were telling the truth and hadn't seen the patrolman, why was he looking for him tonight? The conclusion had to be drawn that he wouldn't have been looking for anyone if his intentions were honest, or at least if he didn't know something was up.

"Listen, Dem…"

"*Sergeant* McShayne," the sergeant said, maintaining distance. "It's *Sergeant* Dempsey O. McShayne, Jess."

"Oh, come off of it," Jess flared. "What the hell are you tryin' to pull?"

"Murder is serious business, Mr. Brown," McShayne said.

"But you _know_ I didn't kill anybody!"

"Calm down, now, Jess, calm down," Spagg said, breaking his silence.

Carlsson, patiently sipping water from a paper cup, and now getting a bit more respect than before, calmly said to Jess, "Ready to empty your pockets, Jess?"

"You slimeball," Jess retorted hotly.

"Just empty the pockets, Jess, that's all," McShayne said. "Just empty the pockets. No names, no accusations. Just empty the pockets."

"Why?" Jess said, calming down a bit. "I've already told you, all I got on me is the day's take. An' it's from my own cash register."

"The pockets, Jess. The pockets," McShayne insisted.

It was something Jess simply did not want to do. True, he did have the Flamingo receipts in his pockets. But Carlsson knew that he had something else. The suspect tried to appeal to his acquaintance.

"Look, Dem...can I talk to you alone for a second?" Jess pleaded.

"Sergeant McShayne," the desk sergeant again corrected.

"Okay, 'Sergeant McShayne,'" Jess said, wanting to make a deal. "Look, can I talk to you?"

"Not until the pockets are empty and all the contents are on the table, Jess."

"All right, then," Jess said, threateningly. "Get Ernie Mulkey on the phone."

McShayne couldn't be threatened. "Empty his pockets for him," he ordered.

Before Pippilo and Spagg could carry out the order, Jess dug into his pockets and did it for them. He slammed the receipts down on the table and waited. Carlsson walked over and whispered something to the sergeant, causing him to say: "All the pockets, Jess. I want you to empty all the pockets."

Angrily, Jess went digging. This time he came up with the items he had taken from Wilson's cellar.

"Sergeant," Carlsson said, "I saw that watch and the other items in Mr. Wilson's display case down in the cellar when I was checking the place out earlier, before Georgie Tetrollini arrived at the store. Since the dead man can't talk, I'll bet Mrs. Wilson can vouch for who owns them."

McShayne didn't need any more evidence. It certainly was enough to put a hold on the man. "I guess that's it," he said.

Jess was flustered. "Them things don't prove a damn'd thing!"

"The prints on the murder weapon should prove to the contrary," Danny Carlsson said, casually moving over and standing next to the dress form. "There is blood on the base of this thing. And you do have blood on your hands, Mr. Brown."

"Book 'im," McShayne ordered.

Jess was livid. He sprang from the chair, shouting, "I wanna talk to Mulkey! Get Ernie Mulkey on the phone!"

McShayne ignored it. "Consider yourself under arrest, Mr. Brown."

"You rotten, graft-takin' sonovabitch! I'll have your job for this!"

Jess continued to rant and rave. McShayne didn't say anything. He strolled back up front to the desk.

As Spagg and Pippilo went to arm Jess to the booking room, he tried to break free and lunge at Carlsson. "You punky sunovabitch! You're behind this! You set me up! You sonov…!"

The two cops restrained him, while the rookie maintained his cool.

"Like the sergeant said, Jess," Carlsson said, unruffled, "murder is serious business. *Anybody's* murder."

He couldn't have felt better saying it. Maybe there was a little more work to do; maybe a little more checking in the Wilson cellar; maybe having it out with Georgie Tetrollini when he checked in the morning. Whatever the case, it was not a worry. A murder was being avenged.

Danny Carlsson looked up. It was as if he were looking beyond the ceiling. He gave a little smile and relaxed.

He knew the Soldier Boy was smiling back.

A few minutes had passed. Up front, the desk sergeant stepped away from looking in the bottom drawer of the desk in the ticket room. He was there rechecking Bucky's bottle. Returning to the desk, he called back to the patrol room, "Carlsson!"

Cap off, jacket still open, Carlsson sauntered up front. "Yes, sir?"

"How are you feeling?" McShayne asked, turning easily in his chair.

The question caught the cop off guard. McShayne, of course, knew that it would. It was a strange question from the desk sergeant, though. The rookie was concerned. McShayne had never asked anyone how he felt, and he certainly had never asked *him*. He knew there was something behind it.

"Fine, sir," said Carlsson, and waited for the other shoe to drop.

"I want to go over a point or two before you leave," McShayne said with disarming casualness.

"Sure," Carlsson said, instead of his customary *Yes, sir.*

"To begin with, why is it you didn't see that opened cellar door?"

The rookie was ready, but took his time answering. "I didn't see the doors, Sergeant, because they weren't open. Tetrollini can bear witness to that. He came down on the security check, remember?"

"And what were you doing when Georgie Tetrollini arrived?"

"Checking the place out. That's how I knew the watch and trinkets were in the display case in the cellar. I was down there."

"And you're positive about that?"

"Yes, sir. You can ask Tetrollini."

The sergeant digested it and asked, "Did you see Tetrollini after he met you on the security check?"

"Only once."

"And when was that?"

"When he came down asking me to keep an eye out for Corbbo."

"And did you ever see Corbbo?"

"No, sir."

"When you called in on the callbox asking for assistance, did you know who it was that went down into Wilson's cellar?"

"No, sir."

"But had it been a burglar — as it turned out to be — and you actually *saw* the burglar going down into the cellar, and you didn't try to apprehend him, wouldn't that be wrong?"

"I don't think so, Sergeant."

"Well, then, you've got a lot to learn."

"Why is that, Sergeant?"

"You don't think it's strange to let a burglar go down into a merchant's cellar, burglarize it while you leave, and then you come back? Expecting him to be there?"

Carlsson could have answered and at least argued the point, but he didn't.

McShayne wasn't finished. "One other thing. It's impossible to see the Wilson store from the box you called in on — the one at the north end. If you were standing near it, as you said, how could you tell if someone were making an entry? I mean, even with that bright moon out there, that would still be a little hard on the eye, wouldn't it? Seeing through buildings?"

"It would be," Carlsson said confidently. "But I think you misunderstood what I said when I made my statement earlier, Sergeant."

"Refresh my memory. What exactly did you say?"

"I said I had a suspect in view, and so as not to arouse suspicion, I purposely remained at the callbox — to establish myself. Like a decoy..."

"Why would decoying be necessary if the man had already gone down into the cellar?"

"I didn't know if the burglar was working alone or not. He could've had a lookout."

"Oh, I see," said the sergeant. "Then what'd you do?"

"After having established myself at the call box, I went back to Wilson's — to check it out again, and then I returned to the box. I had to. There was no other way to call the station. I called for backup on a hunch, and then went back to the store again. It was a decoy tactic that worked."

"But a rather unorthodox procedure, don't you think?"

"Yes, sir. But it paid off."

"I'm sure it has," McShayne said, unconvinced.

The desk sergeant looked at the unbuttoned pea jacket. "Now that that's over, I trust you're going back on post — to stay this time."

It should have been a negative response, but Carlsson didn't say anything. McShayne took note of it. He got a form and started writing. While writing, he quite rightly asked, "You don't think much of this department, do you, Danny?"

"No, sir, I don't," Carlsson said easily, and probably because the sergeant had referred to him by his first name — something that had never happened before. He added, "I don't care for you either, Sergeant."

The rookie was waiting for the explosion, but it didn't happen. McShayne took the words in stride. He didn't even look up. "Not caring for me is a prerogative," he said. "A prerogative as long as you don't transfer it to action, which, I'm sure Jess will agree, you can do quite well."

Carlsson took the implication silently.

For the first time the desk sergeant looked up from the report he was working on. "But now, if you don't think much of the department," he asked, "what do you suppose the department thinks of you?"

"Sergeant," Danny Carlsson said, quietly. "I don't really give a damn."

"And that is precisely what's wrong with the department," McShayne said, patiently deciding to express a view he hadn't expressed before. "That's where the department went wrong a long time ago. Nobody gave a damn. And nobody gives a damn. I think it's time for a change."

Speaking was a man Danny Carlsson had never heard before. It was the first time he had ever heard anyone speak about any kind of concern for the department. The mayor was a dolt, the city manager a crook, the chief was an idiot, and everybody else on the city's payroll was simply wasting time. McShayne was definitely showing signs that he was a long way from being the man the young policeman had thought he was. Maybe there was hope after all.

"You're right, Sergeant," Carlsson said, meaning more than what was actually being said. "It *is* time for a change."

Without further comment, McShayne reached for the set of car keys hanging on the board just off the desk. He tossed them to the young man. "107," he said. "And don't get lost."

Carlsson tossed the keys to the patrol car up and down in his hand. "Why are you giving me these, Sergeant?"

"I think you're old enough to ride. In fact, Mr. Carlsson, I think you're old enough to do a lot of things — *properly*. And I think you can do them for a long time," said the sergeant. He was almost paternal now. "*Be* the future, son. *Be* the change."

Carlsson wasn't even close to knowing how to respond.

McShayne turned back to the desk. He turned again, noticing that the rookie hadn't moved. He was still tossing the keys up and down. "Get out of here with those things before I change my mind."

The young policeman smiled. It wasn't a broad smile, but it was a knowing smile. He buttoned his jacket, straightened his cap and went out to the patrol car.

McShayne sat thoughtfully for a moment. He had long since given up on calling home, and so he wouldn't try it again. With something sorted out in his mind, he turned for the address box, found City Manager Mulkey's number and dialed. At that hour in the morning there was sure to be hell to pay. McShayne was braced for the eruption, but he wasn't about to be intimidated.

When Mulkey answered the phone he was angry. When the desk Sergeant identified himself, the city manager flew into a rage, spit profanity through the line and almost used Jess's exact words in saying he'd have his job. McShayne listened patiently, and when the man was through he calmly said, "Mr. Mulkey, we don't know each other. We travel in different circles. But I'm going to tell you something: Don't *ever* make the mistake of disrespecting me, this desk, or my uniform. I don't give a damn who you are, or what your position is — but don't *ever* do that to Dempsey O. McShayne. Next, I don't like cussin' in the morning, Mr. Mulkey, and I don't like bein' cussed *at*. But, you sonovabitch, I want you to get this straight: I couldn't care less about you, or your threats. If you want my job, take it. Take it and shove it, Mr. Mulkey. If that's not good enough for you, my badge will be on the desk whenever you decide to show up. And if you do show up, I want you to walk straight to the back, to the downstairs cell, and take a look at one Mr. Jess Brown. He's your partner, but he's my prisoner. He's in jail for murder. If he's not convicted of murder, he damn sure will be for B&E and burglary. Now, if this is the kind of sonovabitch you want walking around dropping your name all over the place, so be it. That's your business, not mine. And if you don't like me calling you, telling you this, that's tough. I was merely trying to extend a courtesy to the man who signs the checks."

Mulkey, after a careful evaluation, said, "And you've done it well. I apologize for any discourtesy I've shown you. It'll never happen again. And I thank you very much for the call, Sergeant. When its time for promotions again, be assured I'll remember it."

"Thanks, but no thanks, Mr. Mulkey. But your apology is accepted," the desk sergeant said. "Now, is there anything you want me to tell Mr. Brown?"

"Mr. *Who?*"

The point made, the two men hung up with a clear understanding of each other. The all-powerful Mulkey could be nice when he wanted to, but he was still a snake. He was so much of a snake that he went to sleep feeling better than he had in quite some time. With Jess Brown gone, he had lost a partner and gained a club. Cost-free.

With Jess Brown booked in the back cell, Bucky trailed Pippilo and Spagg back to the desk. En route, Bucky said to Pippilo: "Oh, Frank — I forgot to tell you, your girlfriend called. Miss America. She dismissed us."

"Bucky," said Spagg, coming back to something that mildly concerned him, "What was that you said happened to your eye?"

"I tol'ja. I ran into a door."

"Helluva door," Spagg said. "An' why do y'got those Band-Aids on the top of your head? Tryin' to keep your two strands of hair in place?"

Before he could answer, Pippilo said, "What was that you just said about dismissin' somebody, Bucky? Who called?"

"Mrs. Ina," said Bucky, as he went behind the desk to join the sergeant while the other two policemen moved to idle in front of the desk. "She called and said she wouldn't be needin' our services any longer."

"You're kiddin'!" Pippilo said.

"No, I ain't," Bucky said. "Didn' she call, Sarge?"

McShayne grumbled something.

"What'd you do, drive by an' give 'er a li'l poke, Pip," said Spagg.

"You sure it was her, Bucky?" Pippilo asked, finding difficulty in believing the good news.

Spagg said, "Hey, Frank, you ought'a at least run down and thank the old bag, Frank."

"When'd she call, Bucky?" Pippilo asked, still unable to get over it.

An interesting question. McShayne got involved. "Yes, when did she call?"

Bucky went to the log and checked. "0310."

"After three. Wasn't that after she had called the second time?" a curious McShayne asked.

"The fourth," said Bucky.

"Who did we give the call to?" McShayne probed.

Bucky checked the blotter again. "104."

"Yeah," said Pippilo, remembering. "You gave the call to Georgie Tetrollini. 'Member I was s'posed to be out on lunch, you couldn't find Corbbo, an' Van Dreelan was on the French freako's cat call."

Spagg looked at the sergeant. "But didn't I hear you give Georgie an 88 to the Flo-Control warehouse?"

"Yeah," said McShayne, puzzled, "but there was no fire. Turned out to be a false alarm, and he didn't stay."

"Well, I never heard you cancel the Ina call," Pippilo said.

McShayne looked at Bucky. "We didn't cancel it?"

Bucky went back to the big book and ran his finger down the entries. "No, guess we didn't. But you did tell him to go to lunch. An' we thought Van Dreelan did, too. An' Georgie gave us a signal 16 from home."

"But you called his house, Bucky, and his wife said he hadn't been there," McShayne confirmed.

"That's right, she did," Bucky said. "I spoke to Margie an' she said the soup and sandwich she made for 'im was still on the table."

"Well, either she was mistaken or he didn't call from there," McShayne said.

"But how could Marge make a mistake? She went downstairs an' checked, she said," Bucky added. "An' she wouldn't lie. Not Marge. Why would she? She'd have no reason to lie about a simple little thing like Georgie not eatin' at home."

Spagg's eyes grew a bit shifty, a little suspicious. Suddenly he started laughing.

"Wha'sup?" Bucky asked.

Pippilo caught what Spagg was thinking and started laughing with him.

"You ain't thinkin' what I'm thinkin'?"

Pippilo said, "I'm thinkin' *more'n* you're thinkin'."

The by-play between the two grew into a rib-splitting laughter. Bucky was on a slow grin, but he didn't know why. McShayne, like Bucky, didn't have the slightest clue as to what was going on. He threw his hands up. "Will you guys tell me what's so funny?!"

Spagg and Pippilo were laughing even more broadly.

"Dammit!" demanded McShayne. "Will you two idiots cut it out and tell me what the hell you're laughing at!?"

Pippilo slowed down enough to dab a tear from his eye. "Ho, ho, ho...don'cha get it? Georgie Tetrollini never called you from home!"

"The 16..." gasped Spagg, "...the signal 16 was from ol' lady Ina's house!"

The two cops laughed even harder. Neither McShayne or Bucky had gotten what was funny.

"Don't you get it?" Pippilo continued to laugh. "Georgie Tetrollini is over there with the old bag! He's makin' it with Ina, baby. He's gettin' it on with Miss America."

Spagg held his stomach and said to Pippilo, "Can't you just see 'em? The two of 'em goin' at it."

"An' lovin' every minute of it. An' Spaggy..."

"Wha'?"

"Georgie used to be such a nice, clean boy!"

"Not no more, he ain't. Tell you what it's gonna be like, Spaggy."

"Wha'?"

"R'member the time when the chief was on his knees givin' this lady mouth-to-mouth resuscitation an' his tongue got stuck in her dentures?"

"Yeah," said Spagg. "An' when the ambulance came, the guy saw him an' said, What'cha doin' down there, sir? The chief mumbled: 'I'm giving the woman last rites.' Ha, ha, ha; ho-ho-ho."

"Funny, funny, fun-e-e-e."

It was even somewhat funny to McShayne, but he didn't get carried away. Bucky's reaction was a little more broad, almost matching Pippilo and Spagg. McShayne said to him, "I wish you'd work that hard on the prisoner up there."

"I'll get to her, Sarge."

"That would be nice, "McShayne said, not intending to be nice. "From what I last heard, she might not be around too long. In fact, she's sounding so bad, I think I'll be calling the doctor for her before I get off. Now your dentures, I'm not gonna tell you again: *Put* 'em in. An' *keep* 'em in."

As Bucky sought to comply, Pippilo said, "Hey, Spaggy, I know just the spot where Mrs. Ina's got ol' Georgie-boy."

"Where 'bouts would they be, Pip?" asked Bucky, struggling with the dentures.

"In her attic," Pippilo said. "Hey, I got an idea, Spaggo. Let's go over there an' catch 'em."

"Wouldn't that be a kick?" Spagg grinned.

McShayne cut in, "I don't want you guys to go over there fooling around."

"We won't be foolin' around, Sarge," Pippilo said. "We'll just go over to see if Officer Georgie Tetrollini is there. You want him back, don't you?"

"Yeah," McShayne said. "I want him back. And I also want Van Dreelan and Corbbo back. And I want them back *right now*."

"We don't know nothin' about them," Spagg laughed. "But Georgie-boy. *Va-va-va-voommm.*"

McShayne cautioned them. "All right, if you two do go over to Ina's, I don't want no horsin' around."

"There won't be any, Sarge," Spagg said. "If the car ain't there, then we know Georgie ain't there."

"But if the car is there...ho, ho, ho..." Pippilo laughed.

"What do we got to lose, Sarge? You're missing a car, an' we're going to look for it. We're on the case."

"If you guys do get inside," the desk Sergeant said "gimme a signal sixteen."

"Righto."

Thinking fun-time, the two started to depart.

McShayne added, "And if Georgie Tetrollini is there, I want his badge."

The two cops sniggled to the door.

The sergeant stopped their exit by adding, "Frank, you can turn yours in as soon as you get back."

"Huh?" Pippilo said, coming back to the desk. "What's this?"

"I said I want your badge when you get back here to this station."

The dreary-faced cop was in shock. "Who? Me?? My *badge*??"

"Yes. *You.* Yes. *Your badge.*"

"What's this, some kind of a joke? Wha-what'd I do??!"

"Try thinking about your juvenile, filthy, obscene conduct!" McShayne said.

"What filthy, obscene conduct?! When?! Where?!"

"In radio patrol car 101! Now, don't gimme any lip!!"

"But, Sarge...!"

"Don't *'But, Sarge'* me!! I've had enough crap for one night!"

"I didn't do nothin'!"

"You did! What the hell do you think I am — deaf?! Everything you did in that patrol car came over that speaker, right into this station! I heard you! Bucky heard you! Nine times out of ten, the goddamn FCC heard you!"

Now Pippilo knew what the sergeant was talking about. But he wasn't quite ready to give in. "How do you know it was me? An' in my car?"

"Because, *Officer* Frank Pippilo — we couldn't transmit until you were back in service!" said McShayne. *"'101 — back in service. Time 04:38.'* Remember saying it?!"

He remembered; and it couldn't be refuted.

Spagg followed the heavy-burdened Pippilo out.

Bucky watched them as they left and said, "Boy, Sarge, you really nailed ol' Pip with that one. I heard the radio when it came back on, but I wasn't payin' any attention. I didn't think you was, either. We was too busy. An' when we was able to start transmittin' again, I still didn' put two and two together. You did, an' you really nailed 'im." He laughed. *"'Time 04:38. 101, back in service.'* — Ha, ha, ha. Great."

"Yes, I did, Bucky. I really nailed him." The sergeant of the desk looked at him with a sly eye. "I like nailing wrongdoers."

Bucky laughed again, and again relieved his gums of the dentures. Still laughing and repeating Pippilo's indicting transmission, *"101...back in service. Time 04:38,"* he stepped into the ticket room, leaving the spotted and supposed-to-be-new false teeth on the desk. They were in the sergeant's view, but he didn't quibble. The dentures made him all the more satisfied that he had made that earlier trip to the bathroom.

The sergeant rubbed his chest and waited. He was waiting for a sound that was to come from the small room. It was to come soon, because Bucky had found the main bottle, as McShayne knew he would.

The bottle had a good amount of alcohol in it, and it sent a curious but accepting smile covering the skinny policeman's rubbery face. If he remembered correctly, when he left to go to lunch, the bottle was almost empty — and the small amount of rum had a slightly different tint to it. No problem, thought the policeman. He tilted the golden contents past his gums and swallowed freely. Suddenly his eyes widened. He gasped, "Aaayyygggg!!! *This tastes like pee!!"*

With a sad eye on the corrupt dentures, the sergeant called out in return, "That is exactly what it is, Bucky. *Pee.* And I wish it was good for stains."

Outside in the yard, Pippilo was still fuming. Both men had gotten into their cars, but the heaviness of the consequences and a commiserating silence had kept them from moving.

Finally Spagg said, "Frank, I mean, the whole friggin' thing with you an' the dame was on the air. Not just a little bit of it, but the whole friggin' thing. How could you let a stupid thing like that happen, Frank?"

Pippilo hammered at the wheel of his vehicle. "Some cockamamie jerk snuck up on me an' taped my mike open."

"They did *what?*"

"Taped my friggin' mike open!"

"Mama mia!" said the guilty Spagg, almost overdoing it. "Ooooh, mama mia! What a crock. What. A. Crock. Of all the low-life…!"

"I mean, that was low, wasn't it? Tapin' my mike," Pippilo groaned. "That really went beyond bad taste."

"Sickening!" Spagg consoled. "Dirty pool at its *absolute* worse!"

"What a bunch of animals we got around here, huh? You'd think a guy would think about another guy's wife an' future."

"My thoughts exactly," agreed Spagg.

"You'd think a guy would try usin' a little common sense. I mean, we're the boys in blue. We're the good guys. We're all here tryin' to do a job. We're puttin' our lives on the line every single time we put on the midnight blues an' take to the streets."

"We're riskin' it all, pal-o."

"Takin' chances. An' take me, f'instance. I don't ask for much."

"Hey, you don't ask for nuttin', ol' bud."

"I come to work, do my job. I go home, come back to work, an' put my life on the line again. That's it."

"That's you," Spagg agreed.

"An' when I'm off, I don't go cattin' around, like a lot of the guys. I go bowlin'…"

"At the Elks, or the 'Mercun Legion. Sometimes even up at the Knights of Columbus. But you're always there, palsy. You an' the wife. An' a lot of times, me an' Myrt is right there with you's."

"I live a straight life, Spaggy. I'm a private man."

"Almost a loner."

"The most I do wrong is hit a couppla beers too hard on the weekends sometimes, but that's it. I got a wife…"

"Hey, palsy, y'got a real career woman at the top of her profession," Spagg added. "An' she looks great on that tugboat, Pip. I r'member when she got out of the Marines and got the job, and a group of us had that parade for her. R'member? We marched from here, through the Lincoln tunnel, all the way to the docks there in New York. We was a li'l bombed and marched off the pier, but we was there."

"An' after all these years, I still appreciate you's guys bein' there."

"An' the good news is, we only lost one of the boys in the process. But we sure had a good time."

"It was a good parade"

"A helluva parade. An' the only reason the cops over there let us do the marchin' was because we're all a part of the brotherhood. Brothers in the blue. An' you an' the wife is family, boobala."

"Even my cat and parakeet."

"You're their hero, poopsie! Top dog."

"I'm the engine that pulls the train."

"I can tell you this: You ain't no caboose, palsy."

"An' it ain't always been downhill, Spaggy."

"Lotta times it ain't, Pips. Sometimes it's uphill. An' with a train, you gotta take them U-turns into consideration."

"So, why would one'a these guys wanna put an' end to all'a that? I don't bother nobody. I'm a private man."

"'Privacy' should be your middle name."

"Y'wanna know how private I am, how I never get into anybody's business?"

"Hey, you don't have to convince me, ol' bud-bud. I know how you keep to yourself."

"I don't bother nobody. So why should somebody wanna bother me?"

"You got me, palzo."

"Like, we just got this new neighbor. A broad."

"I r'member when she moved in. You called me when the truck pulled up. An' you called me when it left."

"Right. Now, Spagg, I don't talk to this one *at all.*"

"At all. You don't say a word. You never do, Pips. I'm same-o same-o. We just ain't talkers. Mum's the word, I always say."

"Now, this broad's just moved in. For starters, I can tell she's nosy."

"Nose into everything. I know the type."

"Like I happen to be stannin' next to her trash a few minutes after she moved in."

"Just idling. Killin' time around the ol' trash can. I do it myself."

"Right. An' guess what I overheard this broad askin' somebody?"

"What?"

"What time's the mailman comin' by.'"

"Oh-oh. This one's diggin' deep. Right away I can tell she's a busy-body. She's prying, an' she's done sparked a tender in you. I know you, kid."

"Spagg, I'm steamin'."

"You had every right to be, palsy. An' I wouldn't fault you if you thought about takin' action, 'cause that's the one thing you don't like, Pippo — somebody who's into your business."

"An' I'm gonna tell you something' else I don't like. Cheap furniture."

"That really gets your goat, buddy-boy. Cheap furniture. I know you. You and the wife might be sleepin' on cardboard boxes and have a couple of wooden crates in the livin' room, but they sure don't look like no cheap furniture."

"It ain't. But this broad's got a ton of it."

"Oh-oh."

"Then I discover she comes from upstate, New York. Buffalo."

"Geezus. Almost a panhandler."

"382 Harper Street. She was rentin' a room there."

"Sounds like a hardship case to me, Pippo."

"Her only livin' relative lives in Yonkers. 58 B Street. An' get this,

Spaggy: the broad's got a paid-up life insurance policy with Metropolitan, she's makin' a hunnert and 'leven bucks as a bookkeeper every two weeks; she's fightin' with Social Security 'cause they got her number screwed up, she ain't got no deductions; no car, no phone, an' she's late payin' her taxes."

"Late payin' her taxes! Geezus! You'd think a bookkeeper would know to pay them things when school starts. What a cow."

"An' speakin' of cow…"

"Yuh?"

"She's overweight, her hair is dyed, she's got 80/40 vision, an' she wears a size 12 shoe…"

"Boats, Pipsy. *Boats.*"

"An' a week after she moves in? She goes to New York an' hocks her only ring!"

"You're jokin', Pip. You gotta be jokin'."

"No, straight stuff. I trailed her over there. The guy gave her $17.50 for it. Spagg, this dame spent it in two hours! She spent $17.50 in *two hours!*"

"You're kiddin'! Who's she think she is — John D. Rockerfella? $17.50. Pip, we ain't spent that much money at one time since the war was over! I didn' spend that much money on my honeymoon."

"Seventeen bucks and fifty cents in two hours, so help me! An' what gets me is, she spent it on things that she ain't had no business doin'!"

"She should be arrested, Pippo. She should be tossed in the can!"

"Spaggy, what this broad spent all that money on was sickenin'. None of it was important. You should see the receipts. I'll show 'em to you some-times. An' how do you like these apples: She's paying $37.90 smacks a month in rent — which she can't afford; she buys her groceries at the A&P, her undies at Lady's Wear at 952 Main, mostly on Tuesday between 12 and 2; an' all her other clothes she buys at Sears. An' guess who she's shackin' up with?"

"Spare me, Pipsi, spare me."

"A train conductor."

"A train conductor?!!"

"Yeah."

"Oh, my Lord!"

"The guy gets in every three days, usually 'round 4:12 in the morning.

And, Spaggy — every three weeks…?"

"Yuh?"

"She shaves under her arms."

"*Puleeze*, Pippy, *Puleeze!!*"

"*An' her legs, she shaves!!*"

"*No, Pippo; no! I can't stand it! Anything but that!*"

"I'm telling you, this one's a doozy."

"She needs to be put away. She needs help, Pipperoni, help. It's gotta be the pits havin' a neighbor like that. S' gotta be. 'Specially to somebody like you's an' Helen. You's two keep to yourself. You're homebodies. An' to see a doozy like that walkin' around…"

"We're like moles."

"Practically livin' underground."

"Now, you know me, Spaggy…"

"I know you, kid. I *know* you."

"Besides stickin' to myself, if nothin' else, I believe in my work."

"Work-work-work-work. That's your theme, buddy-buddy. *Work* should be your middle name. You practically invented the word."

"On one of my nights off last week I didn't have anything to do, so I happen to pay a li'l midnight visit to this dame's trash again. I was just lookin'."

"Workin'. Checkin' up. Needin' air, an' payin' a li'l visit 'round the neighborhood, seein' if everything was safe. You're a cop. On duty an' off."

"Uh-huh. An' guess what?"

"Yuh?"

"This broad sticks her nosy head out the window…"

"Same broad?"

"Same broad."

"Oh-oh. I know what's comin'."

"Y'know what she says?"

"Yuh?"

"'May I help you'?"

"*May I help you??*"

"*Yes!*"

"Good grief!! *She said that??*"

"Those very words. On my word of honor."

"What a pryin', spyin', nosy dame! I can't believe it. At midnight —
when she's s'posed to be sleepin', you're doin' a li'l research in her trash, and
she's hangin' out the window askin' can she help you. Now I know she ain't
the kind that uses the ol' bean, but this is unreal, Pippo. *Unreal.*"

"Spagg, as I live and breathe, she said them very words! *May I help you?*"

"Unreal, Pipski. *Unreal.* I can't believe it."

"An' that ain't all."

"C'mon, now, Pipperoni. C'mon."

"There's more."

"Can't be, Pip-pip. Can't be."

"Like later on, she sees me standing at the same spot…"

"Under her window. It's after midnight. The trash is still there. An'
you ain't moved."

"Not an inch. Then, a couppla hours later?…"

"A couppla hours later, an' you still ain't moved."

"Not a muscle. But there she is, back in the window again."

"I can't believe it, Pippy. I simply can't believe it. What's wrong with
people in this world? *What* was this woman thinkin'?"

"An' here's the capper…"

"Oh-oh."

"The next morning she tacks a note on our door, askin' to come over to
the house so's me, Helen and her can talk."

"Say that again, Pipski, 'cause that is <u>too</u> strong. I can't be hearin'
what I think I'm hearin'. She did *what??*"

"Pins a note on *our* front door, sayin' that she's gotta have this talk with
us."

"She's wantin' to come to *the house,* so's you's <u>three</u> can *talk?*"

"Yeah!"

"I can't b'leevit, Pipperoni. I just can't beee-leevit it! I'm ready to faint!
Wantin' to come to my house!"

"Oh, my Lord, my Lord, my Lord. I'm hurtin, Pippo. I'm in pain, kid.
Pain!"

"And get this, Spagg: Helen starts askin' me what do I think? I says to her, 'Helen, f'Christsakes; for once in your life, use some common sense, will you? She's invadin' our privacy.'"

"The broad's wantin' to come over to *your* house, an' you's two's don't even know her. The nerve, Pip; the nerve. I gotta tell you, *that* is gall."

"I don't know what the world is comin' to, Spaggy."

"I don't know, either, ol' bud-bud."

"It's just like that bastard who taped my mike open. It's sick."

"Disgustin'," Spagg said. "So wha'cha gonna do about it?"

"I don't know," Pippilo said, preparing to drive off. "But I'm gonna find him. And when I do, I'm gonna shoot the sonovabitch on sight."

17

It looked as if dawn would have liked to have come to shed light on the city, the snow, the remaining boys in blue, and others, but it was still that time of morning when the night had not fully resolved itself. But although the darkened hours were soon to give way, that hint; that pinch — *that smidge* — of change was still in the air, and the big Beech Street trees stood guarding Mrs. Ina's house as if wondering what to do with their arms.

Pippilo's car had not been speedy, but Spagg's had. The big cop had beaten the short, ruddy-faced cop to the scene and was pacing back and forth when car 101 drove up. Before Pippilo could park, Spagg was over there to help him out of his Hudson.

The big cop was still nervous. "Y'kno, Frank, I was just thinkin' somethin', you just can't take off and start shootin', Frank. It could'a been anybody that taped your mike open, Frank. Frank, it could'a even been a civilian, Frank."

"The hell it was," said Pippilo.

"Why you say that?"

"That tape came from a first aid kit."

"You got any idea what *kind* of first aid kit?"

"Yeah, I do."

"Er...what kind was it, Frank?"

"A *police* first-aid kit. The kind that every single one of us carries in the car. And I know who it belongs to."

The cop wearing the sunglasses and motorcycle uniform slowed his steps. He didn't quite know what to do, whether to run or reach for his pistol. "Whose?" he gingerly asked. *"Whose kit was it, Pip?"*

The short, sad-faced policeman took a few more steps, not saying anything.

Spagg was nearly sweating. "Frank; whose kit was it, Frank?"

Pippilo stopped and turned. *"Corbbo's."*

A greatly relieved Spagg blurted, *"Mickey Corbbo!* I shoulda known it was him all along. Why, that sonova...! Frank, how'd you figger it was him, Frank? How'd you figger?"

Pippilo tapped his head knowledgeably.

Together they said: *"By usin' the ol' bean."*

The police vehicle the two men were looking for was nowhere to be found. It was not in front nor on the side of the house, and so the two policemen sneaked down the walkway and tiptoed back to the garage. There, parked deep on the side of the garage, and partially covered with brush, was a patrol car. They didn't check the small number that was painted on the front fender panel, they were too busy sniggering and congratulating themselves to notice that it was not Tetrollini's 104, the patrol car they were looking for. All they were concerned with was that, with the white top and midnight-blue body with the red light on top, it was a police vehicle.

Bold now, and knowing for certain that they were about to catch Georgie Tetrollini in compromise, the plan was to inch along the side of the car, then yank the door open.

Spagg slowed the action by whispering, "Let's see if we can see anything from the windows first."

Pippilo had a better idea. He wanted to go in back where the dim green light was so that Spagg could first see the lay of the land, then see the coffin in the guest-house. Spagg agreed.

"Some jernt, huh?" Spagg said, keeping his voice low and admiring the partially lit place as they crept along.

"Yeah. She's even got one'a them TVs."

"Whoa-ho-hoooo. Really rich, huh?"

"Loaded."

When Pippilo led him inside the guesthouse, Spagg *Whoa-ho-hoooo'd* again. This time it was followed with expressions of fear. The coffin was dead center of the room.

"Geezus H. Ker-rice!" he whispered.

"I tol'ja she was a nut," Pippilo whispered back.

"An' you said she keeps an Uncle Sam in it?"

"Yeah. You know, the kind they had durin' the war that said, *I want you.*" Pippilo said, as they eased in closer. "I'll show it to you."

"Boy, I'm sure glad this ain't my post."

"She's really a weirdo. One time she had a tombstone in the attic. An' another time she even went over to New York and tried to rent a hearse."

"Let's get outta here," Spagg said, having had enough. "We gotta get to the attic to see about Tetrollini."

"Wait a sec. Get a load of this," Pippilo said, sending his fingers to where Mrs. Ina had sent hers earlier in the night, trying to find the button to release the lid so the Uncle Sam could be exposed.

The cop found the button, and pressed. But the lid didn't pop open as it had done before. This time it creaked open. Now Spagg, for some reason, thought the matter was worth laughing over. He started to sniggle, as did Pippilo. Slowly the lid opened all the way up. The blanket had been removed from the torso and the view had them yelling and screaming. It was not the expected Uncle Sam; it was not Georgie Tetrollini. It was what was left of Johnny Van Dreelan.

Savagely ravaged, his uniform was in shreds, and he was without legs. His head had been crushed, and his face, neck, chest, shoulder, abdomen — everything had been half-eaten by the sub-human creature in Pilar's attic.

18

The mood in the Elton Head Police department had turned into one of somberness. Both Pippilo and Spagg stood in front of the brass-railed desk, still shaking.

Unable to talk, the stunned sergeant of the desk had pushed back in the swivel chair.

Booking completed, Bucky was upstairs, jailing Mrs. Ina next to the badly coughing old woman the sergeant had referred to earlier.

The two radio patrolmen had arrested Mrs. Ina and had departed in such a hurry they didn't call anyone to make arrangements to remove the cop's body. But there was nothing to worry about in that regard. Van Dreelan wasn't going anywhere. The two policemen's main concern was to get back to the desk. In fact, they were so scared they had neglected to arrest the old lady. They had to make a return trip to do it.

It took time, but in trying to piece things together, McShayne eventually came to the conclusion that the only possible way Van Dreelan's patrol car could have gotten to Mrs. Ina's was that someone other than the patrolman had driven it there. Since the blotter indicated that car 105's last call had been to Pilar's house, she obviously had a great deal to do with the policeman's death. The conclusion was helped by Pippilo and Spagg's telling the sergeant about the Christmas tree tracks they had seen in the snow at the woman's house, which to McShayne meant that she no doubt had driven the car to the Ina residence after the killing — a savage killing that came from something virtually inhuman.

Connecting the two women was easy to do. As alluded to by Pippilo earlier, Mrs. Ina was going to fund a little theater group in which Pilar was going to be the sole star — which was well and good, but at the last minute a stunted little relative convinced Mrs. Ina that he should be on stage with the great French actress. This, of course, strained the relationship between the two women.

"Strained" was an understatement as far as Pilar was concerned. Considering the man to be a non-acting, stage-hogging, scene-stealing, posturing twerp who didn't belong on the same planet, let alone on the same stage, with greatness, Pilar invited him over for dinner. Because of her pasty, off-centered look, and the fact that she was an actress, the man naturally assumed he would be dealing with a woman of easy virtue. He arrived at the house with a bouquet of flowers, an appetite, and throbbing hope. He talked a mile a minute, ate heartily, and suggested that they might try having dessert in the nude. Pilar invited him to the attic. Chalking up the uniqueness to an eccentricity reserved exclusively for the theatrically inclined, the runt couldn't finish eating before he was on his feet, looking for the attic stairs.

Hamming it up at the top of the stairs, he stopped, unzipped his pants, shot his abbreviated arms out theatrically, and launched into a version of "Hamlet."

He was terribly dramatic.

But not any more so than Oscar.

As the woman with the fright-night hair and Transylvania looks was planting the twerp's shredded bones in the back yard, it occurred to her that if — not that she needed one, but if Mrs. Mrs Ina still insisted on her having a co-star, why not Oscar? Why not hit the boards with something that the chunky little cop had come up with: *Beauty and the Beast.* In her mind, she was beautiful; and Oscar was...well, Oscar was a beast. He couldn't talk, but that was okay. In real life a beast couldn't talk anyway.

The more Pilar thought about it, the more appealing the idea became. Then the idea became one of brilliance. Beyond not being able to talk, the big O, as she sometimes called him, made no demands, and was comfortable in chains — traits not found in man or beast. As a genuine Big Foot doppelganger from the jungles of Peru, he was a bit shaggy-haired, and his breath exceeded the bounds of putrescence, but he still could be stage-ready. Then, taking into account his golden-hue, hollow eyes and squared, sunken face, and the fact that he kept his hands between his legs, made him all the more qualifying. He was prone to get upset at times — and even she didn't know how far he would carry his rage — but there was another plus. As it was sure to do come awards time, her big O would remind others of another Oscar — that silly little piece of glittering metal that was bestowed yearly on the micro-talented in far-off Hollywood. If they could do that, thought the woman who had been bounced from virtually every stage from Bulgaria to Bangkok, there was no telling what would happen if true talent were ever seen.

Pilar was true talent.

But until the time greatness was fully recognized, or at least until Mrs. Ina came to her senses, it was the woman's task to keep her hominoid fit and fed. It was, of course, the reason why, with net in hand and a bag full of toy mice, a lady with electric-socket hair and a face to match could be seen patrolling the streets and alleyways at night, hopping over fences, attacking garbage cans, standing in the shadows and doing everything else to find soft-bellied cats.

⧗

Mrs. Ina's arrest had been short and sweet, but she looked woefully out of place in the second of the three tiny cells that were nestled under the pitched roof of the place where horse auctions had been held 35 years earlier. Her mind was still warped and disconnected, but the little lady didn't look nearly as frightening as she did at home. Indeed, there was something sweet and dear about her. It helped that she didn't have the slightest clue as to where she was and looked upon her little cell as an extension of her living room. The steel-gray bars had no effect. She was so at home that after Bucky booked and printed her, and brought her upstairs and escorted her into the cramped cell, she invited him to sit in the sitting room. It was the little cell next to hers — the one to her left. The one to the right was occupied by her husband, she said. He couldn't come out because he was busy putting up the Christmas tree.

Mrs. Ina didn't know it, but she was right about the one cell to her left being occupied. Had Bucky done as the sergeant had been requesting all night, he would have known who it was. From where he was standing, however, he couldn't see the woman with the interminable cough, and she couldn't hear him, since her ears were damaged and he was speaking barely above a whisper. Mrs. Ina wanted him to whisper, because she didn't want him to awaken the other person still sleeping in the guest room downstairs.

Although Mrs. Ina had talked with Bucky every night on the telephone, she had never seen him and didn't recognize the voice. Still, she said, he placed her in mind of her husband who was still on a shopping spree in New York, apparently forgetting that he was back and was busy with the tree in the other cell.

Maybe, psychologically speaking, it was good that Mrs. Ina was not all there mentally and believed her husband was alive and close by. Maybe it had kept her alive. But the fact was — and most likely what explained the Uncle Sam connection — that Conrad Ina, in flying combat missions over China with Gen. Claire Chennault's Flying Tigers, had gotten killed long before the U.S. had entered the war.

He had risen to the rank of Lieutenant Colonel; he died heroically.

As Bucky was leaving the cell, in need of a drink and anxious to get to the bathroom, Mrs. Ina had gotten cold and asked him if he had any soup. Always coming to work with his Thermos, Bucky replied that he had some downstairs. He decided to go down to get it before forgetting.

When the policeman returned, Mrs. Ina thanked him, then, struggling with the bottle, she said something about rekindled friendship — a term she had used earlier that morning when she called the station, saying she would no longer be needing their services because she had visitors. She was, of course, referring to Pilar's visit with the remnants of Johnny Van Dreelan's body in tow. But neither Bucky nor anyone else at the station had any way of knowing it. He responded by saying that everybody could use a little re-kindled friendship. He said it in a voice strong enough to be heard in the occupied cell three doors down, and it elicited a response. It was hard and rusty enough to be questioned, but it was a voice — one that was strained from eons of hard drinking.

Between an extremely rough coughing spasm, the woman called out, "Is that y-y-yew, Buck-Buck?"

After the lengthy struggle, Bucky was about to get the bottle back and open it for Mrs. Ina, but he stopped. The voice had a terribly familiar ring to it. Smiling at having his voice recognized, he tiptoed back to see who it was.

Withered, ancient, and, as the sergeant had said, pneumonia-sounding, the hung-over old femme had crooned and coughed herself into exhaustion. She was about the same age as Mrs. Ina, but had none of the charm. She was a tough one, and she was crocked on the side of the cot. Bucky took another look, and it eliminated the need to go the bathroom. If he had been wearing his dentures, they would have flown.

"*MAW!!!*"

The woman, gagging and choking in another heavy series of coughs, shouted in return: "*SON!*"

She would never be that loud again.

⌛

Bucky was a wreck when he returned to the desk. Spagg and Pippilo were still there, but the toothless, beanpole policeman's mind was on the prisoner in the hayloft. Leaving her in the throes of yet another coughing spasm, he should have been calling for immediate medical aid. Instead, he blurted to the sergeant: "*Sarge, how come you didn't tell me that was my maw up there?!*"

"Shut up, Bucky!" McShayne said, his mind locked in woe.

"*But that's my momma up there!*"

"I don't care if it's the Virgin Mary! And for the very last time: PUT — and *KEEP* — your teeth in!!" The sergeant came back to Pippilo and Spagg. "You guys get over to that house and pick up that Count Dracula witch. And if there's anything else that moves in that house that *don't* look like a human being, *shoot it.*"

Their minds were too heavy with thought to move quickly. Not that they were afraid of going back to Pilar's, but a cop was dead. Other than Terry Gillingham's demise at the hands of the so-called sleepwalker some years back, they couldn't remember the last time an Elton Head cop had died on the job.

Pippilo wound up thinking about Van Dreelan again. So did Spagg. "I can't understand something, Sarge. How could this French dame…"

McShayne wouldn't let him finish. He exploded. *"Do I look like Charlie Chan to you?! Van Dreelan's dead, a creep killed 'im, and that nut upstairs had 'im! That's all I know, and that's all I wanna know! Now, if there's any figgerin' to be done, you figger it out! An' while you're figgerin', figger out what happened to Mickey Corbbo and Georgie Tetrollini!!"*

No one knew what to say after that; no one knew what to do. The two patrolmen sauntered out the door.

His mind occupied, and temporarily dropping the thought of seeing his mother upstairs — or even calling for aid — Bucky offered what he thought was a logical reason for Corbbo's absence. "Sarge, maybe Mick's been gassin' up."

It ignited another explosion. *"Gassin' up?!* Gassin' up?! You tell me, Bucky, how'n hell do you spend a whole night 'gassin' up' in a city garage that *ain't* open — and will not open until one half-hour before the change of the midnight shift!!! But even if the city kept the damn thing open every day, 24 hours a day, from sunup to sundown, from dusk to dawn, and that harebrained Mickey Corbbo needed gas, it would only require a *few* minutes at the pump! And that is simply because he's supposed to be operatin' a patrol car, not sailin' a goddamn battleship!!!"

"Well, I just said that, Sarge, because lately Mick's been sneakin' a hose in the car. An' an alarm clock."

The all-but-defeated desk sergeant considered the statement so dumb that he refused to even think about responding. It was so dumb, in fact, that it made him forget about calling home again.

All he could do was slump in the chair and massage his chest.

He also gasped a little.

19

He never thought he would, and it really wasn't that important before, but with thoughts of Korea and re-enlisting in the military pushed aside, young Danny Carlsson found himself deriving a modest bit of satisfaction from casually patrolling in the car. As a vehicle the Hudson wasn't much, but it sure as hell beat walking. Since car 107, favored by the chief, the city council and city manager, didn't have a specific area to patrol, it was free to roam the city. Carlsson didn't know whether the desk sergeant was going to allow him to ride from that point on, but it would make the thought of coming to work more digestible. Walking a post was the pits, particularly in winter. Other than this beautiful, moon-swept night, it was cold, boring, and useless — and to the young patrolman's way of thinking, it didn't really have to be done. He wondered whether anyone had ever checked the records to find out exactly how productive the Post 1-A man had been. It couldn't have been very much. Walking one end of Main to the other with an eye on stores that, at best, were struggling to keep alive couldn't have been very productive for either man or city.

The rookie thought of another idea. If patrolling Main Street had to be done — and, again, he saw no reason why it should be done — but if it had to be done, why not have the man check the doors and then be assigned to a car? As an added measure, the 1-A man could periodically return to the post on Main, bathe the stores with a reassuring spotlight, and continue on to cover other parts of the city. It was a sound idea, but in the end it was sure to be just another slice of common sense that the higher-ups would never employ.

On that thought, though, Carlsson could only fault the department itself. City Hall couldn't be expected to do all the department's thinking. Something had to come from the chief. It was this thought that had the young man delving into another series of thoughts while idly cruising. He wondered how it would be if the department actually had a chief. Oh, it had a chief all right. But he was chief in name only. Maybe even less than that. The rarely seen weasel of a man, who was supposed to lead and direct from the end office upstairs but remained at a bottle-cluttered home that was dominated by a thin-veined wife who could cuss, fight, and out-drink the average sailor, was not a chief. He was a clown who masqueraded as chief. But, the young man wondered, what if somebody came along who had the city and the people and the department at heart. It could even be McShayne. The rookie still didn't think the sergeant was all that hot, personality-wise, but did harbor a lot of deep-down leadership qualities — and he had insight.

It was startling to hear the sergeant say *Be the future, son. Be the change.* That, in itself, was worth the price of admission. *The price of admission?* Hell, it was downright historic.

But what if someone came along who could provide that certain something that could possibly turn the department around? McShayne could do it, but the trouble with him, thought Carlsson, was that he really wouldn't want the job. Also, the really good qualities in him were buried so deep down they might prove to be irretrievable. And, too, the sergeant was old. He was almost as old as the picture of the old-time cops that hung on the wall in the stationhouse. And then there was the problem with his heart.

Danny Carlsson thought about what the sergeant must have been like when he was a rookie, before the department had stunted his concerns and growth. But for the sergeant to have been a rookie must have been somewhere around 1920? Or '21, maybe? My god, thought Danny, that was ages ago. That was when policemen must have worn those funny-looking derbies and wide belts, and treated their nightsticks better than they treated their wives and sweethearts. They were Keystone Kops. He remembered them from the movies he grew up with in Denmark. He pictured McShayne as a Keystone Kop, and started chuckling to himself. McShayne, with his belly pushing and straining against that wide belt, walking up and down a muddied Main Street, courteously tipping his derby to the nicely-frocked ladies as they daintily raised their hems to cross a curbless street. It would have been a sight.

Cops carried no guns in those days. What a wonderful country America must have been then: innocent; leisured in a way, but always energetic in scope and purpose; ever blessed with a can-do spirit. The country had her problems — as he had tried to get across to Soldier Boy's mother — which, admittedly, had been a bit brash, because she knew problems a hell of a lot more than he would ever know, but the USA did have its problems. A main one — and the thing that surprised him most when he came here — was how easily the country sectioned off and very often disrespected and degraded people. Among others, the Irish were not liked, the Jews were not trusted, the Orientals were ignored, and the coloreds were destined to suffer.

But in time, thought the rookie, backed more out of hope, generations would die and they would be replaced by a breed that would believe in unity; the nation's creed. It was 50 years away, but if everyone worked together, perhaps unity could be achieved before the next century — before the year 2000.

The USA also had another problem. This one not quite as serious, but the country wasted a lot of time and resources on the frivolous. It had a tendency to allow the meaningless, the artificial, and the fickle to overshadow things that were truly important. And then there was this terribly destructive thing of having so many freedoms without responsibility.

But that was America, and that's the way it went. And who was he to say? Right or wrong, he was in this country; and, as he had said before, he was here to stay. And now, with a little more thought, he might even be on the department to stay — and therefore to help — thanks to the events of the night and something the Sergeant of the Desk had said.

It had almost passed him by, but it was at that moment when he told the sergeant that he didn't think much of the department, and even less of him. McShayne, who took it in unbelievable stride and had every right to explode, hadn't flared up. He had countered by saying: *That's where the department went wrong a long time ago. Nobody gave a damn. And nobody gives a damn.* Interesting. The sergeant had also said something else. He said it was time for a change. Along with it, he said something else that should never be forgotten: *Be the future, son. Be the change.*

Be the future, son. Be the change. A man in the *Elton Head* Police Department had said that.

In their own way those words paralleled, tied in, and directly connected to something his grandfather had said. The words were worth remembering because McShayne and his grandfather spoke with the voice of experience. They spoke with a wisdom a 22-year-old couldn't possibly have. *"If something is wrong,"* the old Dane had said, *"you make it better. You stay and make it better."* As cruel and as narrow-minded as the grandfather had been on the other matter, the racial one, what he said had a great deal of merit. Same with the old desk sergeant. In tossing him the keys to car 107, the sergeant said — and it was important to remember that this was with full knowledge that as a policeman he had slipped up on two tiny details in explaining how he happened to see Jess going down into the cellar at Wilson's — but, even with that, the veteran sergeant had tossed him the keys to a patrol car and said *"Don't get lost."*

Don't get lost. He wouldn't.

And Danny Carlsson wouldn't ever get lost again in that other way which now loomed as all-important — for himself, and for his grandfather.

Holding a dying man in his arms and hearing the man talk about seeing the face of God had created a strange sensation within the sandy-haired policeman's frame. Soldier Boy had painted an indelible picture in his mind. He wished it could have been done for his grandfather. He wished he could have seen it; heard it; been a part of it. He needed something. The grandfather was terribly old, and soon his end would come. Soon the end was coming to Soldier Boy's mother, too. He had every intention of seeing her again, and it would be often. But even if not, even if something came up and he was prevented from doing as desired, she had something higher to comfort her;

something better to pave her way. She was not lost. She had Godliness. His grandfather had agnosticism and atheism. He was lost; he had nothing.

It was not a comforting thought for the young policeman. He wondered whether there was still time to change the old Dane. It is said you can't teach an old dog new tricks. Perhaps not. But it was worth a try.

⏳

Danny Carlsson was still thinking his about his grandfather and cruising easy when he aimlessly drove into the park and spotted the patrol car sitting quietly alone. His move to the car was not immediate. It had to be Mickey Corbbo, sleeping off post. But the rookie also gave a quick thought to Tetrollini. Not that he felt that Georgie would be in the car sleeping. But in some ways he felt guilty in not thinking more about him before. Maybe he didn't want to fully think about him because he knew that the reticent policeman was not an innocent man.

He had done his best trying to push it out of his mind, but Carlsson was still hurt. Terribly hurt. He didn't know that the policeman had been wounded, but he did know that he had been down in the cellar long before Jess Brown — and that when he emerged from the cellar Mr. Wilson was dead, and that, cursorily, the blood found at the scene didn't look like it could have come from just one body. It was obvious that when Mr. Wilson was hit in the back of the head, and as violently as he had been hit, he went down and couldn't move. Very troubling was the fact that there was blood in other parts of the cellar — and by the steps leading to the metal halves. How did it get there?

Then Danny Carlsson wondered where Tetrollini had gone after leaving the cellar. From what he could see, Georgie wasn't in full uniform and he was hunched over as though hurt. Maybe he went home to rest up a bit, then came back out.

Tetrollini went home because he was hurt? The rookie stopped and thought about how ludicrous his thoughts had become. He was deceiving himself. There was no way that he, or anyone else, could believe that the cop hadn't done something grievously wrong. He was out of uniform, he emerged from a cellar door — leaving the exact place where a dead body had been found, and there was no question that he had lost blood in the cellar. Those were the facts, and all the sugar-coating and dancing around the subject wasn't going to change one thing. Pure and simple, Georgie Tetrollini had committed murder.

The rookie dropped the subject.

He came back to it and wondered what he would say to the cop when they reported in for the change of shifts. Maybe after awakening Mickey Corbbo he would put in a call or go by the once-good policeman's house and have a talk with him. He couldn't just let it go. Something had to be done. The situation was serious. Very serious. Would he turn Tetrollini in? No, no, he wouldn't. He couldn't, now. The setup had already been made, and it would mean freeing Jess Brown of the charge of murder. Jess hadn't killed Mr. Wilson, but he was a murderer. He had murdered Danny's Carlsson's friend. Danny Carlsson had promised his friend that there would be justice. The question now was, was he wrong in doing what he did — for lying and framing a not-quite-so-innocent man? *How* wrong, would have been the better question. Of course he was wrong. He was a policeman; not the law; not a judge and jury. But his conscience was clear. And, in the long run, if no one else appreciated what he did, Soldier Boy and his mother would.

The Soldier had said: *You're gonna start off with a hard one. You're gonna do wrong, but you're gonna be right.* Carlsson had done just that.

And, just as important, the higher good had been served.

Change was in the air, and it was a scenic setting, the park was. Even the debris that poked up and lined the banks of the river looked acceptable under a partial cover of snow. Daylight was trying to peep through the trees, and the snow had begun to fall again. The flakes this time were larger than the ones that had fallen before the start of the midnight shift. Elton Head's park had already been a beneficiary of that earlier snow, but with the added layer, it was sure to enhance that postcard setting. It was not that Elton Head's park was beautiful per se, but the trees, with their limbs still stretched and swooped as though in worship, looked almost as if they defied the laws of nature with their height. Alone, aloof and not near the trees, sat the patrol car. It was in the middle of the park, facing the river.

When the operator of car 107 first saw the outline of the car, the first inclination was to pick up the mike and just call it in, saying that he had found Mickey Corbbo. But from this point on, with his mind set on being on the department for a long time, Danny Carlsson was going to be a good policeman and a good guy — good guy, meaning that he would not get involved in any more wrongdoing. If Mickey were asleep, as he was sure to be, he would awaken him and let him do his own call-in, thus avoiding the charge of snitching. In the interest of patrol-room harmony, that was the best way to handle it, even though Mickey didn't really deserve that much consideration. After all, it was Mickey who was always on him about this or that, always teasing him about his grandfather being a janitor, always coming up with such irritating pranks as putting that police-capped mop in his locker. Given real ammunition, there was no telling what the tubby policeman would do.

Carlsson knew that McShayne had been looking for his errant, trouble-making policeman for the better part of the night. As he cruised in closer under a withdrawing moon, he could see that the newly fallen snow had lightly covered the windshield, and the windshield wipers hadn't been used.

For sure, Mickey was asleep in the Hudson. No one else would be brazen enough to sleep in a wide-open park. Certainly not Tetrollini.

From the rear, and pulling up next to the vehicle's passenger's side, the first thing to grab the rookie's attention was that the cop behind the wheel had his head tilted out the window. Snow had fallen on it, and the engine wasn't running. Unable to see the face, Carlsson glanced down at the patrol car's number painted at the bottom of the front fender. It read: 104.

Mickey Corbbo's patrol car was 103.

Danny was scared. Everything he did from that point on was cautious and deliberate. He fearfully shifted the stick into neutral, pulled at the emergency brakes and climbed out. Slowly he walked around to the other side of patrol car 104, saying to himself over and over: *Please be asleep, Georgie. Please, please, please, be asleep. Please, for God's sake, Georgie — please be sleeping.* Then he saw the icy face of Georgie Tetrollini. He saw the thick, caked blood and the handkerchief that had become frozen in the night.

Except for Soldier Boy's death, in his entire life young Danny Carlsson had never felt sorrier.

20

When Sergeant Dempsey O. McShayne received the news that a second man of his patrol unit was dead, it was just about all over for him. His head was almost matching Tetrollini's head in the car back in the park.

The Sergeant of the desk was not dead, but for a while there was doubt. A scared, opened-mouthed Bucky thought he was dead until the spread-eagled sergeant showed a bit of life by quietly raising a hand to press at the left temple and slowly weaved his head in heavy disbelief. The senior policeman wanted to move the entire body, but the legs weren't there. He wanted to touch the chest, but the hands couldn't move. Sometimes it was a little bit slower, sometimes a little bit faster, but his heart was talking to him. It was saying that it was no longer going to be the dependable instrument that had served him for more than 60-some years. It said more, but the Sergeant didn't get it. The internal-message machine had slowed down on the job.

The old veteran policeman held in that spread-eagle position, then coughed a little. It caused a concerned Bucky to gently inquire, "Anything we can do, Sarge?"

There was no response from the sergeant of the desk. He sat there, molded in that stoic position. He did not hear the question, and his mind could not supply an answer.

Carlsson was deeply affected. At first he stood in front of the desk not knowing what to do, then he stepped up to the switchboard to call the ambulance. But the sergeant's head said "No."

Finally the midnight leader was able to put his hands on the arms of the chair. He lifted himself up stiffly; heavily, slowly. Both Carlsson and Bucky moved in to help. This time the sergeant's body said "No." The two backed away, allowing the feeble-looking man's foot to unsteadily paw for the one step down from the platform where the desk and apparatus sat.

The concern from the two men remained paramount.

Carlsson asked with a great deal of concern in his voice, "Sergeant, can I help you go lay down?"

McShayne didn't hear him. He was nearing the door, heading out.

"Maybe — maybe you should try an' stay here an' lay down, Sarge," Bucky said. There was no response. He added, "You want I should call the house? Maybe get'cha niece?"

It caused a flicker from the sergeant. He almost turned to look back at the phone. But he didn't. Zonked by a weary fatalism, he walked on.

Carlsson, seeing that he had gone out into the cold without his overcoat, quickly removed his own pea jacket, hurried out the door and threw it around his sergeant's shoulders as he continued to stiffly move on. The jacket remained on the shoulders for a minute or so, then dropped to the snow. The rookie quickly retrieved the jacket, raced over and wrapped it around his sergeant's shoulders again.

Like Carlsson, the sergeant had a pickup truck in the yard. He had purchased it many summers ago. McShayne liked the vehicle because it was utilitarian and it was ideal for gardening and hunting, something he was going to do a lot more of whenever he retired. But the sergeant didn't even look the pickup's way when he left. He went straight for the unused railroad tracks that ran in back of the worn station with the tired facade.

His head low, seeing nothing, the desk sergeant was at that point where he was about to trudge down the snow-covered ties when car 101 pulled into the yard with Pilar. As a bona fide cop-killing suspect, she should have been strapped, gagged, handcuffed, and everything but hog-tied in the back seat of the car. But no. Spagg and Pippilo were in the back seat. They were relaxed and chatting amiably as Pilar negotiated the wheels of the Hudson. It had been agreed that she was going to temporarily sign in, then, after picking up a bottle of French wine from who-knows-where at that hour in the morning, she would chauffeur the two men back to her house for breakfast and pleasures unspoken.

As they had been doing since picking her up, the two chauffeured policemen occupied themselves with trying to find out whether the woman had on anything else under that coat-covered, flimsy nightgown.

The only time they strayed from the thought was when Spagg again inquired about the breakfast menu. It was his third time asking. He liked the way it sounded. "An', my li'l darlin', the bo'kay shall consist of…?"

"Freench wine, furry steem rabeet smuuthered in cheese — weeth zee leetle hon-ee on zee side. Zen zee great actrees preeform zee act for you."

"Ooooh-la-la," said Spagg in his best French, but thinking the words were Italian.

"Hold up a sec, hon," Pippilo directed, upon seeing the sergeant and leaning forward to peer into the yard.

Pilar — no whiz at driving in the first place, and even worse with a stick shift — brought the Hudson to a stop inches short of crashing into the building. To be even more accurate, not counting her acting and the artificial French accent, the only thing worse than the woman's driving was her cooking. As witnessed by the still-kicking, half-steamed, meowing "rabeets" she served, Pilar had a hard time boiling water. But both Spagg and Pippilo were untroubled by the near-miss and climbed from the rear seat and focused on the strange sight of the sergeant on the railroad tracks, leaving well before the midnight watch was over. They swung over to Bucky and Carlsson, who were standing by the station's other corner, watching.

"Wha's' up, Buck? Wha's' goin' on?" a bewildered Pippilo asked, and was joined by Spagg.

Bucky made a small circling motion around the temple with his finger. "The sarge is gone nuts."

"Whaaaa?" said Spagg.

"He's gone koo-koo."

"Why, Buck? What happened?" Pippilo asked, dumbfounded.

Bucky shrugged, "I dunno."

Pilar, the prisoner, climbing out of the car window because she couldn't find the door handle, came with the question: "Weel zomebody pleeza teel mee what ees goink on? I must geet back zee house to kook. Zen zee act. I am zee great actrees."

"We won't be long, shug," assured Spagg.

As Bucky proceeded with an explanation to the two, all Danny Carlsson could do was to look at the three policemen and shake his head in pitiable wonder. No answer; no hope; he walked back inside the station.

The thought was slow in coming, but Carlsson concluded that both Tetrollini and Van Dreelan had to have died because of something they had done. Tetrollini's case was obvious. It was a matter of inappropriate behavior. With Van Dreelan, whatever happened to him, Carlsson was sure ineptness had to have been a part of it. But how, he wondered, had these three escaped a similar fate? The kidney-weak Bucky wasn't going to last long anyway, but the other two, Pippilo and Spagg...?

And then there was the still-missing Mickey Corbbo.

Before going inside, the young man had had the urge to again go after his sergeant when he walked away, but, he reasoned, maybe getting away from it all was best for him. And, he continued to think positively, at least the sergeant was on his feet. Obviously, he was on his way home.

Until the change of shift, however, somebody had to man the desk. Danny Carlsson would do it. It was for certain that no one else came close to being capable. It was only right for him to do it, and, all things considered, it would be a good experience for a policeman who would some day bring into effect that magic word *change* — although the way things were going, maybe there would be no one left on the midnight shift to change for.

But the sergeant had said *be the future; be the change.*

The quiet sandy-haired rookie of Scandinavian origin who had found answers and had grown up during a troubled night was still thinking about the strange turn of events, and what had happened to his sergeant, when he came back inside and moved to sit behind the desk. For an instant his mind flashed on something Soldier Boy had said. He couldn't recall everything, but second to the most important — and he wished he had questioned him about it at the time, but it was that thing about being the last man standing. How did he word it? — "Say goodnight to your boys in blue?"...Strange. And there again, it tied in with the word: *Change.*

Had any of it — had any part of what he had said — come from anyone else, it could easily have been dismissed; it could have been chalked up to foolishness, as crazy talk from a wine-soaked old black, shadowed in the night. But no, it came from Soldier Boy. It came from someone who knew things; who didn't preach, but spouted the odd and offbeat; who, with a plate in his head, spoke of Persia, Bulgaria, Afghanistan; who knew of the Lord High Kublai Khan, Genghis Khan; the Viking king Bluetooth, and on and on and on. He even knew something about the arts, and *trigonometry*, of all things. But more than anything else, when the old black was dying, he saw something. And he felt something. He felt spirituality; he saw truth.

He saw the face of God.

Viewing it from the other side, the desk seemed more massive and sturdy than the young policeman had originally thought. He looked at the rounded, chrome-plated mike, the patched switchboard with all the tiny lights, then up at the big clock that hovered over the door, and returned his look to the desk. He thought about what Pippilo had asked outside. To himself, he said what he thought he should have said in terms of an answer. *Why did the sergeant go off?* I'll tell you why he went off. He went off because we drove him off. We drove him out of his mind, and we were close to sending him to his grave. The final hour would have done it.

Why did he go off? Simple. There are a dozen things we'll never know, but how would you like to have a night where you start off by settling a fight between two of your officers? You've got another one wearing the wrong uniform because the other one — made of serge material — shrank in the washing machine. He compounds this by wearing sunglasses — at midnight. Behind the desk, your phones are constantly ringing — not with people who need help, but with two weirdos who should have been institutionalized long ago. You've got a Chinese man walking the streets who bugs you. He's so dizzy he doesn't know what planet he's on. You've got a liver-hardened assistant who can hardly remember his name and hasn't been sober since the start of World War II, and at the rate he's going, he probably won't be breathing in another six months. You've got a rookie — *me* — who's been acting like a child, and a bunch of guys — *cops* — *officers of the law* — who spend their entire night not even knowing the meaning of duty and responsibility, and are known to have some of the most inane conversations ever to strike the human ear. On top of that, you're less than two hours away from the end of your shift and you find out two of your men are dead and another one hasn't called in for hours. And then you send two of your men out to arrest a ditzy, cop-killing, cat-chasing woman with a phony French accent, and they come back — and, trying to put the make on her, they let the fruitcake drive the car.

And you're asking why the man has gone loco?

⧗

When Bucky came back inside, he saw the ruminating rookie sizing up the desk. Not that he wanted to, but he couldn't read Carlsson's thoughts. He couldn't even articulate his own. At this point he was being paged by the hard forces of delirium tremens and the only thing strong enough to answer the call was another drink. If, however, the alcoholic policeman could have formed anything worthwhile in mind, he would have spent a moment or two flashing over his life behind the desk, trying to recall whether he and the sergeant had even come close to experiencing a night such as this. Years and years would have flashed before him, but what he would have concluded could not have been disputed. He would have remembered that, since being on the desk, all the nights had been routinely boring, and that in his long career — the brief stints on the day and evening shifts included — nothing could compare. Even those well spaced times when the odd and offbeat did happen, it wasn't the same; and even at that, the old blood-pumping organ had pulled the sergeant through without chest-rubbing complaint. But not this night. It had been *the* night of nights; the shift of shifts; the watch of watches; Byzantine, cruel, pressured and unremitting — the two of them experiencing disaster after disaster. And, like the sergeant had been trying to get across, unknown forces *had* to have been at work.

Bucky could have said a lot of things, but he said nothing. He had started shaking again. As if giving the rookie room to think, he headed upstairs to the chief's office. The delirium tremens working harder, he needed a drink. A stiff one.

Like any dyed-in-the-wool alcoholic, the need for a drink was always coated by an excuse. Bucky's excuse was that he was going upstairs to the cells to check on Mrs. Ina and chat with his mother, who, unknown to him, hardly had energy to cough anymore. The last series had done her in. She was on her last leg, stretched on the hard bunk, unable to call out, wheezing — too weak even to fan for air.

Before checking in with either of the old women — which, as it turned out, would have made for a happier ending — Bucky decided he would make a stop into the chief's office, get a quick drink, maybe check out the remaining stock, and possibly quench his second-stage thirst with something new. Also, before going up to the loft, he would take a moment or two to work on his dentures. Although in her present condition she wouldn't have known the difference, wearing the dentures for his mother would have been a nice gesture. It would have been just the thing for a fast-fading old woman who would only live for a few more ticks of the clock — although, to be fair, the latter predicament was unbeknownst to him. Wearing the dentures would have been nice, too — and this he really did think of — that in case the sergeant came back, he would greet him with a nice, toothy smile.

But, to go back, if Bucky's wheezing and fast-fading mother had a problem, Mrs. Ina's was worse. It started with the Thermos bottle. It seems that Mrs. Ina had finally achieved success in removing the top from the bottle, but in struggling to pop the cork, the soup spilled out, she slipped, and fell. As she fell, she banged her head on the cot. There the kind old lady with the big house, who fancied a warm body in a cold coffin, was on the floor of a tiny jail cell bleeding to death — a victim of an unmanageable Thermos bottle and the corner of a harsh metal cot. Tragically, she panted her last gasps in a puddle of cold, disagreeable soup.

Fortune had smiled on Bucky's mother.

She simply passed away.

As it ended, and had Bucky not reversed the order — that is, had he not stopped for a drink and put the ill-fitting dentures in his mouth first, he probably would have survived the shift. But he found a Christmas tradition in the chief's office, and it brought about his end in a most unusual way.

It was a new bottle of eggnog, and with the sergeant gone, the chief at home, and a traditional drink in shaking hands, it seemed that a bad night was turning into a holiday. Bucky was feeling good — so good that he tiptoed to the door and locked it. Spiriting himself back to the chief's desk, he plopped down in the chair, put his feet up on the desk, and uncapped the bottle. He was shaking a little bit more now. But he was in control, and relief was on the way. It was a little milky and didn't appear quite as potent as some of the others he had been drinking, but that would be taken into consideration when the bottle was in the right position. A good, long swallow was known to kill all ills. Bucky took his time. In fact, with the bottle in hand, he even looked around the room and thought about the possibilities of him being chief one day. He might even shave for the occasion. Not a bad thought, he thought. He leaned back in the chair, and mused: *Chief Buck-Buck.* Warmed by the idea, he tilted his head back, opened wide, and up went the old chief's bottle to the right position.

Slightly less than two minutes later, down came the old chief's bottle. It hit the floor and rolled a little. The cop's body soon followed. It didn't roll, but when it hit the floor, it went through a series of wobbly, jerky motions.

Pawing fitfully at the air, it looked very much like the new chief with the few strands of hair was waving goodbye. It would have been a fitting gesture, but waving goodbye was not exactly what the "new chief" had in mind. Gasping, one hand flapping at the air while the other hand was grabbing at a throat that was burning with alcohol, the cop was choking. His dentures had slipped and had blocked passage to his esophagus.

Theoretically, Chief Buck-Buck was dead before he hit the floor.

21

Midnight, and its serendipitous collection of a set of moonlit hours that came in on the heels of a series of weird and seemingly satirical winds that augured change, dallied with the night to make it so, and danced away like the clown prince of a black comedy, had ended in the city that had been named by mistake and had the word "Head" appended to give it *body.* What had been omened at the start of night was now becoming clear. If interpretation served well, a *complete* change had been called for. Change that, except for the very new, was to touch — and therefore to claim — *any and everyone* who had been *in* or *around* the old brick building that night.

Of the shift, Pippilo, Spagg, and the midnight sergeant of the desk had not been claimed. They were not new; nowhere had it been said — or, to use Soldier Boy's term, *decreed* — that either would be the *last man standing.* And so although the capricious hours had ended, the midnight melody lingered on.

Dawn and its immediate aftermath had come and gone, the city was bathed in full daylight. In daylight the city wasn't much, but she did have her moments. This morning the snow gave her more than moments. She looked faultless and harmonious; like a Norman Rockwell painting in the making.

But the sergeant never saw any of it. He had long since lost Carlsson's jacket, but he wasn't aware of it. Well away from the station, he was still walking; seeing nothing; hearing nothing. He had left the slippery, snow-covered railroad ties and was trudging along in the street.

In a sense it was too bad that the sergeant was trudging alone, seeing and hearing nothing, because earlier he had passed Charlie Wong.

It would have been appropriate had either of them said "goodbye."

Charlie was walking slower than usual, hardly noticing that morning had come. His head low, he was still a little sore in a certain area, and still there was no "walla" in his voice. But Charlie was not totally defeated by his tryst with the owner of the size 16, triple-E combat boots. But it appeared that his Gung Ho Fat Choy — his *Year of the Pig* — was over, and, owing to the owner of the boots, it looked as if he had brought it in on a pretty rough note. There had been no follow-up encounters with something more to his liking, but he had at least survived the night. And he still had hope.

When Charlie finally realized who it was whom he had just passed, he stopped. A sudden smile snapped across his face. He turned, and started to catch up with the absent-looking sergeant. But Charlie faced a predicament. Across the street there was a figure on the move. It took on the form of a woman. "*Walla!*" said he. The night could be salvaged.

His dilemma solved, Charlie gained energy, shifted gears, waved a crisp, early-morning greeting to his friend's departed back and zipped across the street, looking neither left nor right. His eyes remaining on the prize, in the middle of the street, he hollered out: "I'm still *goooinnnnggg, Sargentoooo.*"

The same could have been said about the bus driver, the one who made the nightly run to Lodi, Garfield, and Passaic. He was winding up his tour for the night. Bored, sleepy-eyed and as stiff as a robot behind the wheel he, too, was looking neither left nor right; he, too, was still going.

Desk Sergeant Demarest O. McShayne was too far gone and had moved too far down the street to have heard Charlie's final salutation. He was not in a condition or position to have heard the cruelty of the bumper's thud, and the accompanying *thump-thumps* that ended the life of the energetic little

Chinaman who now lay splattered in the snow-padded street, flattened by a double set of bus tires that didn't even have the courtesy to skid to a respectable stop after the deed was done.

But like everything else, Charlie's death said a lot about that strange, claiming night in Elton Head. Not that it would have registered with the sergeant — or anyone else for that matter — but, other than the regular shift, Charlie and Jess Brown were the only two to have visited the station during the night. Of course, there was Mrs. Ina and Bucky's mother, but now they were gone. In a sense, Jess's days were numbered, too. He was charged with murder. If all went well — and owing to Ernie Mulkey's avarice, there would be forces pushing hard in that direction — the charge would stick.

In New Jersey the crime of murder carried the death penalty.

And so, in a way, Jess Brown didn't count — at least for the night. Pilar's disposition had to be considered, because she had come close to the building — as had Carol. And then there was Sergeant Elmore Zemora. He had actually been in the building. But, to the point, Charlie's death, as well as the other deaths that occurred in the old building, went a long way towards bringing back something the sergeant had said when he was lamenting over his missing cars. He didn't hit it hard — in fact he muttered it, but still it was worthwhile bringing back to mind. The sergeant had said something like: *this station is a goddamn killer.*

He should have been a prophet.

Prophecy aside, the Chinaman's end — and the impertinence of the end, would have undoubtedly added to the sergeant's woe. Although he never would have admitted it, McShayne liked Charlie. He liked him a lot. Back in the days when they were selecting Air-raid Wardens, McShayne had even recommended him for a job. It was not an easy thing to do because Elton Head was not known for being the most tolerable of places, and was less so when it came to minorities or foreigners seeking positions of considered authority. But the sergeant pushed, and Charlie got the job. Unfortunately, it didn't last. The first blackout did it. New to the country, Charlie had trouble with the English language. When *air-raid* became *air-laid,* the higher-ups decided that the Chinaman had to go.

But, sad to say, the termination of the snappy munchkin who always found a way to add a measure of life to the dull and plodding nights was something the midnight sergeant of the desk would never know.

The sergeant would never know, either, that at the same time Charlie was being dispatched by the bus's bumper and humbled by the *thump-thumping* tires, he was passing the old duplex on Hope Street that belonged to the smug and cryptic Sergeant Elmore Zemora. It was interesting because Zemora, in bed, happened to be turning over to face the young miss who had awakened him a little earlier. It was the ubiquitous Carol, still spreading morning joy, fresh with a new approach, and this time needing money for school. She was just about to sweeten the need by telling the sergeant, whom McShayne never liked and had relieved when he came on duty, that everything she wanted to know about love and *loving* she would like to learn from him. Zemora would have appreciated hearing it, but he was too concerned about whom he thought he had just seen passing his street-level window.

The evening sergeant of the desk rolled over, lit a cigarette, and relayed his thoughts to the teenager. When she heard the words, she bolted upright as if having been jolted by a cattle prod. She uttered an epigrammatic *Oh, migod! Oh, migod! OHMIGAWDDDD!!*

She tore through the door, dressing as she ran.

Sergeant Zemora drifted back to sleep, the freshly-lit cigarette still in his hand.

Some distance away now, with the heart of the city well behind him, the soft flakes continued to cap a robust head of hair already silvered by age. They hugged and caressed the sergeant's taut and stooped shoulders in a light and friendly way.

Sergeant McShayne walked on.

Then, from out of nowhere — sounds, cracking metronomic voices, shattered the morning calm and began to penetrate the sergeant's mind. Instead of coming with the genteel behavior of the fluffed snowflakes that showed sensitivity to a man whose mind had just taken flight, they were rude and obstreperous, hard and incessant. They created tumult in his head by pounding away with every single utterance he had breathed and heard through the night.

Then came the sounds of bells.

Quiet since midnight, the clock atop the library had already sprung back to life. It was melodiously bonging out eight bells. The sergeant didn't hear the bells. They couldn't fully penetrate the metronomic voices, but once again, as they had been at the start of the shift, the bells were wrong. The time was 0731.

After the long, grudging walk, Demarest O. McShayne finally reached the outskirts of town. Automatic with his steps, he marched down a quiet street that looked only vaguely familiar in the night. Soon he came to a house midway of the block. It was 190 Daisy Lane.

The sergeant was home.

The Daisy Lane house was the only one he and his dear departed wife had ever known together. It was the epitome of the American dream. Purchased during those clean, promising, and profane-less days of early marriage, when the future was theirs. The house was well-kept and quaint. Garden State goodness, the wife used to say. In memory of her, he kept it that way.

During the war the sergeant had built two planters on the second floor. Before getting to the garage that was straight ahead and making the turn at the rear of the house where the stairs were, he loved walking under the planters; always walking down the long driveway after the long night, re-claiming that restful feeling that only home could bring.

Except for the back room on the second story, with its pink polka-dot curtains and cuddly teddy bear nesting in the window — done to comfort his recently arrived niece — the house was simple; homey. And while it couldn't have been described as out-and-out beautiful, it was Dutch-looking and cozy, and made all the more warm-hearted because the sergeant had also made it a springtime ritual to varnish the steps and paint the back staircase railing a nice mahogany, which added a richness to it. It also made the staircase look as if it stretched longer than it actually did. If the railing had been painted white, as the sergeant thought he might do some day, it could have — not that he was all that religious — but it could have looked as if one were climbing the stairway to heaven. It was not an exaggerated thought, because McShayne, good with his hands, had also created another unique planter that ran the length of the staircase. In late spring and summer it ended with a marvelous floral display at the top. It was imaginatively done.

Down below, to certify just how good and content he was, sectioned off from the garage that stood alone in the back, there was a little area where he used to grow a few stalks of corn, tomatoes, beans, cucumbers, and other vegetables. It was his Victory Garden; it was something he and his wife had contributed to the war effort. He would have prefered going into service, but he was too old for the draft; too old for enlistment.

But the war was long gone, and so was the beloved wife. It was nine winters later; nothing grew, and icicles twinkled along the second-story window — significant because, shortly after his wife had passed away, the sergeant had built another planter underneath the kitchen window downstairs, which he had filled with tulip and daffodil bulbs. At the beginning of spring, happy little buds would sprout up. The buds were the children the wife had always wanted.

The reason the sergeant had selected tulips and daffodils and not anything else was that they were colorful and perennial. Every year they would sprout, signaling that the gloom of winter was gone, spring was here, and the lazy days of summer were on their way.

Everything at the house at 190 Daisy Lane bespoke a man at reasonable peace with himself.

Making the turn, and ignoring the garage that sat 30 to 35 feet off from the house, the good sergeant started making the long climb up a staircase that occasionally reminded him of a stairway to heaven. For a heart that was already working on overtime, and on legs so unfirm they appeared to bow with every step, it seemed a long and arduous climb. But thanks to the strong railing, vise-gripping hands, and dogged determination, the old sergeant climbed on. When he made it to the top, he cleared a little spot in the snow and sat down in relieving victory. The face became grudgingly alive with the thought that he had at least survived. The dark realism was over. All that had happened during the night was behind him now. It would remain that way. It had to. One more zapper and it was all over. The heart knew it; he knew it.

It didn't take long before both cheeks of the buttocks were getting a little damp as he sat there, slightly forward of the back door. But the dampness was all right. He was home. The pounding in the head had stopped; the cracking, metronomic voices had faded away.

The good sergeant even took a moment out to take note of the winking, blue and white Christmas lights he had put up a few weeks earlier.

Indeed, it was good to be home.

Soon he would go inside, and both head and heart would rest. He was tasting relief. He was hoping the heart would sup of the same plate. One thing the sergeant knew for certain, though, was that the tired old instrument with the irregular beat would never be ill-treated again. Shock, strain and exertion were all behind him. The antics of the patrolmen, the worry over the cars, the coarse language that he had promised his wife he would no longer use, the nutty people of the night, the troublesome switchboard, the concerns of an indifferent city — all, *gone, done, finished. Forever.* It was resolved that the Elton Head, New Jersey, Police Department had seen the last of Dempsey O. McShayne.

For the old desk sergeant with the hair like spun silk, the woe had been so heavy that in trying to put it all away, he slipped a heavily weighted head into the palms of his hands to rest.

— He shouldn't have done it.

Gravity forced the head down and to the left. The garage doors were down and to the left. There was a hose peeping up and through the snow — down and to the left. The sergeant of the night saw the hose that came from under the garage doors and through the snow and was peeping up, *down and to the left.* Then, to make matters worse, from inside the garage — *down and to the left* — off went an alarm clock, kicking with a semi-muted, end-o'the-night *B-B-BRINGGG!!*

Crushed by the memory of his other patrol cars the sergeant didn't need the reminder, but it came anyway.

His voice was first; the belated Bucky's was to follow. *"Gassin' up?! Gassin' up?! You tell me, Bucky, how'n hell do you spend a whole night 'gassin' up' in a city garage that ain't open — and will not open until one*

*half-hour before the change of the midnight shift!! But even if the city kept
the goddamn thing open every day, 24 hours a day, from sunup to sundown,
from dusk to dawn, and that hare-brained Mickey Corbbo needed gas, it would
only require a few minutes at the pump. And that is simply because he's
supposed to be operatin' a patrol car, not sailin' a goddamn battleship!!!"*

"*Well, I just said that, Sarge, because lately Mick's been sneakin' a
hose in the car. An' an alarm clock.*"

With the late Bucky's words hammering, and the sight of the hose that
came from under the garage doors, peeping up through the snow — *down
and to the left,* it had the venerable sergeant of the desk sitting at the top of the
stairs looking as though Charles Atlas had just crushed him with the universe.

Alas, if the good sergeant had been on the other side of town he would
have been crushed even more, for little did he know — and in the interest of
mercy maybe it was good that he would never know, that, at that precise
moment, the operators of cars 101 and 102 — Pippilo and Spagg — the last
of his two radio-car patrolmen, had returned to the socket-haired chef de
cuisine's house and were comfortably sliding their legs under her dining-
room table. Once again the meowing from a sack had been whacked into
something close to silence. The short-eared "rabeets" with the long, hairy
tails had been dumped into a pot, and again steamed quicker than one-minute
rice. Again, the cheese was close by. Everything was in fine form. The
policemen were ready to plunge, and after plunging, ready to cap the shift by
catching a little of the woman's act, then partaking of that which lay beneath
the flimsy nightgown.

"*Ooooh-la-la,*" Spagg was heard to say with happy, roving eyes —
and now thinking he had mastered the Italian language.

"*Ooooh-la-la,*" agreed partner Pippilo, who, since he was Italian, should
have known better.

Sad to say, though, neither the fine form nor the *Ooooh-la-la's* were to
last. Little did the last of the sergeant's patrol-car operators know that hiding
behind the crudely-hung, part-falling Persian rug that hid the attic door was
Oscar, Pilar's man-hungry primate. He, too, was ready to plunge. Mouth
watering, and unchained for the first time since being in captivity, he was
waiting with fork in hand; the salt and pepper shakers were within easy reach.

Having tasted one cop, he was not about to change diets. Jungle instincts at an all-time high, he was weaving from side to side. It was as if the big half-man/half-beast had heard, and couldn't wait to be, the sole beneficiary of what the good sergeant had bequeathed when he said *Some heads are gonna roll.*

The glum but grandfatherly-looking sergeant had said something else during that downhearted soliloquy when he was venting his spleen behind the desk. After saying that the night had *been enough to turn me into a full-fledged cadaver,* he said: *The way things are going, I wouldn't be surprised if every goddamn car on the shift goes out. And the drivers, too!*

— He should have been a prophet.

He was doing well at the table, but upon hearing a strange, hungering sound coming from the attic stairs, Pippilo's mind shot back to the condition of Johnny Van Dreelan's savaged body. Remembering that there could have been a connection between the woman and Mrs. Ina, and that the sergeant had said to shoot anything in the house that didn't look human, Pippilo stopped eating long enough to quietly pull his gun from his holster and lay it on the table — just in case. Suspicious, and on a nod from Pippilo, Spagg followed suit. He was still locked on the woman, and was not nearly as discreet.

Maybe it was because he wasn't a gun-fancier, maybe it was a matter of beastly impatience, whatever the case, from behind the part-falling Persian rug, suddenly the creature roared so loud it froze the cops in place and almost shook the foundation of the house. The big O had lost all aplomb. He went berserk. Snarling and growling thick streams of yellow saliva, the hulk tore through the rug, pounced on the table, ate both guns, and chomped on the two frozen cops with a ferocity so vicious and thorough that even the woman of the house was mortified. While working at the creepshow in Coney Island, she knew that the creature could get a little upset at times, but she had no idea that his rage could be so fierce.

"Fierce" was hardly the word. Sassy, as he was once known, was a raging maniac. After devouring both Pippilo and Spagg, and as if suddenly realizing he had been freed for the first time since being in the heavy, almost battleshiplike chains, the big, hairy, gigantopithecus-descended, bipedal hominid from the jungles of Peru, chomped on everything he could find, to include the tables and chairs. For good measure, he bit the head off the ball-peen hammer, ate the thumbtacks, and bellowed for dessert. Five hundred pounds of grit and muscle, eight-foot-seven from tip to toe, Sassy — the big O — was awesome.

Growling and snarling, and with teeth more pronounced than white keys on a black piano, the beast started stripping planks, bricks and plaster from the walls. He devastated the house, then, by the time he sought to light into his captor, it was too late. Pilar had fled the house and had made it all the way to Main Street. She didn't know where she was going, but her hair on end, barefooted, no coat, nightgown flowing, she was running with new-found abandon.

She was fast, but the big O was faster.

⧗

Ironically, the assault on the woman with the wide eyes and wild hair took place in front of the Flamingo. Never before had an ending been so strange and dramatic. It was like theater; like Broadway on Main Street.

With the big O only having one more block to round before catching up with his former captor, Pilar decided to make her stand. She stopped in the middle of the street, and put up her fists. They were bony and insecure, but posing like Joan of Arc on tired feet — something she had boned up on in her earlier days in Bulgaria — she was ready to do battle. Suddenly, while posing, she became aware of the one or two casual observers who took a moment out to comment to each other that this had to be a Main Street first. One or two others joined the onlookers and were quick to agree.

Snatched by the notion that she had an audience, and that she was center-stage, on Main Street, and that it had the makings of the world's last great proscenium, Pilar changed up. She dropped her combative stance. It became her moment. Like an actress submitting her all to a great performance, she started posturing and spouting dialogue from a multitude of plays. The language was fractured, the scenes disordered, and her acting was campy and seriously over-the-top, but she was delivering the goods with gusto. She had range, and she showed that she could command a stage.

When the big O finally zipped around the corner and caught a glimpse of what was going on, he immediately slowed his steps. Perhaps it was because of the bystanders; perhaps it was because of the woman's dramatics, but whatever it was, it triggered something in his mind. He flashed back to his days in the limelight at the zoo in Coney Island.

Showtime.

With a glint in his eye, it appeared that he wanted to horn in on the act. Apparently Pilar thought so, too. She became even more hammy. Not to be outdone, the beast eased forward with an exaggerated swagger, acting as if he were auditioning for a silent movie. Pilar kicked her act into an higher gear. Sassy did likewise. He started moving with a lilting, melodramatic sway. If he had been wearing a tophat, he would have tipped it. Then, when he was close enough to what was supposed to be the stage, he stopped and swiveled his hips. The handful of onlookers that had gathered had already lost its detachment. Those who weren't still running were ducking in alleyways and cowering behind storefronts and signs. Two, peeping down from a tree, didn't know if they were watching a clown or a beast.

Thinking that the audience had departed because of the woman's bad acting, Sassy leveled an unhappy eye back on the supposed stage. Pilar was still hogging, posturing, and chewing scenes. Visibly upset, Oscar started snorting, and like a stage manager bringing a premature climax to a bad third act, he reared back, bared his long, jagged teeth, and made one the most theatrical leaps ever seen. Worse than he had been with the two policemen, the brute landed on the woman with full body. He flattened her flatter than the bus tires had flattened Charlie Wong.

But the woman deserved everlasting credit. Even with the beast's massive weight on her and his bicuspids planted firmly in her neck, she was Shakespearean to the end. Low-key, fading fast, but spirited with highest of high drama, her last words were: *Et tu, Bruté?*

Later, and certainly more casual and breezy than the circumstances had warranted, when a call was placed to the station saying that a brute of monstrous proportions was down to chewing on the last few bones of a woman, Carlsson was faced with his first dilemma behind the desk.

Although the report of the assault had been blasé, yet all the more confounding because it sounded so brutal — if absurdly farfetched — the rookie wanted to go to Main Street to check, but he couldn't leave the desk unattended or the station unmanned. Instead, he called the fire department and dispatched them to the scene for verification and possible assistance, which, as matters stood, was the right thing to do. But the fireman arrived too late. The beast was already on his way to the George Washington Bridge. Thumb up, he was trying to hitchhike to New York. No more zoo, no more chains, starry-eyed and careful with his thumb, he was walking theatrically.

He was taking his act to Broadway.

Bucky, whom Carlsson thought had gone upstairs, couldn't be found. In going upstairs for a quick look, and only calling up to the loft where the two old ladies were, it had to be assumed that the desks' assistant had left the station. Then going back up to the second floor and double-checking every place but the chief's office, which was locked — and even if it hadn't been, it was certainly off-limits to a rookie — Carlsson was sure that Bucky had slipped out the back door. It was understandable. Sensitive at times, Bucky was devoted and had been with the sergeant for many years, and the poor, defeated manner in which the sergeant left had to have had an effect.

Prompted by a strange quiet that had enveloped the building, when Carlsson returned downstairs to the desk he was connected to the thought that for the first time since being on the job there were no radio calls coming in. He was quick to notice that the phones were quiet, the teletype unit was silent, and that he was alone. He looked around the station thoughtfully. He felt a strangeness, then something Soldier Boy had said reentered his mind.

The last man standing.

Could this have been what the old black had meant? No. No, it couldn't have been, he thought. It had to have been something deeper.

This was the man who had seen the face of God.

Unaware of everything that had happened during the long night, but feeling that something ominous was in the air, Danny Carlsson sat slowly, uneasily. He thought about waiting until he felt that the sergeant had made it home, then give him a call. But, worried about the sergeant's condition, he decided to send Pippilo and Spagg to pick him up, or to act as an escort if he chose to continue walking.

As Carlsson reached for the mike, something else that Soldier Boy had said stopped him. His mind became terribly unsettled, and his hands became cold. Again, he looked around the station thoughtfully. He started to go back upstairs to check it out thoroughly, but he was insecure about leaving the phones at that moment. Somebody had to call. There were four men left that he knew of. One of them had to call.

This is a night of inevitable fates. The hits, they gonna be slow at first, but, Sandy Boy, they gonna keep on a'comin'.

Pushing himself, the rookie reached out again and got the mike. He sat ponderously; apprehensively. Then, with more of Soldier Boy's words echoing, and fighting more growing and unnerving thoughts, he nursed the cold instrument and began calling. He called car after car. The 22-year-old rookie who had assumed the duties of Sergeant of the Desk didn't get a single response. And he was afraid.

When the first few men of the morning shift came on duty, Danny was still at the mike, still calling what had now become his cars. The men collected around the desk and stood bewildered, and it was only when the morning sergeant arrived that anyone did anything. The sergeant, feeling the heavy chill that had enveloped the station, was concerned because he didn't see McShayne nor Bucky. But the sergeant was even more concerned about the beleaguered condition of the rookie. His tie was loose and askew, his hair was mussed, and he was taut and sweaty.

The last man standing was on the edge.

Quickly; gently, the sergeant slipped behind the desk, pried the rigid young hands away from the mike, and with help from one of the men, armed the rookie down the corridor and back to the patrol room. Still, he didn't go away easily. As he was led away, he continued to call his cars. He called them softly.

Sometimes he was pleading.

But the rookie's predicament was something that the midnight sergeant would never know. Desk Sergeant Dempsey O. McShayne would never know, either, that his remaining regulars — Pippilo, Spagg, Corbbo, and now Bucky — had joined Johnny Van Dreelan's and Georgie Tetrollini's entrance along the corridors of death, for as he sat on the porch's top step, breathing as though he had already taken that last lap around the track of life, the back door of his homey house swung open. Popping part way out and bringing full conclusion to a night that had omened a hint — a pinch; a *smidge* — of change, was the sergeant's 16-year-old charge, the one whom he had been trying to reach by telephone all through the night — and who, in her own way, had been as busy as he.

She was wearing a bright smile, and her blonde hair was braided into two springy pigtails with nicely tied bows on each end. Her schoolbooks were neatly underarm — and it wasn't even time to go to school. In her mind, there was still time to catch somebody on the fly — maybe that cute little Scandinavian-looking policeman she had spotted at the station when she first drove by. If not, certainly there had to be a little something stirring on Main Street. Maybe a quick run across the George Washington Bridge wouldn't hurt. The last time she went, she picked up an interesting hitchhiker. They spent the major part of the evening in a drive-in movie.

Feeling good about her prospects, the all-American teenager stood there yawning and stretching a series of nice waker-uppers, giving every indication that she had slept well during the night.

Youth was on her side. With full energy, she bounced from the door. *"Hiiie-e-e, Uncle Dem-Dem,"* she said, cutely bending over to nuzzle her rosy cheeks against the uncle's now frozen cheeks. "Did'ja have a nice night, Uncle Dem-Dem?"

It was good that little Carol didn't wait for an answer before sailing off in her Henry J. Uncle "Dem-Dem" couldn't have answered if he'd wanted to. Like his regular boys in blue, and all who had been shadowed and touched by the moon and all the elements there on the street where his station stood, it was all over.

Unlike his wife, he had never been much for the church or the spiritual; maybe the profane-talking sergeant hadn't even been a true believer in the hereafter, but death understood. It was compassionate. It was charitable and forgiving. Because the soul had endured much, because he had been a principled man — a good and just man — in time you could almost see his tired spirit rise up, take a deep breath, then brace itself for the long climb to the heavens.

Any other direction would have been ungodly.

☒

And so ended the midnight shift in Elton Head, New Jersey; so ended a night that, weather-wise, had been nice and comfy. The morning, crisp and fresh with the light snow that had fallen, had been brightened by a benevolent sun and held fast to the look of a greeting card that promised something to the '50's that the '40's hadn't delivered. But despite the look, despite the sun's benevolence, the staid little city with the weary-faced police station just across the river from massive New York maintained its breath of lethargy; its aura of aloofness — its unyielding malaise. It was saying, in effect, that it was not going to change, and that even though the war was over, innocence and continuity had been restored, optimism was high, Rosie the Riveter had returned to the kitchen, the price of bread, eggs, and gasoline were respectably holding, and that it was the beginning of a new decade, baby-booming tots were teething, apple pie and roses were on the nation's menu, the glory of Christmas was just a few days away, and all seemed right in an untroubled world, none of it was really a matter of paramount concern.

Even when the heart of morning came and there was a hurried Winchell broadcast from New York saying that a young girl's mangled body had been discovered on the George Washington Bridge in a pink Henry J, and that through the night, flying saucers had been spotted in Israel, Hong Kong, and Italy, and that itty-bitty green men with little pointed ears, built-in antennas, and mini ray guns were thought to be invading the planet, the report created neither panic nor concern. Even less concern was expressed over the smoke, smell, and sight of the still smoldering embers that came from Hope Street and had occasioned the life of Elmore Zemora, the only other sergeant who had been in the aged and architecturally destitute little building that night.

And still later, when the full results of the city's most bizarre and ill-fated night came to light and the remains of the departed were being scraped, sacked, pouched, bagged, dragged, and rolled from the various places, no one gasped in horror; no one recoiled in fear. There was no alarm; no trepidation. Few were touched and even fewer tears were shed, and one was left with the feeling that all that concerned the citizenry was that another night had come and gone and short of being whacked by the same bombs that had whacked the faces of Pearl Harbor, Nagasaki, and Hiroshima, Elton Head's head was yet to be aroused.